Hotel Madre Maria

Alexandra Hayes

authorHOUSE®

AuthorHouse™
1663 Liberty Drive
Bloomington, IN 47403
www.authorhouse.com
Phone: 1 (800) 839-8640

Published by AuthorHouse 01/27/2016

ISBN: 978-1-5049-6564-4 (sc)
ISBN: 978-1-5049-6615-3 (e)

Library of Congress Control Number: 2015920218

Print information available on the last page.

Any people depicted in stock imagery provided by Thinkstock are models, and such images are being used for illustrative purposes only.
Certain stock imagery © *Thinkstock.*

This book is printed on acid-free paper.

Because of the dynamic nature of the Internet, any web addresses or links contained in this book may have changed since publication and may no longer be valid. The views expressed in this work are solely those of the author and do not necessarily reflect the views of the publisher, and the publisher hereby disclaims any responsibility for them.

Acknowledgements

I was blessed by contributions from two craftsmen.

Patrick Dunn, my first reader, offered the divine gifts of encouragement, a careful and precise overview, and creative suggestions.

Beth Dickson, my second reader, guided me through the forests of copy editing on old machines, and around various swamps of technical ignorance.

Part One

LET ME BEGIN

Lilies grow beside the hotel swimming pool. They're dramatic. Their scent is powerful, not sweet but penetrating. Their hearts are ruby red. The pool has an ambiance quite different from that of the sea. It promises a turning inward, a private voyage. Visits to the pool, for me, have become meditations; after a few days I no longer see faded grandeur, decay and obsolescence. Instead I enter the calm of another world, a mystery of quiet just around the corner from a crowded beach with its roar of waves, clamor of human voices, hustle of sale and barter.

The pool is the hotel's heart, its history. A large rectangle filled with dirty water; no one swims in it. Around it grow slender tropical trees, the remnants of garden plants, and the Rubrum1 Scattered throughout are scarred lawn chairs and tables. The pool reports: "My time is over. I'm beyond swimming, beyond delight." The furniture adds to this lament: "Real people were here but now are gone forever."

Yet just beyond the curve of the garden, just that fraction out of sight, the blue sea dances and challenges.

As these days go by, I've found this deserted place a refuge. I lie and listen to the rustling sounds of birds moving through trees, draw in subtle odors of decayed vegetation and thick water, a heavy smell but mixed with the scent of lilies. This secret reality has become a temptation, a need, a habit, in these days at the Hotel Madre Maria. I can forget the quarrels, the confusion, the violence my mother and I have encountered on our holiday together. Others have joined us by the pool, but not by invitation. Soon it may be forced to give up its ghosts. Even danger could arrive, a danger we did not expect and cannot avoid. But how can I be afraid beside this pool?

I hesitate. Am I really committed to do this? Writing all this down? I'm at the last few pages in a journal I began when my mother and I arrived in Mazatlan. I don't know why I've done this; remembering seems a hopeless work in progress – no wonder I've avoided it most of my life. Yet I've promised myself I'll try to write down everything that's happened.

As a child I loved stores about people suffering amnesia. I even liked the word itself: "Amnesia" – the sound, the look of it, the meaning – forgetfulness. People forget who they are – their names, ages, family, opinions – everything is gone. Yet they may still be young, still living, breathing, falling in love, making money, watching sunsets. They find work; confess with charming honesty "I don't know what I can do. I can't remember what kind of training I have." Then a small event, a word, a thing, a person – triggers the return of memories that are sometimes terrible.

I especially liked the word "trigger". I thought that memories must be shot into amnesia victims, like bullets from a gun, or vitamin B from a doctor's needle. Good memories then return to you, that is the hope, the belief, the promise. But I found, with a counselor, memory a treadmill without destination and so ran away from mine. He leaned forward in his chair, asked in a calm voice: What are your most important memories?

None came. Yet Mexico has given me some. Memories come to me here, unsettling, yet precise. I've never wanted them, have always resisted them. Even when my mother Sonja tried to talk with me on this holiday, I turned away. Don't remember, don't recall, and don't do anything to stir up the past. That's what my inner being has called out, over and over: Memories are dangerous; I've tried to run away from hers. Yet on this holiday, though we've quarreled, we've also rediscovered each other. I've come to love my mother as never before. Without amnesia, I've learned that there are no gods, no heroes, only people who are pretty much goof balls. Learn still that God never forgets to love us.

·

These are the last pages of the journal I've kept all week, or eighteen days as I now count them. Tonight, I'll walk beside the sea under a friendly moon, and find the courage to go home, for this other mother, the sea, is complete, a whole even as she moves and changes.

Saturday night

I liked Desmond the moment I saw him. Our room was next to the outside door and as I stood half in, half out of it, another door opened at the other end of the hall and he walked its length toward me. It was a distinctively homely hall, with a red stripe halfway up both walls to match the red carpet, but he was big and easy with his body and even there he looked right at home, like a man about to lead a party of hikers on an all day ascent of a mountain.

He stopped beside me, smiled. "I think we took the same flight - not much to eat was there?" He leaned against the wall and looked straight into my eyes. It was a strong man's regard. I hesitated, took a step back.

"They might still be serving in the dining room." He waved a lanky hand at the outside door, "I can walk you over if you like."

He had a craggy face and smiling lips, was around my age, but a head taller. He looked a little like Abraham Lincoln, one of my favorite dead people, but cautious to the bone, I edged further into my room.

"I'm not hungry, thanks. I'm looking for my mother."

"A lost mother. The best kind."

A dangerous remark thrown casually away - I liked that about him too.

He shifted; I caught a clean scent from the chest hairs just visible above the wrinkled, pale green sports shirt he wore. He smelled of fresh shower and soap something I knew I didn't.

"She got in last night."

"There's a casino up the road."

"My mother doesn't gamble."

"The bar then."

"She doesn't drink, not anymore."

He smiled that same Cheshire cat smile he'd greeted me with. I smiled back, but I was tired and leaned against the door.

"Leave her a note. Come on, I'll buy you a drink. Your mother will find you. This isn't a big hotel."

"Thanks, but it's been a long day."

It was his turn to edge away. "I'm off then. Join me if you change your mind."

He was out the door before I could speak. Rude, I thought. I didn't remember him on the plane, nor in the hotel van full of tired tourists airing disjointed conversations. I went inside, closed the door, locked it and turned on the light.

The room was empty. Sonja's suitcase was against one wall; she'd unpacked but left me half the closet - and a note on her bed telling me she was out with friends. I turned philosophical. She was probably gone for the evening. I took a shower; the water was hot and generous and I stood under it for ten minutes, heat eating into the ache in my muscles from long hours sitting in cramped spaces. Relieved to find the bathroom clean and adequate, and more cheerful as I dried myself off, I pulled the last few apricots out of my bag, and stood naked in the center of the room eating them while I looked around. The room was sticky warm, and more down at the heels than I'd expected for what had been advertised as a resort hotel. The overhead light was forty watts. Oh Greg, I thought, what have you gotten us into? My husband had booked the hotel. White painted walls were smudged; the furniture was elderly. A small night table held a lamp and telephone; an old floor lamp stood by the window, a small radio on a wooden table beside it. Hanging over the twin beds was a painting of a bullfighter bowing to a bull while sad eyed people watched in the stands. Not the kind of painting to look at late at night. Outside the window, a road lay just a short ways away, but the silence said everything about it. Nothing and no one was moving out there.

Stuffing the last apricot into my mouth, I dressed in a clean blouse and skirt. Looking for food would be my first adventure. I noticed in the closet the scent of musk, and chocolates. Sophia liked to try them both – perfumes and candy. Familiar emotions were awaking in me - pleasure because the unexpected usually accompanied my mother but also, for the same reason, apprehension and some annoyance that she wasn't in the room. I'd called and left a message – she could have waited.

I tried to reason myself out of the jealousy I often felt toward my exotic mother. Why shouldn't she socialize? Why spend the whole evening alone in an hotel room? Besides, I knew I was carrying news that would upset her. It was just as well she was out enjoying herself – if she were enjoying herself – sometimes with Sonja it was hard to tell.

In truth I wasn't much for holidays or resorts that winter. My life had grown chaotic and I too serious. When my mother invited me to go to Mexico with her, I almost didn't accept. She'd been there several times with my stepfather Josef and liked it. And we'd gone on holidays together in the past and enjoyed each other's company. But this holiday threatened to be different. My mother was unhappy and so was I. She was facing forced retirement and seemed unsettled by the death of Josef, six months before.

I was escaping my husband. Greg was a man who built boats as a hobby, but they were always one-man boats. Increasingly he was engaged in activities that repelled me. The surgery I'd undergone, the severe bout with flu that followed, and above all, the collapse of my marriage had drained me of ambition and hope.

They are never very comfortable, one-man boats.

*   *   *   *   *

In the evening darkness, Hotel Madre Maria looked snug and well appointed. Inside, I found a front desk weighed down by flamboyant floral arrangements, but deserted; the doors to the dining room were closed, yet from behind them came the sounds of castanets and loud voices singing about senoritas, while the quiet bar was smoky, dark and almost empty. None of these were appealing.

A short way down the road I found a small brightly lit casino full of people slinging coins into machines, but didn't see my mother sitting in front of any of them. Nor did I see the tall man with the Cheshire cat smile. I walked back along the road not sure what I thought of this resort. The Madre Maria was a square pink hacienda with small windows and a driveway that swooped past the front door and out again, a style popular in the fifties. From the main building sprawled two octopus arms of motel like annexes. Half the rooms faced the beach, the other, like ours, faced the dusty road. Rooms on the beach side sported patios where guests could drink while looking at the sea, our road side rooms had basic tables, chairs and small fridges which promised midnight bacchanals. The red hall carpets contributed to a sense of an illusion that the halls were disappearing into infinity.

Infinity was not something I was going to be able to deal with in my present state of mind. Especially since everything about my journey had been slow and frustrating. The plane was late leaving Denver so I arrived in Mazatlan at nine instead of six p.m. After a half hour wait for the hotel van, I was the last to get off because the Madre Maria was at the far end of the tourist strip. I was given the wrong room key and had to go back to the front desk to exchange it. Yet my mood lifted when, walking back into the hotel again, I discovered a narrow door near the dining room. I walked through it and straight outside into a sound - a roar that made my heart leap with joy.

It was the sea. I was on the beach. I stood staring at dark waves moving in under a half moon. I'd forgotten the sea's largeness, its purposefulness. Along the night horizon, scattered small ships silhouetted in lights made their passage known while near the water's edge, waves curled in with white crests and thunderous crashes carrying with them the odor of salt and seaweed.

A man and woman walked past me, talking. They didn't notice me in the shadow of the hotel. The woman was short and plump like my mother, and for a moment I thought it was her. The man was taller; they walked toward a breakwater some distance away. Once they were past, I walked down to the shore, took off my shoes, and let the sea wash my bare feet. Oh the pleasure of that!

The first time I saw the sea I was a child of five. Sonja and I had been in America only a few months when we were invited to visit elderly relatives wintering in Florida. For two glorious weeks we slept outside their trailer under what I thought was a circus awning. My mother and I drifted through the orange groves behind the trailer camp, picking oranges from the trees, or went driving with our relatives.

One day we drove along the coast near St. Petersburg. Looking out I saw all around and beyond us a strange blue ripple, a wavering horizon more inviting than the green fields in Iowa where Sonja and I were living then. My great aunt, who seemed to me endlessly old, practicing all night to behave in odd slow motion ways, suggested that my mother and I get out of the car while she and my great uncle, who never spoke, drank tea at a sidewalk café. Dodging swimmers rubbing themselves down and children playing ball, my mother marched me across the blond sand toward the waves. I held tight to her hand as we walked closer for I thought the waves were rushing in to devour us. But Sonja suddenly laughed and ran toward them. I never again saw her run and laugh as she did that day. Nor did we see ever see those elderly relatives after that visit - they seemed to vanish like all our family into oblivion.

We took off our shoes and my mother, carrying our belongings, tip toed deeper into the water dragging me behind her. For almost an hour we waded in the warm sea, even splashed water at each other. Laying down our possessions we grew bolder; we laughed and played together - something we'd never done before and I felt such a lightness of spirit, I feared a wave would carry me away.

The final pin was taken out of our despair.

Now this first evening in Mexico, I felt the same lightness descend upon me.

I ran into the sea. Let the waves smash into me. My blouse, skirt, socks clung to me, as I scrambled to keep my footing against the unexpected weight of the sea. But I was deliciously happy. At last I could be naughty. No one knew me or cared about me in the darkness. Finally I stumbled out of the water, walked slowly along the beach, happy in remembering the past, finding an old safe self after so many years.

It seemed all my thoughts were dissolving in the scent and sound of the sea.

I've never been afraid of the darkness. My eyes see well in the dark. My step sister Irene used to insist I was a cat, that I stole light from her. She'd whisper at me in the darkness of our bedroom. "You stole my light, yes you did; you know you did." I said nothing, just pretended to be asleep until she'd drifted away, then got up and went through her side of our shared chest of drawers. I put my hand down into each drawer and groped around to find something, anything that she might have hidden there. Sometimes I found things: games, dolls, books, whatever she was trying to keep from me. When she was older, it was letters she wrote to her girlfriends, then from her boyfriends. I'd take them down to the bathroom and read them. There were no secrets from me, not for Irene, not until she met Mick and married him and then everything, all of her became a secret, but soon she was gone, gone so completely out of my life that when I met her at family gatherings, I stared at her because she simply wasn't Irene anymore, but Mick's wife. Sonja and I capitalized it in our minds: "Mick's wife, his woman, his little wifie, his doll." My mother even said, "his slave".

When I needed my sister, she wasn't there, not anymore; she was a space, a hole in the air, torn out pages in a book, or those photographs which she deliberately took out of an album so there was a blank spot. When she spoke she prefaced everything with "Mick says" and "Mick thinks". All those years we'd slept in twin beds in the upstairs room, breathed the same air, played jacks together and paper dolls – interminable hours together - gone as if that had never been.

I stopped, shivering. Where did all that rattling nonsense come from? I haven't thought of Irene in months. I looked around. I was in a stretch of empty beach, ahead I could see a single bright light, behind me the lights of the hotel.

I turned, walked back, went to bed. At 1:30 a.m. Sonja swept in, heavy with scent and excitement; she leaned down, kissed my cheek. "I am happy you are here, my darling. Tonight I had a phone call from New York. Martin - my cousin Martin in Prague – he is dead. The last of my family." She waited but I didn't reply, instead pretended sleep, the deep drenched sleep of someone just off a plane.

How many days were we there? Such long full days that first week - the sand white, sometimes burning to the feet, yet at night cooled enough so that some preferred to walk outdoors, while others lingered in the bar built on the sand, a terrace without cover though the floor was tiled. Beautiful blue tiles, blue like the sea, blue like a man's eyes, like earrings wrapped in tissue paper or marbles lost behind hospital walls.

*   *   *   *   *

Sunday Day 1

I like this place," she said, our first morning at the hotel together. "I will meet interesting people here; I know this." Interesting was one of her favorite words. As long as I could remember, Sonja began the day with a cup of black coffee. That first Sunday morning she'd brought one over to my bed, tapped me on the shoulder, and said, "Get up. Here is your coffee." She plunked a pink plastic cup on the nightstand beside me.

I struggled up, looked at my red plastic Huey, Duey, and Luey travel alarm clock. It was 7 a.m. "It's early, Mama."

"While we're here, call me Sonja." She whisked into the bathroom, emerged, came over, sat down on her bed, and looked at me. She was wearing a shocking pink negligee. "I met some people on the plane from New York. I like them."

"What were you doing last night? You were out late."

"Yes. Last night. Other interesting people." She hesitated, stood up, went back to the bathroom, and splashed water on her face.

I sipped the coffee – instant, and weak. When she came out still wearing the pink negligee, she went to the chest of drawers and put on a silver and turquoise necklace. Setting the coffee on the nightstand, I sat up straighter.

"Were you out walking? I thought I saw you walking with someone last night."

Abruptly she turned to look at me then went back to staring at herself in the small mirror above the scarred chest of drawers. "I was in the casino –queen of the casino Dr. Herchmer called me." She gave a little chortle of pleasure.

I let it go. Why argue on our first morning?

"You look rested, you're sleeping better, I think."

"I had a facial before the trip." She stared at me, my mother; she held one hand between her generous breasts - a gesture familiar to me.

"Well, you look good, Mama."

"Remember."

"Sonja."

"He is a dentist. Dr. Herchmer."

"At least you know what to talk about."

"He does not talk about his work." Sonja said coyly. What kind of trouble was she getting herself into?

"What's Mrs. Herchmer like?"

She looked suddenly shy. "She was in the camps."

I stared at her." You talked about it?"

She looked away. "No. She saw."

"Never mind."

"She is a good person. We understand each other. We can talk."

I had trouble believing her. My mother was a complicated person. I changed the subject. "Well anyway Sonja, I think you look good."

"Were you surprised? To learn of my retirement?" She looked at me without expression.

"Yes. You like that job."

"I was asked to leave."

"Fired?"

"No, not fired. The word is 'laid off'- too old."

"You're only sixty."

"Too old; the great dentist needs young people around him." Her voice was bitter. She walked over to the window. The sky was widening into a high golden haze. Our window overlooking the road faced south; we would only guess at sunrise and sunset. Tomorrow, I promised myself, I must be outside on the beach for both.

My mother examined me from across the room. "You, Karin, do not look good."

"Tired."

"I will shake that man. Sometimes Greg is a fool."

"No, my husband is very smart. At least, everyone he works with thinks so."

My voice was sharper than I'd intended. Sonja came back over to my bed, sat down beside me and touched my cheek, then rose and went to the closet.

"What time did you get in? Two times I came back to the room."

"Not until after ten. The plane was very late."

"Karin, I left a message for you at the front desk."

Sonja took a flat square cosmetic case from her purse and opened it.

"There was no one at the desk. I looked all over for you."

I saw it contained make up brushes and circles of eye shadow. She chose colors and with an air of great concentration blended them like an artist, leaning forward to peer into the mirror. I was still sitting up in bed watching her, smoothing the covers as I had in the hospital, all of which seemed familiar, though nothing else did that first morning together in Mexico.

"Mama, last night it was wonderful to see the sea after so long."

"You walked on the beach?"

"For a little while."

Sonja stopped applying rouge and looked at me. "That is dangerous." She went into the bathroom, came out a few minutes later wearing a low cut black swim suit and a turquoise necklace.

Her legs were fleshy but firm, the rest of her plump and curvaceous. She snapped the makeup case shut, thrust it into a big carved leather handbag.

"I like your purse." I said.

"Josef bought it for me on our last trip to Mexico." She sat down on the side of her bed to thrust her plump feet into black sandals. "You should not do that - go on the beach at night."

"I was there only a few minutes Mama." I got out of bed determined to say nothing more about the evening before. "Did he buy you the necklace too?"

"No."

"It's beautiful."

"I hope you will not do that - go out at night alone." She watched as I marched past her into the bathroom. "You have no nightgown?"

"Too much trouble." Even as I said those words, I knew my mother would not let the subject go.

"I gave you a pretty nightgown at Christmas."

"I haven't worn one since I was sick, Mama. I had a high fever."

"So you said." She picked up the red plastic Huey, Duey and Luey alarm clock. "Where did you walk on the beach last night?"

"The sea was so beautiful. Do you remember Florida?"

"I came to find you, Karin. Eleven o'clock I came. I thought you will be in bed. I was worried I tell you." Sonja's eyes, with makeup, were huge, dramatic. She put down Huey, Duey and Luey. "I do not like this clock. Time is not a joke." She went into the bathroom, returned carrying a small bottle of cologne, and once again leaning into the mirror, anointed herself with White Shoulders cologne. My mother looked attractive; her curly black hair was only faintly streaked with gray. Now she wore a wreath of delicate scent.

"I will go to the beach."

"No breakfast, Mama?"

"I ate last night. The midnight buffet, it is excellent, a good meal."

"Who took you to the casino?"

"Dr. Herchmer - he said I brought him luck." She dimpled at me, waited for me to ask about him. I resisted, instead looked out the window. From the bed all I saw was an empty road and pale mountains in the distance. Sonja went to the door, came back, took a long terrycloth sweater out of the closet. "Karin, you will dress now?"

"You smell fantastic, Mama."

"I want to introduce you - such nice people the Herchmers. Drink the coffee I made for you."

"I'll come in an hour or so, Mama. Where's the dining room?"

"Close. You will find it," she said, and was out the door.

I lay back shocked by her nonchalance. My mother had never so precipitously abandoned me before, not on the rare holidays we took together. I got up at once. Who were these new friends? I dressed in shorts and prepared to go out, but first sat down and put through the call I'd promised myself on the flight down. "Greg?"

"I told you not to call me at the university."

"I need my money."

"Today? I thought you were in Mexico."

"I put the ticket on my credit card."

"Your mother paid for it."

"It's my money, Greg."

"You'll get it. Say hello to Sonja for me."

He hung up. I slammed down the phone and went outside. Furious, I walked into the small garden by the swimming pool and sat down on an elderly chair.

What forces moved through me to create such anger? I hadn't even asked about the girls yet Greg was taking care of them for the week. The small garden was quiet and gradually my temper cooled. No one came by for a few minutes then up wandered the big friendly man I'd encountered the night before. He smiled and strolled into the garden space.

"Hi lost one. Did you find your mother?"

"Barely. She's already on the beach."

He sat down beside me. "The dining room's closed. But you can get coffee and rolls at the outdoor bar. Name's Desmond Nicholson."

"Karin Carter"

'Karin - a German name."

"Czech."

He settled back into the lounge chair and stretched his legs out so I noticed how strong they looked. He wore black shorts and a black tee shirt. We sat in silence for a minute, staring everywhere except at each other.

"Did you make it to the dining room last night?" I turned to find myself looking into wildcat blue eyes.

"I ate in the bar and watched a bad French movie and learned about greed. Beautiful half-naked women are greedy but if you put lots of them in a movie you can make up for a bad script. Going to the beach this morning?"

"I don't think so. I can't handle too much sun right away."

"Or too much mother."

"That was naughty."

"What about night swimming? Can you handle that?"

"Have you tried it?" My voice sounded as shy as I suddenly felt. He raised his eyebrows in disbelief. "Put my body in the sea at night? A mermaid might kidnap me." He stood up. "I'm taking off for the morning. Anything you need from town?"

"I haven't even unpacked. Thanks anyway."

"Karin, right?"

"With an 'i'."

"You should always smile." With his cat grin in place and his hands in his pockets, he strolled away. I sat for a half an hour after he left. Conversation with a pleasant, lighthearted stranger seemed to heal the bitterness that rose in me whenever I talked to Greg. Toward my husband I held an anger I couldn't control, couldn't banish and which seemed to harm me more than him.

I went for a walk. The beach front was half empty; attendants were laying out towels and setting up chairs, only a few guests had arrived burdened with the day's supplies. Nobody cavorted in the sea. It was too early, the sun too pale, the line of waves like a razor enveloping us. I walked down to the water, took off my sandals, and dipped my toes in – cold. The sea seemed that morning to be the cold heart of the earth itself. But its salt smell enticed me. I let the water wash my feet, looked out at the small islands that lay along our horizon. I wanted to learn their names. Perhaps I might go to one. There must be boats. These thoughts pleased me. I'm here, I thought - never mind what's coming next, enjoy each moment. 'Experience the now.' the counselor had said.

His words stayed with me. I'd come on this holiday determined to try. Yet already there were complications; my emotions more volatile than I liked. For years, I'd preferred calmness, had practiced discipline, been reassured by a feeling of indifference to everything that seemed to creep up on me. I'd worked hard to appear the same way to everyone, even my mother. But some part of me was making that more difficult to sustain; a second self was pressing against the walls of the old, forcing a breakout, a breakthrough, even a breakdown – an escape route out of what seemed to be my destiny.

In the airport in Denver, waiting for my flight to Mazatlan, I'd walked into a restroom and straight into blood all over the floor. A woman had either cut herself badly or was menstruating heavily. The sight of that bright red poured out across the white tile floor astonished me, and then abruptly for the first time, I felt my own loss - the monthly reminder of nature's hold, the known pain of a crimson flow rising up out of a mystery. That mystery of my blood was gone forever and there was no one to console me. Now I must submit, not to an internal clock, but to the hours and days of the world's time, must risk myself against things external not internal.

Mexico might be the beginning of this new challenge. I prayed. I stood in the sea and prayed for help. Prayed to a God I barely believed in.

Then I walked down to the outside bar on the west side of the building, took a coffee and sweet bun to a table and sat slowly eating and drinking everything in - the sun, the sky, the sea, the air, the coffee, the sweet bun.

*   *   *   *   *

I'd missed the sunrise that first morning, but the sun was still pale when I went for a walk. The smell of the sea seemed life itself, and its roar a deep cry from the earth. I walked slowly, breathing it all in. I was happy, not myself at all.

"Do you want to run?"

I turned, startled to find a young man had walked up behind me. I stopped and looked at him. He was a dark strong looking young Mexican. He'd halted too, stood waiting, muscular arms on muscular hips.

A new brave self spoke in me. "Yes. Yes I would like that."

At once he jogged down the beach. I didn't think, just followed him. It was the first time I'd run on sand, soft dry sand, bleached white.

How odd, I thought. I don't know this man. But my body exulted.

"Swing your arms. Let your hands hang loose."

I did as he ordered. We ran on past the boundaries of the hotel beach front into the next area, that of a small motel where Mexicans sitting on the beach stared at us. I was beginning to breathe hard.

"Control your breath." The young runner dictated. "Own it. Let it out in small puffs like this." He demonstrated and I obeyed.

I felt the energy of my body. We ran in and out of the incoming waves, shifting from white sand to cool shallow water. We turned and ran back to the place where we'd first met beside the hotel wall.

27

He stopped. "I must work," he said. He had a dark, ferocious look, but dignity.

"Thank you." By then I was breathing with effort.

"Let me see you again." He didn't look at me when he said those words and so I didn't think much about them. "I can run with you tomorrow morning if you wish."

"That would be great." I managed still gasping for breath. Without another word, he walked away. I stood in the shade of the wall until I'd cooled down. I saw the young man down by the water with two other men. They were fitting a hotel guest into a para-glider harness.

*   *   *   *   *

"There you are, Karin. Come. Sit with me. Why no swim suit?"

"It's already too hot, Mama."

"It's eleven o'clock."

"It's too hot for me."

"If an old lady like me can sit in the sun, a pretty young woman can."

Sonja sat in a row of lounge chairs under umbrellas with little tables. Each table held an iced drink complete with straw. On the beach, chairs were claimed early in the morning by towels draped across them. Sonja was sitting with a couple of her own age, a man and woman in their sixties. Next to the man was a younger man, stocky, with close-cropped hair. He stared at me but didn't smile. Sonja offered me her coke. I shook my head. Behind her the sea with all its mysteries rolled in.

"She has a new suit, Mrs. Herchmer, such a pretty bikini. When I was her age I couldn't wear a bikini."

"Nobody could, Mrs. Mika. It was against the law. It was like being naked."

Mrs. Herchmer gave me a friendly smile. She was thin and wore a big sun hat and sunglasses. She was working embroidery with fingers that were long and elegant.

"Karin, when you have a good figure you show it. Go put on that pretty suit."

"It's too hot, Mama."

"I will buy you all a drink," Dr. Herchmer put down his book. "What would you like?" He was big boned and slow moving. He had a wide, full face and wore glasses. When he talked, his chin fell into folds.

"Nothing for me right now, Dr. Herchmer." I said. "But I promise you, I'll come back later and take you up on that offer." I went to stand beside my mother. "I'm going to read for a while, Mama. I'm still tired from the flight yesterday."

Sonja took my hand, but looked at her new friends.

"She is always reading, Dr. Herchmer. She is a scholar but enough is enough. Come, Karin, sit with us. This is our holiday. We have been laughing. There are some funny people here, believe me. We are having a good time. Tell her, Mrs. Herchmer."

Mrs. Herchmer looked up from her embroidery - a pillowcase.

"A wonderful time; your mother is great fun, Karin, a lively lady."

"Where are you going, Karin?"

"To the room, Mama."

*   *   *   *   *

Sonja refused to grieve. She avoided talking about Josef or about her retirement, or even the death of her cousin Martin. With her new friends, she was determinedly gay, or what passed in Sonja for gaiety - a drive to be everywhere, to watch and comment on everyone, to dress relentlessly in the dramatic clothes she invariably chose. For our first dinner together in Mexico that evening, she wore a ruffled black blouse, shocking pink cummerbund, and floral skirt - a long Hawaiian splash of pink, pale pink, green flowers and leaves. Her nails were longer than I remembered but not false. She'd piled her discreetly dyed hair on top of her head which made her look taller, as did the white high-heeled sandals. She looked deeply interesting.

I doubted I did. But I was rested. I'd slept most of the first afternoon, and thought about my future. How would I survive if I left Greg? I'd stopped going to classes at the university and would soon have to leave. What about my daughters? Should I ask my mother for help so I could keep custody of them? It wouldn't be easy to win her support. Our years apart, the different lives we'd led since my marriage, our very different views on success would all have to be overcome.

Our first dinner together passed agreeably. We chose a quiet corner where we could talk and avoided speaking of the past. I talked of my daughters, how well they were doing in school. How both dreamed of going to university. That pleased my mother. She briefly spoke of my step sister Irene, but mainly we planned how we wished to spend our time together in Mexico. We drank glasses of white wine.

The pastas we ordered were excellent, our waiter friendly. He was a plump middle aged man with a wide, anxious face. He spoke no English but smiled at Sonja when she fussed about whether to order a dessert or not. Sonja was so pleased with the evening, she smiled back and patted his shoulder in a motherly way, then hugged him goodbye and with unprecedented generosity gave him a large tip. The waiter looked shocked. When we walked back to our room, he followed us. But he looked unhappy. At first Sonja did not notice him trotting obediently at her heels but when we arrived at our door, he followed us into the room.

"No, no, no," Sonja said, when he stood looking at her with sad eyes. He didn't move. She physically pushed him away from her side several times, then when he still didn't depart, she gave him a great whacking shove which propelled him out the door. "What did he want?" she demanded of me in an excited voice when he was gone.

"He was a strange waiter." I laughed, but said nothing more.

Everything about that holiday was unusual. Mexico seemed a destiny as well as a destination. I went there seeking renewal, and rediscovered my mother and the sea.

Sunday, Night, Day 1

Flowers are strong. They grow not just in rich soil and public gardens, but in desolate spaces, they bloom in hidden places. They need summer soil and warmth but endure rain, heat, drought and wind. They go on blooming even after they are plucked and their fate seems certain.

To follow this story of Mexico you must know something about me. I ran toward trouble at times, instead of from it. I did what I was warned not to do. This is probably not courage, but the actions of a fool.

I was told a terrible story by a man who experienced it. He was standing near a young woman at a cocktail party. They were outside on a patio in a high rise apartment. And the young woman sat on the edge of the balcony. The host said, "Be careful sitting on the edge like that. Be sure you don't lean back." The girl, a little drunk, laughed and said," You mean like this?" Then she leaned back and fell to her death.

I understand that girl.

Sunday night, after we talked in the room for awhile, both Sonja and I went to bed but I couldn't sleep. After an hour or so, I got up, dressed in shorts and a shirt, and made my way through the mysteries of the Madre Maria Hotel at night - along blue tiled floors, beside thatched beach umbrellas onto the lighted beachfront of the resort. There was only a small moon and beyond the hotel beach complete darkness edged in.

As a teenager I wandered almost every night, partly for exercise and partly to test myself against fear. Our first years in the U.S. were good ones: Sonja obtained work as a secretary in the Slavic Languages department of a university in a small Iowa city. We both felt safe. By my teens, when Sonja was busy in the evening I went out by myself. I ran on the campus walks near our apartment, or went to the student union where the activities' rooms were full of students, or even into its cafeteria where young men and women in black sweaters debated the sins of the world. Sometimes I walked from dormitories to classrooms along paths where I found lovers embracing against trees or lying together on the grass. No one bothered me. I wasn't afraid though sometimes hid when I saw someone coming toward me in a dark stretch. Sonja never knew. It was part of my rebellion against her claustrophobic parenting.

Later I absorbed more caution and rarely went out alone at night – too dangerous everyone said - until Mexico, when that first Sunday night, restless and sleepless, I once again dared myself into darkness. The night watchman sitting at a table on the hotel terrace reassured me; otherwise so close to midnight there was no one moving except me. The sea wave sound was so loud and stern it seemed a wall against fear.

I'd not swum that day and suddenly I could stand it no longer. I rushed toward the water and waded in further and further until, caught by an incoming wave, I was overwhelmed, my shirt and shorts drenched. Shocked, I backed up, then laughed and walked forward until another wave washed over my head. I turned my back against the incoming waves but still walked forward against them, enjoying the taste of salt on my tongue and on my face, feeling a naughty child. I swam heading away from shore. Above me a crescent moon smiled down. Some way from shore I stopped, treaded water, and feeling the weight of my clothes, unbuttoned my shirt and pulled it away from my body, yet held on to it. Wave after wave came in - I weakened as I felt their strength and became alarmed at my own bravado. What on earth was I doing swimming alone in a dark sea? Would anyone be there to rescue me if I grew too tired to swim to shore?

The waves carried me back into shallow water. I stood up, struggled back into the wet shirt. I was not cold. This was Mexico in

March; the wind was warm. The night watchman still sat motionless on the terrace; otherwise I was alone. It was still too magic a night for me to retreat. I began walking slowly along the edge of the water away from the hotel, and as I did so I saw in the distance two figures. They appeared to be embracing - or was it a struggle? I slowed, waited; at last they vanished.

I walked up the beach to a stone breakwater. Built on a curve along the coast where the beach narrowed and the water deepened, it was surrounded by broken concrete slabs and stones. The water around it was full of foam. No Swimming and Danger signs were posted nearby. I climbed up and walked its length to look out at the horizon. The largest island was just visible. Two toy ships moved across the horizon. Then almost by accident I looked down at the foaming water below me. A body was tugging against the stonework.

Shivering now, with fear and horror as well as cold, I bent down to see more clearly and almost fell in. Attempting another look, this time more certainly planted in the center of the stonework, I saw it was a young man, fully clothed, lying on his face. His body was bobbing in the action of the waves as they struck the stonework. The smell was of seaweed and sewage. Was it also of the corpse?

My teeth began chattering. I stumbled back across the breakwater, walked as fast as I could to the hotel. There was no sign of the night watchman on the terrace so I rushed inside to the front desk. The desk clerk was reading, slumped over almost out of sight, but he got up when he saw me stumble in blinking in the bright light.

"There's a body in the sea." I said.

"Where?" His hands came down hard on the registry book, as though to keep it from flying away. "Where is this body?"

"By the breakwater."

"Tell no one," he said. "I will call the police." He waited, dark eyes on me, then lifted the phone, since I wasn't going to move until he did call them. Still wet, I stood at the desk while he spoke rapid Spanish into the phone, then he put his hand over the receiver. "They will be here at once. As I said, please say nothing to the other guests."

"No, no of course not."

"You were outside?"

"I couldn't sleep. I went for a walk."

He stared at me a blank look still in his eyes, but his voice was firm.

"You must stay in your room. At night, the beach it is not safe."

He sounded so much like my mother I immediately decided to disobey him. Resisting advice is a difficult habit to break.

"I thought at first it was a swimmer but the body was in street clothes. Perhaps someone was taken ill."

"Thank you, Senora. The police will care for him." His voice was brusque. I didn't bother to challenge this narrow faced young man. He had a right to believe that anyone dumped into the sea was a man, not a woman. I was so tired by then I could barely stand up. I turned away without saying anything more, went back to the room and prepared for bed. Sonja was asleep, her face to the wall; I too lost myself in sleep.

Monday morning, when I thought about that night adventure, I wondered what made me do such foolish things. Was it rebellion against my mother's myriad warnings? A need for excitement, for danger? Did I believe that because I had been saved so many times before, I would always be saved? Or was I despairing of my life and tempting fate? Do I really want to die and am looking for someone or something that will make that happen? No. I thought. I can never believe I will just give up.

Monday, Day 2

Despite my late hours the night before, I was up and dressed early Monday morning. I was meeting Roberto to go running again. He'd left me a note at the front desk - that's how I learned his name. I slipped out of the room while Sonja was still asleep since I'd decided not to tell her about this adventure with a stranger.

That morning we ran up the beach past the breakwater and well beyond the last of the houses and hotels. At one point Roberto stopped and led me up the hillside to show me, behind a jumble of rocks, a small hidden cave. Was he suggesting a sexual tryst? I'd been faithful to my marriage. I didn't know how to discourage him, but like everything in my life then, I was unable to make a decision and so instead surrendered myself into the hands of fate.

We walked most of the way back to the hotel. By then we were talking. Roberto spoke of his family and of his mother who'd disappeared when he was a child.

"How can you know nothing, nothing at all?"

"All my family will say is that she died when I was a child. But there is no grave, no photographs. I think she is alive somewhere, and so I look for her. I look for her everywhere I go." His voice throbbed with emotion. Out in the bay, a fine mist stretched over the sea. It was still early morning. The sea smell was stinging to my nostrils.

"You'll find her some day." I was getting bored with the topic of his mother. Roberto was wearing white, which set off his brown skin and eyes and that morning he looked young and happy.

"Maybe. But I look for her always. I look in every woman's eyes, especially when they are beautiful like yours." The mist drifted across the water, away from us. "Sometimes I think God is a woman too. God is both man and woman, so I am held safe there in the womb of God, part of her being and his dream."

"That's beautiful. How beautiful you are." The words fell out of me unintended. Warmth of feeling engulfed me. I looked at him with new respect.

"So are you," he said in a soft voice, but I didn't meet his eyes, looked instead behind him at a bright blue sea, a pale blue sky.

When I got back to the room, Sonja was gone, having joined the Herchmers on the beach. I went back to bed. It was nearly noon when I found the three of them sitting in a row in beach chairs. Dr. Herchmer looked up from his book and smiled a benediction; Mrs.

Herchmer commented on how rested I looked; Sonja organized me - or tried to. "Where are you going, Karin?"

"For a swim."

"Sit down, I missed you all morning."

"I want to swim first."

"Please, darling, I want to talk with you."

"O.K. but I'll get us all some coffee, then I'll sit down."

At the outdoor bar, the young man who'd sat with the Herchmers the day I met them was drinking a beer. He had the beginnings of a black beard, and his green eyes seemed harsh, his smile off kilter. He hadn't spoken to me the first day, so I was surprised when he did in the bar.

"Getting some swimming in?" His voice was an injured sound.

I smiled politely, but didn't reply.

The heavy set Mexican bartender brought four coffees on a tray. Behind him a radio at the back of the bar was tuned to a murmur of voices. A cluster of bees buzzed dizzily by the beer taps.

"Take it easy in those waves," the beer drinker called out as I turned away with the tray. "They can be rough at night." The words seemed to hang in the air behind me. I took the coffees back to Sonja and the Herchmers, then sat down and took out a small notebook. I'd decided by then to keep a diary, a dream diary the counselor had called it. I'd refused in Boulder, afraid of what might come, but I felt safe in Mexico. Just dreams I thought – or odd thoughts.

I'd brought books with me too - nothing heavy, just anything I'd put off reading as not serious enough. Yet in those first days all I wanted to do was enjoy the new world I'd been plummeted into. In the mid day heat, the beach was a room, a busy, crowded restaurant of sun and sand full of people in constant motion - sleeping, talking, walking, swimming, playing, buying, selling. But it was the color of the sea that astounded me most, a blue so clean and vivid that as I lay dozing under a thatched umbrella, I suddenly thought of two possessions I'd treasured as a child. My older brother Stefan had kept a small leather bag full of marbles. Two of them were in my pocket when we were separated; they were as blue as my brother's eyes. I sat up. It was an odd memory.

I opened the notebook.

The hospital

I had the blue marbles with me

If I held them I would see my brother again

There's an unending sky outside and Stefan's safe there

If I lose the marbles something will happen to me

Better hide them

I *dropped them down the little hole in the wall behind my bed*

A *horrible lost feeling passed through me when I did that*

Part of me just disappeared into the darkness of the hole

Enough! I slammed the diary shut. Why remember all that? The camp was a closed space, the hospital, a terrible place; smells were of disease and death, sounds, fear and pain. I was frightened there. Once I was told I would be sent away, another time that my mother was dead. Every time I was sent to the hospital I grew more frightened, convinced that I would never leave again. I was afraid to tell anyone, to cry in case they noticed me. But the marbles told me I would see my mother again.

I'd learned something about myself - that in the hospital I was afraid I'd vanish.

I felt more and more that way as the days passed in Mexico.

*   *   *   *   *

By late afternoon Monday, Sonja was packing up her things.

"I will rest," she said. "Will you come with me, Karin?"

"I want to sit by the pool for awhile. It's cooler there."

"Is there a pool?" Mrs. Herchmer looked up from her embroidery. "I didn't know that. Where is it?"

"It's not very clean." Dr. Herchmer who'd been dozing opened his eyes and half sat up. "You wouldn't want to swim there."

Walking toward the garden, I sensed someone behind me and turned to see Dr. Herchmer, a tense half-smile on his face, following me. I didn't speak. He passed by me and went into the hotel. I sat down on one of the battered chairs by the pool.

I was annoyed with Sonja. She'd discussed me with the Herchmers. Told them what a silent child I was, how I'd said nothing for months when we first came to America, how I was like my father - an apology she made for me when she felt my social failings.

"Silent people, they worry you. What they are thinking, if something is wrong. They do not tell you their feelings." She'd confessed, not for the first time, that she did not know why my father was arrested. "Why not tell me what he was doing? I was his wife." Sonja spoke of my father with a veiled contempt for his guilt that angered me.

I'd thought him a hero.

"Anton was taken the year before - with Stefan our son. Anton was a talented man - brilliant many people said – he played the organ, a musician, a real professional musician, but he threw his life away, threw our life away." Sonja's voice had assumed its deepest tone. "He joined the resistance. Became obsessed with it. The whole war he contributed nothing to our household, only suffering he gave us, like all the resistance. They thought nothing of the consequences.

They did not know the Germans, not at all. The war – you know this Greta - it was a struggle to stay alive." Sonja sighed.

She was sitting in her beach chair, wearing dark glasses and a large straw hat, looking the epitome of a suffering European intellectual. Only I knew better. My mother had a secondary school education; my father had not had that.

Mrs. Herchmer was sewing, looking up now and then to nod sympathetically, but Dr. Herchmer was mesmerized. His book had fallen on the sand; he'd sat up, pushed away his drink for the first time that afternoon, and was staring steadily at my mother.

"What was your badge?" he asked.

"Red. Anton was a communist. But when we reached the camp we were marked lavender."

"Better for you," Greta Herchmer said, picking through her embroidery threads in search of a new color.

"Yes. Jehovah Witnesses, we worked in the kitchen, then later..." she paused. "Never mind, "Greta said. "You have said enough. I understand."

Sonja fell silent. We all did.

Alone by the pool I thought about the conversation. I was four years old when the war ended, five when we came to America. I wanted nothing from the past - an obsession but my truth. All I knew as a child was what I thought was a normal world whether in a camp or in America. When I was sick I was taken to a special place for sick people. When I was separated from my mother, some adults were kind to me, others were not. Sometimes there were children to play with. Those are the appropriate memories – the ones that will allow me to live my life as a normal person. Who wants to remember cruelty, death, barbarism on a massive national scale? Sonja and I had survived but my father and brother Stefan were taken to Buchenwald where they perished. The unfairness of that haunted me as young woman, but as I grew older I no longer thought about them. So why now have I thought of those marbles?

As the afternoon drifted into late sun and stilled heat, the pool seemed more stagnant, the trees more shabby than before. But the rubrun lilies thrust out their blossoms with assurance and slowly the garden worked its magic on me. My thoughts grew more ordered; my mind no longer assaulted me with questions about my husband and daughters, and how I must solve all the problems life was presenting me.

I still didn't know what to tell Sonja. I knew what she would say, the questions she would ask. "You want to be unhappy? Why leave a good man? Have I not suffered enough for both us?" We'd planned one shopping trip into town; I'd tried to convince her to tour the countryside with me too, but she said she'd seen enough on her previous trips. She did mention visiting friends in Mazatlan. I had thought away from the hotel we might find a place to talk. But we didn't need to go away for fireworks to begin between us.

* * * * *

That evening, as Sonja and I rested in the room before dinner, she suddenly got up from her bed and began to dress for dinner.

"Where are you going?" I was half-asleep.

"I thought to see what happened to Andres before dinner," she said.

"Andres? Who is that?"

She was patting cream on her face, rubbing it in with tender strokes of her soft hands. "A nice young man. We talked here at the hotel. A repair man. He came to the hotel to change the pool, or drain it, or something to do with the pool." Sonja took out her gold jewelry, a short roped chain and matching clip earrings. "I thought I will see him again, but he is not here."

I got up to dress too since my mother liked us to walk together to dinner. I'd decided that in order to win my freedom at night, I would be obedient to her every wish at dinner. That evening we planned to eat in the bar.

"I can see why the pool needs repair." I said, as I combed my long hair and re- braided it. "I can't imagine anyone ever swam in it."

"Impossible, so dirty, yes. So …what is the word?"

"Murky. You haven't seen him? Andres?" I laid out my single long dress.

"Not since the night you came. We talked, he was…" she hesitated, "complimentary. But since then I do not see him." She put on a long black dress almost identical to mine. I'd never seen it before.

"Where did you get the dress?"

"I bought it today at the shop here. Not expensive."

I opened my suitcase. What else did I have to wear? I didn't like playing what I thought of as "Tweedledum and Tweedledee" with my mother. I pulled out the only other dress I'd brought, a green sundress.

"Is that warm enough?" Sonja asked.

"We're in the tropics, Mama."

"Sonja. You forget to call me Sonja."

"Okay, outside you are Sonja. In our room, I call you Mama."

Sonja sighed. "Oh, you are so stubborn, Karin."

"I take after you, Mama. Was Andre wearing a red plaid shirt?"

Sonja picked up her White Shoulders perfume bottle, looked at me. "I cannot remember. Yes something red, his shirt, and yes, red. Why?"

"There was a dead body in the water wearing a red shirt."

Sonja's mouth opened. Her mouth formed a wide O, and she put down the White Shoulders bottle. "What are you telling me?"

"I saw a man in the water."

"When was this?"

"Last night."

"Oh my God. You might have died too." She was genuinely distressed.

I didn't reply, but put on my green sun dress. My mother insisted on lending me a white shawl to cover my bare back.

It was a mistake to have told her. Sonja would complicate what I thought then was simple. "You must ask," she said urgently, "Ask who this man is. I have not seen Andres. He said he had work at the hotel. Please, Karin, ask."

I looked at her sternly. "Why do you care?"

"He was a nice man, a good man. He told me he was working here; he would be here for several weeks. He said he would help me."

I was puzzled. "Help you how?"

Looking in the mirror, I saw the white shawl was perfect. My mother came over to adjust it. She was talking in a low nervous voice.

"Help me find my friends. I have friends here, old friends from Europe. I have an address, but I do not understand where it is. Andres said he would help me. He lives in Mazatlan. He knows the town. He said he would help me find these people."

Her voice and face revealed an anguish disproportionate to her acquaintanceship with the mysterious Andres.

*   *   *   *   *

The bar was noisy and smoky that night. After supper Dr. Herchmer invited us to their table for Spanish coffee. Sonja began to ask guests sitting nearby if they had heard about a body found off shore. No one had. To please her, and curious about the dead man, I went to the front desk.

"The body in the sea – was it a swimming accident?"

The desk clerk, a tall, handsome black man I hadn't seen before, looked at me blankly, "A body?"

"I reported I saw a man's body in the sea last night."

"I don't know about this, what you talk about here." He moved uneasily. 'Please, you must explain what this problem is. I am only just come to work."

"There was some kind of accident. Last night I saw a man's body by the breakwater. Did the hotel find out anything? Was he a guest?"

"I am first here only this morning. I will ask."

"Please do." I waited while he left the desk and retired to the office behind. In a few minutes he returned. His response surprised me.

"Was it a matter for the police?"

"I left it up to you, to the hotel. All I did was report the body."

"Ah yes, a report. You alone made the report? We have no record of it."

I was offended by his stupidity, his tone of disbelief. I'd seen a body the night before. I'd reported it, and the night desk clerk had made a note to include it in their hotel book and then called the police. This clerk informed me that he knew nothing about it. I had to struggle not to let my anger show as I walked away.

I found myself looking for Desmond. He was such a calming man. How strange that he'd totally disappeared. He had a room in our annex the night I arrived. Or had he? I hadn't seen him since Sunday morning, but I remembered him saying he was going away somewhere. I joined the others in the bar. When we rose to go, on our way out, Dr. Herchmer murmured words that Sonja and Greta couldn't hear. "I shared something very special with you last night."

I didn't understand him and must have looked my doubt for then he put his arm around my shoulder and leaned closer. "I saw you swimming in the sea." He had a little smile on his face, "Like a nymph you were. I will never forget."

I blushed, and pulled away. Sonja and I said goodnight.

We walked out on the sand close to the hotel and stood for a few moments looking up at stars that had spread with great efficiency across the entire universe. The sound of the sea was overwhelming, but so was the three-piece combo in the outdoor bar playing mambo hits. We retreated back to the annex. I tried to say goodnight by the door, but Sonja objected to my staying out alone. My temper was short by then. "Mama, I like to wander around. That's good for me. Leave me alone."

"I do not bother you," Sonja said, in an offended voice. "If we take this trip together, I wish to spend some time with my daughter."

"I am spending time with you. I think you are worried about losing your job. And I'm sorry about your cousin in Prague." But I sounded more sarcastic than sincere.

She pressed her lips together, "My job? I am too old. That is what everyone thinks. That is what you think. And this cousin, he cooperated. With everybody he cooperated. And helped no one. Why should I grieve for him?"

"But you are, Mama. I know you are. He was part of your life."

"What do you know? Nothing. You are too young, Karin, too American." We went on arguing stupidly until Sonja broke away to snap goodnight and vanish inside. We'd spent the entire day together. It was already too much togetherness. I went into the hotel, to the front desk where the nervous young clerk was holding court and booked a tour for Wednesday, then called home. The girls were cooking spaghetti with their dad and sounded happy. I walked up and down the beach until my own contentment returned; even sang a little when I was sure the waves would drown out my song. Twice I thought I saw Desmond striding purposefully in from the untamed stretch beyond the hotel, but it was too dark to be sure.

How I loved the night there! The shadows made by the walls of the hotel, the beach equipment, the floodlights were a chessboard of geometry, and I, like all mutable people, could force myself into the design around me. Loss of self isn't keenly felt after midnight. Near the edge of the hotel, on a deserted stretch I sat on the beach and looked at the stars. Lay back and dazzled myself with them. Very late, near that same empty stretch beyond the hotel, I slipped off my sundress, and this time holding on to it, swam naked in the sea. No one saw me. After a few minutes I slipped into my clothes, and back in the room, after toweling dry my hair and body, went to bed.

Tuesday, Day 3

A vision of clutter stretched all along the hotel beach: chairs, umbrellas, towels, plastic cups and glasses, candy bar wrappers, shoes, straw hats with and without distinction, wadded Kleenexes, squeezed flat suntan cream, paperback books, magazines, cans. All temporarily essential yet easily erased - one sweep of the waves would make it all disappear. This domestic clutter was coated with fine bits of pure white sand and was a potpourri of timid smells on a wild sea breeze.

We were sitting on the beach - my mother and I - Tuesday morning. I was reading 'Lord of the Rings' by Tolkien, enjoying that landscape artist of England; the pages turned easily and I was far away. My own adventures were unfolding too – earlier I'd been running with Roberto; he'd again led me down the coast to look at the cave. This time we'd climbed up the embankment to peer into a body sized hole between slabs of rock. What he wanted was becoming clearer. Breaking my marriage vows was not something I'd thought about before Mexico. Yet events – and my own actions - were leading me in that direction. But why was I so dreadfully conscious of it all? Why didn't mindless passion step in and take over? I was faintly resentful. And sitting next to Sonja an activity as revolutionary as an affair seemed far away.

My mother straightened up. On her face was harshness.

"They look German," she said.

She was watching a young couple, part of a group that had just arrived. All were talking and laughing, but an invisible chord stretched between the young couple; occasionally they reached out to touch each other. Both were tall and strong looking; both had blond hair streaked with the sun.

I looked at them too. "You see, Mama, that's the length I want my hair."

"Oh, no, no, your hair is good.'"

"It takes forever to wash. Besides braids are not in style. I want to cut it."

"No, no. You have pretty hair. You must not cut it. Nathan, speak to her. Tell my daughter what you said: How beautiful her hair is, how different from other young women she is."

Dr. Herchmer looked up from a history of World War II with a smile directed at me. "It doesn't matter how she wears her hair," he said.

The young couple - the magic pair - rose and walked, like a beach advertisement, hand and hand, into the sea. He was graceful with a muscular, smooth chest; she was thin and tight-muscled in the California way. They were both in bikinis.

"Look," Sonja said in a sharp voice. "Like movie stars. Do they work like the rest of us?" She said this to Mrs. Herchmer who didn't reply or look up from her embroidery; her hands were rarely still. She was a quiet person and graceful.

"You wife does such beautiful work," I murmured to her husband when a few minutes later he came over to sit near me.

"She likes to make beauty," he said. He was drinking gin neat from a small glass, and soon summoned a waiter to order another. "From her hands will come something new and perfect – or so she likes to believe. If what she makes is not perfect, so should we care? No one knows that but her. She gives away what she makes." He nodded his head emphatically. "More of us should be like her. Of course for those of us who are practical, who must struggle," he shrugged his shoulders, "if that seems a little self indulgent, so what? We are all self-indulgent one way or another." He flashed an oddly ugly smile at me but I pretended not to notice. Sonja looked stunned after these words, but I watched Mrs. Herchmer more closely. Expressionless, she let her hands move swiftly like humming birds so that colored threads were coiled into shapes, into patterns.

*   *   *   *   *

Nathan Herchmer was not a lucky man. Sonja told me he lost money every night gambling. That afternoon when he invited my mother and me to go to the casino with him after dinner, Greta Herchmer objected. She never went to the casino, only rarely ate in the dining room, and retired to their room early in the evening. For the first time they argued in our presence.

"You are foolish, Nathan. This is not a good way to spend our money."

"I disagree, Greta, I disagree. I've been warned enough times by you, by others, and then found out I might have made money, a great deal of money, if I hadn't listened to you. But from now on, I will do without your advice; I will not listen to you." Dr. Herchmer's voice didn't change but he picked up his drink and downed it.

Mrs. Herchmer stared out to sea; for some moments her hands were still. For the first time I recognized how much he drank, and how rarely she spoke. Yet that first week in Mexico I was mainly concerned with negotiating the difficult shoals of my relationship with Sonja, plotting how to tell her what was happening in my life in Colorado, yet not telling her anything about my adventures at the Hotel Madre Maria.

"How dirty this beach is - so much garbage." Sonja suddenly said in a loud voice. "Why leave food like this, so flies come?" She pointed to scattered trash near us. I turned back to my pages; this was not a complaint I would reply to. "Did you hear me, Karin? The beach is dirty. There is garbage everywhere. Why are we at this hotel, such a dirty hotel?" She said this looking at Dr. Herchmer, who avoided her eyes. "I think there are cleaner beaches and hotels where such people do not bother us."

This was said as a desiccated old Mexican man approached us. He carried trays of rings; we waved him away; he was followed by a solemn eyed woman selling rugs.

"I will buy you a ring," said Sonja loudly. The ring man turned back; the rug woman departed.

"Mama, I don't need anything."

"Pick a ring, please."

"I don't want a ring."

"Karin, I will buy you a ring, and you will wear it," she said, and her voice was fierce. What did she think - my poor mother - that made her so angry?

After we examined tray after tray of rings, and I found nothing that pleased me, we released the merchant. A few minutes later, Sonja abruptly rose.

"We will eat inside today," she announced in a stern voice. "Karin, come to the room in ten minutes. We must change for the dining room." One look at her face told me not to argue. Besides it was by then quite hot and lunch in the dining room sounded appealing. The Herchmers said nothing. He'd fallen asleep and she was staring blankly out to sea, embroidery in her lap. My mother went over to her and touched her shoulder.

"Greta, be careful of this sun. Promise me: Not too much sun." My mother's voice was gentle. Mrs. Herchmer looked at her, face still blank, then a softened curve appeared in her lips and she nodded; she picked up her embroidery and began to work again. Sonja stalked away. I sat for a moment longer writing in my notebook.

Those who survived the camps recognize each other

How I do not know

They are together for a while

Then reveal to each other the secret story we share

Some times they burst into tears

Other times they never speak again

I gathered up my things and was about to follow my mother to the room when Mrs. Herchmer called me over.

"I never guessed," she said softly.

My lips tightened. "No one ever does. I never tell anyone."

Along the sea front, young children dashed toward the incoming waves, then scampered out of reach. Their shouts were joyful laughter, even when they fell down.

"How old were you?"

"Three and a half when we were arrested. I spent months in the camp hospital.

"Were the doctors and nurses... kind?"

"Some were."

"They didn't...didn't...hurt you?" Her voice was a whisper by then. I could feel my resistance growing. I didn't want to talk about any of it, ever, not even to this gentle fellow survivor.

"I remember nothing. I had pneumonia seven times."

"Yes, yes that must be what saved you. Once past the gates, after the selections, yes, all sorts of oddities emerged." She looked into my eyes, took my hand, for a minute I let her, then slowly, carefully, I drew every part of myself away from the conversation, and from her. She and Sonja had told each other their stories.

I want no pity - that thought was screaming in my head. I smiled pleasantly, said goodbye and walked away. But I was angry at Sonja for dragging me into such dialogues.

*   *   *   *   *

"The confusion is going, Mama"

I was slow in my preparations, irritable from fatigue, from the heat, and my emotions. "From a fever - I told you several times, I had severe flu."

I was in the bathroom, re-braiding my waist length hair. It made me feel like a child, my long hair. Sonja was sitting on her bed watching me.

"That long winter in Colorado - you need a holiday. Greg must take you on a holiday every winter. You tell him I said so. These hotels, they are not expensive."

I turned my face away. "I appreciate you taking me, Mama."

"You are my little girl." Sonja came over to stand beside me. "I would do anything for you, my sweet Karin." Paused together, we examined ourselves in the mirror. In some ways we looked alike; in others we were very different. I was tall and she was short, I was thin and she was plump, but our eyes were the same dark brown, our noses long but not too long, chins narrow, cheekbones high, lips acceptable. In many ways I was proud of Sonja, still so feminine, so attractive to men. I wanted to be like her – yet I didn't want to be like her at all.

She touched my cheek. "You are all I have now. I am happy you are married with a good man. I will tell him you must have more holidays, more fun. I will tell him that."

At once I pulled away from her, yanked on my attempt at a braid, "Oh, this hair. I've become so clumsy with it."

"Let me braid it for you." Sonja reached for the brush, but I stalked away.

"It's too much trouble. I want it cut."

"They cut it off in the camp. So ugly you looked, like a little rat."

I walked to the window and looked out at an empty road across a dry landscape.

"It's quiet here."

"Your father loved your hair. You have beautiful hair. You should wear it up. Does Greg like your hair up? There are many pretty ways to wear your hair now – find a new style. Why do you still put your hair in braids?"

Sonja's hair was short, thick, and well mannered. She had it cut in whatever was the style of the day; she said for her job in a dentist's office she must look up-to-date, as if she knew what she was doing. I, for some reason, in her mind had never had such necessity. Still at the window, I turned and looked at her. Her face was soft. She looked beautiful. I wanted to be close to her, walked over, and touched her shoulder.

"Tell me about my father, Mama, You never talk about him, never."

"So long ago," she sighed, "Too long ago, too sad." She wrinkled up her face in a way that was familiar.

"Why do you make such a face when I ask about him?"

"I do not want to talk to you." She turned her back, went into the bathroom. "Not about him."

"He was my father." I said between tight teeth, but in a voice so soft she didn't hear me. When she came back out, I was waiting by the door. She picked up her handbag and followed me out.

"Are you going shopping?" I snapped.

"Maybe,"

"Why did you say red?"

"What do you mean?"

"The camp badges. You said red - political. We were Czechs."

Sonja stuck up her nose. "Now you know so much. You know about colors, badges. What is 'a badge'?"

"You know what I'm talking about." I caught sight of someone sitting in the garden as we passed, thought, that is my place; the garden, the lilies belong to me.

"Now you are interested. Before never, now suddenly you know everything."

"We were not political."

"Anton was a party member." We were quarrelling seriously by then, as only Sonja and I could, refusing to give up, to yield to the other.

"He was not German. Why weren't we green, foreigners?"

"We were Jehovah Witnesses."

"Yes. Yes I understand that. But before – you said red. Political. Germans. How could that be?"

"This subject is closed. Please, I wish to eat in peace."

The dining room was full that day; the heat had driven many guests inside. Across the room we saw a new acquaintance - Mrs. Smith. She was eating alone. Sonja rushed us over to join this older lady with faded, flattened hair and spectacularly wrinkled face; she smiled a lot and talked entirely about where to shop in Mazatlan. Sonja listened intently. I looked around.

The wide, many-windowed dining room looked out on a terrace facing the sea. These windows were often opened up during the day to catch the sea breeze; that day we were fortunate to sit beside them. At a nearby table sat the young man and the young woman we'd noticed on the beach that morning. They were still enamored with each other. They sat by the window, looking only at each other, around them hung brilliance, as though they reflected the sun. When Sonja saw these lovers enter, she shifted restlessly. After Mrs. Smith left, she changed her seat so she didn't have to look at them.

"Too early in the day," she wrinkled up her nose. I watched as they kissed over their coffee cups, cast radiant smiles at their indulgent waiter. When they left, on their way out they passed our table and I caught a whiff of the woman's musk scent, heard the murmur of their shared laughter. I liked sharing their sexual tension if only for a moment, but Sonja studied the menu. Once they had passed, she looked up.

"They are not married."

"They look like honeymooners."

"They are not married of that I am sure."

Her flat tone of voice annoyed me. "How can you be so sure?"

"I know these things." She picked up the lunch check, took from her summer straw bag a pair of harlequin glasses. I felt an odd clutch of fear. They were the pair she wore when I was in high school, glasses with sharp pixie points.

"Where did you get those?"

"This old pair?"

"I dreamt about a woman wearing glasses like that." I stared at her as she put them on. In my dreams the woman's intent had been to hound me.

Sonja laboriously read the check then looked up at me over the glasses; she was smiling. "That woman is German. The man I am not so sure."

"Does it matter?"

"To me it does. To you, who knows? You care about nothing. The glasses are old, yes – they were with clothes I packed away after Josef died. I bought them that last summer with him in the Catskills. My God, what a summer - Irene was briefly there, rude as always." She signed the check with a flourish and gave it to the plump young waitress hovering behind her, then took off the glasses and tucked them into her purse. She looked at me sharply. "My eyes are the same. I should buy new glasses?"

She pushed herself away from the table. I rose too. When we reached the lobby, we saw the magic couple kissing beside the front desk. Sonja swerved violently to avoid them and I started to laugh. "Why do you dislike that couple so much? I think they're darling. I admire them."

"What couple?" she said looking straight at me - an old trick. She forced us both through the front door. Outside the sun beat down; the asphalt road bubbled in the heat.

"So beautiful they are," she purred. She stroked my cheek, "Now my darling I shall rest, then go back to the beach. Perhaps I will go in the water this afternoon." She didn't ask me to join her, but walked away. I sought solace in the pool garden and to my relief found no one there. In the heat of the day the scent of the rubrun lilies was strong;

they grew wild, crowding out other plants except for sturdy bushes of thyme and mimosa.

I lay on one of the dilapidated chaise lounge chairs and stared up at the trees. How I disliked Sonja sometimes! Four days in Mexico and she'd already found Germans. How simple Roberto and his lost mother seemed compared to my mother and her hated enemies. And yet I loved her too, loved her tender soft face when she was happy. I took out my small diary:

I believed that when she died I would die too
Though knew even as a child that her questions
Her sideways glances at reality changed mine
What if someday I could just be me?
Just breathe in and out freely
Thinking that never seemed fair.

I remembered her anger when Josef died, not unexpectedly, of a second heart attack. I came down the first night after the funeral and saw her sitting in the living room. I could just make out her face in the sheen of the street light - Sonja holding her arms against her chest, calling out in a voice I didn't recognize.

"You bastard," she was rocking herself gently. "You bastard leaving me with nothing, no money, no friends: Taking the easy way out, coward, coward, you damn coward." Her voice rose, fell, but she didn't cry. Not that I could see. She was letting out that core of anger she usually hid, a safer expression than tears. Only rarely did she cry. Sitting by the pool, I noticed again the penetrating smell of the rubrunat ho lilies, noticed once more the tropical sky high above me was not a vivid turquoise, but a pale blue skin, saw too that after I looked up at the sky, the pool beside me seemed to move, so that when I looked down it was right beside me.

It had become commonplace in Boulder to think about giving up, taking myself out of the appointed circle, the appointed time, and instead, lacing myself into an ending. I could leave behind everyone who had expectations I could not meet. It seemed at times that simple. No worry about losing Greg, my failed work, the anger of my mother, a separation from my children. Only an easy surrender to what was to be anyway. It had been a battle at home to drive those thoughts away, a daily battle, here, by the pool for the first time they came again to me. But as always, my daughters reminded me of the love I shared with them.

I fell asleep. When I woke a half hour later it was to stare up at Dr. Herchmer. He was bending over the chaise lounge, his eyes fixed on me.

"You look very sweet lying there," he said. "But I wasn't sure you were all right." I moved slightly to break the mood of intimacy, "Just taking a nap."

He went on staring down at me. Into my mind came a vision. Dr. Herchmer was a dentist and I was in the position of a patient in a chair, looking up at my dentist's full face bending over me. A bubble of laughter trembled inside me. I thought I should open my mouth.

But I didn't, instead sat up.

"It's been a wonderful holiday," he murmured.

"Yes."

"We went on a tour this afternoon."

"How was it?" I felt stupid conducting a polite conversation in such an unusual arrangement of body meeting body. I noticed for the first time what a distinguished gray his hair was, how wavy, how lacking in definition he was otherwise.

"Adequate." He continued to stare down at me, as he must often stare into the open mouths of patients, yet there was something overly intense in his posture.

"I'm glad." I didn't trust him, but refused to be afraid. A few minutes later, he was gone.

* * * * *

That night Sonja and I went to dinner in the dining room which at night was warm, noisy, and bright, as intense as a squawking parrot, but the salt wind brought in a reminder of the sea and of the tropical night deepening outside. The terrace wall of windows was open and the many small candles on the tables fluttered in response to the breeze. There was a smell of spilled wax and broiled fish in the air. Black-attired waiters glided around tables, shoes squeaking on the polished black and white parquet floor. When the hotel band, a trio of men in black pants, green cummerbunds, and yellow satin shirts, entered, they were greeted with applause by the nearly full dining room, which changed to laughter when they played their first song, a Latin American version of "When the Saints Go Marching In."

Our plump waiter stammered as he gave highlights of the menu; he took our orders for fish and chips and shrimp pasta, rushed away not to reappear until many minutes later. Sipping wine and avoiding quarrel, Sonja and I were silent at first; we looked around at our fellow guests and commented on them, but when our dinners came, I tried to talk seriously with my mother.

"Mama, truly, it was such a high fever; 104 for two days. I don't usually run fevers, but when I was ill I saw everything clearly. Saw what my life will be like if I stay with Greg. I haven't said much, but you need to know."

Sonja put down her fork. "Do we talk about such things on a holiday in Mexico? You have a chance to be happy. That is what I want for you, to be happy."

"I know that, Mama, but I'm not."

"I will order ice cream; those dessert carts have nothing special."

"It's over, Mama. I know that." I sat back knowing she wouldn't listen.

"Little dry cakes. Nothing with cream. And the chocolate is not good. Not like Europe. Your hair looks pretty tonight, Karin. Spumoni, that is the ice cream I like."

She was relentless that evening in her refusal to listen. Finally I gave up.

When we were nearly through our meal, the German tourists, six in all, strolled into the dining room. The women wore long glamorous dresses that showed off their figures and tans, the men were in tuxedos; they all laughed and spoke German in loud voices. Everyone in the dining room watched them as they smiled and joked. They sat down at a reserved table near the band. The magic pair held on to each other tightly, behaved dramatically; he bent her back and kissed her passionately before they sat down.

Sonja's face changed. "Germans, I told you," she said and drew her black shawl around her. "That one's name is Marian Eissel. His I don't know."

"How did you find out?"

"I looked at the hotel register. Are you ready to leave?"

"Not yet, Mama, I haven't finished eating."

At that moment Desmond strode into the room. I hadn't seen him since the first morning and I was glad he was back. He didn't see us but marched straight to the table where the three couples were ordering amidst raucous outbursts of laughter. The band was playing "Vaya Con Dios"; the new arrivals were urging each other to dance and finally one couple – an intense looking black-haired woman and her muscular escort – got up and danced. Others joined them. Desmond sat down in an empty seat next to Marian Eissel and took her arm. He was speaking rapidly but she shook her head and yanked her arm away; her companion leaned forward and said something to Desmond who remained seated still speaking to Marian. Her companion rose and stood over Desmond until he too was on his feet.

The tension was so apparent to everyone in the room that most people stopped eating to watch them. Desmond was taller, the other man heavier. After a long moment, the two men walked out of the room. A few minutes later the German returned and sat down. Marian leaned across and spoke to him and he nodded.

I threw down my napkin, muttered something about going to the restroom, and rushed away before Sonja could object. I went looking for Desmond - first to the front lobby where the desk clerk was being harangued by an elderly couple - then to the bar where a crowd of sturdy drinkers were listening to a guitar player murder jazz, and out into the front of the hotel where I saw thousands of bugs circling the outdoor lights. I was too disheartened to look further. Back in the dining room all the Germans were dancing; the band attempted a polka with frightening results.

"What a rowdy party, those people." Sonja said as we left the dining room, she to join Dr. Herchmer at the casino, "To give him luck," she said, and I to wander out to the beach, "for a short stroll." That night we didn't question each other's plans but parted without another word. On my way out I saw, at the outdoors bar, Jason, the husky young man who'd been with the Herchmers the first morning. To my relief he didn't notice me.

I did meet a man walking in the sea. He was older than I, with a stout body and severe face. We were both wading in the shallow flow after the breaking waves and so encountered each other on the same path. As a way of greeting, he asked me, "Should I leave my wife and live with my mistress?" and without thinking I answered him, "What will do the least amount of harm?" We said nothing more but pursued our separate ways along the dim edge of the hotel beachfront. I thought later that by answering his question I'd answered my own. Later that night I began to run alone in the dark.

Wednesday, Day 4

It was just after six. I woke out of a strong dream. My heart was pounding. It was the first such dream I'd had in Mexico. I got up at once and dressed. Sonja was still asleep; she didn't hear me go out.

Only a few people were on the beach. I downed a quick coffee and roll at the outdoor bar, saw by the boat dock and parachute launch men straightening life jackets and arranging equipment, but Roberto was not with them. We were meeting later to go running so, barefoot, I walked slowly along the beach for some distance than back.

The tide had withdrawn. I was half-awake, wrenched out of some other life to be here on a quiet morning, the sea beside me, the sting of its odor weaving a spell around me. Finally, sitting at an outdoor table to wait for Roberto, I put on my runners and took out my notebook. I was keeping a record of my dreams and wanted to remember one from the night before.

Light - a sparkling brilliance- is spreading across the horizon

I hope it will engulf me now

Will take away the dread I feel

In that dream I was waking from a sleep

Around me many people on a great polished floor

All sleeping, separate and apart

A few like me were awake

One or two sat cross-legged

Or were rising to their feet

But most were deep in sleep

Smiling like babies

I liked them – in the dream I liked them -

But feared the black clad figures weaving among them

Prowling through people like panthers

Knocking over those who tried to stand

Dragging sleepers away

In the dream I knew evil was awake and good was asleep

I tried to stand but couldn't

In the dream I had only enough strength to stay wake

To watch evil men moving through sleeping people

Writing the dream down, I felt my usual joy in the morning rolling out with the waves, out beyond the sea into the horizon. I rose, paced along the edge of the sea, and found a bird in the sand. Not a living bird, but the bones of a pelican naked and exposed – laid out as though a mosaic. It was beautiful, untouched. Half an hour later when I walked back, the skeleton, once plunged with perfection into the sand, was gone.

The tide had taken it away.

Roberto ran up. Smiling broadly, he didn't stop but motioned me to follow him.

We ran long and hard, I could now keep pace with him. This morning we ran past the cave and didn't stop. Once again, on our way back, we walked and talked, or rather Roberto spoke of his plans to finish university when he had enough money, that he would become a lawyer and fight the injustices of his country. I listened respectfully though he said nothing I hadn't heard at university from other young students, except that he claimed the cultural treasures of Mexico were being looted. His voice trembled when he spoke of the illegal trade. I told him I was leaving on Sunday, and he asked me to meet him in the bar that night at ten o'clock. He planned to drive to Mexico City for the weekend.

I went back to the room. Sonja had already left for the beach. I lay on my bed and tried to rest for an hour, but I remembered the dream, the dread and certainty that I'd seen a real world, and finally I gave up and went out to the beach.

*   *   *   *   *

Desmond was wearing a bright red bathing suit that showed off his body. I watched him ram himself into the waves and rise smoothly, swimming out against the fence line of waves - a big man, Desmond, and not afraid of the sea.

Beside me, Nathan Herchmer sighed, "I'm jealous," he said. "Your friend is a good swimmer." That morning both he and Greta were holding books but not reading.

"I'm not sure he's a friend." Nor was I sure why Nathan had called him one.

"I don't swim at all." The good doctor pursed his lips. "Ever since I was a child, I feared it. A gypsy or some such person told my mother I would die by water, and she refused me swimming lessons."

"That was a mistake," I couldn't help blurting out. "You should learn."

"Don't try to change his mind," said Greta "He is too stubborn. Everyone's told him he could learn but he refuses."

"It is such a pleasure on a hot day – to swim." Sonja's voice was a cooing sound. Sitting beside her I could smell the banana scent of her suntan oil. She'd been tanning all morning. "So smooth and calming for the body; too bad Nathan, you don't enjoy such things. You should try swimming here."

77

"In those waves?" Dr. Herchmer made a mocking sound. "Such waves are not smooth and calm."

"There is a swimming pool." Sonja sat up straighter. She wore dark glasses and looked interesting. "Every hotel has a swimming pool."

"Have you seen the pool here?" Nathan snorted. "Not fit to swim in."

"We asked about that dirty water." Greta stroked her knees with a long elegant finger. "The hotel clerk said they are improving the pool and have closed it for two months. Next time you come, Sonja, you can swim there."

"It's too small." Sonja wrinkled up her face. "Maybe they are planning to enlarge it." She didn't mention she'd met the swimming pool repairman. "Has the work started?"

"Yes. Someone came. Then that someone went away without telling anyone." Nathan shook his head. "It's not like New York."

"There it is worse." Sonja laughed, "Nobody wants to work in New York," Yet still she said nothing about meeting Andres.

Nathan patted his stomach. "I plan to die without swimming a stroke."

I was annoyed by his stupidity. "There was a drowned man's body in the sea. Perhaps that was the repairman."

Was it my imagination or did Nathan's smile freeze on his face? That made me feel good. But he didn't miss a beat in the conversation.

"Workmen have a habit of disappearing when they see the size of the job." Looking the wise elder statesman, he rose and came to lean over Sonja and I. "Coffee, anyone? Or a drink?"

"The repairman was here the first night. We know because Mama met him. Didn't you Mama?" I liked watching his usually placid eyes twitch. Was that alarm?

Sonja pulled down her sunglasses and looked daggers at me. I'd forgotten and called her Mama. Or was she still reluctant to discuss the now famous Andres? But she said nothing. I looked out at the water but couldn't see Desmond anymore. Perhaps he'd swum way out or along the shoreline. Nathan still hovered over us; he rubbed one hand against his bare chest. He had a dark overworked tan. "Mexican beer is good. Let's all go to the outdoor bar."

"It's too early." Greta lay back in her chair, "Too early to drink."

"I will have a margarita." Sonja sat up. She'd only been in the sun a few days but had an olive skin that tanned easily. "I am in the mood to celebrate. Such a good holiday we are having."

"There you go." Nathan smiled at me. "Karin, what about you - a drink?"

"Thanks, no." I said. "I'm going for a swim."

"It is not too hot for you?" Sonja had a sharp edge to her voice that concealed a growing anger with something - or someone.

"Not yet."

"I must wait, Nathan. I must watch my daughter swim."

"She's in danger of drowning?" He raised an eyebrow, looked at me.

I shrugged. "Meet my mother, Dr. Herchmer," I said. "Don't swim too far out. Don't go near the edge. Or walk at night, or get into cars with boys."

"That's a good mother." Greta smiled at me. "You're lucky to have a mother who cares so much. For you she cares more than for herself."

"Yes, yes, you are right, Greta." Sonja took off her dark glasses and leaned toward this marvelous Greta who had said all the right things in the right tone of voice. My mother sighed and leaned back in her chair in imitation of Mrs. Herchmer. "You are right, that is what a good mother does. Now, with Josef gone, Karin is everything to me. Everything." Her voice grew deeply dramatic. "When I die she will be comfortable. I will make sure of that. And will help her daughters to have a good life too."

"My children also," said Greta. "I want them to be comfortable."

"You have children?" Sonja asked Greta.

"I see I'm on my own. Off to drink a beer." Nathan walked away.

"From my first marriage," Greta said, "Three sons. I was a young widow but I had married a rich man. Our sons had the education they needed."

"How fortunate for you," I disliked the bitter tinge in Sonja's voice. I stood up, looked at the swimmers in the water, hoped he was still out there – Desmond. I'd lost sight of him, hadn't seen him come in. I got up, walked down to the water, thought perhaps I'll encounter him in a wave.

The water was colder than I expected, but still warm enough. I padded along on my hands through the shallow water until the first waves rippled in. The tide was still out and the waves were mild compared to the night of my arrival. Our arrival - I thought of how I met Desmond that first night. I was thinking about him a little too much, perhaps because he was so thoroughly ignoring me.

The waves were testing me, pushing me backwards and forwards. I resisted and sailed over them one by one until I was far from shore. There were only a few swimmers beyond the breakers, all of them men. That made me proud; I knew how to swim in the ocean; Sonja had made sure of that in Florida. And then he was treading water beside me.

"Karin isn't it?"

"Yes. How are you, Desmond?"

"There's a shark warning up, Karin."

"Are there sharks in Mexico?" I looked around.

"Hard to believe with oil tankers going by. The notice is posted near the front desk, but there's no date on it."

"Could it have anything to do with the body they found?"

He stopped treading water.

"What body?"

I was swimming small circles around him. "You didn't hear about the dead man found by the breakwater?"

"I haven't been around much." He ducked, spat out water.

"I noticed." I said and smiled my best smile.

"I'm going in, Karin. I've got to meet a man about a dog. Keep a sharp eye out for sharks." He swam away toward shore and I lost interest in treading water. After a few moments I followed him in.

Sonja was standing at the water's edge, arms akimbo, but waved when she saw me. Desmond had pulled himself out of the water near her and stood dripping, talking to her, but he walked away before I could join them.

"What were you two talking about?"

"He wanted to eat lunch with us today. I said you were busy."

"I'm not busy."

"Today you go on a tour. You told me you booked it."

*　　*　　*　　*　　*

"You want to give up the life of the intellect?" She followed me out the door of the annex. We were already arguing that fourth afternoon when we left the room for lunch. We planned to eat in the dining room so we could talk before my tour of the countryside but we were stalled by the garden. "You have left the university?"

"I didn't say that. I said I must."

"You think such a life is not important?" Sonja was rubbing her hands and arms, a gesture I knew meant rising agitation. She'd always wanted me to get an advanced degree. Now I'd told her I wouldn't.

I couldn't stop myself. "University is not an intellectual place."

"Culture is nothing to you?"

The smell of the rubrun lilies lingered in the air - delicate, insistent. We'd come to stand beside the pool. Around and above us were warmth, sun, and open flowers, yet she and I were full of cold and darkness.

"What culture? Mama, I know more than you do about universities."

"Be careful of me," Sonja's voice was angry, "and what you say." Sonja had never been given the chance to go to university, and I knew that rankled.

"There were three suicides at the university this month. This month! The university is a place of competition and malice. The few that are cultured withdraw into themselves or their research. Or have affairs - I ought to know." A middle-aged couple wandered in; caught by our angry voices, they stared curiously at us. We moved closer. The couple walked out.

Sonja lowered her voice. "I do not want to know about your life."

I brushed the flowers, throwing them against each other. "Yes, you do. My first year as an undergraduate there Greg put moves on me. You knew what happened."

"That I should have a daughter so weak," She was hissing now. But she sat down beside the pool, and I sat beside her. She refused to look at me.

"Oh, I fell in love. Don't worry. He was everything refined, intelligent, all the things you taught me to value." "He is a smart man. Greg, I think he is a good man."

"Yes. Smart. Maybe cultured. Good? Good and smart are not the same. You of anybody should know that now."

"Stop it. Stop talking about this." But she didn't move, and I knew at last she was listening.

"Some professors think sleeping with students is just fine thank you. There's another young woman right now. That's why Greg leaves me alone, Mama, why I can't concentrate on my studies. He's too busy with other women. He will always have someone else. So you see I have to get away, have to do something to make my life right. But I have no money."

"Such a situation - how could you be so stupid?"

"Because I am stupid! I can't do anything but stupid things. Because I've believed what you taught me! I love my children. I married for that love."

We were silent then having finally agreed on something. I could hear the quick friendly voices of the small birds that sometimes visited the garden, their discussion more cheerful it seemed than our own. I never saw them in the trees, only occasionally like at that moment, a small blur of yellow or green would flick through the air, more like a thought than a passage of something living.

My mother stood up as though to go. "When did you make this decision?"

"This fall I enrolled for a graduate course on the Holocaust. It was a mistake. I knew that right away, but it was a graduate credit and I thought I should learn more and at first I persevered but it was too much. It brought some memories."

"Do you want to eat now?" Sonja was walking away from me, out of the garden.

"Yes," I followed her. "My tour leaves at two."

"A course in the holocaust. What kind of a fool are you?"

We were inside the hotel, out of the heat, the sun, our tempers cooling.

"I'm sorry Mama. You don't want to know all this, I know that."

"Never mind," her voice was calmer. "Did you not live it - as I did?"

"It's what I owe you, Mama - or thought I did: To understand it as an adult. But such knowledge is beyond me. I remain locked into being a child lost in it."

For several minutes we waited by the door of the dining room.

"You owe me nothing. That garden is not so bad. So close to the beach, yet you cannot see it. Only the pool, the pool is ugly, the water so dirty."

"Mama, I don't trust the intellect. Smart people have smart plans for everyone else. In their own minds they are never wrong. They think they should make up the world for the rest of us. I would rather be with ordinary people, not so smart people. Maybe I will train as a cook. I like to cook. Or be a florist."

Sonja's mouth widened with astonishment then tightened but she didn't speak as the maitre d' approached us. The black man from the front desk of a few nights ago, he didn't smile as he led us to our table. The room was pleasantly noisy, a buzz of people enjoying conversations after the morning sun worship. She sat down at the table the maitre d' had taken us to without complaint though it was a small table, away from the terrace. The maitre d' gave us the menus and departed. We were some distance from an open window, close to the kitchen; the air was overheated and we breathed in all the good smells of the kitchen. I hesitated. Would Sonja complain? But she opened a menu.

Suddenly I was ravenous. I sat down across from her and examined it too. I was ready to stop talking, to start eating, but she wasn't.

"Karin, do not speak to me of ordinary people." Her voice, her eyes were angry. "Ordinary people put us in hell. They built the hells, they ran the trains, typed the lists, baked the bread. Yes, ordinary people. I know them."

"Mama, let's not talk about it any more. Do you want to go on the tour?"

"No. I will rest this afternoon." She looked sternly at me. "You had plans, ambitions."

"Yes, I thought I wanted to study the camps. I've read many records of suffering, Mama; I know now the cruelty and evil human beings are capable of. And I'm no closer to knowing anything. That's what makes me sick, Mama. I've tried to understand,

I wanted to do that for you, to be useful, but I can't. I guess I need to learn more about life, not death."

I looked up at the waiter who, by then, stood waiting with pad and pencil, but Sonja ignored him. Instead she leaned forward and took my chin in her plump soft hands.

"Why do you say this? This too late?"

"Before I'm too old, Mama. I'm almost forty."

"No one told you to wait so long, to go to university so late."

Then she paused so that we could give our order. When the waiter had left she started in again. "Were you not a fool to work six years and all those travel jobs?"

"We didn't have the money. You know that."

"I told you I would help you. No, no you said, no university, that's not for me. I remember this. And Josef, he said he will help you too, and still you say no. You made money, good money, and you spent it all on traveling."

We were talking, Sonja and I, after the heat of anger; we were for the first time in a long time, talking and listening to each other.

"Let's enjoy lunch, Mama." Yet I wanted the conversation to go on, this new communication to continue. I wanted so badly in those days in Mexico for my mother to understand me.

She opened her roll, and buttered it. "That young life guard, he was watching you today when you went in swimming. He is handsome. And he is more interesting than that tall thin man you talk to."

Her tone was triumphant. I could feel my temper rising again. I changed the subject, and, handing my mother a brochure of my tour, let her pronounce on it as long and as vehemently as she liked.

*   *   *   *   *

In New York, where we moved, after Sonja married Josef, my mother began to experience terrible rages. Unpredictable and dark edged, they descended on her suddenly. Sometimes she wouldn't speak for days; she took pills so she could sleep. On those days, she wouldn't sit down to eat with us, but served us food in silence then left the room. I never knew what was wrong, but her unhappiness and unpredictable aggression against everyone in her life deeply disturbed me. We'd been just two for so many years, and she had been so reliable and creative in our life together, that I was dependent upon her. Now I know there were medical reasons for this, but as an adolescent during that period, I felt I no longer received any love from her. And perhaps her behavior may have hounded Josef into his weak heart, and subsequent early death.

He was a quiet sad man, a little man both in stature and in his life, but he loved Sonja doggedly. A Czech from Prague he'd emigrated before the Nazi invasion. A school teacher of French and German in a private school not far from our apartment, he liked his work, liked young people, many of whom were Lutheran. I learned about God from Josef. Sonja found work, first as a part time subway station attendant in the mornings, then full time as a dental receptionist.

Yet so dark continued her moods, I rarely brought friends home. Once when I did, we were met at the door by my mother who told us in a high excited voice about Nadya, the two headed swan who was jealous of her sisters and lost the sight of one eye as punishment. Sonja announced, "Nadya grew more and more jealous of the beautiful plumage of the other swans." She then dragged my friend and I into the dining room to see where she'd mounted a piece of driftwood that resembled a swan and on which she had placed buttons as eyes – one green and one rhinestone. The girl with me stood dumbfounded and left shortly afterwards.

I was helpless in the face of Sonja's anger and unhappiness. There seemed nothing I could do, and yet it seemed also I must do something, that I was responsible for Sonja's despair. I thought it came from her past. Perhaps that's why I began to look for employment that allowed me to leave home. But as time passed the dark moods vanished. She took up hobbies, found new friends, traveled with Joseph.

* * * * *

What I liked best about the tour was that Desmond went on it. When I saw his tall, angular figure waiting for the tour bus in front of the hotel, my heart gave a little bump of joy. He wore a pair of dirty white shorts, a brown and white striped short sleeved shirt and disreputable sneakers, and stood with his hands in his pockets. He looked big, ragged and bleached blonde by the sun.

I walked over to him straight into his smile. "You decided to take a tour." I said.

"You recommended it."

I smiled at that, I was happy. "I hope we can sit together."

"Let anybody try to stop us."

Someone did.

When the elderly tour bus pulled up, a blonde woman with sunburned face and bare legs moved between us. I took hold of Desmond's hand and said sweetly, "Come dear, we'll be late if we don't get on now."

She jumped away as though stung, and Desmond let himself be led on the bus. I dropped his hand, but he picked up mine. "Let's keep doing that," he said, "just in case she attacks again."

Such a wave of happiness went through me, I was startled. I didn't know this man. Why did he make me feel buoyant, unsettled, yet content? He was so easy to talk to, to be with. "What have you been doing?" I asked.

"Chasing women." I laughed. I thought he meant me.

When the bus was three-quarters full, we drove off. The tour started with the town of Mazatlan, making brief stops there to several landmarks, a marketplace, then a coffeehouse. Finally we were out in the countryside, all of us staring out at picturesque huts with TV antennas dotted over a spare dry landscape. The bus filled with oil fumes and we leaned closer to the half-opened window to breathe fresh air. My arm rested on his, my bare knee against his. "You said you were divorced."

"Yes. And you're married."

"I think so."

"Not going so well?"

"No." My throat felt tight.

"Mine was rocky most of the time, partly my fault; Traveling too much."

"And partly hers?" I looked sideways at him.

"Yes" But he said no more and I liked that about him.

The tour took the group on a raft ride. Thirty-six people scrambled onto a raft meant for ten. We floated out on the river, the guide pointed out places where alligators were sighted. The river was slow, surrounded by banks that were overgrown with bushes and trees. The raft rode very low in the water; Desmond called out: "How many people on this raft can swim?" Only eight people claimed they could, including Desmond and I.

After that, he kept his arm around me until we were back on shore.

On the way home, Desmond sat for a time next to an elderly man who was traveling alone. He'd spoken to no one, but Desmond learned he was a widower traveling on a round the world trip he and his wife had dreamed of, and saved for, but she'd died one month before their departure date.

"That's sad." I said to Desmond as we climbed off the bus. But we watched the widower taken away to another hotel with three elderly ladies; one sat by him, while the other two chattered away. The widower appeared to be listening.

Desmond held out his hand. "I enjoyed this."

My surprise must have showed. "You're not coming into the hotel?"

"I'm down the road in your basic cheap motel. I come up to the hotel to talk to sane people. You qualify. Thanks. It was great to think about somebody else beside myself." He shook my hand, then walked away up the asphalt road. Irritated by the ease with which he abandoned me, I spent the next hours arguing myself into ignoring him next time I saw him, which I hoped would be soon.

After I'd telephoned home and the girls told me they were off to a movie with their dad – never mind it was a school night, Sonja and I ate a light supper in the bar. Desmond was there. Sonja pointed him out. He was deep in conversation with the beautiful German we'd seen him with in the dining room. I saw his hand touch hers.

"So arrogant that man," Sonja said. "I do not like him" She brushed her hair away from her face. "I play cards this evening. I can walk with you now if you like."

"Not tonight Mama, I 'm tired. I think I'll go to bed early."

I lied.

*   *   *   *   *

"Your mother should not go on the parachute," Roberto said when we sat down to share a drink. The bar waiter had not yet arrived. It was the first time I'd come to the outdoor bar in the evening. A rectangular dance floor was marked by hanging lights, colorful piñatas shaped like animals, and a guitarist hard at work inciting guests to dance. No one ventured onto the floor. Beyond us the sea rolled out its dark message.

"You don't think it's safe? She's been talking about going up."

"How old is she?"

"Sixty-five. She likes to dare herself to do things."

"When I'm not there, Luis or Manuel may let her go up. She is a delightful lady.

But it is not a good idea; a man of her age had a heart attack up there this summer."

The waiter came and we ordered rum and cokes. I'd surprised myself by coming to meet him. I'd said I'd join him when he'd told me that morning that he usually had a drink at the outdoor bar around ten o'clock, but I was tired after a long day.

"You like rum?" Roberto smiled and sat back in his chair.

"I never drink it."

"And you are drinking it now."

"I'm doing a lot of things I don't usually do."

"What things?"

He leaned forward, flashing a smile. His shirt was open several buttons,

at his neck hung a silver necklace shaped like a heart.

"That's a beautiful necklace."

"It was my mother's."

Roberto talked of his plan to return to university in Mexico City. He was a law student and was driving to the city the next day to register for the following semester.

"I am here for three months only to earn some money."

"It's a beautiful place."

"For the tourists, maybe," he flashed another smile. "Would you like to dance?"

The music was Mexican and lively. I hesitated. "Yes."

There were others on the floor, and dancing seemed harmless, but as soon as we were dancing he held me too tightly, pressed his hard body too certainly against me, and he smelled of cheap cologne. The invitation was unmistakable, and my own response to him was one I didn't trust.

"I think you are lonely," Roberto said in a soft voice. Once again he had eerily read my thoughts, "a lonely lady."

"Perhaps."

"You are a lady. Any man can see that."

I didn't reply, but when we walked back to our table, I refused another drink. Roberto suggested we walk a short way together along the beach. The sea was calm; there was still a half moon. I took off my sandals and let mild waves swirl across my feet.

Roberto said. "I've never met anyone like you."

I wanted to believe him." You've got quite a crowd of admirers."

"The lifeguard -" He made a small disparaging motion with one hand that I liked. "Tourists on holiday." His voice was sharp, but I didn't want to be warned away.

"Remember the day you asked me to go running? Why did you do that?"

"It came into my mind."

"I was just at that moment thinking about running."

"Run now."

In the darkness we paced together along the sea. Small wavelets, ripples of sensation from the sea, flowed across our feet, erasing our footsteps as we made them; we were running, not fast, but with a sharing of the night; and I enjoyed, once again, being in harmony with someone, without words and without fear. But then Roberto left the hotel beach, and we were out on the wilder stretch.

I slowed. "That's enough for me."

"A little farther," Roberto urged, "there is that place…the small cave."

"I should go back."

He stopped at once, "O.K."

"Maybe another time."

"O.K., sure."

We turned and ran back, this time faster, began darting in and out of the sea like small swallows chasing the waves. I was laughing, though Roberto was not. At the edge of the terrace I said goodnight. "That was fun."

"You run well now," he murmured.

"'I've had a good teacher." And I walked away without looking back.

The room was empty. Sonja was still out playing cards with Nathan. I took a bath, climbed into bed, took out the notebook. I was beginning to enjoy keeping it, though I'd had only one dream. But odd memories seemed to float by, and I was catching some like butterflies to pin on my pages.

I stole the blue marbles from Stefan

In Prague when I was three

I wandered at night even then

Stefan was downstairs

I got up out of bed in my parents' room and went into his

He had a tall bureau. I opened

The bottom drawer where he kept things

All his toys - the little train, the box of soldiers, a leather bag of marbles

I put my hand down into the bag and took out two big ones

Ran back to my bed, hugged them

I had two exactly alike, both blue

Then, in the middle of the same night, different memories came. In total darkness, I sat up and scrawled them out: Memories that belonged to Desa, my child self.

The hospital was in another part of the camp. Her mother, who worked in different places in the camp, never visited her, so Desa's most important memory is of being alone. She has no memories of arriving there, though she was brought, ill with high fever and pneumonia, seven times in the two years she and her mother were imprisoned. She remembers the hospital as grey – everything in it grey, even those who worked there. She remembers other children as white, pale and thin. She remembers one little black-haired girl in a cot beside her – a beautiful little jew – three years old. Desa knew those facts because she heard the nurses, most of them prisoners, talking about that child. The little jew child screamed as soon as anyone came near her. Every night they held her down – four people – because she threw her body around as she screamed, thrashing like a wild thing to avoid the needle one of them was holding. For days and days, it was a horrible, peculiar, and relentless night event, until one day the little girl wasn't there.

Desa remembers too, a man lying beside her on her cot. He was a prisoner working in the hospital but came there to sleep. The crew of four with the big needle began to come to Desa – shots in the buttocks every four hours night after night. She was too afraid to move, never screamed nor thrashed around, never told her mother.

The ragged intern couldn't nap there anymore.

When she read this in the morning she saw how formal it was, a sign that Karin, her university self, was gathering up this memory. But it belonged to Desa – the name the workers in the camp hospital called her, the name she told them: DESA - her grandmother's name. It's still her name, a secret from everyone, though she was tempted to tell Captain Hernandez. These memories are rare, but sometimes arrive abruptly and in full color. They never told to Sonja, because Desa could never bring them forth. Sonja had her own terrible memories which she shared with no one.

THURSDAY, Day 5

The hotel annex had thick concrete walls; our room was soundless. In the early morning I rose in silence. When I emerged, I heard a faint roar; turning right and past the garden, I walked along blue tiled paths, down a sandy incline. I walked out of silence and into a sound that owned everything, louder and louder – until there - I glimpsed water - bright blue, white crested waves, and the sky - all the distances of blue, familiar shapes of the small islands along the horizon, and the sea announcing itself with its roaring. Closer, closer, up to the water, into it, against me came the forceful push of water, waves up against my knees.

Each morning I loved it more, loved it beyond reason. Relish it now, in memory. I can close my eyes and be there. My life had been tamed early, been obscure for so long; I'd been frightened into obedience. But the sea confronts everything, comforts us, stills fear and regret, anger and melancholy, and does more - incites risk, promises adventure.

That Thursday morning I ran with Roberto across soft sand, than arranged to meet him again that evening. I sat down on the beach with a coffee and took out my diary. By that time I was carrying my string bag everywhere, as my survival kit. In it: my diary, a pen, my sun hat, and a poetry book. I'd remembered more of yesterday's dream.

Those that were standing
Didn't move like the black clad prowlers
But oh they looked beautiful
I knew in the dream that just by standing up they protected the
others
The sleepers didn't know perhaps they would never know
A battle was being fought.

It was more and more interesting to write thoughts down, but only certain thoughts – dreams and sometimes those that came suddenly out of nowhere.

When I got back to the room, Sonja was up and dressed in white trousers and a white blouse. She took out a wallet, sat down on her bed, and patted a place next to her.

"Come here darling."

I sat by her, unsure of what she was doing. She opened the wallet, held out a wad of bills. "Take this: For your ticket and for some shopping today. Buy yourself something – something you like – a gift from me."

"That's a lot of money, Mama."

"Never mind," She laid the bills on the bedclothes, got up from the bed. "I want you to have it. And I will give you more to finish your university course. Never mind what Greg says or does. He is a foolish man, not a bad one. Tell him I will help your daughters go to university in New York."

"New York?"

"Yes, why not? They can stay with me. And so why not let me pay for your next semester's tuition too?"

"No." I was shaking my head as I stood up, went into the bathroom. "No, I can't take money for that."

She stood on the other side of the door, still talking. "You are a person without resources. Let me help you."

"I'm through with university. And I'm not going back to my marriage, not now, not ever. I will only take money for my daughters, but they are still in high school."

"You have no money. You said this yourself."

"I can find a job overseas. I've already applied for several."

I came out of the bathroom dressed in my green sundress. I'd put on lipstick.

"Aren't you going to go out on the beach today, Mama?"

"Later," she said, "I have a meeting this morning. What do you mean overseas?"

"A meeting - that sounds important." My voice was more mocking than I intended. "Europe. I have languages, Mama. I can get work there, I know I can."

"I do not want you to go overseas. You are my life now. To be so far from you -. no. Not now. Where would you go?"

"Germany. My German is good, very good."

The look on her face told me everything. I felt some guilt. I knew she wouldn't like that idea, but I persisted. "There are places I want to see, Mama. I studied European history. I'm able to write and teach. I can do it, Mama. Don't you want me to do something with my education? Aren't you proud of me?"

"And what about your daughters? Your beautiful children?"

I stuck my chin out. "I'll take them with me."

"With no money?"

"Well, give me money for them then."

"You go to Germany – I will never speak to you again. I promise you. I will not. It will be over between us. And no money for that. Never."

We were walking out the door. It was nine o'clock. We'd planned to go to town for lunch, but I knew now we were not getting along well enough to do anything together. By then we were fighting about the most improbable of all acts – my going to Germany. The idea hadn't even occurred to me until she'd attacked my plans, which weren't plans, only pipe dreams. Suddenly they had become the most important thing in the world for me to do. The next twenty minutes were silent ones.

"Did you walk last night?" Sonja finally asked at breakfast.

"Yes." I was buttering toast. I had an appetite that morning.

"You know it worries me."

"There were other people out, people walking, a man riding a horse."

"Who was on a horse?" She was curious now.

"Old Juan."

"That old man? Late at night he rides a horse?"

I changed the subject, suggested that we still go into Mazatlan together another day. We had only two left on our holiday. Sonja said she might. She said nothing about her meeting and I didn't ask. We claimed two chairs and a beach umbrella. Sonja read a mystery with a lurid cover she'd brought from New York; I fell asleep in the heated air. When I woke I saw Roberto and his helper Manuel erecting the parachute apparatus. I waved but he didn't see me; he was busy buckling a tourist into the harness. I opened the poetry book I'd brought – a small paperback Walt Whitman that I carried whenever I traveled. But I opened it to the wrong page, the last lines about a shipwreck:

"The beach is cut by the razory ice-wind....the wreck guns sound,
The tempest lulls and the moon comes floundering through the drifts.

I look where the ship helplessly heads end on....I hear the burst as she strikes. I hear the howls of dismay

they grow fainter and fainter.

I cannot aid with my wringing fingers;

I can but rush to the surf and let it drench me and freeze upon me.

I search with the crowd....not one of the company is washed to us alive;

In the morning I help pick up the dead and lay them in rows in a barn."

I put down the book, leaned back and closed my eyes. I was trembling.

The Herchmers arrived. Greta looked tired, but the good doctor was his usual expansive self. When Sonja came back from swimming and sat down, he invited us to be his guests at dinner than evening. Sonja then announced she had things to do and would rest most of the afternoon. I must go alone into Mazatlan. I was happy to do so, for as we walked to our room together before lunch, Sonja and I walked into another quarrel.

"Listen to me," she said. "To leave your marriage - this is a mistake."

"I don't want to talk about it, Mama."

"At first in the camps we thought that way –to die – to run into the wire. Then you saw you must live. In whatever way you can – you survive. You must. For others."

I erupted. 'We are always climbing it. Up the big mountain. We were in hell. We suffered. I'm sick of it, Mama, sick of carrying the rock."

"What rock is this?" Her voice was scornful.

"The biggest mountain of pain the world has ever seen. We are so important carrying that rock. I don't want to be there. Don't want anything to do with it anymore." I was trembling with anger. She walked away, turned into garden by the pool, sat on the edge of a chair, face tense. I followed her; sat down on a chair beside her. "You hear me, Mama? Not one second more. I don't want you there either."

"I am, God help me." Her face was averted, arms crossed over her chest.

"You think about it all the time, talk about it too much."

"I did not choose this life." Her tight voice told of her anger.

"Every day that you choose to be there, you are there."

She turned face white with anger, eyes blazing in that white. "You know so much. Nothing is what you know." She bent forward, breathing into my face, breath acetone. I was afraid of her. "Listen fool. Someday you will be in hell. That is waiting for you if you stay a fool." She sat back.

I flinched inside, remembering the furies I saw in my mother as a child, had encountered as an adolescent; Sonja could bring up darkness from the earth through the soles of her feet. I had always run away. Yet in the garden of lilies, I stood my ground. "Mama, everybody who knew the camps is dying."

"It was a fact."

"Facts are slippery – especially facts that are too terrible. The camps - I know, I know... I do remember – a little. But Mama - I want to forget like everybody else."

Why had we chosen to sit down beside lilies, that hot day, the sun dazzling, the sea frolicking just around the corner? Sonja's face whitened even more, a dreadful drawing in, as though she was taking away blood, withdrawing life from herself.

"I hate you," she said, her lips pulled together like a trap closing. "Sometimes how much you cannot know."

"I don't hate you, Mama." I looked over at the rubrun lilies - they were leaning over, bending down, seeking their reflections in the pool. She looked at them too.

"I promise you. I would like to forget. But I know what was, what is now. Here is a fact for you – Mrs. Herchmer is not happy. That is a fact - a today fact."

"Because of her husband?"

"She is not a Mrs." Sonja hissed. "You hear me, Karin, she is not his wife. His first wife killed herself." Sonja's face was stony. "She also was in the camps."

I reached out to touch her arm "People do that."

She pulled away from me, "Only the weak."

"I tried to do that, Mama - this year. Yes. After the flu I lay in bed and stopped eating. Finally they put me in the hospital; they force fed me. I had counseling. I'm leaving Greg. I must. You want me to survive?"

"Can I stop you? Yes, I too kept you alive – many times. That is a fact. Now please yourself. Run into the wire. Say to everyone, what does life matter?"

She stood up. "You are young, strong. You can talk about everything. Forgive everyone. O.K. Do that. You want to kill yourself, go ahead. Do what you please."

She stood staring down at the pool. Its surface was scummy, opaque – no longer a swimming place but some forgotten pond in a wilderness. Small parrots disturbed by our voices were squawking, a harsh sound. Sonja had entered a room I'd long wanted to share with her - How had she kept us alive? Against all odds? I tried again to put my arm around her shoulder. She didn't pull away. "How, Mama? How did you get me to the hospital so many times? I want to know. What kind of power did you have?"

"He was sometimes crazy. Most of them were...once and a while...like a clock." She turned to me; blood was returning to her face, her voice no longer a strangled sound.

"That clock in the kitchen in Iowa – Remember that clock that went crazy? Once a year - there on the wall, for no reason - it made a loud noise, a big buzzing like a hive of bees in the grass when you walk by and shake the grass - that buzzing, louder and louder. I could hear it in the other rooms, at the other end of the house. Why does a clock go crazy? Seconds rushing into each other, time – does it go mad like people?"

Abruptly she pulled away from me again, sat down again. I sat next to her, tried to hold her hand, but again she yanked herself away.

"I took it off the wall - the clock. Remember? Put it face down on the counter. Still it buzzed. I left it there for three days: three days it rested - like God I thought. He must need that clock. Only God needs three days to force time into obedience. When it was quiet, I put it back on the wall. It worked fine, that clock was silent for another year. How many years did that clock go crazy like that? It never stopped that madness, that noise, but it never stopped telling time either. So one day before it went crazy again, I smashed it. I broke the clock into a hundred pieces and threw the pieces into the garbage. They took it away - the garbage men. That was the end of it. No more waiting for a crazy clock to begin again."

She stood up, walked out of the garden as in a trance. I followed her into the annex, into our room. She sat down on her bed. "I am not a coward like you, Karin. You have always been weak. Forget you say? Forget the crazy clocks? The whole world was like that. I will not forget that. I will remember everything. And forgive nothing."

I thought then that I could hate her. Hate her energy, her mysteries; hate the world she insisted on presenting to me when my own had just begun to seem manageable.

"What's the point of that stupid clock story?" I said, still standing staring at her. But now I drew in the raw silk scent of the lilies. That morning I'd plucked two and brought them into the room. They were beside our beds.

"The guards in the camp: Many were like that clock. Once and awhile going crazy. Some were afraid, yes; some stupid or lazy; but some, some were crazy all the time." Then it happened: Anger left her – suddenly - as it often did. She lay back on her bed and stared at the ceiling. "Nathan. He is a little crazy."

"I thought you liked him." I looked at the two lilies in the glass beside me. Why were they bending down that way? Thought: There are questions I want to ask and dare not. There are feelings I cannot share with you. I sat on my bed, waiting for my mother to say more, to say anything, but she'd closed her eyes, appeared to be resting. I wrote out instructions to myself:

E*at in town, go shopping, spend the day away from this dialogue.*
But didn't you ask for it?
Didn't you start it?
You are weak
A weak woman
You want to kill yourself, go ahead
Those words won't go away

My mother appeared to be sleeping. I thought then of her age. It was easy for me to forget her age. She opened her eyes, spoke in a weak voice.

"Karin, I must sleep. I do not want lunch. Please go. Go to town. And take a little money, please. I want you to buy yourself something pretty."

I did as she asked – took fifty dollars from the wads on the bed and walked out onto the beach. I was shaking. Above the sparkling sea, a small cloud – a dark blur, a smudge of concentration – hovered on the horizon. I looked at my watch, walked to the front of the hotel -: the bus to town was waiting there.

Driving into town with other hotel guests, looking out at the dry, unforgiving landscape, I thought about the angry confrontations with Sonja. Liberation, it seemed, was managing to escape everyone and everything that bothered me. I grew determined to do that. And so that afternoon, I made sure I got into wonderful trouble.

I bought a dress - black with flowers the color of pink and blue, a low cut, seductive dress. Then after I wandered through the old town of Mazatlan and visited the port, I went into a small beauty shop in the central square, and got my hair cut by a pretty, longhaired Mexican girl who mourned its going. "Such beautiful hair," she said, "Why do you do this?"

"I must." was all I could say. My feelings were mixed - regret but relief too.

While I sat under the dryer, I wrote in the diary.

Hate being the knife edge of love

Yes, Mama, sometimes I hate you but only

When we persist in misunderstanding

Or when you stand too close

Because I hate most what others did to you

And to my father and brother and to all

The sleeping people who wanted nothing more than

Peace, who even now want nothing more than

Not to awake and see bad things happening

Why be a see-er when that is seeing?

I was beginning not to understand what I was writing. I put the notebook away, thought instead of all that Sonja had done to keep us alive. How she had always found food - dry bread, porridge, scraps of vegetables, rotting apples or pears. Hunger was always with us, but she always found food. I asked God's forgiveness for not remembering that, for not honoring her for keeping us alive.

It was nearly six when I got home; Sonja was sitting under a beach umbrella talking to the Herchmers. She was dressed for dinner, her pretty new black dress.

She saw me and her face changed.

"Why do you do this?"

"Don't be angry, Sonja."

"Your hair so ugly."

"Remember that story you used to tell me, Mama - how you cut your own hair when you were a little girl?"

"That was different."

"How you lied to your father and said you got up in your sleep and did it, so it was not your fault, but must have been a dream?"

"Greg will not be pleased." Her face was stony.

"I don't care." And I didn't.

The Herchmers were diplomatic and wouldn't be drawn into our quarrel. Instead they described the behavior of the two young German women we'd seen the day before. Greta and Sonja had overheard them talking in German, which both could understand; Sonja was fluent in the language. The young women were making fun of some of the guests, and had come around to laughing at Greta and Sonja.

"Zwei alten krachen –'two old crows" they'd called them – "a thin one and a fat one." Greta and Sonja were both wearing black bathing suits and large sun hats. They were not amused by the young women's mockery. We watched the German group play beach volley ball - badly we were pleased to see. It seemed my mother had forgotten my cut hair but I decided not to wear my new dress just in case.

The hotel had a small dining room which was reserved for private parties. The Herchmers had booked a table for six; Jason, their hard-faced friend we'd met the first day joined us; the sixth seat remained empty. The menu was more elaborate than in the main dining room and the service seemed intense. All through dinner, Sonja stared at me; several times she interrupted a conversation that was ranging over many topics to say she couldn't believe what I'd done but the others ignored her comments. Jason said little. A second bottle of wine was opened with the dessert. Jason chose that moment to announce he was a Nazi hunter. "Yes. I have found these men, several men. I make it difficult for them - the women too."

We all stared at him. His words were absolute, threatening. Sonja seemed entranced. "You think so?" she asked. She refused Nathan Herchmer's offer of more red wine by placing one ring-studded hand over her glass.

"Nazis in Mexico? How is this?"

Jason smiled thinly, "A good story."

"Which you won't tell," Nathan said emphatically. He smiled, poured himself a glass of wine. "Another of your deep dark secrets, Jason?"

Her face white with fatigue, Greta rose and excused herself. I stood up too, nudging Sonja but she at once suggested we go to the outdoor bar for coffee.

Sonja and Jason, still engrossed in their dialogue about Nazis, led the way.

On our way out of the dining room, Nathan stopped to light a cigarette and, pulling on my wrist, once again halted me beside him while the others walked on.

"I can't forget what I saw." His voice was low and smooth so the others couldn't hear him; when they were some distance ahead, he kissed his fingertips, and touched them to my forehead. I shivered and pulled away.

"I have to make a phone call."

"I'll wait." He put his hand on my waist.

I moved away, called over my shoulder, "Tell Sonja I'll join you later."

I was angry with her. How could she get involved with those two men, with their exaggerated stories of Nazis? I regretted my contrariness, decided I would spend more time, not less with my mother. Calling home proved to be a mistake. I needed to find out about the girls but a strange young woman answered; she had a warm voice and was laughing. I didn't tell her who I was, and she didn't ask. Greg was talking in the background and laughing too. I hung up.

The outdoor bar was not large, but when gaily lit looked like a ballroom because of the terrace patio floor and the string of lights surrounding it. That night every table was full and many people were dancing. The combo was made up of younger livelier players, two guitars and drums beat out popular music, while a hefty woman in a splashy red dress alternated between shaking castanets and singing about love in a husky voice.

Though the bar was crowded, the night wind bathed us with salt sea air. I made my way through the packed tables looking for my mother; through the music, I heard a woman shouting. "Leave him alone! He is a good man." At a table near the dance floor sat Sonja, Greta, Nathan and Jason; they were all drinking. I sat down with them. The black haired woman shouting was one of the German tourists, the one with a rough look and ragged hair. She was draped protectively across her muscular boyfriend who smirked drunkenly as she went on hurling words across the dance floor at our table, "You old crows. He is not a lousy Nazi. I am the lousy Nazi. I am a lousy Nazi bitch."

No one paid much attention to her – no one but my mother that is.

Sonja sat forward in her seat. She called out to the young woman "You are proud of what you are? What is that?" To my surprise, Greta, face stark white in the shadowy light, was standing up, swaying back and forth. She called out in a gentle voice: "Go home, please go home, please." People at other tables were watching her, and eyeing Sonja, who was sitting next to me. They were looking with shock at all of us. The two men and I said nothing. But I was ashamed. What was happening to my mother?

The band came to the end of their music; the players spoke to each other, then the woman singer announced they would take a break. As they left, Sonja stood and shouted at the German couples. "You go too. Go home. We don't want you here." But she sat down as the silent disapproval of the other guests became more evident.

We were in the same, noisy, dark friendly outdoor bar where I'd met Roberto and danced with him. The mood was very different this night. The black-haired young German woman with the raucous voice was by far the most aggressive, but my mother, was a close second. Now the young woman stood up, fists on hips; beside her the drunken man's smirk seemed fixed and he closed his eyes.

"I am the lousy stinking Nazi bitch."

"Go home." Sonja was out of her seat again. I tugged at her arm.

A second woman – the cool blonde half of the magic couple at the German table had said nothing. She leaned against her lover. She was calm, smiling at him, seemingly uninvolved with the other woman's raucous campaign. She kissed the slim blond man with soft, steady passionate kisses. She looked infinitely seductive; a wave of jealousy rose up in me. I recalled Desmond trying to talk to her, bending over her chair in the dining room, face sweaty with eagerness. Though Sonja had immediately disliked these tourists, I'd admired them for their open sexuality. Now I grew less sure. I watched Marian Heisel reach up, grab her lover's head; and kiss him with open mouth, then climb up to lie on his nearly prone body as he stretched back across the chairs. He was laughing with embarrassment, but he was not drunk, nor was she. It was deliberately provocative, or so it seemed. Sonja erupted with rage.

"Get off him. Get off. Get out of here." She was booing now. I couldn't believe this was my mother, my sophisticated Sonja. And Greta had joined her. The magic couple looked over at our table and laughed. Sonja stepped forward. She stopped in the middle of the dance floor. The bar grew very quiet.

"Mama, calm down." I said loud enough so she could hear me. But Sonja refused to look at me or listen. For the first time since Josef's death, she'd drunk too much.

"You!" She was aiming words at the blonde woman now - the perfect face, the perfect body. "You are a slut."

Everyone was silent, the tension was noticeable. Greta, without a word to any of us, slipped away. Nathan and Jason were standing behind a table now, as though to prepare for a fight. Sonja didn't notice. She was walking across the now empty dance floor. The magic couple watched her come toward them and their smiles faded.

Above us the stars didn't notice any of this. They were too far away, too indifferent. I thought, if I concentrate on them I can pretend I don't hear or see my mother. The black haired woman was sitting now and had turned her back on us to talk to others at her table. Marian Heissel and her companion seemed unconcerned. She lay on the lap of her lover and stroked his hair. He was sprawled in his chair at the edge of the dance floor, passive; she stroked his thighs and he leaned back, smiling. I thought both couples were deliberately provocative, daring Sonja to continue her attack on them.

Sonja shouted in German several times that they were dirty pigs. How many understood her? I looked around but could not see the faces of the other patrons in the shadows. The black haired woman didn't turn around but Marian sat up. "Leave us alone," she said to Sonja in a low, intense voice; she too spoke in German, "If you do not leave us alone, I will call the manager. You will be sorry I think."

"Do we care what you think? What you think is not important. Not anymore." Perhaps only I and the German couples understood Sonja – but no one could mistake the anger in her voice. Nathan and Jason looked at her with surprise.

This is my mother, I thought.

Then the band returned, were playing again – people at the tables, as though released from some magic spell, hastened on to the floor and danced. My mother stood in the midst of them transfixed. The music was dreamy and slow, calming. Nathan, his face in shadows, was raising his glass to his lips when he caught my eye. He tipped the glass to me and drank. The dark-haired woman and her mate rose. Swaying drunkenly they danced a tight embrace, gradually mingling with the others on the floor. I walked over and touched Sonja's arm, pulled gently at her; at first she ignored me. Instead she moved toward the chair where the blond woman half leaned, half lay against her lover's body murmuring into his ear. As Sonja drew closer, the man straightened, pulled his companion against his chest and looked up at Sonja. "Hey, hey, we are friends," he said in English and threw out his hands and smiled, but his female companion did not. The blonde rested her head against the man's chest, but looked with hard eyes at Sonja. "You jealous old crow," she hissed in German.

Sonja's clenched her hands into fists. I held my breath, touched Sonja's arm one more time. "Mama, please." Then I turned and went back to my seat, reluctant to do more, to stay involved, but unwilling also to let my mother do something vile in public.

Sonja turned and stumbled back to our table.

The dark-haired German woman and her lover were dancing strenuously, heads butted against each other, hips moving in exaggerated rhythm. Sonja sat beside me; she picked up her glass and drank, but when she put it down I put it under the table. Jason leaned over and said something to her I couldn't hear. Gradually the tension eased. Ten minutes later the three musicians put down their guitars and drums and strolled away as a spotlight over the band corner flared into brightness. In the sudden glare, dancers blinked, stood dazed, than dispersed. The German dancers drifted to their table and spoke quietly to the magic pair. A few minutes later, they all left. Recorded music came on. Sonja muttered angrily to Nathan.

I could stand no more. I got up and walked away - out onto the beach. I lay down on the damp sand by the edge of the sea, put my head on my arms and cried.I felt the great chasm that lay between my mother and me was that awful anger. Since the arrival of the Germans, Sonja had targeted them as the enemy. She'd watched them, on the beach, in the hotel dining rooms. At that moment Desmond came up. He sat down beside me. "Not a good evening."

"Did you see?"

"Some of it. Are you all right?"

"Nothing a little quiet won't cure."

"Do you want to walk?"

"Yes," I said, "Yes I do."

He put out his hand and pulled me to my feet. We walked along the waves, their roar in the darkness a night animal, ferocious. I held my long dress away from the water and pulled my white stole close. When we reached a dark unused stretch of sand, tiny ghost crabs hastened before us. I turned to him.

"Desmond, why haven't I seen you?" The words came out unbidden. I didn't know why. Then when he took my hand I thought I knew. The curling waves seemed like white smiles in the darkness.

"Tomorrow," he said. "Let's have dinner – you and your mother." We walked back up the bar. He said, "You cut your hair."

"Yes."

"Was it a burden?"

"Yes."

"Then you did the right thing."

He said goodnight and walked back into the bar. I watched him stride over to sit with the Germans. They were back at their table drinking. He leaned forward to chat with Marian and I thought - not for the first time - that I knew nothing about men at all.

Friday, Day 6

The next morning it rained, just after sunrise - a sudden hard tropical pelting down which moved across the water. Yet the sun shone too, the air brilliant with light. I dressed, rushed out, walked in bare feet on wet sand. We were leaving the next afternoon and I didn't want to miss anything of the last day. Roberto found me on the beach. He was leaving early the next day and didn't want to go running, but made me promise to find him that night to say goodbye.

Desmond was meeting Sonja and me for dinner – an early dinner so Sonja could go to the casino with Nathan. At mid-day she was shopping in town with friends. I looked forward to an afternoon alone, but was determined to make peace with my mother. I'd incited some of her anger Thursday night, had been deliberately aggravating in many ways. Still I loved my new short hair, felt younger, more desirable, and somehow stronger. As I walked the beach I picked up small shells to take home to the girls.

I was eager to see them, to set my new plans in motion. Sonja and I had agreed Nadine would attempt university in New York City next year. Despite the tension with Sonja, my life seemed to be moving. I could go home and face the decisions I must make.

Sonja was dressing when I entered the room about nine. She scowled at me. "This morning I am not eating."

"Come to breakfast with me, please. This is our last day together."

"Only coffee," She wound a scarf around her rumpled hair.

"Look I'm wearing the ring." I held out my hand to show her a green turquoise ring, I'd bought with her money. "I like it, Mama."

She looked at the ring and seemed pleased. As we walked out, I couldn't resist teasing her. "No perfume this morning?"

She frowned, then smiled sharply and pinched my cheek as she used to do when I was naughty as a child: "So smart the girl is this morning."

Sonja seemed hung over; she ate very little but drank coffee, which she didn't usually do. She watched me eat my way through another big breakfast. I made her talk. We sat a long time in the dining room. She spoke for the first time about her boss. "Dr Fitzgerald thinks to retire next year." Sonja looked at me with swollen eyes. "So many years in business he was - a good dentist. Everyone liked him."

I had thought on my odd visits back to New York, that there was something between my mother and the dentist she worked for. Dr.

Fitzgerald was a tall, cheerful man with a bald spot and wrinkled shirts. Married with two sons in business, he spoke of them, but never of his wife who was an invalid.

"He has taken a partner, a young man." Sonja played with a teaspoon.

"When did that happen?" I was eating Scottish oatmeal; my eating regime in those days required my ordering obscure health foods.

"Last month." She reached out with beautifully manicured hands to tear off bits from a sweet roll on a plate resting between us. "They both want me to work there the next six months. Before I came here - the new man himself asked me." She went on taking mouse-sized crumbs of sweet bun. Her fingers were trembling.

I touched her wrist. "That's good, Mama; you stay six months - or as long as you want. See if you like working for him. This is delicious oatmeal, want to try it?"

She gave a little shiver of disgust. "No. Please. I do not like the smell. This new man, this Grabner…" She demonstrated more disgust when she pronounced his name. "He says he wants me, that Dr. Fitzgerald thinks highly of me, that…" She paused, swallowed, "he himself cannot imagine the reception desk without me behind it."

"What a thing to say!" I tried to look indignant, but sounded melodramatic.

"I am a piece of furniture to him." She was not eating the mouse pieces, but rolling them into small hard balls, then placing them on her bread plate. Sonja's voice deepened. "I am to serve that... He looks ...no, I do not speak of him. But I do not think of working for him."

"He sounds pretty tactless. What about someone else? Another dentist?"

"I do not have to work. Not any more."

As I listened to her I thought how much I loved Sonja. One way or another, complicated as she is at times, I always have. I love her courage, her physical energy, her willingness to try anything, go anywhere, love her ability to charm men, to adopt women as friends. I love and respect her deep concern over my happiness, my success. We are very different, and as she and I grow older, we understand our differences more clearly. But she has known me better than anyone else. I hope my daughters understand me in the same way. Somehow I doubt it for Sonja and I share that terrible secret world that no one talks about now - places so inhuman that all the rest of a life in the world should seem a garden, a place of ease.

On the holiday in Mexico, whenever Sonja smiled, I still saw sadness in her eyes; sometimes she laughed but not often. My mother never had a strong sense of humor, but silly behavior, especially with others, could make her giggle. That was how we healed the growing rift between us that Friday morning. After breakfast, we went swimming together after breakfast. I wore the green turquoise ring and pranced into the waves in my shorts and shirt, splashing and shouting which made Sonja smile. She tried to follow more cautiously; she was wearing a swimsuit, but still had on her terrycloth jacket. A big wave rolled over her, knocking her down; she struggled up and was knocked down again. Three times this happened and then, trying to rescue her, a wave broke over me totally drenching me, and we grew hysterical with laughter. Like two children we bounced up and down as wave after wave hit us until Sonja threw up her hands and marched to shore.

"I wet my pants, I laughed so hard," she announced when I followed her. She had joined Nathan and Greta under an umbrella. I went on dancing in the sea, wet clothes plastered against my body until I too staggered out and up the beach. Sonja was sitting with a coke in her hand chatting to Greta. In the distance, old Juan rode his horse up and down the beach trolling for customers. He invited tourists to climb up behind him and ride along the beach. A woman ran up. After a conversation, she climbed up behind him, and the horse, which looked as old as the man, ambled away. Why should I warn her? My mood was a happy one.

Why not run along the beach? One last time – go as far as the cave- a glimpse of it in daylight – yes I wanted that. Roberto would soon be in Mexico City; nothing but my own mood would challenge me. I ran lightly, skillfully - proudly too – how well I'd been taught and by a lifeguard. I felt young, strong, full of purpose. How much seemed changed after one short week. I was grateful to Roberto for inspiring me to run; grateful for the Hotel Madre Maria and all its charm, and to Sonja for bringing me there. I even remembered to thank God. I thought of the pelican bones in the sand - everything working toward the momentarily perfect. Even conversations with Sonja seemed to be leading somewhere. Surely my return home would be marked by growth and renewal, my need for independence accepted by my children.

It was not yet the hottest part of the day but only a few people shared the sand with me. Heat struck at my back, I slowed to a walk. That morning the sea was dazzling; all the small islands clearly visible; there were three ships on the horizon. No one sat outside the seedy Mexican motel. Rounding the bluff, I was by then walking the open empty stretch. I'd come this way most mornings with Roberto. Mid-day revealed dirty sand, a few cabins - yes, there - a second motel and several houses high on the cliff above the beach; then, beyond the bluff the sandy enclave where Roberto had shown me the cave. There was a chair or two on the sand below; others knew about this place, perhaps knew about the cave. I had liked believing it was a secret, enjoyed that secret.

I walked back, running the last few yards to impress my mother. But she'd already left the beach. I waved to the Herchmers, and then went on to our room. Sonja was gone; she'd left me a note promising to back before six when we were due to meet Desmond. I ate lunch by myself in the outdoor bar.

There were more cooking smells outside than inside: delicious aromas of chicken and fish grilling, butter and garlic, hamburgers and fries, tortillas and refried beans. Memories of Mexico must surely include the taste and smell of limes. Sounds were lively at the bar too; the radio played at all hours and there was a constant knot of love struck bees by the beer taps; multiple human conversations floated about and laughter, the sudden loud laughter provoked by the telling of good stories. In the evening, the dance floor would be laid on the sand but during the day sand and bare feet prevailed.

Occasionally I heard the distant clash of voices and dishes from the kitchen behind the bar, and out on the beach half-drunk tourists teased each other in and out of spite and arguments. How I wished I could take those life sounds back with me.

On the beach a small Mexican boy fearless in the incoming tide examined his toes as if they pointed to the universe; nearby his parents sat stunned by their own inertia. Under brown thatched umbrellas, hotel guests baked brown were sucked dry and speechless from the demands of sun worship: they sipped drinks and stared out to sea. Some were reading, others packing up, moving lazily toward their rooms for afternoon siestas, stopping to wash their feet under the primitive showers, yet still leaving trails of sandy footprints along the blue and yellow tile floors. The parachute equipment had been carried away so that sand stretched open and empty, yielding slowly to the waves with their necklaces of white foam. The afternoon breeze was just stirring; the clouds had lifted into streaks of white in a blue sky.

I took a brief dash into the waves, sat talking for a few minutes to Greta. She was alone that afternoon and told me about her embroidery in a soft voice.

How I loved all that day! The Hotel Madre Maria was precious now because I was leaving. When I went back to the room to rest, I took out my little notebook, and waited for words to come. None did. I sat notebook ready and my mind a blank for long minutes. Finally I gave up, tried to read, but instead fell asleep, and dreamed:

A white lady in a white light

Tall and beautiful

She came close to me

Touched my head

Said nothing

In that dream everything was silence

She led me away

Showed me high mountains and narrow green valleys,

Water flowed in twisted channels

I asked questions

*   *   *   *   *

When I woke I could remember none of the questions or their answers.

*   *   *   *   *

"I did not do what I went into the town to do. I had no time, no time at all." Sonya picked at her shrimps; one by one she pulled them out of their fine segmented selves and then cut them into pieces with her knife and fork. "These are too big, these shrimps."

"They're perfect, Mama, delicious."

"So you say. Always you say things are 'perfect, so wonderful'. Why? Things are not perfect, and almost never are they delicious."

She looked so cross that I glanced at Desmond and saw he was smiling.

"Yes," he said, "Mrs. Mika, you are right. Nothing is that delicious. Except perhaps your daughter."

I blushed and looked away. Sonja stopped dissecting her shrimp and looked, first at Desmond, then at me. She didn't quite understand the exchange, but she knew, or at least so her facial expression implied, a severe sense of shock.

"You are kind, Mr. Nicholson."

"No, I'm not." he said.

For some reason that particular remark made my whole body flush. It was the way he looked at me when he said it, and the tone of voice he used. Sonja didn't smile. Her eyes were red rimmed from the sun.

"Those women, Mrs. Smith and Mrs. Allan, they went into every shop. In every shop they are looking for one thing – plastic flowers. I tell you - tall plastic Calla Lilies. They are taking them to all their friends. Every shop they bought ten or fifteen of these flowers. Now they have fifty plastic flowers and they are searching to find a big box to carry them all home -unless they themselves carry them on the plane. What a business. I had other things to do, but they would not let me go alone. They said, Sonja, it is not safe, you will get lost, stay with us. They gave me two big plastic Calla Lilies but I said no, too much trouble. What do I want with plastic flowers on an airplane?"

She was cultivating her most dramatic voice, but clearly relishing the afternoon trailing around with two eccentric elderly shoppers. "Mrs. Smith will take them on the plane – she will carry twenty-five and Mrs. Allen will carry twenty-five but another lady we met who was buying them has arthritis in her hands and said she couldn't carry so many. She bought one! I never saw such shoppers." She put down her knife and fork clearly abandoning the struggle with the shrimp and turned to Desmond, who looked startled. "Mr. Nicholson - Do you like Mexico?"

"Desmond. Yes, I've been here before." His eyes had begun to stray across the room. Looking for Marian I thought but didn't say. The dining room was barely a third full; we were determined to eat early enough in the evening to go on to other events.

Desmond, like Sonja and I, had plans. "Sometimes, I like it very much."

"This hotel?"

"Yes. Good hotel. Relaxing."

An odd thing to say. Except for swimming, I'd never seen him lolling on the beach or in the bar. Sonja said, "Are you in the main building?" She was developing a determined push to her questioning.

"No, I'm staying down the road. Shall we go to the bar for coffee?"

Sonja shook her head. "Sorry. I am meeting about a dog."

"A dog?" I asked, laughing. Sonja laughed too and pushed her plate of shrimp remains away. She took a sip of white wine. Desmond had treated us to a bottle and we were working our way through it.

"Tell me about yourself, Mr. Nicholson."

"Desmond. There's nothing to tell." He sat looking into Sonja's eyes, and suddenly I wanted to reach over and hit him just strongly enough to get his attention. Why wasn't he looking at me?

"It is a name I don't know – Desmond." Sonja said. She was sitting still as stone staring straight back at him. A duel of stares. Oh dear, I couldn't help thinking, these two are not getting along.

The band was playing slow dance music – fox trots, romantic last hour together numbers like 'Begin the Beguine'. Desmond leaned across the table and touched my mother's hand. "Would you care to dance, Mrs. Mika?"

"You may call me Sonja," she said, then fumbled for a handkerchief, "Not yet. Not so soon after dinner. The stomach…" She patted hers.

"Ah yes," said Desmond, "the stomach must rest." He leaned over my shoulder.

"Karin, what's the state of your stomach?"

Now it was real, the strong urge to strike him, preferably with something large and wet like a fish. He saw that reaction in my eyes, smiled, took my hand and said in a warm voice, "Do you want to dance?"

"Yes." I said, and stood up. He waited a long moment, than rose as well.

"Excuse us, please, Sonja."

I turned and said. "Are you O.K., Mama?"

"Yes. Go. Dance. The music is not so bad."

Then we were dancing, Desmond and I, smoothly, both tall, we could move together and stay in harmony.

"I knew you would be a good dancer," he said, and gave me an awkward push to make me whirl.

"I love to dance."

"I don't," Desmond said, and tried another awkward push; this time I was ready and managed nicely. The music was neither fast nor slow and we danced four in a row, Desmond talking about his children and my mother.

"Your mother is very determined you won't be taken advantage of."

"You think so?"

"It's obvious."

"She knows I'm not happy right now."

Was that my imagination? Did his arm tighten around me? I thought - Don't tell him anything. Don't tell this attractive man all the unhappy trashy facts of your life. But the words came out anyway.

"Can I talk to you about something?"

He looked faintly alarmed, but smiled. "Yes."

"You're sure you won't mind? I'm in a little trouble."

"What kind of trouble?" He stopped pushing me around the dance floor, stared down at me. I froze but he waited patiently.

"I spotted that dead man's body in the water and reported it. But I haven't heard a word since then. We're leaving tomorrow. I don't know if I should do anything more."

"Good God, leave it alone. The police are working on it, or not working on it. The less said the better in Mexico."

"O.K. Thanks." We danced in silence for a few minutes. Desmond spoke first.

"You said you have children. Where are they now?"

"Daughters - fifteen and seventeen: They haven't been answering the phone much. Maybe that's a good sign. Their dad is paying attention to them."

"That's why I'm here. Visitation rights are worth jack all. Marian said she left Carla and Martin with someone she knows but she won't tell me who that is."

"Marian?"

"My ex wife. She's here with that German party. It's been six months. They're lost to me, or will be if I can't shake some sense into the woman. I caught up with her at the hotel – but she won't tell me, too enamored with the lout. – that's typical." I could hear his anger and his pain but mainly I felt my own surprise. Marian Eissel was his ex wife. The night before was fresh in my mind. I didn't want to talk about her but Desmond clearly did. "She's a nut case: A totally unreliable mother."

"I'd like to sit down." I managed to say. Could Greg say that about me?

We went back to the table. Sonja was rubbing a wine glass, her arms covered with silver bracelets that gleamed in the candlelight; her face was anxious, but she managed a smile when we walked up. "A very handsome couple you make."

"Let's go to the room, Mama. We've got to pack."

"Of course, darling," Sonja said and summoned the waiter so she could sign for the check. After offering to pay and being refused, Desmond walked us to our building.

"How do you like her new ring?" Sonja said. I held it up so he could admire it, which he did. He said goodnight and, touching my hand lightly, walked away, once again up the beach, out of my life, without looking back. Beside him, white ripples of sea smiles still rolled in with eccentric precision, but beyond them the water was black and heavy. A few boats bobbed on the surface; to the north the lights of Mazatlan scarred half the horizon. It was our last night but I had no desire to run alone in the dark.

"Where did you buy that dress?" Sonja asked in the room. I'd worn my new seductive flowered dress.

"In town."

"Very pretty. You looked very fine tonight."

"Thank you Mama."

"I don't like that man."

I said nothing, but began to pack. Sonja wandered out and down the road to the casino in search of Nathan. When I was satisfied I'd done all the packing I could, I read Tolkien for awhile. I'd nearly finished the second book and promised myself I'd start the third once I was home. I'd begun to like reading heroic adventures. About ten, I took a shower, put my seductive dress back on, and with my mother gone for the evening, decided to tempt fate.

The sky in the tropics is a blue-black – the sheen of a crow's sculptured body or the smooth precision of a ripe plum. There is nothing flat or forbidding about the night sky above the sea of Cortes. Sometimes there is cloud or haze, the white slippery passage of fog, but when clear, the sky is a black that opens, not closes its being, but only if a visitor goes out into the night and disappears into it.

I went outside. It was half past ten. Wandering down beside the hotel to look at the waves, I saw Roberto watching me from the edge of the outdoor bar. We looked at each other, waved, and without a word or sign, walked up the beach to the beach below the cave.

He started out first, strolling down by the cliff edge, while I, taking off my shoes, waded in the water, drifting along, seemingly without a destination. Yet I knew he was waiting for me. By then I was certain I wanted to break my marriage vows, needed to break my life apart. Looking up, I gazed at the stars and felt their benedictions;

they were dazzling that night, the sky clear. I was still young enough to believe that everything that happens between men and women is destiny.

Have you ever noticed hard difficult it is to remember lovemaking? The actual facts, the practicalities, the smells, sounds all these disappear after the fact. Perhaps our brains go on hold when our bodies take command. What I do know is that true memory seems to relinquish all sense of right and wrong, and instead provides only a bracing sensation of being with someone you trust. I was consciously breaking my marriage vows with someone I would never see again. That night, it seemed to be something I had to do.

Black and white – that's what I remember. The beach of white sand, the black moonless night, a black sea with white ripples on its breasting waves, Roberto's white shirt and my black dress. The sound of the sea was a heartbeat, loud and steady, its wind a giant breath. Taking such deliberate, ceremonial steps to betray my husband, I was entering what I hoped would be a new selfhood, one that broke a bowl of indifference.

Someone might say you are seeking revenge; you want to pay back a husband who has betrayed you. But being with Roberto was different. There was something strong between us, not exactly attraction but something larger, in a way more certain. He had guided me into greater confidence in myself. Why he sought me out I do not know, but I trusted him. And he seemed to want to trust me.

Here I tell the truth, an awkward truth. I could not yield to the man, but wanted to yield to the cosmos. To strike sparks with eternity, destiny, God, all the names for the fateful power that guides us, even drives us beyond where we want to go. I did know I wanted to stop hating my husband, to start finding new ways of loving others: daughters, friends, mothers, sisters, lovers. Did Roberto want that too?

He sat in a chair when;I approached. For some reason, I knelt on the sand, yes knelt before this handsome, young, not particularly interesting Mexican lifeguard. In doing so I was submitting to the night, the sea, the sand, the wind, and to a new self with a future still to be carved out by me. Roberto said nothing, and neither did I. It was, I confess to my shame, a romantic moment.

For long minutes we paused there, held by the black and white, and the roar of the sea. Then he rose and led me up to the cave. The entrance was narrow; first he slid in on his side, then, holding my hand, pulled me through. Inside, the small space was suffocating and close. He pushed me down on the ground; there was a blanket already on a section of the coarse sand and rock, a small bundle of clothes, or rags, which served as a pillow. Others had been there before us; a smell of seaweed and sweat and semen was caught in the rags. I breathed in Roberto's cheap cologne and his breath too, which was not unpleasant. Inside the cave, the sound of the sea was a faint roar.

Roberto said, "Are you O.K.?"

I said, "Yes," in a brave voice; but didn't feel brave at all. It was such an unusual place to be introducing your body to a stranger. But he kissed and stroked me, and soon I warmed to the task of fulfillment, my own as well as his, and we did come, both of us, in tiny shivers of pleasures that satisfied; the cave was too confined though, and so we lay together as close and warm as twins only for a few moments. Then he was a stranger with a strange smell and an unknown body, and though we lay in the tightest of dark spaces, a hollow in a rock wall, that strangeness became more powerful than our closeness.

There wasn't a pinprick of light. The thought passed through my mind that he could kill me there and nobody would know. I moved, edged away, tried to roll outside.

He moved to win me back. We had held each other tenderly and Roberto had said, "Now I have found you," absolutely the most romantic words I could imagine - but at the same time I was still thinking: This is a perfect place for a murder; nobody would find my body for weeks. I thought: What am I doing here, a mile from the hotel, in a secluded cave with a man I don't know?

But to trust to destiny is to trust in destiny. I lost my fear, was able to whisper, rather melodramatically "And I have found you." This seemed the right thing to say, though, at least to my own ears, a bit redundant. Because he may have been talking about his lost mother.

Roberto went on to pronounce, "We are one. Nothing is lost. Everything is found." I didn't exactly know what that meant, so I didn't say anything but soon admitted, "I'd like to go back. My mother will worry." It was true and the right thing to say considering the roles both our mothers were playing. But briefly thought too we'd forged a connection to all the people in the world engaged in the same act of male - female reconciliation, body and spirit. So powerful were these thoughts that I will never forget them; they go with the cave, and the night and the man.

Yet as soon as we rose and left the cave, all the practicalities flowed back; I knew both guilt and regret. Roberto would feel none of that, I thought, he might even forget me as he drove off into the night with his friends. Once again the stars comforted me. They were blazing away their distant identities in a night sky with nothing else as companion but a sliver of the moon. As we walked the empty beach beside the sea, we met the old Mexican with a handlebar mustache and battered sombrero who offered tourists rides. He raised a hand to salute Roberto, and eyed me with sly recognition.

"Why is he out so late?" I asked Roberto.

"Old Juan? He is often here. He is harmless. He never speaks to anyone."

"Except you."

"Oh, he knows me. I tell you, he is always on this beach. Day and night he comes to ride here. My bosses, they don't mind." He said good night with a formal kiss on my forehead, and walked away. I went back to the room which was empty. Sonja wasn't back from the casino. I undressed, thinking I will never hate Greg again, slipped between the sheets and fell into a dreamless sleep.

Saturday, Day 7

Sonja was angry, spitting angry.

"They took me to a room high up in a hotel in the town. It was hot, the fan did nothing. He was living on the bed, some old man, such a decrepit old man, two teeth in his head, one on each side, talking nonsense, a senile old man. He talked of flying upside down over airfields, of drinking beer with his comrades, all sorts of nonsense I did not care to hear, but everything a whisper, so old, in his nineties I think and no mind left."

"What are you talking about Mama?"

She was sitting on my bed. From the gray light, I knew it was early morning. It was clear she hadn't slept much – she looked dreadful. Still barely awake, I struggled to sit up, blinked: 5:38 according to Huey, Duey and Luey.

"The room stank. It was horrible, the whole evening - horrible."

"Why did you go then?"

"I wanted to see him. Jason talking of Nazis and finding them in Mexico and this man was German yes, I think, or Lithuanian or who knows what. So I went. I thought I want to see one, I want to hate one up close and it was impossible to hate such an old man, living a pointless life in a small hot room. And how could I know he was a Nazi, there were no papers, nothing to show what he was, what he had done; to be German that is not a crime."

I listened. Heard her say what I'd suggested only a few days before.

"How long did you stay in his room?"

"Not long. They gave him money – a few pesos - we left him still talking nonsense. He talked about fishing - catching a big fish – taking beer up to ten thousand feet to cool it. I heard him speak of a camp, putting people there; then I was afraid. I did not want to hear more because yes he might be a Nazi. We went to a bar, then Nathan asked me, - Karin, he asked me - if I wanted to kill a Nazi. He said that they would help me kill one – maybe that old man. For revenge, they said, no one would know. I looked at him - Nathan was drunk, but I believed him. He would help me do that. He was smiling at me, saying to me: 'It would satisfy you wouldn't it - to kill one of them? That man was a camp guard; he killed hundreds, probably thousands; would you like to kill him?" I was horrified – yet I whispered –'yes'. I cannot explain this, Karin. 'Yes,' I heard my own voice say this. Jason was not sitting with us. I asked when? Whenever you want, Nathan said, tonight, tomorrow night, whenever you want."

She sat, staring at me, stunned, exhausted, repentant, and yet also excited. I didn't know what to say. After a few moments, she rose and went into the bathroom, ran the water, stumbled out of her clothes; there was silence, then a sound I'd not heard for many years - Sonja crying in the bath, loud sobs. She ran water as she always had to drown out the sound, but I heard her sobbing because I knew what to listen for - Sonja was afraid. I got up and went outside, thinking everything is getting too intense. I have my own problems, my own guilt; we need to be ready to go to the airport by 1 o'clock.'

The sea was gray blue and soft in the early morning light. I didn't have much energy but once outside, grew calm enough to run. No one sat outside the seedy Mexican motel or walked the empty beach. I passed the breakwater, rounded the curve of the shoreline, saw the chair where Roberto had sat. How dilapidated, how ordinary a chair can look. Last night may have been a mistake, even a sin, yes, perhaps, but in my mind the experience lingered as brief magic, my chosen test of strength and courage. And it had been simple and true fun too.

I looked up to my right and saw the outcrop of rock behind which the cave opening was concealed. To take a last look, I climbed up the rocky promontory and peered into the opening. The dry fishy smell of the cave reminded me of the night before, long before my eyes adjusted to the dim light. But I saw something that hit me like a fist.

Someone was in the cave – a woman, a blonde, lying naked, sprawled askew, head jammed against the cave wall. I felt faint.

- The camp, our hut - Mrs. Sjolik - sleeping next to me, crumpled -

Then reason prevailed. This was a young woman. I knew her. Yes: Marian Heisel. I knelt half in the cave, half out, not believing. *What's wrong with her?* Some new part of me was speaking, adding a correct, analytical assessment to my more familiar emotional response. The crooked angle of the body - she must be dead. *Oh God no. The distant muffled sound is the same as when Roberto and I were here, but now Marian and I are listening to it together.* A fly crawled over her wrist; if I leaned forward I might hear it buzz. Yet awkward as her body looked, she was still beautiful.

Don't touch her. I backed out of the cave and stood up. I was trembling. *Flies don't crawl that way over living people. She's dead.* An accident? Or sick. *She's dead.* If it's an accident or she's sick I should get help. *It's murder.* I should look again, check for signs of violence, see if there are wounds or blood. *A gag over her mouth?*

I crawled back into the cave. "Hello." There was no answer, no sound of breathing. I should look for blood? *Are you crazy? You fool. She's dead.*

My mother's exact words when I asked her about Mrs. Sjolik. I stared at Marian, now become 'the body'. There was no blood. She lay as lovely and calm, as perfect as when she was alive. I'd found her – Marian. No one else knew. *You're in trouble. If you tell anyone they will ask why you came here.*

I put my head down against the sand and lay there in the cave for very long moments while all sorts of thoughts uncurled in me, most of them slow and ugly. Was she murdered? *Probably.* Why do you think that? *Gut feeling.* Who would murder her? *Don't be stupid.* Why did I come here in the first place? *If that isn't stupid what is?*

Who did it? Roberto? *He knew about the cave.*

Once again reason took over. Roberto was gone, and anyway I couldn't imagine him doing such a thing. Surely other people knew about the cave - locals, tourists. And a number of people knew Marian Heisel. *Heisel means hot in German.* Now memories of the camp came – the dead in the morning lying frozen in their unhappiness and pain. Curled over oddly like Marian, mouth shaped open and awry. Memory also came of the two German women shouting in the bar, shouting at Sonja!

Could she have been angry enough? I crawled out of Marian's tomb, stood up. Below me Old Juan sat on his horse beside the sea. I turned my back, stood long moments in front of the cave staring at nothing. I was still in a state of shock when I saw the square cosmetic case on the ground. I couldn't mistake it – purple - Sonja's favorite color. I don't remember what I thought then or if I thought at all; I simply jammed the case into the top of my shirt; a reflex so automatic I was looking out to sea again before I realized I'd done it. Old Juan was still there, now looking up at me. I squatted down, waited, crawled back into the cave.

In the gold gloom of the sand cave, the body lay as though poured into amber.

I made myself look more closely. There was no blood, no bullet wounds, knife slashes, bruises. How did Marian get there? Did she die in the cave, or was she carried there by someone – the person that murdered her? Her face was closed, aimed away from me, from looking at the world ever again. The cave surrounding her body seemed to protect her right to do that, to be that helpless, to be dead forever and forever.

The same thought came again and again – *Don't report this, don't get involved.*

It's nothing to do with you. I thought out explanations. I happened to stroll by and was poking around when I found a cave. Too bad I found it on the very morning that a dead person was lying in it. Yet, could I get away with that explanation?

What about Sonja? The trip to town to see a Nazi, the plan to kill one?

I backed out of the cave one last time, looked again at the cosmetic case. It was my mother's. I opened it – smudged makeup, brushes – yes it was Sonja's.

I jammed it into my pocket. Below me, Old Juan was riding away. I waited long minutes, and then took off running, out of there, as far from the cave as I could manage – and from the thought that my mother might be a murderer.

The next hour I sat by the pool looking at the cosmetic case. Thought about what to do with it, about my mother: What exactly did I know? *Not much.* What should I do? It was like incest - as an adult you could declare your freedom from a person by a rediscovery of yourself but what then? How forward, how public do you take the truth? *Sonja was preoccupied by Nazis. So were her friends. She got into a screaming fit with some German hotel guests.* Those were the incriminating facts.

The body in the cave was Marian Eissel, I was sure of that. I couldn't imagine my mother dragging a body there, or even being in such a place. Other arguments came defending her - her goodness, my knowledge of her, and the fact that she didn't even know about the cave. Someone else must have taken Marian there.

I couldn't escape the memories of my mother's rage in the bar, however, the evening confrontations with the German women, how provocative they'd been, especially the one who kept admitting to being a Nazi. I remembered, too, historic Sonja rages, times when she'd seemed out of control. Thoughts of camp experiences I shut away as swiftly as they came.

I don't remember how long I sat by the pool. Finally I rose determined to remain silent, to protect my mother. I owed her a very special allegiance. My stepsister Irene used to insist Sonja stole light from me in order to see. She'd whisper at me in the darkness of our shared bedroom, "She steals your light, you know she does."

That was such an absurd accusation, I said nothing, just pretended to be asleep. I didn't understand what she meant – Irene was six years older than I and impatient with everyone, including me - still I thought she was wonderful. She knew everything, could answer every question, was highly charged, wildly dramatic. And she wasn't afraid of Sonja. I tried to absorb everything I could of Irene's wisdom.

When I went to our room, my mother wasn't there, nor had she put on her travel suit. She'd packed her bags. We planned to have lunch together but she'd spoken of going to the hotel shops that morning; I finished my packing but was too upset by the morning's discovery to do much else.

I thought about calling Irene. I needed to talk to someone who knew Sonja.

I thought too I could contact Greg, but knew he wouldn't help, wouldn't take charge or help me out of fixes as he once had. In the end I headed out to the outdoor bar to get a coffee and once again find comfort in the sun and sea. I was sad, both to be leaving a place I'd come to love, and because I was now trapped in a disagreeable situation, one in which I was going to have lie. What was happening to my new resolve to tell the truth? I sat with a coffee on the beach and watched the waves. The morning wind carried a mixed smell of grilled steak and raw sewage. Then up along the curve of beach by the breakwater, I saw a group of five or six people moving in my direction. They were bearing a burden. They all wore shorts and shirts; it was still early, still cool, but the light was full day.

At that moment I preferred the dark, the mirror in which you never saw yourself, a darkness in which a worrisome heavy makeshift being, that aggravating blob called you disappeared and all that was left seemed slight, a mere thought, or only a scent, a sound.

The distant group drew closer. They were carrying something covered with a blanket. A woman? Was she naked? My hands went to my face. To hold back what? A cry? No one was looking at me. *Be like before. It's just someone that's dead.* They mounted the incline, up away from the water, carried their burden toward the hotel. Then the wall against a sea of memory dissolved again and I remembered dead people in the hospital, in our hut. *Mama will tell me when to look.* Sonya had tried to save me from ugliness, from the sight of death as well as death itself.

I stood up. They'd found the body. But we were leaving – I need only keep quiet for a few more hours. In the room I pulled the blind down on memories, stopped them. I'd learned how to do that long ago. But could Sonja? Her memories were beyond my comprehension.

*   *   *   *   *

"This was left for you," the desk clerk said dryly and held out a small tissue wrapped gift. Sonja was already in the hotel van chatting to acquaintances. After a quick lunch, we'd said goodbye to the Nathan and Greta who were staying two more days. Our flight left at 3 p.m., we were at the van early.

I took the tissue paper and unwrapped it. Inside was a pair of earrings - turquoise blue stones set in circles of silver - blue stones the exact color of the morning sea - or a child's marbles. I couldn't remember telling anyone about Stefan.

"No card," the desk clerk said when I asked.

I got into the van. It was hot as we waited for other guests to arrive. Sonja was still chatty but I sat silent, intent on our getting away, hoping we could leave chaos behind. The van drove off. We left the Hotel Madre Maria.

I stared out at the brittle landscape with its dry somber earth and trees like crucifixes. I was still afraid. What had been magic would vanish; I would come away only with guilt, old and new. I touched my arms. Sometimes I'd done that on the beach. My arms and legs felt different, silky; I was losing an old coarse skin and finding what lay beneath. *That's a scary thought.*

I must fight for this new me, this hidden being. *But what about Marian Heisel?*

Let others find the truth. No one cared about the swimmer by the breakwater; why would they bother about Marian? In the van I used all the arguments I'd mustered earlier that morning as the body was carried into the hotel. At the airport, Sonja and I climbed down with the others, claimed our luggage and walked to the airline counter. Three Mexican policemen stood beside it. Two were in police uniforms, the third, a slim handsome man in a white cotton suit, introduced himself as Captain Hernandez and waved every Madre Maria hotel guest out of the departure line.

He explained an investigation was underway, escorted us back to the hotel van, and told the two policemen, both short somber looking men, to ride back to the hotel with us. While our fellow guests broke into a blizzard of complaints and curses, Sonja and I said nothing, but watched Captain Hernandez return to the counter to cancel our seats.

An hour later Sonja and I were in the dining room looking at each other, but saying very little. We'd had nothing to eat except a light lunch, and now back at the hotel had retreated to the dining room bar to order nachos and margaritas. The dining room windows were open to catch the breeze but it was a hot day and the room was empty; a solitary bartender dozed behind the bar, but reluctantly rose to take our order. From my chair I watched the sea, dazzling in the afternoon sun; a few strollers waded in the shallow water; beyond them swimmers bobbed up and down tempting waves to knock them over. The empty dining room smelled of fish and lime - I was oddly happy we were still in Mexico but Sonja was angry.

"Why do we stay here? You must tell them I work. Tell them anything. They can telephone us when we are home." Her eyes were swollen and her lipstick smeared. It had been a long day and she was tired. I cursed the police captain who'd requested we stay in the main building until he called us in for questioning.

"You go first, Karin. You talk to them."

"We go in the order they call us, Mama. The police are running this."

"What do you call this?"

"An investigation."

"Do they have power to keep us here?"

"I don't know and I don't feel like asking. It would make us look suspicious."

"What do you mean suspicious?" Her voice was tense. She was drinking the margarita cautiously but steadily. "Are you going to order another one, Karin?"

I nodded. She ate nachos, one by one, chewing with cow like concentration, a habit that usually annoyed me. That afternoon I didn't care, but wanted to warn her..

"Mama, be careful how much you drink. And what you say. Try not to attract attention. We should look innocent."

"We are innocent," she paused, a nacho halfway to her mouth.

The bartender woke and I nodded at him; reluctantly he came to take our order; I praised the margaritas and when he returned he put down, with our two glasses, a small one filled with sliced limes. I picked lime slices up one by one and sucked on them, throwing the skins into my glass.

"Where was the hotel you were at last night with Nathan and Jason?"

"I don't know the name," she said "Why do you ask?" She stopped eating, stabbed a glance sideways at me.

"Just wondering - they might ask you that, and about the night in the outdoor bar. Everybody in the place saw how angry you were."

"I was not myself."

"You were drinking too much."

"An ugly evening, Karin, I do not wish to talk about it."

I concentrated on squeezing the remaining limes into my drink. Sonja shook her head when I offered her one.

"Jason bought you a glass of wine."

"I was not drinking that night, nothing."

"You had a glass in your hand. Tequila can really hit you if…"

"Ginger ale – two, three ginger ales. I do not drink alcohol with that man."

Would she lie like that to Captain Hernandez?

"I thought you liked Jason."

"You think a lot, Karin. Too much."

"Your behavior – I thought you'd had too…"

"No." She looked down at the table, brushed nacho crumbs from her fingers and pushed the dish away. "They drank - those Germans - all of them too much. Someone should study that at your universities. How many of them were drunk when they did the things they did – the camp guards, the killers. Study that you scholars. Drinking all the way through the war, so there is no conscience, no guilt."

She paused; we both knew this was a dangerous moment. We chose silence and stared out to sea.

*   *   *   *   *

"I have a headache tonight." Sonja's voice was quiet.

I looked over at her with surprise. Sonja never had headaches. It was a few hours later and we were resting in our room. We'd waited all afternoon, but hadn't been called by Captain Hernandez. "Too much sun, Mama?"

"Yes. I was without my hat." In a spirit of irritation she'd insisted on waiting for our summons outside on the beach, a summons which had finally been phrased as 'be available at 10 o'clock tomorrow morning".

"Or perhaps tequila doesn't agree with you." I didn't want to admit that it had agreed splendidly with me and I felt less worried than I had for days. We were both lying on our backs on our beds; we'd pulled the curtains and the room was agreeably dim. The air conditioner was rattling away full blast. I was dozing off when Sonja spoke again.

"I lost my handbag." Her eyes were closed, hands clasped on her stomach.

"I noticed that this morning - the carved one. The police may have it."

"I lost also my cosmetic case." Her voice was weak.

I sat up, looked over at her, "Your purple one?"

"Yes. On the beach I had it to show to friends."

"What friends? Why?"

"To show them how pretty the colors are. Will you look for it, Karin?"

"Of course. Where do you think you lost it?" I kept my voice neutral.

"Maybe on the beach – away from the hotel – toward that stone wall."

"You walked way up there?" I looked to see if her expression changed, but her eyes remained closed.

"Yes," she said feebly. "I walked with Nathan. It was in my pocket. I may have dropped it." She raised one arm and stretched a palm across her forehead. "That handbag I do not like to lose. Josef bought it."

"Buy another one tomorrow. I saw some like it on the beach."

"They are too small or too large, never right those handbags."

"There's more than one seller on the beach. I saw some nice ones in the hotel gift shop. Also they had cosmetics."

"I bought already a cosmetic case."

Why didn't I tell her I'd found it? Give it to her? I'd put in my suitcase, slipping it into the pocket of a jacket that was too warm for Mazatlan. I'd planned to look at the case again before I gave it back to her.

"I'll look in the morning, Mama."

"Thank you," her voice was stronger. "Do you want dinner, Karin?"

"Not really. Not for awhile anyway."

"I am tired."

"All right. Let's sleep. Skip dinner."

"Yes. Thank you Karin."

Outside a wind had risen, coming from an unusual direction, stirring up dust from the road.

"I remembered for the first time something from the camp, Mama."

"It's all there," she said. "I told you, it is there inside you like all of us."

"I remembered Mrs. Sjolik."

"Oh. Her. Why her?" She turned over and opened her eyes to stare at me. "She was always lamenting. She died there, typhoid."

"That's what I remembered."

"I'll eat a good breakfast in the morning," Sonja said. She closed her eyes again and fell asleep. So did I. When I woke she'd changed into her nightgown and lay on her back snoring slightly. I looked at Huey, Duey and Louie – 9 o'clock. I was wide-awake and hungry. Ever since I'd come to Mexico I'd been hungry. I got up, dressed in jeans and a shirt, and went out quietly. But I didn't go into the hotel. Instead I went to the outdoor bar, ordered a hamburger, and took it into the garden and ate it there. I looked at the stars; they were, as so often, a safety net I could fall into. I breathed in the stagnant dank smell of the pool at my feet; at night it was black with a slight surface gleam. As always its opaque utterly still surface lured me over, to look down, to see a hint of blurred shapes but nothing more, while in the distance the sea roared on.

I thought about my children. I'd left a message on the answering machine. At seventeen and fifteen, the girls were capable of taking care of themselves but they still needed supervision. He'd be angry; he'd talked about 'a heavy week'. Exams, papers, meetings ruled his life - Greg was competitive, arrogant, unhappy. I didn't want to talk to him but I did want to explain to Nadine and Ona what had happened. That evening I longed to hear their cheerful voices; wished I were home with them. But what could I tell them? We hadn't even been questioned.

Someone came into the dark garden and sat down at the other end of the pool.

A man. He said nothing. Finally the silence disturbed me.

"A beautiful evening," I murmured. There was no reply. I debated walking out past him, but at that moment he rose and noiselessly slipped out of the garden.

I followed him at a safe distance. It was a dark night, the water almost black, slashes had appeared in the sand. But under the hotel lights he was easy to spot. Could this man have something to do with Marian's death? He disappeared into the distance, into shadows. I walked faster but saw no one, then too late spotted three men running down an embankment toward me. I turned around, and fled toward the safety of the hotel. I turned to check. Were they following me?

Yes. And they're closer

One man had outstripped the others. I ran as fast as I could but suddenly was grabbed from behind, thrown down, my face bruised against coarse sand. I yelled for help; a rough blanket thrown over my head shut off the sound. My heart was beating wildly; I couldn't breathe. I tried to speak, but all that came were moaning sounds that surprised even me. My captor pushed the wool blanket harder against my mouth; it smelled horribly of sweat and human feces. Then I was pulled up and forced to walk a short distance, then again pushed to the ground. Astonished and frightened, I lay still for some minutes; heard footsteps and voices of men approaching.

Rape. They're going to rape me. *Please god no.*

I squirmed, tried to inch away, but my captor kicked me hard and I lay still. The three men spoke Spanish together in low voices. I was still breathing in the foul blanket odor. Is this really happening? What do I do? *Pray.*

Then I was praying for help, words I didn't know I had in me poured out.

Oh God save me. Help me. I am your child.

Help came. The men fell silent; someone walked up the sand, feet crunching noisily in the silence. There was a brief exchange in English.

"Let her go."

"No. She is here every night. She is trouble."

Someone walked up and squatted down beside me.

"Listen lady. Do you want to go home?" The voice was familiar but I couldn't place it. "If you want to go home, keep quiet and let us do our work. Say nothing to the police. This is nothing to do with you. But you must not walk the beach at night. That is a bad habit. A bad habit can kill you." There was more conversation in Spanish, then I heard them move away.

I lay for long moments listening. Silence except for the sea. Finally, when I heard only waves murmuring below me, I struggled out of the blanket. I was high up on the beach. There wasn't another soul in sight. I looked at my watch: One a.m.

I stumbled back to the hotel and went directly to our room. I didn't want to talk to anyone, to report anything. I wanted to be safe. Once inside I leaned against the door.

Sonja had left the bathroom light on. She was asleep, on her back, mouth open. I undressed, examined my body. My whole right side was bruised, my right cheek scratched. I put disinfectant on the scratches, washed, turned out the light and sank into bed thinking for the first time, that I too might not get out of Mexico alive.

Sunday, Day 8

I woke up afraid - really afraid.

You wanted to lose your indifference didn't you?

Shut up.

I hated that challenging voice. I'd started writing such thoughts down. I'd warned the counselor that what came up might change me, might even be unpleasant.

Once again the morning light was pale gray, Sonja asleep nearby, Huey, Duey, Luey warning: 5:17 a.m. No change here in this room – not yet anyway. But I'd had a bad dream and I thought about writing it down, thought almost an hour, meanwhile dozing off, dipping back into the same dream, and continuing it. When I woke again, I leaned over and pulled the notebook I'd tossed on the floor the night before. I sat up and wrote:

Bad dream

Where is the white lady now?

Something happened in the hospital

In the first dream I lay beside Sonja

A black cat jumped on my chest.

I pushed it away and woke up

In the second the cat waited just outside the door

A wildcat desiring to attack and kill

Yet I couldn't wake up

When I did, I sat up, my heart pounding. I thought: that's enough of that. I'm not writing in this diary anymore.

I got up, threw the notebook into my suitcase, which I'd barely opened the day before, and slammed the case shut. Take that you doorway to hell

Too bad you can't say that to hell.

It appeared the voice I'd unleashed might take a little longer to destroy. I certainly didn't feel lonely with it around.

Most of my memories of our second week in Mexico are braided together, like my long hair before I cut it, because every day was full of dialogues with myself, with people who knew more than I, or with discoveries about others that I barely understood or even wanted. Add to that, the effort Sunday morning, not only to escape both the diary and the dream, but to find something to eat. I woke up hungry. After months of not eating I was, at the Hotel Madre Maria, often ravenous - not just for food, but for love, for meaning, for anything and anyone I could taste, touch, and feel.

Dressed in shorts and a shirt, guided by a vague memory of a food-dispensing machine somewhere on the hotel premises, I slipped outside. Energy fuel for a run on the beach was what I'd promised myself. I wore the mystery earrings with the blue stones. I didn't know who'd given them to me, and that made them a gift from the universe; I felt safer with them on. By then I needed not only courage but good advice. I'd been in trouble before. But now my concerns were more urgent - defend Sonja if she's the murderer, protect myself from getting attacked again, and find something to eat. A candy bar no longer seemed an enemy. I'd gone so long practicing amnesia, control, and indifference, these new facts on the ground seemed all too terrifyingly real.

The garden was quiet, the light still soft, but the sea was her usual noisy self. The threats last night – should I tell my mother? Perhaps they had to do with her. Should I give her back her cosmetic case? Yet it might have something to do with Marian's death. My suspicions of Sonja had grown. I wanted to be careful what I said at our interview with the police at ten that morning. Before I submitted to hunger, I yielded to curiosity.

I went back into our room and removed the cosmetic case from my suitcase where I'd hidden it. I put it in the string bag. Sonja lay sleeping. I went outside into the garden, sat beside the pool again, and examined her case. It was old, the clasp scratched. I opened it. Some circles of color were smeared with use; Sonja obviously liked blues and purples. Several circles were missing and all three brushes looked well used. There was loose powder in the basket below the colors. How long had she had the case? I'd never seen it before but nothing in it suggested anything out of the ordinary. Yet she'd carried it on the beach – to show it off - or so she'd said.

I fiddled with the basket, jiggled it and then pulled it out. Underneath were two small envelopes. I opened one.

Two photographs - one of a young Sonja beside a young man in German uniform. They were smiling, standing close together, behind them trees were in blossom.

The second photograph was a picnic scene. In a landscape of trees, two women and three young men sat around a picnic cloth spread on the ground. The men wore German uniforms. One of the women was Sonja. They were all smiling. Loaves of bread, plates of meat and cheese, and bottles of beer were spread out on the cloth.

Stunned I stared at the two photographs. What did they mean? Why did Sonja have them? Who were the people? I turned both photographs over, on the back of one in crabbed handwriting was written Sophia. On the other: Hans and Sophia.

I jammed the photographs back into the manila envelope. My hands were trembling – I remember noticing that even as all my other thoughts became chaotic.

Sonja had another name – Sophia. And who is the man? Why the German men?

I put the envelope back in the case, and opened the other. One hundred dollar bills - I counted them – ten one hundred dollar bills. I took the money out, replaced the basket, and closed the cosmetic case. When I ran I wore a travel wallet, a yellow cloth armband with money and my key in it, and so I jammed the one hundred bills in it, stuck my key in my pocket, and walked out of the garden. On the beach I put the string bag with the cosmetic case in it behind a beach chair and hid it with my straw sun hat. I'd forgotten about food, or needing energy for running. I had energy from my panic. But as I ran I remained heavy, joyless. Fatigue soon overtook me and I stopped to catch my breath.

I was just beyond the breakwater. On that stretch of beach, rock outcrops were ragged yet aloof; in some places natural rocks formed protective walls; others were reinforced with cement, so that the modest haciendas and small hotels of moderate height and pretension on the ridges above all had glimpses of the sea. I stood and watched four toy ships pressing the edges of the horizon. The photographs - why was Sonja with Germans? Was it her? Did she have a second name, one I didn't know about?

Other questions impressed themselves upon me. Why two deaths since we'd arrived? Why the threats on the beach? I needed advice, but not from Sonja. I didn't want to talk to Greg. Desmond had problems of his own. Roberto wouldn't be back from Mexico City for two days, and besides was too young and too ignorant to appreciate the mess I was in. I thought of Irene.

My stepsister was a down to earth woman. She specialized in messes. I trusted her despite her battles with Sonja. Yes I thought - I'll call Irene.

I turned to go back to the hotel and just then saw a tall lean figure standing on the breakwater looking out at the islands. I walked closer: Desmond. I caught up with him just as he was climbing back up the piled rocks where the breakwater met a rock-strewn wall. He stopped when he saw me; his face was white, haggard.

"Was it here they found the body?" he asked.

"You know? About Marian?"

"Yeah." His voice was strained, eyes somber. "I heard somebody was dead, but I didn't know it was her until last night. Was the body in the water?"

He looked ill. I touched his arm. "Desmond, are you all right?"

"Yeah, I'm o.k. The body – did they find her by the breakwater?"

"That was somebody else – a man - a swimmer maybe. Desmond, I am so sorry."

"She wasn't in the water?" His voice nearly broke. "I'd hate to think that."

I hesitated. "Have you spoken to the police?"

"No."

A middle-aged American couple in white tennis shoes, white shorts, and blue t-shirts with blue visors to match walked by and glanced at us. Desmond pulled me against the rock wall. In silence we watched them climb the rough path up to a small café above the beach. The sand around us testified to the cafe: paper cups, cigarette butts, and candy wrappers were strewn along the path and the beach. The land directly above the breakwater was covered with weeds; to the right, the cafe with tables on a terrace looked out over the sea. Beyond this point the land sloped upward and was bare of any protection, boasting only dry raw earth and harsh grasses.

Desmond leaned again the wall. "That dark-haired wench with the mouth Frieda - I think her name is – she told me last night. I thought you'd left."

"Your wife's companion – does he know? Where is he?"

Desmond pulled away from the wall, straightened. "Have you had coffee?"

"No. I was waiting for the restaurant to open. What's his name?"

"The lout? How should I know? Did you miss your flight?"

"We're being questioned. We have to stay – I don't know how long."

"When's your interview?"

"At ten. In the hotel."

He lurched away, toward Hotel Madre Maria. "Come on, I'll buy you coffee."

We sat together for an hour - sometimes talking but mostly sharing silence as we drank coffee, ate sweet buns, and looked out at the glorious abandoned water dancing a tango toward us, utterly indifferent to our miserable human affairs. I ordered a Mexican omelet and forced him to eat one too. Eventually, I sought advice.

"I got into a situation last night." My voice was dry.

"So talk." He didn't bother to look at me, just stared out to sea.

"Some men attacked me."

He turned at once, grabbed my arm. "Attacked you?"

"Yes. It was late, really late. I was on the beach."

"Are you all right?"

"I wasn't hurt, just shook up"

"This was on the beach near the hotel?" He didn't let go of my arm.

His hand felt warm, strong. I was looking into his eyes, and that felt good because talking about the attack was bringing back the fear.

"They threw a blanket over my head, made some threats."

"Why on earth were they picking on you? The bastards. How many? Were you carrying money? That's not safe on the beach."

I shoved back my chair. "You know, I think I'll go."

Desmond put his hand on my arm. "Sorry."

"They said I should leave the hotel. Get out."

Smooth as liquid silver the sea that morning – I remember it was cloudy and there was no wind. Sometime during that morning conversation with Desmond I saw – by the edge of the sea – a middle aged nun dressed in white coif and short skirted dress talking to two small girls. I remember thinking that they matched the day, because despite her smiles, the little girls looked away.

"Did you report it to the police?"

"That's what I need advice about. Sonja and I were asked to stay because we're being questioned about Marian's death. Would reporting this attack make more trouble for us? What do you think, Desmond? You know this place, how things operate."

He looked uneasy, let go of my arm. "Report it to the hotel management. They have security people that take care of that sort of thing. It's usually robbery so they try to hush things up. I don't know about an unusual death, especially of a tourist. The police dealing with that are probably Federales from Mexico City."

I was happy to be with Desmond. He was so big and noisy and full of life I felt stronger when I was around him. His sorrow was obvious, despite his estrangement from his wife, which was natural after a sudden death like Marian's. I hesitated, stayed longer. The waiter brought more coffee and plates of fruit and sweet buns, filled glasses of water from a jug. Desmond was staring out to sea again. I sipped my water.

"Are you worried about your kids?"

He turned to look into my eyes and for the first time that morning smiled.

"Of course, thanks for asking. I've got a lead. What I don't know is if I'll be able to collect them anytime soon."

"She told you?"

"No. Stringing things out – that was her style. No wonder somebody aced her."

My shock must have showed on my face.

"Yeah - but it's true. She had friends in Germany that she left the kids with. Her parents didn't know she was in Mexico. I had to notify them. She didn't tell them because she was up to something; she was always up to something. So I don't know if she brought the kids. They may still be with the friends in Germany. Want to see a picture of them?" He'd already dragged his wallet out, a shabby brown leather one, and pulled a photograph of two blond angels.

"They're adorable. You must be very proud."

"I am." He put the photographs back, the wallet away. "What about your kids? Who's taking care of them while you're here?"

"Their father. They're very sensible girls. Mostly they take care themselves."

"Marian had more than one boyfriend." He leaned forward, his face harsh. "Marian was a professional boyfriend collector." His face tightened.

I sat back. "Desmond, I am sorry."

"She was a bitch, grade A." I wasn't ready for so much anger so early in the morning. My face must have changed.

"Sorry," he said, "Believe me, I wasn't a threat to her."

We sat in silence for awhile longer. Desmond let go of my arm, ate two more sweet rolls. "So what are you two up to - you and your mother?"

"We're waiting for the police call us in.. What time is it?"

He looked at his watch. "9:30."

"I'm not dressed for the interview." I stood up. "Thanks for the coffee."

"Marian had another friend in Mexico." Desmond said softly "I think he lives around here. Somebody she knew before this other guy, an older man."

"He wasn't German?"

"No, but anyone can rent or own a house along here."

"Do you think the police know about him?"

"They don't know about me."

Alarm bells went off in me, "Why not?"

He stretched back in his chair. "Let's meet tomorrow for a drink."

Once again, he was staring out at those tango driven waves. The nun had moved away, and the little girls were gone. All the clouds had lifted but the sand still gleamed like old burnished mirrors. Tourists strolled up and down the beach; peddlers carried armloads of sale goods, in big bags, or on their heads. In another hour, the beach symphony would be playing full tilt. Our waiter arrived with more coffee. I shook my head. Desmond got a refill, took another sweet roll.

"These are good. I don't usually like stuff like this. I'm glad I ran into you. You're a nice lady. I'll pay for all this; you probably can't run a hotel bill now.'

"I don't know what our status is. Thanks. You seem to know a lot."

"I know about hotels." He was chewing the buns with his mouth open like a kid.

"Thanks for the coffee."

"Report what happened last night. And stay off the beach like they told you."

"I don't know if I can. I tend to be disobedient."

He looked at me, still chewing. "How come I knew that?"

I walked away. *You're falling in love with him.* Forget it. *When he touched you, you practically fainted.* Please, I've got enough trouble.

A burly middle aged Mexican policeman in a baggy unhappy looking uniform was talking to the assistant manager, Senor Moreno.

"Excuse me. I need to speak to the police. I've been attacked."

"Yes, but can I help you, Senora?" the policeman who had a baggy unhappy face too, grated words out past a toothpick. "I think you must go into the town." He and Senor Moreno looked at each other but neither smiled.

"I wasn't robbed."

The policeman looked severe. "We are here to investigate a death. Rape or robbery they are for the station in Mazatlan."

Senor Moreno hadn't taken his eyes off me and now nodded in agreement.

"Yes, yes, Senora, the local police."

"I was not raped."

"No, no of course not," Senor Moreno murmured, "That cannot be here. It is a quiet place, safe this hotel, this beach, no crime."

"An attack is a crime." I said in as firm a voice as I could manage. "I was thrown to the ground, covered with a blanket, threatened."

Senor Moreno assumed a look of anguish. The policeman looked at me with indifference. Was it my imagination or were his eyes bloodshot?

"I felt..." my voice was trembling, but I carried on, "I should report it." I met Senor Moreno's eyes but spoke to the policeman. "It happened near the hotel – on the beach. The men told me to leave. My mother and I should go at once. We're in danger."

The policeman straightened, "Senora, you must stay until the interviews are over. You must speak with Captain Hernandez." He turned his back with measured rudeness and, motioning to the office behind the front desk, directed the manager to lead him there. The two men closed the door and left me standing by the desk. A surge of anger shot through me. A woman is murdered and Sonja and I are not in danger?

A few minutes later, Sonja sashayed up, shopping bag in hand.

"My darling, I found some wonderful blouses, an avocado one for you and a red one for me, unless you want the red. I will give you the red if you want it." Before I could reply we were called in by the police captain.

"I imagine you have some questions," Captain Hernandez said. The senior police officer was from Mexico City, a handsome man of about thirty-five. His white suit was in fine shape, though slightly wrinkled. He sat behind a makeshift desk, a table pulled close to the window overlooking the garden. The room smelled of flowers; a large vase on the floor beside him was filled with calla lilies and bougainvilleas. He stood up, introduced himself then sat down again, motioning us to sit as well. "You ladies must ask yours first, and then I will ask mine."

Sonja shifted in her straight chair. "Why are we kept here?"

"We have questions to ask of everyone who knew Marian Heissel."

"We do not know her." Sonja said stoutly. "The woman was a stranger to us."

"Everyone has said this. Still…" he shrugged immaculate shoulders. He reminded me of an acquaintance at university, a sophisticated, tidy and very certain Egyptian. "We must ask a few questions of everyone."

"It is not convenient." Sonja said, "Already I am two days late for my work."

"We regret your inconvenience. We hope to be through soon," he smiled briefly. "A woman is dead. We must find out why."

I like this man. He's an actor, acting the part of a police detective.

We sat a moment longer.

"She was murdered." Sonja made it a statement not a question.

"We hope to find that out too." He turned to me. "Do you have any questions?"

"No."

"None?"

"I don't know enough to ask."

"Yet you found the body."

Surprised, Sonja looked at me; her mouth fell open.

I was startled too. "How did you know that?"

"It is our business to know such things." His words were gracious but he looked intimidating - a slender, graceful, courteous, authoritative man. "We must talk to you two ladies separately. First Mrs. Mika, - Sonja looked worried. - "Only a few questions, I promise you. Mrs. Carter, will you wait outside?"

"Of course, I'll sit in the garden." A familiar space - the garden, but that day, I could not enter its mood. I was too worried. How had Captain Hernandez known? Old Juan? It would have been better if I'd volunteered the information. I stood looking into the opaque water of the pool. I hadn't yet seen the bottom. In the deeper end I could just make out a blurred shape, square like a big rock, a very big rock. I leaned over but couldn't make out what it was and so gave up and rested on a lounge chair.

I soon dozed off. When I woke, it was with odd dream like thoughts in my mind. Then someone was leaning over me. Sonja. It was my turn. I went back inside.

"Your mother said you often go out late in the evening."

"I enjoy a late walk, yes." "A dangerous practice for a woman."

Captain Hernandez's cool eyes didn't leave my face.

"I don't make a practice of it, but here it seems safe."

"Safer than it proved to be?" He smiled a thin, almost human smile and imperceptibly sat back. "I understand you had a bad experience on the beach."

"Yes."

"We will pursue it."

"Thank you." I shifted, determined to be assertive. "Captain Hernandez, I saw the body. I don't know if I would say I found it."

He raised his eyebrows slightly and I felt a fool.

"She was a very beautiful young woman," he said.

"I thought so."

"Not everyone did?" He touched his cheek with one finger ever so slightly. "Your mother and another woman," He opened a folder, looked inside. "Greta Herchmer. They are reported to have argued with the dead woman in the bar."

"Not an argument - more a kind of frustration. They thought the young women behaved badly. The two young German women said provocative things, calling them names. Then they all started shouting at each other. Names. Insults. That sort of thing."

"Shouting. And you? Did you join in?"

"No. And Marian didn't say or do all that much. She was pretty preoccupied."

"How long did this argument go on?"

"Half an hour."

"You had some drinks?"

"Not me. At dinner yes, but not in the bar. I don't know about the others."

"Why preoccupied?" He raised his eyebrows that slightest microscopic bit.

"She was bold."

"Bold." Captain Hernandez seemed to like that word. "Bold about what?"

"Playing up to the man she was with. She was very…," I hesitated, "passionate with him."

"And the older women didn't like that."

"No. they thought it rude: To be so public with her feelings."

"Did any of the rest of you speak to the dead woman? Did any other guests?"

"For myself – no, no I didn't. But I can't speak for anyone else."

"Did you know your mother spoke to the dead woman later that evening?"

"No." My heart sank, but I soldiered on. "Mostly here people talk about the weather or the food." I tried to smile, "Maybe they were trying to be polite."

"Your mother asked some questions about the past."

"The young woman's?"

"About the war."

"What war?"

He was genuinely surprised by my question, I could tell by the miniscule quiver of his lips. "The second World War. I've gone over some of this with your mother."

"What did she ask Marian? I doubt it was important."

He stiffened in his chair. It appeared I'd made another mistake. "Mrs. Carter, it is my job to decide what is important. Your mother asked what part of Germany the women came from, also about their families." He tapped a pencil lightly on the table top. "You have said you walk at night on the beach."

"For exercise. I've been running too - in the morning, sometimes at night."

"What about that particular night?"

I felt myself blushing, "I'm not sure I know what night you're talking about. No one's told us anything. As I said before, I ran every day, walked almost every evening." I was pleased with myself. I'd practiced projecting ignorance.

"You discovered the body. Or rather you 'saw' it. And you told no one."

His voice was sarcastic. I sank down in my chair. My skin was beginning to itch -an allergic reaction to the flowers in the vase, or to the questioning.

"No. I didn't."

"Why not?"

"I don't know."

"Would you like coffee or tea?"

"Coffee, please."

We waited in silence while he went to the door and spoke briefly to someone outside. When he returned he took out a single thin cigarette. "Do you mind?"

"Not at all," I watched him light the cigarette with a slim silver lighter he'd taken from his inside vest pocket. His every movement was quiet, yet graceful.

"You discovered Marian's body while you were out for a walk?"

"I saw her body, yes."

"The morning of..."

"Saturday."

"Let's go back to your walk on Friday night. Were you alone?"

"No."

"A friend?"

"Yes."

"His name?"

How did he know the friend was a man?

"Roberto Hermano." I hesitated, "A lifeguard at the hotel." Captain Hernandez's face didn't change. "He was giving me running lessons." *A lame statement*

The door opened and a short smiling waiter entered with two cups of coffee and a plate of small sweet rolls. We waited while he brought me a cup and held out the plate.

I took two and gobbled them down. Captain Hernandez regarded the rolls with disinterest, but stirred quantities of sugar into his coffee. He nodded at the waiter who left the room.

"You met Roberto Hermano and went for a walk. Along the beach."

"Yes. Past the breakwater."

"How long were you out together?"

"We walked about fifteen minutes then we spotted a cave." I pushed it out, past the timidity and nervous exhaustion, the specter of disapproval. Captain Hernandez didn't move but his voice lifted slightly.

"You spotted a cave?"

"Yes."

"The same cave where you later found – saw - the body?"

"Yes."

"About what time on Friday night?"

"Well before midnight. I was back in my room at one."

"Did you see anyone?"

I hesitated. "An old man on a horse - Old Juan - Roberto called him that."

"An old man on a horse," somehow Captain Hernandez made that phrase as implausible sounding as my running lessons. "What about your mother, did you see her?"

I took a deep breath. "She was in bed asleep when I returned to the room."

Captain Hernandez put down his cup. "Mrs. Carter, the morning you went back to the cave. Was that Saturday? Why go back?"

"We were leaving that day." *That sounds suspicious.*

"Did you recognize Marian Eissel?"

"Yes. From the hotel."

"What did you do when you left the cave?"

"I ran away. I was horrified. Ran all the way back to the hotel."

A small thin smile blessed the expressionless face of Captain Hernandez.

"Walking and running - you are an active person, Mrs. Carter."

He sipped his coffee in silence. I looked at my watch. An hour had gone by.

Captain Hernandez put down his cup. "We have a witness."

"Old Juan?"

"Yes. He reported he saw both you and your mother near the cave."

"My mother! When?"

What's going on? Is he lying? Is this a trick?

"Friday evening."

"I don't believe it. She never goes on the beach at night. What time was this?" "Thank you for your time, Mrs. Carter. We will speak to you and your mother again tomorrow. Please don't leave the hotel for the next twenty-four hours."

He stood up. I was dismissed. Stunned, I left without saying anything more. I went back to the room, rescued my diary, sat on the bed and wrote in it.

Captain Hernandez is a trickster.

In my hurry to get to the interview, I'd forgotten my string bag and hat underneath the beach chair. An hour later, when I went back to collect them, the hat was there, the string bag was there, but the cosmetic case was gone. I looked up and down the beach. There were plenty of tourists lying on towels, gathering drinks, putting on sunglasses, sun hats and suntan lotion. Some were strolling up and down near the water, others standing in it. It didn't seem likely that any of them would take one item out of my belongings, but leave the rest. Someone had wanted the case. *Sonja?*

My mother wasn't on the beach, but I did encounter the Herchmers in the outdoor bar. They were at a small table drinking beer and eating small plates of mussels.

"Hello. Those look good." I said.

Greta smiled. "They are." I was glad to see her and went to sit beside her, but Nathan leapt up and pulled over a chair from an empty table beside him. "Sit down, sit down. Have you been questioned? What did they ask?"

"Haven't you been called in?" I replied.

"Yes, yes, right at the very first, they called us in. We knew nothing, nothing at all. Greta was brave weren't you my dear? Very brave. You said everything very well. I kept quiet; that was important because I was indignant, very indignant when I saw how many people they were inconveniencing - you – and others about to leave, who had other plans. We didn't mind, because we were staying anyway." He paused to drink his beer.

"It's sad," Greta said, "such a young woman."

"What about her friends. Did any of them stay on?" Greta looked confused, though once again words poured out of her husband.

"Yes, yes, two of them. They had alibis, air tight alibis. The young woman I don't know what her name is, but she was with someone and the young man, he was away, somewhere, then in an accident and in the hospital. Airtight alibi, both of them, all very strange, very strange, don't you think Greta?" His wife smiled and said nothing.

I ordered mussels, and spoke of eating them years before on the Brittany coast.

Sonja found me in the room. We didn't talk about the interview, or the cosmetic case. We didn't talk about anything much though we spent the rest of the afternoon together. Late in the day we went out on the beach. I went for a swim. New arrivals took over our favorite spots, discovered and discussed what we had discovered and discussed the week before. We felt old and wise. Frieda, voluptuous in a red bikini, walked on the beach looking neither old nor wise. Mrs. Smith came up to tell Sonja that all the guests from last week had been cleared to leave except six who would be questioned again on Monday. Since the Herchmers, Sonja and I, and Frieda were all there on the beach, we went on to speculate as to who the sixth person was.

That evening Sonja wanted to listen to music. We ate at the outside bar, just the two of us; the band played songs she remembered from past visits with Josef - Vaya Condias, and La Conchita, the little swallow. She remembered Anton, my father, with the music, when one evening we ate in a Spanish restaurant and he'd called Stefan and I his 'little swallows'.

"He cared about us, didn't he?" I asked my mother and she made a small face.

"Yes, your father - he was kind to you children – when he had the time."

"Did you love him Mama?" She pretended not to hear me.

We talked about her handbag. She'd found it with one strap broken. She hadn't carried her wallet in it, only suntan lotion and cosmetics. It was nearly nine when we got back to the room. I was impatient to be away, having decided to risk a short walk, but I waited while she got ready for bed. I turned out the lights.

"Take care, my darling daughter," she crooned in the darkness as I left the room. I hesitated about going far from the hotel. I'd received threats. But some part of me always wanted to defy warnings, to refuse to be manacled into whatever system was operating. No one was out walking. So I stalled: I called home, no answer. Then I called Irene. There was no answer there either. I went back outside, paced up and down the brightly lit hotel area. A security guard stood by the stairs to the beach. I smiled at him. It was Manuel, the tallest of the parachute crew. I was tempted to ask him if Roberto had come back, but decided not to. A few people wandered around, mostly new guests. Was I really in danger? I scoffed at my self-imposed restrictions. The moon was nearly full and, like a dog chained to a post, up and down, up and down, I walked the beach, snarling at one plump woman who asked me the way to the casino. I will go running tomorrow I thought. *Tomorrow risk more, risk every day more*. Finally I was tired enough to go back to the room. Crawling into bed I relaxed. Sometimes half way into bed I was already asleep; I no longer lay awake, thinking or worrying about anything.

I woke shuddering - A dream, a bad dream. His face is close. I can see the strain in it as he lunges for me. I feel his fury as much as see it; he is breathing hard and he smells of sweat. In that instant of struggle, before I break away, I know I am being taken back to the camp; the soldier is pulling me away from my mother. Sonja is shouting that we are privileged prisoners that we have papers; she is shrieking; she holds out the papers, but the guard has snapped me back against a wall and I fall against it. I can feel his anger, a tornado of emotion directed at whatever he can grasp, claim, maim, and destroy. I do not understand that emotion, can only run from it, and now I am running, running hard away. I feel the terror of the child. I am the child. Then I wake up. The room is dark; why are the curtains drawn? I pull one open, see the beige of a beginning sky. A new day is arriving. I look over; my mother is there, in the other bed, asleep.

Part Two

Monday, Day 9

I sail across a dreamer's sea

Floating on eternal waters

Oh then my darlings, I remember you

All who I have known - father, brother, sister, lovers, friends

Those now lost to me - even my mother is drifting away

Everything, everyone departs

Yet how can I be alone

When my other mother, the sea is holding me, rocking me?

I move toward the unknown, unremembered, unimaginable

On these inner waters I become my own prayer

I began that second Monday with a second, calmer awakening. I was dreaming more and more and the dreams were haunting me. When I woke, the room seemed all shadow, wrapped in deep silence, beyond the window lay only a gray dawn. Saying the Lord's Prayer and the 23rd psalm over and over led me back to sleep again, but this time I dreamed of my father. I was mourning him, the dream was full of emotion, I cried out my grief and pain. It was a long wild dream lament for a man I barely knew.

After I woke, I wanted to tell Sonja all that I'd dreamt but couldn't find the words. I'd lost the habit of yielding memories, of crafting them into speech. Instead I tried to write it down, even as it began to vanish. I took the notebook out again to report the dream. Some good thoughts were coming too. But that day too was wild – full of confrontations with others.

"I will go to breakfast early this morning," Sonja was wearing the gold and green wrapper she said she didn't mind going to the dining room in because it looked like a sundress. I thought it looked like a wrapper and told her so which made her cross.

"This is a nuisance," she fumed, "this staying on." She hesitated in front of the mirror, rearranged and smoothed the wrapper front. She wasn't wearing makeup. "I will change when I know if we will spend another day on the beach."

"We can't leave, Mama - not until we're given an okay from the police."

I threw on my shorts and shirt. Roberto was due back; perhaps he would have time to run with me.

Sonja was dawdling in the bathroom. "Will you see that tall man today?"

Impatient, I was already by the door. "Desmond? No. Come on Mama, let's eat."

"Where did he go?"

"How should I know?" She saw my face, picked up her carved handbag which she'd found under her bed, and met me at the door. I didn't expect to meet Desmond.

He'd disappeared after our coffee together. Nor had he given me a telephone number, a room number, or any way of contacting him.

At breakfast in mornings on the terrace, the few guests seemed on board a half empty ship bound for a distant shore. The dazzling sun never struck the terrace tables sheltered by an overhanging roof; we ate in shadows - and in silence. But in the sea air, everything tasted delicious. I fell into the habit of a fruit plate; Sonja subsisted on coffee and buns.

The service in the morning was slow. Though the young girl hostesses chattered together like brightly colored birds, the male waiters were slow flying magpies, clustering in corners and niches on their own private errands, coming out only when guests acquired looks of desperation. When they approached us, they stood well away, unlike their evening performances of solicitous hovering behind chairs.

I refused to join Sonja on the beach. That morning I didn't want to go anywhere, or do anything with anyone. I'd liked being on the sea of memory, and by then wanted to run on the beach with or without Roberto. Sonja and I parted in silence. Sonja was reluctant to seek out the Herchmers. Instead she went off to find Mrs. Smith and Mrs. Allen. I stood out on the terrace and saw a parachute blossoming on the beach below.

Roberto must be back. The equipment had stood largely unused while he was away. The first parachute sailed out over the sea, than circled in; as it came over the shore, the man in the harness, legs wide, arms spread-eagled, began screaming. He and the parachute plummeted to the ground. The parachute crew could do nothing until he slammed into the beach and lay still, then they ran over shouting. Guests, gasping, stood up, moved closer to see what had happened. Two of the crew knelt by the injured man while the third sprinted toward the hotel.

I ran down to the beach; the two assistants I knew by name, Manuel and Edwardo, and a half dozen hotel guests were gathered around the crumpled basket wreckage. Manuel turned the injured rider over - Roberto.

His nose was broken, his face covered with blood. Manuel took his pulse, said something in Spanish, then English, "He is breathing. Find a doctor." Two guests ran off while we stood around. I didn't know what I should do. I cared about him. I couldn't claim to be a friend, yet I'd known his vitality.

"What happened?" I whispered when I was able to approach Manuel. At first he didn't answer, only looked at me with stunned eyes. Then he recognized me.

"The equipment, it was okay," he said. "And Roberto, he is not afraid; he runs this thing, so I don't know why he yelled, why he fell." Edwardo held Roberto's head as he gasped for breath. He was alive, but perhaps only just.

Old Juan was standing on the edge of the crowd. He was on foot and in those moments seemed to me not frightening or ominous, but sad-faced and old.

"Look," Manuel pointed to Roberto's chest. Close to his heart, we saw the sly feathered edge of a dart.

We waited, silent, this band of about ten or twelve people. Gradually more guests came over to stare down at the crumpled body, the bloody face – we all heard the sounds of the gasping man that seemed in unison with the hiss of the incoming waves. No one dared pull out the dart. Suddenly I felt sick. I was going to vomit. Turning I walked swiftly away from the beach, ran to the annex. Rushing inside our door, into our bathroom, fear, shock and anger coiled up and through me; I vomited violently everything - breakfast, supper, my very self. Afterwards, I lay on my bed trembling.

When I could sit up, I remembered that the annex, our whole long block of rooms was probably deserted except for me, and with that thought, got up and locked the door, which I'd forgotten to do in my haste. For some reason I thought of Old Juan. He was always around the hotel. I remembered how one afternoon I'd seen him in the front lobby. Yes, the afternoon I went on the tour - he was in the front lobby. Why?

I pushed my memory. He'd been standing by the front desk as though waiting to have a conversation, or having just concluded one. Then one of the guests came and stood near him. Did they talk? I didn't think so. Did the guest speak Spanish? No, Old Juan could limp through the truncated choppy sentences of a Spaniard speaking English. Which guest had been talking to him? I stretched and teased my memory.

Mrs. Herchmer. Greta. How odd. What an odd person to speak to Old Juan. Yes, I recalled her standing beside him. What had they been talking about? I couldn't guess.

I needed to find out about Roberto. Why was he attacked? Roberto's fall was the third act of violence in the week my mother and I had been at the Madre Maria. Though no one spoke of the drowned man, I was now certain that his death had not been an accident either. And how had Marian died? The police hadn't said.

A light rap on the door - my heart started pounding. I went to the door, put my head against it, listened but could hear nothing until the soft rapping began again. The person on the other side of a thin easily broken through slab of a door didn't want anyone else to hear the sound. Then abruptly I became aware of just how ridiculous I was being.

"Mama, is that you?"

A silence, then: "I am sorry to disturb you, Mrs. Carter."

I didn't recognize the voice which held a sliver of accent. "My name is Peter Baden. I am a guest at the hotel. May I come in?"

"I'm not comfortable letting a stranger in. How did you find my room?"

"The front desk. Please I understand your concern. I am a friend of Marian Eissel. I will sit at a table on the terrace. Join me for a coffee. Please. In ten minutes. I will explain my intrusion."

He waited, but I said nothing. I didn't know what to say. This whole experience, these days after our departure date, was beginning to wash together into a non-time, a time not matching the sun's passage but instead hanging motionless in the sky until nightfall. I didn't want to meet this man. Was there a connection between his request for a meeting and Roberto's accident? Was the accident connected to Marian's death?

I wanted to escape into a dream world again.

"Mrs. Carter, will you come to the terrace?"

I felt breathless, alert. He rapped on the door again. "Mrs. Carter."

"Yes. Ten minutes."

"Thank you."

I heard the slight noise of his departure and rested my head against the door and went on listening but the silence was complete. A moment later I opened the door to peer into the hallway. Empty. I walked to the outside door, opened it, and looked out - no one around. Everyone was in the other annex or the main building or on the beach.

I combed my hair, put on fresh lipstick, gave myself courage. Blotting my lipstick, I stared at myself. I looked better than I had in a long time; the sick pallor had departed; perhaps I needed danger, needed excitement.

Stop it. Let Sonja provide the dramas. Stick with the safe and sane.

I gave myself these firm instructions looked straight into my eyes, knowing I'd already violated every safe and sane promise I'd made myself before the Mexico trip.

There was nothing safe and sane about watching a lover fall out of the sky.

* * * * *

I liked the terrace. It had a parquet dance floor, and slim wrought iron tables. Seated at a corner table was the handsomest man I'd ever seen: Marian Eissel's lover. He was not tall, but white blond, with perfect almost severe features. If people were diamonds, he was fourteen carets. His eyes were sharp blue, diamond white blue. He smiled, a low key, subtle smile that was too perfect. As I approached his table, he stood up and bowed slightly. "Thank you for coming. Mrs. Carter."

"Peter?" I didn't sit down.

"Baden. I am Swiss."

"I've never been to Switzerland."

"It is a very pleasant country, boring but nice. Please..." He gestured to the chair opposite him. I sat down - not quite on the edge of my seat.

I introduced the subject of Roberto's accident by asking him first how he knew my name. He replied that Roberto's co-workers had told him. He insisted he knew nothing about the accident. He was exquisitely polite.

"I appreciate you speaking with me, Mrs. Carter. It is about my friend Marian."

"I'm sorry about her death."

"Yes. This death is shocking to me. Do you mind? I ordered coffee. And some rolls. Have you had breakfast?"

"Yes, but I'd love a cup of coffee."

He put on his sunglasses, drank delicately from a glass of water.

"We were good friends. I cannot believe she is dead. Impossible I think - Marian so full of life - even now I think this."

"How long did you know her?"

He took another careful sip of water, "two weeks."

The waiter arrived with a pot of coffee and sweet rolls. In silence we watched him lay out the service; when he left we picked up the conversation again. The sun was higher in the sky, the day warming. Peter Baden poured out two cups of coffee. Beyond him I could see swimmers jostling in the waves. The tide appeared to be going out.

"Yes. So short a time I knew her. We met on a plane from Frankfurt. We talked and laughed…yes laughed…" He looked out at the beach, into the distance, then in the direction of the cave. "Tell me, Mrs. Carter. How did she end up there - in a cave? That I cannot understand - why her body was there."

"I don't think anybody knows."

"You have seen this cave?"

I hesitated. How much did he know, or not know? "Yes."

His chiseled model handsome face softened slightly. "Will you take me to see it?"

"The police have probably cordoned it off."

"How far away is it?"

"A crime scene they call it."

"It was a murder? That is what the police believe?"

I was surprised by doubt in his voice. "Haven't you been interviewed by them?"

"They came into my hospital room the morning they found her."

"I'd forgotten. You were injured in an accident."

"A cracked rib: Painful but I was lucky." He took another sip of water, reached across to touch my arm. "You were walking on the beach earlier that night."

"I beg your pardon." The abruptness of his statement caught me off guard but I was quickly angry. "Mr. Baden, I have no intention discussing this with you."

"Marian was alone that night. Others here at the hotel told me you were on the beach with someone that evening. If I offended you I am sorry. I hoped you saw her, or someone with her. This is mystery yes; it is for the police but still I want to know. Is it a murder? I am not a policeman. I do not know how to ask such questions. Forgive me when I am rude."

We'd emptied the pot; Peter Baden held it up until a slight pretty girl in a pink nylon uniform that crackled when she moved sidled up and poured hot fresh coffee into it - the smell nudging memories of a thousand mornings or afternoons spent thus - talking at a table - only this was not a friend, and we were discussing an unreasonable death.

Peter Baden held out the plate of rolls again. "They make excellent breads."

I took one, bit into it, sat back. I didn't like this man. Too perfect.

"The accident on the beach this morning…"

"Yes?"

"The person walking with me Friday night was hurt in that accident."

"I am sorry." He didn't sound sorry.

I picked up my room keys. "I must go."

"Will you take me? To the cave?"

"I don't understand why you are asking me these questions, or why you want my help. It's best to leave things to the police here." I stood up.

He rose too. "May I call you Karin? Karin, I am a simple man. I came to Mexico on business. I am a dealer in antiques and primitive art. Americans, they like antiques, but Europeans desire primitive art. They are…how you say it… crazy for primitives. I am here to buy Mexican art. Marian was interested in this art. That is what brought us together." He had been staring out to sea, now he turned and fixed those startling blue eyes on me. His face was serious. "She wanted to help me. She liked to shop. We agreed she was to work with me. After my accident the others left but she waited for me to return. Perhaps she had some ideas for me, some things she had bought. The police said they would check her possessions."

I didn't want to listen to him. I didn't believe him, didn't like him. The sea breeze was stronger, the waves higher. I wanted to be on the beach.

"I must go, Mr. Baden." I walked away, down the terrace steps. Peter Baden followed me. "Karin, I cannot believe she is dead. I must see the place where her body was found. Maybe I will believe then. Do you understand that I have some emotion? That I cannot leave unless I am certain Marian is gone."

I stopped, turned. "Believe me, she is very dead."

"A woman from the hotel found the body. Was that you?"

"Yes."

"How terrible for you."

"Yes." I avoided his eyes, looked beyond him. On the beach two Mexican workers were adjusting the parachute harness on a plump blonde tourist. They were strangers. Where had Roberto been taken? Were Manuel and Edwardo with him? Perhaps he was dying - while I stood discussing primitive art with this coldhearted man.

"You know where the cave is. Will you show me, Karin?"

I let my anger show. "Leave me alone."

"Please," he said, and added as though reading my thoughts, "I am not so without the heart as you think. I did care for Marian. She was a beautiful woman. Please, I will not trouble you further if you take me to see the cave today. Perhaps I can tell you more about the accident this morning. I did see it, but from a distance."

The sea smell was strong. I caught ever so faintly the scent of the lilies from the garden behind us. I was interested all right, curious, but also worried, suspicious, and a dozen other emotions. Still I thought, perhaps I can learn from him more about the Hotel Madre Maria mysteries. Why had he come here? Why had Marian?

"O.K.," I looked at him standing on the terrace steps. "We'll have to go now. I have a meeting at ten." I didn't want to tell him it was with the police.

He nodded, and came down the stairs with princely precision. We walked side by side under a hot sun. Sunbathers lay on lawn chairs under sun hats and thatched hotel umbrellas. We trudged side by side across the sand, reached the end of the hotel beach, entered the scruffier beach where no one lay out in the sun, passed the breakwater. How different it was walking with this stranger than with Desmond, or running with Roberto. No silly attempts at humor, no sense of adventure, no exuberance. Those more carefree days seemed a long time ago.

We passed the smaller, smarter hotel. Here there were a number of bathers on the beach; we dodged round their chairs and drink stands. Peter Baden walked with such solemn care in his blue and white striped seersucker suit that he attracted attention; his expensive shoes made scrunching sounds in the sand that caused sunbathers look up. We came to the undeveloped stretch, than the scattered cabins and vacation homes, around the corner, to where the bay curved and the resort area ended; saw people gathered beside the hillside below the outcrop of rock: A whole gathering of fully dressed tourists wandering around taking photos. Perhaps a bus had stopped on the road above.

The face of the rugged hillside had no visible path and no one was close to the large rock which hid the entrance of the cave. A stretch of tape across the entire rock indicated the police had staked it out.

"We can't go up there now with people swarming all over. That's where the cave is." I pointed to the hillside.

"Perhaps later," Peter Baden said.

I didn't reply, only turned, and retraced my steps.

"It is up in those rocks?" He lingered, staring up at the hillside.

"Behind that large one. Mr. Baden, I'm quite sure you won't be allowed to go up there. The police won't let you. And it's not a good idea to try to avoid them."

"Is there light here – at night?" He stood examining the terrain.

"A beach light here below. You can see reasonably well. Now I must go back."

We walked the way we'd come without speaking again. Peter Baden stepped carefully in his loafers and his seersucker suit.

"What kind of art have you bought this trip?" I asked, remembering my daughters' purchases of skeletons and papier-mâché demon gods on a long ago quick trip into Mexico. We were standing beside the terrace again.

"In Europe they want a clay pot, an animal jug, some ugly jewelry - something savage - with teeth - you might say." He smiled, his teeth very white, took off his sunglasses, looked at me with those violently blue eyes. "Thank you for taking me there."

"Good luck with your work." I said, as he bowed slightly and strode away.

*   *   *   *   *

"Does your mother see herself as a victim?"

Captain Hernandez was sitting at his polished table.

"You mean now?" I sat on my usual hard chair.

"Yes." He was not smiling that morning.

"I don't know, Captain Hernandez."

"I think you do." Had he caught my thought? He was tapping his pen against the wooden desktop – a sign of impatience I'd learned to recognize.

"She was a victim. She isn't one now - unless she lets herself think so."

"Thank you, Mrs. Carter - gives herself permission in other words."

"It's not that simple."

"I am sure you are right."

"Her suffering, her survival is part of her. It will never leave her."

"Do you believe being a victim gives a person certain rights?"

"I don't know what you mean."

"Are victims allowed to do things that people who are not victims are not?"

"Of course not."

"Are you sure? Think."

I hate these questions. I want to scream at him. – Don't tell me to think. I kept my voice steady. "It depends on the circumstances."

I looked at my watch. An hour had gone by - a long time for Captain Hernandez and I to tilt lances. As usual I was losing confidence.

"Of course," He stood up, put his hands behind his back, walked slowly up and down the room. "To make myself clear - I meant after the circumstances of the victimizing is over, when they – the victims- are back to normal, what about then?"

"They're never back to normal! Not after those camps."

"I am sorry. You misunderstand me - I meant back living in normal circumstances. I hope I make myself clear."

"Is this ever going to be over? This interviewing?"

I was twisting in my chair, trying to contain my anger, physically exhausted by sitting in the hard chair in front of him.

"Soon, Mrs. Carter, I regret that the process seems tedious to you, but it is an important matter – the murder of an innocent young…"

"Innocent!" The word shot out of me.

He stopped, put his hands in his pockets – something I'd never seen Captain Hernandez do before – and walked to the window that overlooked the garden.

"A beautiful little garden."

"Yes."

"You like to sit there."

"Yes."

"Restful."

"Yes."

He turned, took his hands out of his pockets, went back to the desk, and stood fiddling with his pen, rolling it up and down. I was cursing myself for the outburst.

"Do you know something I don't, Mrs. Carter?"

"What do you mean?"

"You don't think our murdered woman was innocent?"

There was a long silence. I couldn't think what to say. My mind was blank.

"You are tired, Mrs. Carter." He smiled briefly. There was no offer of coffee that day." Shall we meet tomorrow at the same hour?"

I wanted to ask about Roberto's accident but was a coward. Tomorrow, I thought.

Tomorrow I will ask. But bitter words came out.

"How many more days will we be trapped here?"

"Until we are convinced both you and your mother are innocent."

He emphasized the word innocent, and dismissed me without a smile.

*   *   *   *   *

If you have amnesia and your memory comes back, does it come back neat and tidy and logical or does it come in dribs and drabs, a name here, an idea there? Is it messy and illogical for a long time, or does it spring together almost immediately?

My current theory of choice is that memory – Total Memory - is God. And we all are suffering from amnesia, due to get a jolt when we rejoin God. We will have to remember everything, good and bad - a heavy load to carry around for an eon or two.

So life on earth may be a brief holiday from all that knowing, allowing us to have a little piece of memory, selective and selfish, tidy and manageable, like a small efficiency apartment after a huge house. On earth our lives may seem cramped, unmanageable, even troublesome, but who knows, afterwards maybe they're considered relaxing, the equivalent of a sanatorium stay.

In the hotel room that second Monday afternoon, my mother and I rested after a short tense lunch. We'd quarreled about anything and everything over hamburgers in the hot and noisy outdoor bar. Yet once in the room we floated on a silence as complete as a tomb. When we'd first arrived, other guests – including Desmond - had walked up and down the halls, opened doors, talked in loud voices, but this week no one else was in the annex but Sonja and I. Even the housemaids – a younger and an older woman - came in only after we'd gone out.

I lay dozing, thought about Marian's body in the cave, the gleam of her nakedness. I too had lain in that cave naked. And into my mind came a strange memory. When I was about twenty, Sonja and I visited friends in upper state New York. I slept in an old dark paneled room with one entire wall covered with mirrors. In the night I woke, and sitting up unexpectedly saw myself. That night the moon was shining; its light had penetrated the room through an open window, and was a gleaming silver that sweetened the mirror. But I sat, wide-eyed and frightened. Was I dead? That was the first thing I thought because I was naked. In the camp the dead were vulnerable. Their valuable clothes were usually stolen so even as a young child I recognized the white reproof of the dead. I sat up, tried to write the memory down.

My opposite is there - in the mirror

A creature, silver with promises but in a dark womb

Who is it, I myself or some other?

I lay back on the bed

Knew the pressure of pillow on face, slide of sheet across side

These were the real self – solid and warm

But at any moment some agreement might be broken

A promise betrayed

I could slip with a long sigh into the mirror world

I moved, waved my hand, the maid in the mirror waved back.

Sonja didn't believe softer emotions should be revealed to strangers. Vulnerability was dangerous. "Tell no one anything." had been her warning

It was a vow not easily forgotten. Yet a woman's naked body is the most vulnerable sight in the world, even in a woman's camp. When my mother felt the camp mood had grown dangerous, she took me to the kitchen or her workplace; she never let go of me. The few memories I have are of her reaching out for my hand, holding on to me; we slept together, ate together. Did we become each other? Did that seem the only hope we had?

No wonder we are linked in impossibly intimate ways. Yet we grew apart too – often ill, in the care of others - I forged a separate identity, one that taught me to hide my fear and discipline all thought. And I learned to keep that silence with Sonja too. Is silence overwhelming me? Has the mirror begun to devour me?

I got up. Now for the first time in Mexico, dark thoughts were welling up.

I had to get moving.

Sonja, who'd been sleeping soundly, woke and dressed for the beach. She invited me in her most charming voice to go with her but I resisted. Instead I walked up the road to the little souvenir shops, and then into to the hotel gift shop. I found nothing I liked that I could afford. I was down to twenty dollars. I thought about asking Sonja for some, after all she'd offered me money. But I'd turned her down, and now rejected the idea once again, still it tempted me all afternoon.

At the front desk a message from Greg – he and the girls sent their love; hoped we'd get away soon. Did I want him to come down and challenge the police? Also a note from Desmond suggesting we meet for coffee the next day. I called Irene. At first my stepsister was pleased to hear from me. We hadn't seen each other since Josef's funeral. She had two boys a little younger than my two girls and we agreed they should finally meet. She was worried about Joel, her younger boy, who was suffering asthma attacks. Finally I could stand it no longer.

"I need some advice, Irene."

"How's it going with your mother?" she replied right away. It was always 'your mother' with Irene though she'd lived with Sonja for three years. She was used to being in charge and adjusting to Sonja had been difficult for her.

"That's why I called, Irene. I'm worried about her. She's changed."

"How?" Steel came into her voice.

"She's…I don't know how to say this…"

"Angrier."

"Yes. No, not exactly. Have you seen her lately?"

"Not much. Has she changed?"

I lost my nerve then. "It's complicated."

"I'm sure it is." Irene said coolly, "What's she been doing to you?"

"Nothing. Not to me. That's not it."

I shifted in the closed phone booth, feeling ever more cramped by the conversation. That was the way I often felt with Irene, something relatively uncomplicated could escalate rapidly.

"I just wanted to know if you think she's changed."

"I never see her if I can help it. She's got all that money now. She can do what she likes. I hope you're having a good holiday."

"What money?"

"My father's money. We didn't see a dime of it."

"I didn't know there was much."

"Well then you didn't get any either. Let's not talk about it, Karin. I'm angry. I saw how she treated Father. She hit him a few times. Did you know that? She could be mean. Plus she was always threatening to leave. She could devastate him."

Looking out of my glass cage, I could see people coming from the dining room, happy, smiling people. They must have eaten well because they looked contented with life. How had I gotten trapped in a telephone booth?

"Irene, I just wanted to see how you and the children were."

"No. You called because you're worried about your mother. The truth is that it was psychotic the way she treated you. 'Women's Cruelty to Women.' - I'm reading a book about that."

"O.K. Irene."

There was no point in telling her anything more. I had the answer I'd sought which made feel sick to my stomach, but Irene wouldn't let go.

"How's university, Karin?"

"I had to quit. It was too much for me."

"It's your mother that's made you do all that 'face the past'. She wouldn't leave you alone, Karin. It used to disgust me."

"It's not her fault, Irene."

"I'm glad you quit university. You need to enjoy life. Those damn enemas. She'd stand at the door telling you what to do. She tried that on me once. Just once. That was it for me. But you did it. You were down on your knees following instructions. Stick it in. You remember all right. She was nuts. Psychotic."

"I don't remember."

"I hate it when you say you don't remember. You don't want to remember."

No, I don't." I was shrinking down in the telephone cabinet, hermetically sealed like Eichmann in his booth in Israel, confronted with truth behind glass.

A large friendly-looking Mexican lady tapped on that glass.

"Irene, someone wants to use the phone."

"I'm frightened about Joel's asthma. His attacks are getting worse. We're not strong our family. Father wasn't strong; I'm not either. Not like you and Sonja. Nothing bothers you does it?"

"I'll have to hang up now, Irene. Say hi to your family for me."

"Call me again," she said, "any time.'"

Fat chance, I thought as I hung up. The Mexican lady was gone. I sat on the small stool inside the booth. I had known as soon as I enrolled for the graduate course in the Holocaust that I couldn't sustain it, couldn't make myself think systematically about its horrors and its banality. I tried to take notes but my truths interfered.

They threw babies

Into the fat trays

Babies boiled alive

That was something I didn't know

Until I took that class

I couldn't stand it

Would Irene listen then, really listen if I said that?

Forget about enemas and never getting any money?

Treating horrors like facts

Like the walls of the telephone booth

Containing us both

The phone rang. It was Irene. I knew she'd call back. I've never known her not to call back once her attention was on something.

"Karin. Is that you? Listen, I'm sorry. I didn't mean to come down on you so hard. It isn't easy for you, I understand that. But you have to remember we know now."

"What do you mean?"

"What people once did. What they still do. Governments are working on changing that. We're not so stupid now." She was talking faster and faster. "You don't have to do anything, Karin. Don't write about it, think about it. You've suffered enough. Just believe in your own life. You've got one life. You know something? My seven-year old kid's asthma attacks matter more to me then a pile of corpses from an old war. That's the truth, Karin. But that may not be true for you. But give it a rest. Take care of yourself. Promise me. I need you. I love you. You're the only sister I have. Believe in that."

Outside the booth, the Mexican lady tapped on the glass.

After Irene hung up, I wandered into the garden and lay down beside the pool. Closing my eyes, I felt myself drifting away, moving into a wall of withdrawal and silence almost as though I entered the pool, the cool rim of self slowly closing over me like its waters covering me. When I woke, the light was dim, it was evening. I saw someone in the garden, by the bed of flowers. I sat up. It was Edwardo. He turned to look at me, did not speak nor smile, but slipped quickly away.

The time was past our usual dinner hour. I went back to the room, changed clothes for dinner. Sonja was already dressed. She'd put on an old pants suit she hadn't worn before; it was too tight now. We've been eating too well I thought. After I changed into a skirt and blouse, we walked to the dining room and ordered a drink before dinner. Sonja was cross.

"With a murder at this hotel, you want to play hide and seek."

"I fell asleep, Sonja. I'm sorry."

"You fell asleep! I made the desk clerk look for you. I myself ran up and down the beach. I was asking people about you. I was scared I tell you: Because of that murder." She did not sound anxious, nor afraid; she sounded only irate. Don't go near men in uniform, strangers, the water, the road, the edge of a cliff. My childhood had been full of my mother issuing safety edicts.

"Why didn't you look beside the pool?"

She watched the waiter lay out our glasses, and a plate of nachos. There was a small bouquet on the table and she played with the blossoms. I looked around. We were both determined not to quarrel. The band had not yet arrived.

"That garden I do not like," she said.

We ate a plate of nachos with a glass of wine. The dining room gleamed with satisfied light; at the early hour there were few diners, Sonja and I and two other tables. At one of them I saw the German woman, Frieda, sitting with a man I recognized. I watched them, deep in discussion; neither was smiling. I remembered him – the man she'd been with in the bar, with Marian and her lover. Was he the sixth guest?

"Karin," Sonja said. "I worry for Greta. I remember the camp, the deadness that came to people. That is in her. And she has suffered already so much."

Sonja's voice went up. She let herself fall into emotion - anger, grief, remorse - I couldn't tell which one was being expressed. Swept by a ghost of feeling, not a feeling itself, I looked at my mother. I'd never understood what the roots of her emotions were. Were they deep and passionate, or close to the surface and always open for business? I hadn't told her about Roberto's accident or my own mixed feelings about him - that old safe habit of mine - tell her nothing important – but, as often before, I began to doubt my emotions were any more authentic than hers.

Through the half-empty dining room marched the dance band; tonight - a cucaracha ensemble that had played before and were popular. The few people there applauded but they sat glued to their chairs once the music began; no one danced, afraid perhaps of being conspicuous. Many were new arrivals wearing their best clothes.

"I am happy to have these extra days with you." Sonja announced, buttering her roll and not looking at me, "So long since we have been together, only talking on the telephone. I called my neighbor today. I told her to water my plants."

"I hope you won't have to stay much longer, Mama."

The band members were jumping around; the leader played rattles and a noisemaker. In bright red satin shirts and shiny black trousers with cummerbunds, they were almost - not quite - cartoons of a Latin American rhythm band. A waiter took our order; we sipped white wine. We were on good behavior by mutual consent.

A brave, quite elderly couple got up and began to dance sedately. Sonja and I watched in silence. Alone on the floor the elderly couple

223

persevered in a fox trot for some moments, even though the band urged everyone into Latin rhythms.

"How did you find the body?" Sonja asked in a low voice.

"I'd rather not discuss it."

"You can tell me."

"Just leave it alone, Mama. Some day you will know everything."

"Like God." Her voice was sardonic. The waiter arrived and I ate fresh caught turbot surrounded by beautifully prepared vegetables. Warm buns arrived on schedule. We were on such good behavior that night!

"I hope God is a little like you, Mama."

"There is no one. Trust me. No heaven with pretty little angels. Nothing."

I looked at her severely but made no comment. My mother and I could not discuss God without a fierce argument, and that night I was too tired to attempt one.

Slowly, steadily the elderly couple toured the floor. Their cheeks were pressed together; by then they were attempting a tango. They were so old, skinny, slow moving, so pressed against each other - they became a metaphor. We cannot let life go they seemed to shout, so we must not let each other go. If we break off our embrace - we will vanish.

"Why were you at this place where the body was found?" Sonja didn't look at me, but delicately cut her scampi with knife, fork, and great attention.

"Why did you shout at the dead woman?" I concentrated with determination upon my fish, not daring to look at her.

"Shout?" Sonja's eyebrows went up. "When did I shout?"

"On the terrace dance floor – you and Greta."

"I do not remember this occasion."

"Then we'd better agree not to discuss the death."

"I asked you about finding a body, not creating an argument, Karin. Why are you so difficult? Always you are difficult." Sonja's voice grew deeper, sterner.

I didn't care. I was watching the elderly couple with fascination. Were Greg and I that macabre, that self-strangling? Who was it for - the children, for ourselves? The creation of a web, a gossamer net of mild deceit, accumulated half-truths and necessary euphemisms all in the aid of safety. So finally after the years go by, no one knows any longer the perimeters of truth or the definition of a lie.

"Did I tell you?" Sonja pushed away her plate. "Nathan found my cosmetic case." "Really? I'm glad. Where is it?" But I sounded ironic and suspicious to my own ears. What kind of game was being played now? Had he taken it from my bag?

225

"He has it still. I have not seen Nathan today. But he left me a note. He will give it to me." Sonja looked around, but nothing seemed to catch her eye. She turned back to me. "What's wrong, Karin? Your face is sad."

"Sorry. Your handbag - did Dr. Herchmer find that too?" I called him by his full title again.

"In our room I found it. Under the bed - Twice I found it there. Such an odd place. My money, my passport were in it. I was worried, I can tell you, but there it was - under my bed."

"Did you count the money?"

"I only found it this afternoon."

Sonja gathered her evening purse, stood up. "Will you walk with me, Karin? I am doing nothing tonight. Please, I am not snooping on you. I do not believe you killed her if that is what those policemen think."

I looked up at her with some astonishment. "They don't think I'm guilty. They don't like the fact that I didn't report the body when I found it."

"Why not report it?"

"I did. Report it. Just not everything."

"Why not?" She looked directly down at me, dark eyes challenging, voice deep. She could stand very tall, could Sonja, be stern and proud, repel as well as invite.

"I found something near her."

"What?" Sonja's voice pounced, had talons like an eagle.

"Something."

"You cannot tell your mother?"

I was suddenly weary, eager to be out in the cooler air of the beach, to address the waves and curry their favor. I threw down my napkin, tried out a lie.

"I promised Captain Hernandez I wouldn't discuss Marian Eissel." I stood up, "You taught me to keep my promises, Mama."

"If we walk, first I will go to the bathroom."

She left me at the table. I sat for a few minutes finishing my glass of wine and listening to the band. Frieda and her companion were still deep in conversation. They had not danced, nor did they appear particularly affectionate. I rose, and pretending to walk out, passed their table. I paused and they both looked up.

"I wanted to tell you how sorry I was about the death of your friend."

Frieda looked at me with expressionless eyes and for a moment or two I thought she didn't understand me, but then she replied in flawless English.

"Thank you. Marian Eissel was not a friend. I met her only a few days ago."

"Yes, I remember your group. You are all from Germany."

Her companion, a big, square faced man with brown hair like a helmet, and a broad chest, gave a brusque smile. "I live here in Mexico. Please sit down."

He motioned to a seat beside Frieda who eyed me unsmiling. I hesitated.

But the man pushed the empty chair toward me, attempted another smile.

"Please sit down. My name is Carl Boetcher. Let us decide what is going on at this hotel – to make you stay – that is inconvenient."

I sat on the edge of the seat, "I have only a moment, I promised to meet my mother for a walk."

"Yes, I understand you are both energetic women: You especially, an athlete. You like the night hours. I have heard that."

"From whom?" I didn't like him, detected scorn in his voice.

"This is Frieda Heinze. I followed your advice. Yes, good advice." He smiled a big toothy smile that I hated at once. "I left my marriage for my mistress. My wife was very angry. I told her it was your fault."

"What do you mean?"

He went on smiling, and then I recognized him. It was the man I'd encountered walking in the sea the week before. I flushed and he looked delighted.

"Yes, yes I see you remember. Oh yes, you did cause me a great deal of trouble."

"I'm sorry. I don't ordinarily do…"

"I am not sorry. Believe me. But you are staying on. Are you being questioned by the police? Do you know why?"

"No." I lied. I was uneasy. The mood continued unfriendly and Frieda continued her hard eyed stare. The musicians stopped playing, trotted off on a self-appointed break.

"I have objected to these extra days." Freida said. She had a harsh voice for so young a woman. She took out cigarettes and, lighting one, sucked in smoke. She picked at tobacco crumbs on her white dress. With her red hair she looked gorgeous in white and the dress was strapless. But I thought she was not as sophisticated as she thought herself. "Why I must stay I do not know. Marian was a friend of a colleague, Peter Baden."

"I met Peter Baden today." I said.

"You know him? Peter is here? In the hotel? He is not in the hospital?" Frieda looked surprised.

"I had coffee with him this morning. He said the police questioned him in the hospital about Marian. He had a broken rib in the accident." I was pleased to be the owner of information.

Frieda was determined not to be impressed. She blew out smoke.

"Yes they ask me about his accident too. We were all little drunk. Most of the time we were here, I think. So much fun. Now it is over. Back to work. Yes, Carl?"

He kept on smiling that big white toothed smile. "Yes, my dear, you have work to do. Did you tell the police about the drinking?"

"I told the police many things. Not all of them were true." She smirked at him.

"But please I wish very much to speak to Peter. I will ask for his room. Carl, thank you for the dinner. I will see you later I hope."

"If you are a very good girl," he growled, and took out a cigar. She rose; he rose with her and gave a slight bow. I sat tight. Carl sat down, lit the cigar. "Yes, your advice was good. But Frieda was angry and my wife too." He chuckled."Both of them. Very, very angry. I had work to do I can tell you. Those women wanted to kill each other."

"Have you any idea what happened to Marian?"

"She was beautiful, no? Even in death, very beautiful, very calm. Of course when a person is dead, they have to be calm." He gave another hearty chuckle and another strong puff on his cigar. He was waving it around and for some reason I suddenly remembered a stick figure I'd played with in the camp. I poured my world into that funny little figure; no doll ever meant more to a child. Worlds opened up in my head as I danced the stick figure, whose name changed along with his or her part. He laughed, when I didn't. She cried, but only a few soft sobs. The stick figure was very brave but rather stupid. I lost it when we left the camp. But that seemed right. It belonged there, a stick figure among stick figures.

I stood up. "Mr. Boetcher."

"Carl."

"I should go now. I only wanted to ask about Marian."

"Sure, sure, but let's talk again. I like angry women. Very sexy - angry women. Do you get angry? What is your name anyway? I forget it. Yes, we will talk about Marian. Marian was a bitch, but sexy. She wasn't angry much. Most of the time she was calm, all the time, so…like a statue …"

He was puffing away on his big cigar and I hated him.

"Do you know anything about the lifeguard accident?"

"The lifeguard?" He scowled, his face darkened."That fool Roberto?"

I wanted to get away, saw Sonja across the room looking for me.

"I have to go." I dashed off.

*   *   *   *   *

Sonja and I strolled along the beach in silence. The sand was littered with the debris of the day's sunbathers. We walked close to the hotel terrace and wall. My mother liked to be near lights and other people when nightfall emptied itself into the world. She paced slowly beside me.

"Have you told the police what you found?"

"Not yet."

"Will you?"

"I don't know. The fact that I picked it up may get me into more trouble."

"Yes, that is true." Sonja nodded her head.

Why doesn't she ask you what it was or where it is?

"Why you are a suspect, I do not understand."

"Not exactly a suspect."

"They said you cannot leave."

"I suppose if I insisted I could."

"You told me different."

"I don't know what to think, Mama. And if I found an important clue, should I look for the murderer?"

"No, no, that is for the police, Karin, that is dangerous." Sedately we continued our walk, in silence turned back, retraced our route, inched closer to hotel. In the dining room, the tables were cleared; soon guests would be lured back in to play canasta or bridge. Sonja wanted to play cards but I longed to get away so we parted. She touched my cheek. "Give me what you found. I will hide it. Or if you wish, give it to the police."

I drew back, shook my head no, retreated to the room, and as I opened the door, saw on the closet shelf, my old string bag with the cosmetic case in it. The sight of it in plain sight infuriated me. Did she look inside? Does she know the cosmetic case is in it? Who put it up there? Did I, groggy with sleep?

I took the bag and the case out to the garden and with my bare hands dug into the earth beneath the nest of lilies and buried the bag and case in the ground. The lilies sprang nicely back over the mound of earth.

Confront Sonja. Ask for the truth. Go on ask her.

No damn it. It might be Desmond or Nathan who put it there.

They can't get into our room. A maid? Who knows? Perhaps it was me in one of my fits of terror? No, you are growing much too sane to do things like that.

Back in the room – I undressed, crawled into bed, fell at once asleep.

Tuesday, Day 10

When I woke that morning, I saw Sonja lying asleep on her back, mouth open. We were embedded in absolute silence; the annex was still empty. It was just 6 a.m. I'd been keeping to a schedule of running every morning so I got up and dressed in shorts and a shirt. But I moved reluctantly, a morning run didn't seem a good idea. The imperative was deciding what to do with my mother's cosmetic case. Yes, it was safely buried. But who took it? Who returned it? Why hadn't Sonja noticed? Or said anything? What is she guilty of? That was the thought that kept pouncing on me, a thought I kept rejecting.

Is my mother guilty of murder?

I had the money from the case in my wrist band. I'd slept wearing it, intending to return it to her first thing this morning. I didn't know what to do with the small black address book I'd found tucked in with the money. I didn't really look at it except to note the entries were in English and German. Tempting as a thousand dollars could be for my future, the money might be Sonja's. Yet I wasn't sure. Perhaps it belonged to Marian's killer, or perhaps Sonja was involved in something complicated in Mexico. If only Sonja would tell me more about what was going on. Yet I wasn't telling her anything either.

The morning warmed, and I ran. Took off my sneakers and stayed near the sea, close to the hotel. Sometimes I placed a footprint in and out of the water, as though a person stopped here, then there, here, than vanished. A game I'd begun to play with myself. I heard kitchen clatter from the hotel, people chatter from the dining room, and smelled food cooking. Someone was singing, a man, not a good voice, but he was singing opera, and I found him - a burly dissipated man sitting on a retaining wall at the edge of the hotel - singing for sheer joy.

All my despair vanished. I hovered nearby until his song ended and he wandered away. When Sonja found me, she was dressed in black slacks and a colorful green shirt, was carrying her handbag.

"I am going to town today. I have business." she announced.

I barely replied. I waited for her to mention the missing case but she didn't.

All through our breakfast together she said nothing, which only increased my tension. The whole hotel dining room, though full of guests, was unusually quiet. Just as we finished, the maitre d' hotel, a tired older man with a smooth seamless face, brought a note to the table. The police wished to interview us again immediately after breakfast. Sonja made a face, but agreed and went to sit with Mrs. Smith, a stout older woman who'd traveled many times to Mexico. There was another message at the front desk from Desmond. He'd come around later that day. 'Come around' sounded pretty vague. It was about nine thirty.

I could put it off no longer. On my way out I touched the thick nest of lilies to make sure the string bag was still there, then walked into the front lobby. I found Senor Moreno at the desk, a look of harassment on his face; he was talking to the policeman that I'd reported the attack to on Sunday. He didn't look any friendlier.

"May I speak to you?" I asked him.

"Senora?"

"Can we leave tomorrow? My mother and I have a seat on the afternoon plane."

I was lying, skillfully I thought. The policeman was not impressed.

"Your alibi is not perfect, nor is your mother's." With measured rudeness, he turned his back to speak to the manager.

I was sullen by then, and consequently braver. "We've told you all we know."

"Captain Hernandez is not through with you."

* * * * *

"She is old…she may have had her reasons." Captain Hernandez shrugged.

"Which were?" I was angry.

"The war? The irritation of some betrayal? These are the real mysteries."

"You think my mother murdered this woman?"

I grew more and more astounded by this Captain who sat across from me, hands folded neatly on an empty table. He didn't sweat, though the afternoon was warm and the air conditioning not working. He'd once again taken control of the discussion, had revealed how much he'd heard about Sonja's verbal attacks upon Marian and Frieda.

But for a policeman to suggest that my mother was the murderer had shocked me into a defensiveness that might make me look guilty as well.

"Mrs. Carter, I have made no accusation, only a suggestion -a hypothesis for the purpose of discussion."

Captain Hernandez looked like a man who enjoyed strategy. I had to curb my temper, find my own strategy, and not reveal my growing fear.

"Do you play chess, Captain Hernandez?"

He unfolded his hands, took out a cigarette and a cigarette lighter. "As a matter of fact I do." He waved the cigarette. "Mrs. Carter?"

"No, thank you."

"Do you mind?"

I waved a hand. "Please yourself." I was angry. "Captain Hernandez, what possible reason would my mother have? We did not know the woman, or any of the others. Yes, my mother was angry, but nothing happened. I can vouch for that."

"Let's leave the reason alone for the moment."

"Leave it? How can I? You can't make statements like this and expect me to walk away. What kind of a person does that make me?"

"Let us talk again tomorrow." Captain Hernandez smiled his thin permission granted smile and rose. Once again I was dismissed. When I went out, I saw Sonja waiting with a nervous smile.

I remained suspicious of Captain Hernandez. He was trying to entrap me, but why? I liked the Captain, admired his coolness, precision of speech, and the correctness of his behavior behind which there seemed to rest a humanity I could not doubt. He'd called me in first but didn't keep me long, while Sonja he kept for over an hour. I waited for her, taking a coffee to sit near the front desk and read magazines. Bored, I went to the gift shop and bought two paperback mysteries. They didn't look inspiring but they were in English. When I came back to the front desk, Senior Moreno was no longer there; instead the narrow faced night clerk I'd reported the dead swimmer to was throwing papers around. I pounced on him.

"Senor?"

He looked up, blinked. "Buenos Dias, Senora," then looked at his papers.

"I'm the lady who reported the man in the water last week."

"I remember." He gazed at me with a blank face.

"Was the dead man the swimming pool repairman, a technician I guess you call him? I heard he was here to repair the swimming pool. He disappeared suddenly. Did he have an accident?"

"Yes." His hand hovered over the telephone as though he could make it ring.

I leaned over forcing him to look up at me which he did, for a brief moment.

"What do you mean yes? Did you contact the police?"

"It was an accident, Senora, as you yourself said."

It helped that I was a head taller than the clerk. I leaned a little further and once again forced his eyes to meet mine. "I found the body. I want to know what happened."

The clerk picked up the phone, began dialing. Then he stopped, held the phone against his chest, and leaned toward me. We were - as they say in the movies - eyeball to eyeball. "Senora, there are accidents in Mazatlan. That cannot be helped. Sometimes people, especially tourists, are not careful: they do not take care of themselves, do not listen to warnings. Maybe this man did not listen to a warning. Maybe he went out on the beach at night where it is not safe."

I managed a feeble, but face saving, "Well then, he's dead."

"Yes." He was dialing. Not looking at me anymore.

"Did he drown?"

"Yes." Then he was speaking into the phone. I stood several minutes longer before going back to my seat. I picked up a paperback mystery about murder in San Francisco. He ended his phone call. I turned a page.

"The district attorney addressed the jury in a deep voice. 'A woman's naked body is culturally valuable. It has become the symbol of vulnerability - asleep, lying passive, waiting, inviting - but inviting violence as well as love. What if all you have to give is violence? What if you have no love to give? Must they rule the world then, the violent? Is there no answer to the orchestration, the elaboration, the magnification, the glorification, the triumph of violence? Isn't that what law was created to punish?"

I abandoned the book at the front desk, saying "Read this." to the clerk.

Sonja came out from her interview. She looked relieved instead of worried. We agreed on the buffet in the dining room.

"Have a nice day," I called to the desk clerk as we walked away.

"Senora," he said firmly not looking up from his appointment book.

In the dining room, the talk was of Marian's death – new guests were full of theories. It had been a drowning, poisoning by jellyfish, shark kill. The hotel was suppressing information. Sonja and I barely spoke as we took our places in a long line of new arrivals, many of them marveling at the heat and array of food. In the midst of their buzz, when I did speak to my mother, my voice sounded stern, even to my own ears.

"Where are you going all the time? Who are you going with?"

My mother's head snapped back. "Why do you ask?"

"You can't be doing much shopping. Some nights I come back to the room and you aren't there." I turned to catch her expression, which was anxious. "For example, where were you last Friday night?"

Her face was pale. "Are you a spy now? Do I follow you? I do not like this behavior, Karin. It is not your business what I do. I am your mother not your child."

The woman behind her, a plump blond, smirked at us. She was listening so I didn't reply to Sonja. The line moved forward; we came at last to our part in this march of a privileged few, those who eat from a wealth of dishes, debate the quality of delicacies, choose from mountains of food. Once my mother and I had been less privileged - a

241

fact no one can ever entirely forgets, but which can lie in the belly forever.

"The food – so much." Sonja said as she took her plate and began piling on food. "I am not hungry."

I took a plate and looked at the food. I wasn't hungry either. But here we were faced with mountains of it. "Friday night. Thursday night. Some nights I came back late and you weren't there. And who are all these friends you are visiting?" I muttered these allegations so that the plump blonde could not hear me.

"I go to the casino with Nathan. You know this. He teaches me to play blackjack." Her voice was a murmur too. She hesitated in front of the salads. I poked a few shrimp and moved on. "Don't say too much to the police. If you lie they will know." I said.

"I do not lie." Her voice had dignity, but she didn't look at me.

"The police are asking a lot of questions, especially about what we were doing Thursday and Friday nights. Why did you get so angry Thursday night?"

"When? When was I angry?" She went before me, dishing up more and more on her plate. "I have no time now to be angry, believe me please – no time."

Was she being deliberately annoying? Was I? Staring at plates of chow mien, Mexican frijoles, tacos, tamales, refried beans, guacamole, sour cream, fried chicken, vegetable crudities, tomato slices, deviled eggs, sliced ham, cheese squares, fish and chips with lime slices, lettuce salads, pineapples, mangoes and papayas, cheeses, little iced cakes, sweet buns, apple strudel, and chocolate éclairs, I lost my appetite.

As a child I cried from hunger. Once, Sonja snatched a piece of bread from a bench where a woman had left it. The woman found her bread gone and she and my mother scuffled, but the other was too weak to do anything but bow her head as my mother struck her several times; all the time I watched, gobbling bread – get it down, eat your food fast so no one snatches from you. My mother taught me that because others took from children – some - but others gave to us too.

I was never quite sure as a child which adults to trust. Sonja did not believe in the softer emotions. "Trust no one," was her motto. Perhaps she was right. Somehow, she managed to feed me. My silence helped. I rarely cried, no one important noticed me. The children who cried vanished.

I took some shrimp, bread, butter, and cheese. A plate of fruit tempted me. Then I was through the line and finding a table in a quiet corner. On the wall I saw a sign advertising church services and sat under it. As I watched my mother walk across carrying her tray - her plump body, smiling face, nicely done hair were all familiar to me I knew her so well.

"I love you my darling."

"Love you too, Mama."

"So much food I have taken. I do not like these buffets. Always I take too much."

She began to eat her way through the many salads piled on her plate - salads and desserts – those were her favorites.

"That Nathan - first he said he had found my cosmetic case, then he said he did not. Such a man – what should I think? It was not in my handbag. Did you look for it?"

"Yes. You're sure he didn't find it?"

"I said this didn't I?" Her voice was cross. She tossed a glance at me. "Why do you eat so little?"

"I'm not hungry, Mama." I looked out the windows. The sea was still there, my friend, my other mother.

"I bought a new lipstick, some shadow, but here there is not much choice. My case – where did you look? Did you go on the beach up by the tall light?"

"Yes," I lied. "Yes, all over the beach."

"Too bad I lost this case."

"Does it have sentimental value?"

That forced her eyes up to meet mine. "Yes. For me sentimental value it had."

"Was it from Europe – the case?" Wrong question – it forced her eyes down.

"Why don't you eat – such good food, so much of it – I will go back for dessert. Today I saw black forest cake.**"**

I felt myself withdrawing from the place, the food, from my mother as thoughts and feelings I couldn't articulate, inexplicable and frightening began to boil up in me. I wanted out of the confusion, of the sense of betrayal and my own growing fear. By then I wanted out of Mazatlan and the Hotel Madre Maria.

The Herchmers wandered in. Greta wore a huge wide brimmed hat, a Victorian lady affair that hollowed her cheeks and submerged her eyes. They sat beside the windows and ignored the buffet; nodded somberly when they saw us.

"Perhaps she's ill." I said to Sonja, who having skipped breakfast was still eating steadily everything on her plate.

Sonja stopped chewing, put down her fork. "She is dying."

I was shocked. "You don't mean it."

Sonja looked uneasy. "That is what he said. Cancer he said."

"How awful. Why did they risk this trip?"

"She has had remissions. Two he said. Like a miracle. He said she prays all the time. A Christian she is. Before a Jew, now a Christian. Does it matter?"

"No. I like her, don't you?"

"Yes." Sonja turned away, looked toward the windows. There was no breeze, but the view was the same dazzling light on incoming waves, and the crowded beach. "I cannot believe in God," she said, drumming her fingers on the table. She used to do that staring down at the streets in New York. "Believe that God would create this and then watch us suffer, watch us die – I cannot, no."

"Maybe God doesn't think like us."

"Then he should." Why did she pursue such a gloomy topic on so glorious a day?

"I am beginning to believe in something." I said. "Against my better judgment – what I was taught as better judgment."

"Judgment – that is good. I believe in judgment."

How I wished I could say, 'I believe in amnesia - The great white Goddess Amnesia', but didn't dare. We returned to the subject of the Herchmers.

"I thought they were Jewish."

"Nothing he is. She is Christian. I told you. Are you listening?"

"Are you upset about something?"

"No." She was watching Greta, who looked pale and suppressed in conversation with Nathan. "I am telling you it is not fair that now she should be in pain. Should this happen to a woman who has suffered so much already?"

I tried to placate. "I agree with you. It is dreadful. But are you worried about something else? You seem nervous."

"I did not sleep last night."

"You were asleep when I came in."

"Still you go out every night."

"Just to walk – you know I like to walk – I didn't go far last night."

"So late, always you go out too late. It is not safe."

"Yet you were with Nathan Herchmer. You were with him weren't you? Why do you keep mention how dangerous everything is for me? Do you trust him?"

She picked up her fork and returned to her plate, eating potato salad.

"Karin, today I do not want to talk with you anymore."

"I thought you wanted to get home. You must think through your answers before we meet with the police again, Mama. If we say the right things we'll be able to leave."

"It is not so bad to stay. I have now things to do."

"What?" I was annoyed by then.

"I want to find some people. Friends."

She was stuffing in deviled eggs, spreading some of the egg on crackers. Deviled eggs smelled of home, of the egg salad sandwiches I made for my daughters. And then I was exquisitely homesick for them, for my old life, for my work, for excursions and conversations with friends, even my quarrels with Greg seemed predictable now. To be anywhere but a place where people were attacked, murdered, where my mother could eat her way through a huge mountain of food with absolutely no guilt and obvious relish, at the same time insisting on improvements. "This macaroni salad -they must put more pepper and lemon on it." She pushed her plate away.

"Who are these friends?" My irritation grew with her ecliptic sentences, her air of mystery, her ability to devour. "Someone you met at the hotel?"

"Have you talked to the girls? Next time I will speak to them. Ona in school - is she a better student now? Does Greg take good care of them?"

Senor Moreno was moving from table to table talking to guests. He came to ours and, avoiding my eyes, informed us in a soft murmuring voice that we were asked by the police to be available to answer questions the next morning at ten o'clock.

"Questions. Already they have asked us too many questions," Sonja snapped.

"We need to go home." I added trying out a smile. "I've run out of books to read."

He smiled a painful practiced smile, "Senoras, for the police there are never too many questions. We have a small library; you are welcome to borrow books. There are a few in English." The dining room was slowly emptying. The waiters moved with lethargic grace clearing dishes with great clattering sounds, then carrying them to the kitchen talking and laughing.

"Was the woman murdered? Was it suicide? What about that other death - the drowning?" I wanted to be annoying. I didn't believe he had any readable books in English in his library.

"The police have already arranged with the airlines that some of you will not leave for a few days. Consider yourselves our guests." He gave a slight bow and moved away, this time to the Herchmers' table. Across the room I saw Marian's friend, Frieda, come into the dining room and examine the remains of the buffet. Sonja noticed her too.

"She will be questioned first, that German." Sonja said. She got up and went to the dessert table, came back with a plate full of cakes. "She will crowd to the front."

"Mama, please. Be patient. Sit on the beach."

Nathan Herchmer came over to our table. "This is outrageous. They are forcing us to stay some days longer. All because of that stupid scene at the bar," He glared at Sonja who assumed a look of innocence.

"Nathan, I go to town tomorrow."

His mouth tightened, "Of course." He backed away.

"You promised to help me, you must go with me." He fled back to his table.

After lunch, I surprised Greg at his university office.

"You found a body?" His voice was incredulous and quarrelsome. He was tired already of taking care of the girls. Staying home every night didn't suit his style of life.

"It's a long story, Greg. Let me tell it when I get home."

"I've got a business trip this week. What are you going to do about the girls?"

I nearly hung up on him. From that faraway resort I was to organize the family? What was he doing on a trip? It was middle of the term. What was his excuse?

He had a lover. I'd heard from others she was young and blonde, and hung on his arm at the theatre, the opera - places Greg had always been too tired to attempt with me. I said nothing however. Only told him I'd call again. That I'd talk to the girls.

Lying on a chaise lounge by the pool, I stared up at the clear blue sky. I couldn't rest; talking to Greg for more than ten minutes was impossible without tension building in me. Why had I called him? It eroded morale to live with someone who sought out others, who acted as though marriage didn't matter. I was eight month pregnant with Nadine when Greg brought the first one home, a sweet young schoolteacher, recently widowed. He'd explained to her that I understood but I don't think she did. She would never have entered the house otherwise. I left the room after greeting her, went upstairs and watched TV. When I came down half an hour later she was gone.

Years later he admitted she'd refused him but he'd found others. I listened to Greg explain that he needed more than one woman, that his appetite was too gargantuan. He sounded convinced, though I knew he wasn't that libertine; no, I suspect it was the power of two that he needed, which made him less vulnerable. He said he would be open, that I could meet every one of them if I wanted, but I didn't. Most of his young women were graduate students. Brief encounters, he said, mere acquaintances. I would always be his wife.

I was dumbfounded. Still, I went on to give birth to Ona, even to think of having a third child. I had no friends and couldn't tell Sonja. She thought so highly of Greg, and of marriage. But my feelings for him were gone. Greg didn't particularly notice at first, and when he did and tried to warm up our relationship, I was truthful. I didn't think it could ever be the same. His jaw set against the idea that he change.

Resting beside the lilies, I understood that some good had come for me at the Hotel Madre Maria. Despite the deaths, the threats of violence, and my concerns about Sonja, and my own future, I had discovered I was still a woman, still desirable, could even feel desire for another. – it had been so long since I'd believed that.

About four thirty I called the girls. They said they missed me. Their voices were cheerful and breezy. School was okay, Dad was doing things with them. Saturday they went skiing. They were making a cake. I thought again how much I liked my children.

I put on my swimsuit and started down the terrace walk to the beach. It was cool enough that I didn't need my sun hat, though I carried a towel and the second paperback I'd bought under the theory you should read mysteries when you're entangled in one. Sonja was sitting under an umbrella with Mrs. Smith and Mrs. Allen. I joined them. The two women were older than Sonja, both stout, kind somewhat dull women. They clearly adored Sonja.

"I'm glad you came, Karin, so glad. You look lovely." My mother smiled, introduced me, spoke of gifts they wanted to buy their grandchildren. But then Sonja urged me to tell them about my problems with Greg and university. Annoyed, I changed the subject. Greg's obsessive behavior was far too complicated to explain to those dignified older ladies. At last, bored with their conversation, I stared out at the sea. Every day it displayed the same dazzling waves dared by swimmers, the same toy ships traveling a blue gray horizon. The tide was either coming in or going out. It seemed so ordered and predictable at a time when I felt highly unsafe and disorganized. Every now and then in Mexico a clear lilt of happiness would overwhelm me and propel my mood upward. That day was no exception – happiness came in upon me like the tide. Of course,

Desmond arriving at that moment may have had something to do with it.

"I want to see that smile," his voice from behind my right ear.

"No." I said without turning around. Nearby, Sonja, Mrs. Smith, and Mrs. Allen, in great blossoms of straw hats, were discussing the hotel and its deficiencies.

"You look good sitting there." Desmond came around to sit on the sand near me.

I smiled wanly, "Only pretty good?" I liked his clean soap smell.

"Your interview?"

"Over the coals. Confusing as usual."

"You can't leave."

"Captain Hernandez suggested I'd better not. I'd found the body but didn't report it. He said I was more than a simple bystander. I was 'entangled in the event' - that was the word he used - entangled."

"Marian's body? You found it?" Desmond looked anxious.

"Not exactly. He said more about Sonja too."

"You want to drink coffee?"

"I've had too much already."

"A walk then."

"Yes." I stood up instantly, squashed on my head a battered hat I'd bought in Mazatlan, and away we marched, up the beach. Heads turned. People watched us. Desmond was an attractive man. I looked back. Sonja sat surrounded by her friends. My mother's ability to draw people to her, to make friends easily and to say goodbye to them without tears had always impressed me. She waved, I waved back.

"Was the good captain rude?'"

"No, he's very correct. But smart - too smart for me."

"No cop's that smart."

"You haven't been interviewed. That one is tricky."

"They haven't caught up with me yet."

"How did you manage that?"

"Avoiding the cops? They don't know who I am. I moved out before Marian was found." His face sagged, "After the murder." He stumbled over those words. "Can you keep quiet about that? I shouldn't have told you. I'm planning on moving back into the hotel in a day or so."

That made me feel a little funny, but the look on his face made me say, "Sure."

Desmond strode methodically along; I had to run to keep up with him. We were heading in the direction of the casino, a part of the beach with few buildings along it. The sand was coarse, the hillside steep and dry. People commonly walked above the beach along the roadway.

"In mysteries 50% of the time the person who finds a body is the murderer. That's where cops get all their good ideas." Desmond said.

Avoiding questioning was even more suspicious, I almost said, but didn't. I hadn't yet thought through the fact that concealing Desmond's relationship to Marian would be as incriminating for me as for him. I was definitely giving him more than the benefit of the doubt, a clear symptom of my growing attachment to him.

"I discovered something - some facts - about her." I said.

He turned toward me, "About Marian?"

"Yes. Slow down will you?"

He slowed abruptly to a near halt. "I thought you liked to run."

"This isn't running; this is walking and we're trying to talk."

"By the way, her boyfriend's alive. Not even hurt in that accident he was supposed to have had. That's why she didn't leave with the others. She was waiting to hear about him. What'd you find out about Marian?"

"I talked to him – her boyfriend, Peter. He insisted he didn't know anything. I don't like him." By then, we were stopped facing each other, the waves beside us declaring themselves.

"I didn't like most of her friends. That woman friend is something else."

"I talked to her too."

"Captain Hernandez is from Mexico City."

"I knew that."

"Federales. Special Investigations. Marian's was no ordinary murder."

Desmond began striding along again. I tried to follow.

"Are there any ordinary murders? I have a headache." I slowed, stopped. "My head's splitting. I don't feel like walking anymore, or lying on the sand baking. That leaves swimming and drinking, both of which I'm not particularly good at."

"Sit down." Desmond stopped dead. "I mean it, sit down. There on the sand." His voice had taken a commanding tone. Hardly bothering to think why I was obeying him, I sat. He squatted beside me. "Stay still." We waited a few minutes.

"What's the matter?" I whispered.

"There's someone hiding behind the beach cabin above us. I can see part of his body. Pretend we're having a deeply meaningful conversation."

"We are. So what if someone is standing behind a beach cabin?"

"There's been one murder and one near miss. The guy's shifting around so we won't see him." Desmond stood up. I sat on the sand looking up at him. He was shielding me from the line of sight - from the line of fire - I thought suddenly. A curious sense of contentment filled me. I struggled to my feet.

"Look why don't we get out of here."

He pushed me back. "Just sit there and talk. Give him a chance to move away. And don't for God's sake look up there." Desmond was serious. He thought we were in danger. I sat very still and looked at him.

"You know something, Desmond?" I murmured. "You're beginning to grow on me. I definitely like having you around."

He stared back, a slight wry smile formed on his lips. Around us the sound of the sea and its smell existed as surely as the sea itself. Something passed between Desmond and me at that moment. Looking back at those oddly intense moments on the beach, I see that love inevitably refuses to be denied. Love will go on no matter how we flee it.

Desmond didn't move, his back was still to the cabin, but he reached down to help me stand up. "Get up slowly, and as you get up, look casually up at him. Is he still there?"

.I rose, glanced. "Yes." We were now standing close together, Desmond still shielding me. "Desmond, do you know something I don't know about this place?"

"That may be that man watching you."

My shock must have showed because Desmond put his arm around me "Start walking," he growled through clenched teeth. We walked in silence back toward the safety of the Hotel Madre Maria.

"Watching me? What about you?"

"Never mind me. I've noticed men keeping an eye on you."

"When?"

"While you're lying beside the pool sulking."

"I'm not sulking."

"Whatever you're doing, they don't like you there. I saw a man standing in the shadows there watching you. I've seem him twice."

"Dr. Herchmer. He's does that. He's a bit strange, a dentist…"

"This was a young man."

I thought of the night attack by the breakwater - shivered a little remembering the menace of that night. We walked without another word and in mutual agreement over to the outdoor bar and sat down.

Desmond beckoned a waiter to our table. "What about a margarita?"

"What a good idea."

The waiter came up. The bar was full; it was nearly six.

"Two margaritas," The waiter, an older man with a pleasant smile, vanished. Desmond looked at me. "I was watching you last night. A man was staying within shouting distance of you. Someone's keeping an eye on you."

"I think I knew that, but I don't know why. Do you?"

"I barely know you, my darling. But that is the question. Another one is how dangerous is that attention."

"Dangerous?"

He looked at me; he was not smiling. "Now why would they want to watch you? I can't imagine. Or can I? You were the first to discover Marian."

"But I didn't tell anyone."

"Why didn't you? And did you find anything there, Karin? You said you found out some information. About Marian? If so are you going to tell me?"

He stared at me. I didn't know what to say. I didn't want to talk about Sonja.

Our drinks arrived. I sipped mine and looked down. I was beginning to dislike Desmond again. Why was he micromanaging my life? Didn't he have problems of his own? I still didn't know how much I could trust him. I decided to leave.

"I have to change for dinner."

"Why?"

"Ordinarily I go back to the room about six and change clothes. Sonja likes that -- sometimes we wear long gowns. It's very much old world."

"You should tell me what you know, Karin."

"I don't think I can right now. Besides I don't know much."

"Do you have something they want?" He grabbed my arm.

I put down my drink. "What do you mean?"

"Did you take something when you found the body?"

I didn't reply.

"You took something. Karin, admit it."

"Yes."

"What?"

"Nothing important."

"It is obviously important or people wouldn't be following you around."

"People - one man."

"Last night. This morning."

"It might be important to me."

"What is it?"

"Makeup," that did puzzle him. I could see it in his face.

"The cave is very small. I was crawling out. You have to crawl in and crawl out. It's more like a tomb for two than a cave. When I came out of the cave I noticed a cosmetic case."

He eyed the waiter, debating whether or not to order again. "You want another?"

"Nothing."

"Karin..."

"You're as bad as Captain Hernandez. Why are you asking me all these questions? It's not really your concern." A mood close to anguish entered his blue eyes, a slow glacial stillness. I'd forgotten this was his ex-wife who had been murdered. "I'm sorry, Desmond.

It is your concern. Anything that has bearing on Marian or her death is."

We were silent together. I looked at my watch. "Sonja will be waiting."

"What else did you find?"

"Nothing. Really."

"So you picked up the case."

"I did it almost without thinking. I thought maybe the cosmetics belonged to the dead woman so I gathered them all up and put them in the makeup case but then I got back to the room." I was lying glibly, quite beyond my usual powers.

"Karin." he interrupted me. "Where is the case?"

"When I got back to the room I thought…I'd seen the case before so I…"

"Where is it, Karin?"

"I've hidden it."

"Where? Why won't you tell me?"

"I don't want to tell anyone."

He came around to my side of the table and pulled up a chair to sit beside me.

"What else did you find? It may be important, Karin."

"Leave me alone, Desmond. Just stop asking me questions." I heard my own voice as though a stranger's – high, tremulous, anxious.

"What's wrong?" He put his arm around me, and I did what women so often do, melted into the strength, that warm sense of protection that comes with men.

So I told him – that my mother may have lost it outside the cave where Marian's body was found and how that was worrying me. I told him everything and almost immediately regretted having done so. He didn't say much. Got up went back to his side of the table and drank another margarita. I was being careful with my second, having discovered what a potent drink they were. I started babbling away.

"I'm reading a mystery from the library here about women at war. How they learn to fight and kill. They learn to protect each other against a common enemy."

It was such a neat lie I believed it.

"What did Marian's body look like? What state was it in when you saw it?"

"I'm not talking about any of it, Desmond. I told you for me this concerns my mother. And that's as important to me as Marian is to you."

"You may be in danger, Karin. How can I get that through your thick head?"

He stood up, stared down at me.

"You haven't bothered to tell me why you're avoiding the police. You are aren't you? Why won't you talk to them? Why are you're asking me all these questions? Maybe I'm in danger from you."

I was deeply angry - and a little frightened. Everybody was getting too complicated for me. I stood up and faced him. "I'm leaving Desmond, thanks for the drink. You could be in Captain Hernandez's pocket for all I know."

"Do I look like a cop?"

"I don't know. But I'm sure you know how a policeman thinks." I started to leave, turned around and gave him what I hoped was a dazzling smile. "I don't like complicated people. I've got enough of them in my life already."

He stared at me with those blue gray green eyes; his mouth was set.

"I've said the wrong things obviously."

"Yes."

"I like the way you look when you're angry." His eyes changed – lifted and lightened, his mouth relaxed just a fraction. And suddenly I too turned reckless.

"I'm going for a swim."

"With your clothes on?"

"You don't think I could?"

"No."

"Dare me?"

"Yes."

I walked over to the water's edge and waded in. The water was warm; I felt the tug of the waves, and around me foam boiled up as step by step I marched into the sea.

On the beach, Sonja stood up and took rushed little steps toward me - Mrs. Smith and Mrs. Allen were watching as well as other guests. I didn't care. Incoming waves began tugging at me; I turned my back and, walking backwards, looked at Desmond with a triumphant smile. Ha, I thought, you think I'm a humble little housewife.

Desmond watched for a moment, then, as I continued to wade in backwards, he stripped off his watch dropped it in his shoes and grinning, stepped into the sea after me. He was wearing a sports shirt and slacks. I started to laugh; just then a large wave swept me off my feet and I was swimming. Desmond dove into a wave, and came up beside me. We could still touch the ground.

"Well, well aren't we bohemian."

"I like the way you swim." I said and splashed him. He splashed back. Then a large wave overwhelmed. When it left us behind, completely soaked, we were both laughing. We were two idiots sharing a comic bath when I spotted Sonja on shore, waving frantically.

"Are you crazy?" she shrieked, "What are you doing?"

We began to wade in, stood side by side on shore dripping wet.

"That was fun, Desmond."

"You're nuts, you know that." But he moved closer to me. So did Sonja.

"In your dress, your pretty dress."

Desmond took hold of Sonja's arm. "Mrs. Mika, you have a very unusual daughter." Sonja smiled slightly. She couldn't tell from his sardonic tone of voice whether he was making jokes or pointing out a great truth.

"You are wet, Karin."

"You don't have to tell me that, Mama."

She glared. I'd forgotten to call her Sonja. We wandered, the three of us, across the sand into the hotel.

"Desmond, what about your clothes?" He was still dripping.

"What about them?"

"You haven't any others with you."

"I'm drip dry. I'll, change clothes, come in and book a room when I look respectable." He walked away. Back in our room Sonja fussed over me. I let her.

"That man, he is not a good influence, Karin."

"Remember you went in with me too, Mama. You're not a good influence either."

She relaxed. I'd said the right thing.

*   *   *   *   *

A confrontation had developed further down the beach and on my way to meet Sonja for dinner, I stopped to watch. Five or six men had surrounded another man and were pushing him. The group were all Mexicans but the man they'd surrounded was blond and taller. It was just at dusk, the beach largely empty of strollers. Old Juan was sitting nearby on his large, long-maned gray horse. He too was watching; he looked like a general directing his soldiers. Yet he was an old man, a decrepit old man, I reminded myself how, earlier in the week, I'd accepted a ride on his horse, then felt his fingers shoving into my bathing suit - a disgusting old man, not comic, not cute, but predatory.

"Watch it," the distant blond man's voice was loud, a stormy sound in the distance. "You don't know me." But the others went on shoving him around.

It was Peter Baden.

The Mexicans were not hurting him so much as impressing their strength on him, whacking and shoving him, but never so hard that he fell down, yet not releasing him either. Two young couples passed by the group, and the attackers broke off and walked away. Peter Baden stood looking after them, than hiked up toward the Madre Maria. As he approached, I saw he was dressed in ragged shorts and a sleeveless T-shirt; he looked confused and completely unlike the sophisticated man I'd talked to on the terrace. Was he drunk? More likely stoned, I sat down under a beach umbrella so he wouldn't recognize me and waited for Sonja. That evening we planned eat hamburgers on the beach.

I passed the time by writing in my diary. I'd barely opened it for days. I wasn't dreaming, wasn't even thinking about the past. It was a small blue notebook, with pages warped from exposure to water and air. My meandering thoughts were written in a scrawling handwriting without punctuation or corrections; I was determined not to be intellectual. But as well as writing down scraps of memories and dreams, by that evening I'd begun to keep track of the people I was meeting, and what they might have to do with the deaths at Madre Maria. I wrote down questions too.

Wild cards – Sonja, Jason, Roberto

Unknowns – Edwardo, Manuel, Senor Moreno, Frieda, Carlos

Bad guys(seem so) – Nathan, Jason, Frieda, Peter

Good guys(seem so) – Greta, Captain Hernandez

Possible allies – Desmond

Out of the loop – Greg, Irene, Nadine, Ona, Marian

*   *   *   *   *

Irene likes to bring up facts like enemas – facts that shock

What happened to Roberto? Andres, the pool repairman?

Why was Marian naked in the cave and how did she get there?

Love has the ability to erase all traces of what went before

The bones of the pelican were like remnants of memory

Does love erase memory?

Our identities rest on memory - a scary thought?

* * * * *

Later that evening I sat cross-legged on the sand watching white flecked waves roll in. I prayed. Somewhere, somehow I'd learned how. That seems to me the best of all miracles - prayer waiting within - whether we tap into it, or even recognize its existence, when we turn to God, we already know how to pray.

I prayed because I was growing confused and frightened by what I was experiencing, and also what I thought and wrote about. I didn't want to think. I'd been fleeing thought for nearly a year.

God is not love as we know it.

Who says?

Tolstoy

Is God all knowledge, all memory, all emotion, all creation?

Does God live through all human beings - even wildcards,
unknowns, bad guys, good guys, possible allies, out of the loops?

That evening it was like all the questions and ideas I'd been suppressing for years came flooding in, even as I wrote them down, I knew they were unanswerable at least by me. I lay back and stared up at the stars. There was the thinnest sliver of a moon but my favorite, Venus, was smiling down.

Why did Tolstoy say God was not love? Well, he was dying in a railway station! But he also said that when we love we more fully experience God, and when we more fully experience God, we are more truly alive.

I went to look for Sonja. I didn't find her, instead Nathan Herchmer found me. He sported a red handkerchief and boating hat. His eyes were bloodshot. Though he wore white cotton trousers as he did every evening, that night he had no shirt on. Only his face and neck were tanned. He was walking toward his room, which had a small patio looking out over the sea; he was carrying a glass of what looked like scotch. In his rapid-fire way he harangued me, "I've been listening to others far too long, Karin. I listen only to myself now, especially not to my wife. She is so good, so very, very good. Have you any idea how annoying someone is who is always patient, kind, loving? They become like a white hole that swallows you, that makes the 'Who am I?' disappear. I'm used to not knowing the answers. I don't want to know them."

Surprised by his vehemence, I walked along beside him.

"I exist very nicely, Karin. I am definitely smarter than my wife, yes much smarter. And I've seen everything you have, and done everything your mother has. She met that fellow. He was a Nazi. She didn't believe me."

His voice was soft, dull, expressionless and enthusiastic; everything about him seemed sedated, subdued, yet I felt heat near him, a sense of rising agitation.

"Goodnight Nathan." We were at his patio.

He held out the glass. "Where are you going? Have a drink."

'Not tonight."

"Where's your mother?"

"Where's Greta?" I responded. "I haven't seen her for days."

"Asleep," he said pathetically. "She's always asleep now. I'm alone every night. How about a scotch? Sit here on our patio" We both sat down. "She was sitting right here on this patio. She was having a drink with me, waiting for her boyfriend and she said she didn't want to be alone – a very beautiful girl – Marian. Beautiful but strange. Very strange. Greta didn't trust her. Greta said don't have anything to do with her. But I did. I poured her a couple of drinks. Right here on the patio. The young woman who died in the cave: Marian. Don't know her last name, but I talked to her -the night she died."

I shook my head when he again waved the glass. "Did you tell the police?"

"Of course." But he turned away and I couldn't see his eyes.

*   *   *   *   *

"Where did you go tonight?" Sonja asked. We were crawling into bed.

"Sitting on the hotel beach."

"Why?"

"Because it's safer than walking."

"Nowhere is safe, Karin. I have told you that. There is no place that is safe for people like us."

What kind of 'people' were we? Different, I gathered as an adolescent, victims. That's what she meant after those years in the camps, even though we were privileged prisoners compared to many. But why were we 'privileged'? Especially since my father and brother had died.

"Is that all you did?" she asked in a muffled voice. Her back remained to me; she was hesitating to get into bed, smoothing her sheets, delaying so that this conversation could be fulfilled. "Walking?"

"Walking, talking to people."

"Alone?"

"Why do you ask?"

"Were you alone?" My mother turned around abruptly. She wore an elegant nightgown, old, patched, but satin; it was her wish to be found dead in elegant attire.

"I'm not a child, Sonja. I don't have to hear all your secrets and you don't have to hear all mine. We can be two friends. That's what we said before."

She sat down on the bed. "I am afraid for you."

Outside a car labored along the road, the sound breaking the silence we'd become accustomed to at night.

"I like this room." I announced. "I shall miss it."

Sonja didn't turn out the light. As usual, the bed covers had been turned down by the two housemaids while we were eating. I was reluctant to surrender myself to such beautiful arrangements. Even beds now seemed suspect.

"What do you like about our room?" Sonja was watching me delay going to bed.

"Well, you're in it. We're together."

"That is good. I think that too."

"And it seems safe," I lied.

"Does it?" Her voice was subdued.

I turned out the light beside me, slipped between those commanding sheets.

"It is far from the lobby - and no telephone." Sonja said, still standing; the overhead light was on; she walked over and turned it off.

"That's what I like. No one bothers us. There's no one in this wing except us."

"That is what I do not like." Sonja said in the darkness.

"I thought you liked quiet. You're always complaining when it's noisy."

"I do not like this annex with only two of us. That is too quiet. It is not safe."

"There's no safe place for people like us, Mama." I mimicked her voice. She tried to laugh. "Where are Mrs. Smith and Mrs. Allen's rooms?"

"They are in the main hotel. They do not like annexes."

"I'm not afraid of a murder," I announced, turning over to sleep. I stretched my legs out in the luxury of the clean bed, those sweet sheets. My surrender was total.

"They said that dead girl was in the other annex - on the beach side."

"Who told you that?" I turned back, waited for a response, but there was none. I yawned, began to drift out on the dream sea.

"The Herchmers - their room is on the beach." Sonja sat up, peered across at me in the darkness. "I am worried about Greta. I do not see her for days. She likes the sun, every day on the beach, she was, remember? All day she is in her room now."

"Didn't you tell me she was sick?"

"I went to her room but she would not come to the door. Not one word from her."

"Maybe she was out."

"I heard some sounds. Someone was there; the radio was on but soft. I heard it but she did not answer my knock. They haven't been together that long."

"What does that have to do with it? They seem happy enough."

"Seems is not good enough. Her first husband was rich, a rich man."

"Dr. Herchmer's not?"

"He converted for her, to make things right for her. A mistake."

Sonja turned out the overhead light, sighed, lay down. For a moment we were silent together in the darkness of our room.

"Believe me, Karin, that young woman was German, I know these things. Mrs. Allen said her body was in a cave, a little grotto and a cave that was known only to the locals. The guests here would not know about that cave. Mrs. Smith said she thought the murderer was a local - maybe that old man and the horse."

Old Juan. I'd forgotten Old Juan. He'd seen me emerge from the cave. Was he the murderer? Did he report me to the police? Old Juan and I shared our one important fact - I'd seen him; he'd seen me, outside the cave. He knew I'd been there with Roberto.

We'd shared another fact too. When I jumped off his horse, his response was to turn around and smile. He and his horse had rambled away. I'd shouted after him "I'll report you." I wish I had. Maybe he's my enemy now.

Half asleep, I heard the outside door open, then close and someone walk up the hall until at the other end, a door opened and shut. I thought - we're no longer alone in the annex. I jumped out of bed, went to our door, and checked the lock – O. K.

I climbed back into bed, turned over on my side, told God how I loved him, and went to sleep.

Wednesday, Day 11

Early the next morning, outside, the sky was full of sea birds, their cries like confetti fluttering through the air. Above them, the horizon was still pink, and a bank of clouds was melting into emptiness. I ran, the exertion felt good; I thought of Roberto, how he'd taught me to run. Still astonished he was gone, I didn't like thinking about him. After half an hour, I stopped by the parachute launch, neither Manuel nor Edwardo were there, nor did anyone else come to unpack, so I walked to the outside bar for coffee and sat drinking it. I asked the burly waiter about Roberto, but that gentle man pretended ignorance. Or perhaps the ignorance was real. Then I saw, on the beach, a horse and rider – old Juan. As always, he paced his horse along the edge of the water. What did he know? Determined to find out, I rushed down to the water's edge, and stood in his path. Old Juan tried to ride around me, but I took hold of his horse's bridle.

"Roberto? What happened to him?" He sat looking stupidly at me, said nothing.

I forced more words out. "The lifeguard in the accident - I saw you there. I know you know what I'm talking about. Where's Roberto?"

"Por favor, Senora." He shrugged his shoulders, clicked his tongue, and at the same time kicked the sides of his horse, which obediently moved forward. I backed away.

"Where do you live?" I called as he rode past me. "I'm planning to report you to the police. I'll tell them what you are doing with tourists. You're molesting them!"

He turned in the saddle and gave me a big gap toothed smile - a fat happy smile. The leather saddle squeaked as he moved; both he and his horse smelled of rank sweat.

I went back to the room to prepare for the interview with Captain Hernandez. Sonja was up and already back from breakfast. She was dressed for an excursion in white slacks and blue blouse, with lots of white jewelry and perfume. She made no comments on her plans for the day, nor did I ask, mostly because I thought she wanted me to. Once again I put on the mystery blue earrings.

My mother admired them. "So pretty your earrings. I looked for them; many shops I looked. A gift you said." I didn't pursue the subject, instead went to the window.

"It's a beautiful day." I said looking out. As usual the road was empty. Though buses, taxis, and cars arrived at and departed from the hotel, somehow magically they never ventured up the stretch of road in front of our room, a road that appeared to dwindle into insignificance and die out in distances.

I decided I needed to walk down that road.

Sonja said nothing about the cosmetic case. Had she stopped thinking about it?

What did the photographs mean? Would I dare ask about them if I returned the case to her? We were quarrelling more and more even as we tried harder and harder not to. Why not leave the case under the rubrun lilies? I needn't tell anyone I'd found it.

I decided that morning to do that, just keep quiet. A mistake.

Sonja did mention Frieda.

"I saw her – that German woman." She was bending into the mirror, putting on makeup, slowly and carefully – bright red lipstick, plenty of rouge. Where was she going so dressed up? I bit my lips to keep from asking.

"Frieda?"

"This morning - in the restaurant I see her. She was with your friend."

"You were out this morning?"

"The tall man with the bad manners," she turned to look at me. "Just now I see them - sitting together, - talking away, two blue jays - Chat, chat, chatter. They do not speak to me. They do not look my way. I drink my coffee and go. Where are you this morning so long?

I looked for you this morning. Always I am looking for you here. I am losing weight looking for you."

"Stop it, Mama."

"What?" she said in an innocent, pleased voice. She packed up her makeup, thrust it into her new red cosmetic case. "What are you talking about?"

"Picking on me," But even as I said it, I knew I sounded absurd. "I have to go. I have another interview this morning." Without saying anything more, I left her in the room, getting ready to go an unknown somewhere with an unknown somebody - another mistake. Leaving Sonja to her own devices was often a mistake.

I went to the restaurant. Sure enough they were in the big dining room, sitting together over coffee – Desmond and Frieda. Instantaneously I erupted into jealousy.

I marched over. "Hello" I said. "How are you two today?"

At once, Desmond stood up. "Join us."

I made another mistake. "No, can't. I have another interview with the police.

"And you?" I said in a sweet voice to Frieda. "More interviews for you?"

"Yes." She said in her deep, rough edged voice. "Yes, they see me every day."

"But they don't see him, do they?" I indicated Desmond. He sat down, looked at me with tight blue-gray eyes. Frieda frowned, puzzled.

"What do you mean?"

Desmond shook his head slightly. I stumbled over the next words, and thought better of what I was doing but couldn't stop talking."They don't call in the men do they? Just us women. Funny that – I mean only women –why us? That's what I'm asking."

"I do not understand." Frieda said slowly. But I saw by her eyes that she did.

"Karin, what time is your interview?" Desmond was as smooth as silk, but he shot me another warning look

"Now," I said and rushed away.

I was furious and still jealous. It was stupid really but there it was - feelings were erupting all over the place. I went to the garden, eyed the shadowy shapes still in the pool – did no one notice them but me? - took out my diary and wrote three sentences:

I'm not going to write anymore. It's not good for me. It riles me up.

I went to the front lobby, slid into my old friend the Eichman booth, and called Greg at his office. He had ten minutes to spare.

"You know damn well, Karin, I didn't have anything to do with that attack on you coming out of the hospital clinic. I was sorry. I tried to help."

Greg sounded sorry. I didn't want to hear sympathy in his voice. "I know you wanted another child, but it's just as well. And it was years ago, four years ago. Please forget about it. It happened, it was nasty but you survived. I know it still bothers you."

He was being so rational. He sounded like my mother. In fact, I no longer cared about an event that had happened years ago, that I'd thrown at him during our last argument before I came to Mexico. An old bitterness, an old anger– which must have disappeared into amnesia so completely, I was surprised he remembered it. I let the silence build up.

"Karin?"

"It's tense down here, Greg."

"I appreciate that."

"I'm still a suspect."

"I don't understand why."

"I have to go, Greg. I have a police interview in five minutes."

*   *   *   *   *

"Coffee this morning, Mrs. Carter?"

"Thank you. May I have a sweet bun too? I didn't have time for breakfast."

He nodded, a slight slice of a smile, "Of course."

He went to the door, placed the order, sat down again. "While we wait we will talk. I understand from your mother that you had some problems as an adolescent."

"What do you mean?"

"Some eating problems, some problems with…what is the word?"

"I don't understand."

"Adjustment. Yes that is the exact word. You had counseling for this problem - your mother told us - counseling that was successful."

"When I was nineteen at college."

"A second time also?"

"Not for the same reason - the second time – a problem I had to face. One that is over now. I'm surprised my mother told you."

He waited but I was not about to say more.

"Were you ever arrested?"

I was startled, "Of course not."

"For shoplifting?"

I shrank from the word. "I never took things from stores, only from houses of friends, little things, things that…"

"That charmed you."

"Yes."

"And that you thought wouldn't be missed. Your mother indicated there were other times when your behavior..."

The old timid voiceless self was gone. "Captain Hernandez, I know my mother. You intimidated her. She's afraid of authority. You could ask her any question and she would answer it. I have no idea why you are probing into my life and I refuse to answer any more questions until I know why you're asking them."

The coffee service interrupted us. After the waiter had left, as we drank coffee and I nibbled buns, Captain Hernandez changed his tactics. He went over again my finding of Marian's body, asking the same questions he'd asked in previous interviews. I tried to give the same answers. Suspicions were shifting from Sonja to me. Captain Hernandez stated that Sonja could depart whenever she wished; I must stay a few more days. He let me go with the request that I make myself available for another interview that afternoon. My patience was exhausted by then, but at the door, I stopped, and turned round to ask about Roberto.

Captain Hernandez blinked. "He is better, much better, I believe."

"Where is he? In Mazatlan?"

"The police ambulance took him to a hospital but I do not know which one. I will inquire if you wish."

"Please."

Sonja had waited for me outside the dining room; despite the good news for her, she was sullen all through lunch.

"I cannot believe this. I go but you must stay. You cannot. To be here alone, I will not let you. Who knows what they will blame on you? If you found a body, so what?"

"I'm a suspect, Mama."

"You killing that woman - it is nonsense."

"You know that and I know that, but the police don't. Not yet anyway."

With no buffet that day, the newcomers were ordering fish, salsa and chips, soup, and Mexican dishes of every sort. Waiters skipped, hopped, dashed about, happy to inform the ignorant, satisfy the hungry, and encourage the greedy. It was enough to make me lose my appetite, but I loved the smells lofting through the air. Fried fish was my favorite or was it fried potatoes? Also lemon, stewed tomatoes, garlic.

"Where is that tall man you walk with?"

"Desmond. I don't know, Mama."

"I think he is too fast for you. Karin, you are a married woman. Your reputation is important, an important possession for a married woman."

This was the Sonja I remembered, jealous of everyone. A friend, a boyfriend could part us. The knot was tight. Once, I too could not imagine our parting. But that belonged to the past. Why was she going on that way now, attacking my friends and acquaintances?

"Mama, it's none of your business."

She got up from the table as though stung.

"Where are you going?"

"To rest," she snapped. "I am tired after the interview, and after this lunch with you." She grabbed her purse and marched away.

A secret part of me was pleased, but ashamed also. My resources as a young woman, when fighting being submerged into another human being, were weak words of malice.

On my way out I checked the front desk. No messages from Desmond. Or from home. But Sonja had had a call from New York. She'd sworn she'd stay with me as long as it took, but I thought if she wanted to look for a job, she would have to go home.

I went back to the room to tell her about the call, but she wasn't there. After a rest I wrote post cards to the girls, then a letter to Irene.

'Dear Irene, Stuck in Mexico in the middle of a murder mystery and since I don't read murder mysteries, I can't pretend I know how it will end. But I found the body, and though not officially a suspect, I've attracted attention. P.S. The body was of a woman.'

I changed into a swimsuit and headed out the door to mail the letters, but forgot money for stamps, and went back to get some. As I opened the door, someone grabbed me from behind, a hand was pressed again my mouth. I tasted tobacco.

"Quiet," a voice I recognized but couldn't name. "You're in danger. You need to know. Stay close to your room."

Then I was released, but when I turned to look, the person was gone. Trembling, I picked up my coin purse, walked over into the hotel, mailed my letters. But I was still in shock. I headed toward the beach but as I walked past the garden, I saw Desmond.

He was sitting alone, staring into the pool. He was wearing his increasingly tattered sports jacket. I wanted to call out, to tell him what had happened, my mouth opened to form the words when I noticed there was a cigarette in his hand. Desmond was smoking. I stopped dead and blurted out, "I didn't know you smoked."

He looked up, "Only on bad days." He rose, "I'll catch up with you in a few minutes." and was gone.

I thought about the stranger's hand that tasted of smoke, and his voice. Desmond had an even mellow baritone, a halfway up, halfway down voice. My encounter's voice was dry, harsh and light. It had not been Desmond.

On the beach there was no sign of Greta or of my mother. I swam, fell asleep on my towel. Why couldn't I become a beach rat, a simple creature of the sun with no worries? Lying close to the waves, I fell asleep in the cradle of their roar, woke when Desmond slid down on the sand beside me. He had a deeply tanned chest that I couldn't help staring at since it was so close. He wore a gold chain with an eagle on it.

"How's the sun?"

"Hot."

"You're not very tan."

"Sorry."

"Any word when you can leave?"

Silence overwhelmed me. He lay facing me.

"You're seeing the Captain again this afternoon."

"How did you know that?"

"I have my ways." He smelled of sweat and shaving lotion.

I shifted back a little. "Tell me how you knew."

"I guessed that's all."

I turned over so my back was to him.

"Hey, don't do that."

"I can't think of anything to say."

"Turn around so I can see your face."

Reluctant to confess my fear and confusion from the morning events and now suspicious, I turned to face him. He touched my face gently. "What's happened?"

I sat up. So did he.

"Tell me, Karin." He put his arm around me. "What's wrong?"

"Someone grabbed me and said I'm in danger."

"Do you know why they're warning you?"

"First explain to me why I should tell a stranger I just met everything that is going on in my increasingly complicated life. Telling you doesn't really make sense."

"Actually it does. Make sense."

"Says who?"

"I do." He stroked my bare leg. "You need my help."

Inexplicably, tears formed in my eyes. *He's right, but how can I trust anyone?* He lay back on the sand, and pulled me down beside him. We lay side by side; at our feet waves roared in promising eternity. In the past I hadn't liked sunbathing because it reminded me of the hospital, of bodies lying in neat rows, passive, vulnerable. But with Desmond muttering words beside me, I felt at home. I stared over at him. I wanted to lean over, put my head down on that expanse of tanned chest and fall asleep with absolute trust. As though he'd caught my thought, he looked over at me. "Has it ever occurred to you that Marian's death was a mistake?"

I sat up. "You think someone wanted to kill me and murdered Marian instead?"

"No, not at all. What if it were an accident?" The waves were quiet that morning. The wind was hiding. It seemed there was a pause in the universe so that Desmond and I could speak. Then, for some crazy reason, I started telling him about my childhood. I told him that I was 3 years old the last time I saw my grandmother and I wore a new sundress and she said I looked pretty. Then I announced. "She cooked me an egg in a little egg cup. I was her precious little darling." Desmond looked intently at me.

"My own special egg cup. It was hot in her kitchen because she was baking. She was always baking and cooking, stirring pots at the stove and putting big pans of things in the oven. She was a wonderful cook. Her name was Desa. She called me little Desa."

"She sounds like a good Grandma."

"She was. I loved her. There were red and white embroidered curtains hanging over the cupboards and big stone jars that stood like soldiers against one wall. I was afraid to look in them." I was talking faster and faster, my voice, high and excited, "I like thinking about my grandparents. Someone with grandparents like mine is not going to be murdered."

"Were they Sonja's parents?"

"No, no, my father's."

As we lay facing each other, more and more memories rose up in me, bursting out into insistent words. Desmond listened.

"My mother never liked to cook - too boring she said. She'd wrinkle up her nose and make a face when she talked about it. Only food that was dramatic - flaming desserts, roast lamb with tiny paper hats – that's what Sonja made."

"I bet you're a good cook."

"I am." Soon, holding hands, we fell asleep in the sun.

*   *   *   *   *

I remember, I remember the stick doll

I made hair and a face, found scraps of cloth

Wrapped them around the stick

I talked to it

Told it I was afraid

Everybody was going to die and my mother too

Most of all I was afraid I wouldn't die with them

Everybody I loved would leave me behind

The stick figure told me that that wouldn't happen

Everything would be good again and Sonja and I would be happy

Whatever the stick figure told me hummed away in my head

A sweet little voice promising hope

After I left the beach, I wrote all that memory down. I stayed in the room, rested, fell asleep. Perhaps Sonja would arrive to tell me her news. It seemed strange to be at the Hotel Madre Maria without her. I thought I'd leave a note for her at the front desk and wrote one out before my interview. When I saw Captain Hernandez again that afternoon I followed Desmond's advice and became more aggressive. "Captain Hernandez, you must understand. I've run out of money. The costs are high to stay here an extra four days and there doesn't appear to be an end in sight."

He sat motionless. He was a disciplined man and that gave him power. Captain Hernandez spoke quietly. "Mrs. Carter, you were seen leaving the cave where the body was found and you were part of a demonstration against Miss Heissel." Desmond had also suggested I not say too much, nor be too friendly.

"Demonstration! That's a bit strong."

"You survived a death camp and she was German."

"I was a child. I remember very little. Only the hospital."

Captain Hernandez shifted in his chair. "Mrs. Carter, as the survivors grow older, only they remember, while others forget. We must respect they may feel the need for revenge. I do not wish to belabor the point for that would be insensitive. You are a suspect - that is true. You must remain at the hotel until the matter is fully investigated. All we can hope for now is that we gather evidence, that we acquire some idea of what happened. Only then can we make a judgment."

"You must be joking. You can't hold me here." My voice was shrill. I folded my hands in my lap, forced myself into calmness. "I am not a murderer and I don't have any special feelings about Germans, Miss Heissel in particular."

"But you do about Roberto Hermano."

"I like him if that's what you wish to ask."

"We already assumed that." Dry words said without a ripple of expression. "There is a rumor that he is dead. That he died in hospital."

I gasped. I couldn't help it. "I thought he was better."

When I went to the hospital Sonja hid the stick doll. She said at the hospital they took everything away and gave nothing back.

"You can go, Mrs. Carter. We have finished for today. I understand from the hotel management that your room will be at a reduced rate. Or even free - but that may only be a rumor." He smiled a last thin smile and ushered me out.

I went down to the outside bar, and ordered a margarita. I debated calling Greg and asking for help paying the hotel bill. Or I could ask Sonja. But somehow I shrank from asking either one of them for anything, even though I was down to my last pesos. Sitting in the bar, I saw Frieda walking slowly along the water's edge. Of medium height, full bodied and already hippy, she had a jagged face and hair as black as a raven. I thought about catching up with her, asking her more questions, but she was out of sight before I could make up my mind. Besides, she seemed a restless, angry sort.

I sipped my margarita alone. No sign of Sonja. I was surprised. I wasn't quite sure where she'd gone but usually she joined me before dinner. Greta Herchmer came into the bar and sat down beside me. She ordered a small coke. There was no sign of Nathan and I didn't ask about him, but did about her health. She skimmed over the subject with brief words about not sleeping well, than surprised me. "He's still trying to get me to pay his debts. Nathan is gambling. I said no. I wouldn't. I'm leaving my money to my children – I've changed my will. I don't owe him my life or my fortune." She soon excused herself and left the dining room.

Sonja didn't arrive, and finally I ate a light supper alone in the bar. Mrs. Smith and Mrs. Allen sat down for a half hour, and told me a story about our hotel. Apparently, thirty years ago there was a sighting of the Virgin Mary on the deserted stretch of beach beside the hotel. Most people forgot this event, but Mrs. Smith who was Catholic said if the sighting had been significant a chapel would have been built there, instead of the hotel next door. Mrs. Allen, who was

Lutheran and more cynical, said they'd built the hotel and a casino so people could go up the beach to see the Holy Mother, only she'd never reappeared because there was too much sinning going on.

I began to worry. Sonja didn't call or return to the room. Desmond came by and suggested a walk. It was dark by then and as we strolled out on the sand, I gasped. There was no moon; it was the darkest night I'd encountered; the black sky was filled with brilliant stars. Only the hotel beach lights obscured their wonder, and as we moved into darkness, we stopped to stare up at them. "Let's go up the beach. Look at the cave." Desmond said. There were only a few strollers out that night.

We walked past the motel up to the breakwater. At the small hotel we encountered Carl and another man smoking and talking with an older woman, dressed in black, and Frieda still dressed in white, holding her high heels in her hands. They ignored us. We walked on. We were alone on the beach. Desmond stopped to light a cigarette.

"They're beautiful, aren't they – the stars? I'll miss them." I said. That's how I'll remember Mexico I thought to myself, the scents of the sea, tobacco smoke, the rush and roar of waves, a murmur of human voices, brilliant stars, soft sand underfoot. Desmond stood beside me looking up. When he spoke his voice was low. "Karin, I have to tell you something. You made me wish I were married again. You are everything my wife wasn't and I knew you were married, and so I thought why not give it one last try and sure enough, despite all the grandstanding with that guy, who by the way is ten years younger she than she was, and not all that smart, I got Marian into the sack again. It was a big mistake, first of all because it was over, and I couldn't keep my end up, and second, she was already high, and had been high almost all week and that put me off because that was the way her life went. Drugs came first." It was a long speech for Desmond. He was looking down at me and I thought, not for the first time, my goodness he is tall. I wondered why he'd told me so much. What night had he been with her? Shouldn't the police know all that? Yet with his speech had come a sense that everything was all right, which was crazy considering his explanations, the fact that I hadn't known him long, that he wasn't even staying at the hotel, and there had been two murders and several accidents. Then he said, "We should have a light. I'll get one from my room."

We'd turned back and were walking past the group standing under the beach light. Carl looked sharply at me but made no sign of recognition. He was listening with great attention to a short, older woman who was talking animatedly to the entire group. Perhaps his wife, I thought as I caught a whiff of her heavy perfume. When we reached the first motel stretch, Desmond loped away. "Wait here. I'll get a flashlight, a jacket too. You'll be cold." He vanished.

He was right. I was cold. My sundress was too flimsy for a walk late at night. I peered at my watch: After eleven. Then I had a horrible thought. *Desmond killed her - Marian. Strangled her and took her body down to the beach or paid someone to do it. He had several reasons to kill her.* I hated that thought, but it wouldn't go away. Desmond came up with the flashlight and his battered sports jacket.

"I thought you could wear this. I don't have anything else."

"It's late for a walk."

"Do you want to skip it?"

"No. Let's go."

I slipped on the jacket. It smelled of tobacco and sweat. Then to my dismay, as we continued to stroll, by then hand and hand, he kept talking about Marian. "I thought I could woo it out of her if I took her to bed, that she'd relent and tell me where the kids were, but she was so stoned nothing got through. Plus I realized she hated me. And I hated her. I didn't before but the way she'd dragged the kids around taught me she didn't love anybody but herself."

"How are your kids?"

"Haven't seen them for a year." His voice was tight.

"I can see why you're avoiding the police."

"Avoiding?"

"I'm sure they'd like to talk to you."

He didn't reply. Instead strode ahead, away from the hotel. I was getting tired. He had a long stride and I had to work to keep up. The gringos were no longer standing beside the sea; we passed the breakwater into another empty stretch where it seemed much darker, but ahead was the beach where Roberto and I had gone, and the cave. The memory of Roberto was there in me; by then I felt only sorrow for what had happened to him. The death of such a young man was a mystery I wished I could solve.

I touched Desmond's arm. "This is where the cave is." I said in a low voice, "Up there in the rocks."

"Let's go up there." his voice was soft too. I thought how crazy it was - how dangerous – out there with him when there had been three deaths but somehow I couldn't see Desmond as a killer even though I wanted him to stop confiding in me.

I walked ahead of him up the path. The light no longer beat down on the sand, there was far more black than white. I went up along the edge of the outcrop and walked straight into a man. He wore shorts and was large, yet looked exactly like a six-year old, the same chubby undifferentiated body of Freddy, a kid in my first grade class in Iowa. that I remembered with a shudder. *Freddy had the mentality of a rhinoceros.*

"Vamos," this Freddy said, in a husky voice. I expected Desmond to answer but he didn't. I turned around and there was no Desmond. He'd vanished. My heart seemed to drop past my shoes, plop - right into the soft white sand.

"Vamos, lady," The large man repeated.

"O.K." I said, and backed away. He watched me, a big bulky shape in the darkness. Perhaps he would do nothing. Perhaps he was just a passerby - or a night watchman. He was not Mexican. He was a big beefy North American killer boy type.

"What the fuck are you doing here anyway?"

"Walking." I moved away, acting the innocent tourist.

"What the hell for?"

"This is a public beach. And I have a couple of friends with me." He looked unconvinced. "I'm from the Hotel Madre Maria."

Freddy's fists were pressed against his hips. Without Desmond I was vulnerable. Rape occurred to me. I took several more steps backward down the slope. "My friends are just behind me," I said in an unconvincing voice.

"This beach is private," Freddy said and followed me down the path.

"Well, I didn't know that. I'll tell the others." I speeded up, reached the bottom of the slope, and walked quickly away. On the darker stretch beside the water, I slowed down. Out of the shadows next to a small bathing hut, Desmond emerged. I was frightened until I recognized him.

"Thanks a lot. Where were you?"

"It would have been worse if he'd seen me."

"You know him?'

He nodded his head. "And he knows me. I'm sorry I had to duck out on you." We walked back to the hotel in silence. I was angry.

"Forget about the cave. I don't want to see it ever again."

"Karin, I was watching. I could see you. If there had been trouble…"

"You would have come running."

"Believe me, I don't usually dodge trouble."

I didn't really want to know anything more. On the face of it, what he'd done had been fairly cowardly, but he seemed a tough enough man and so I gave him the benefit of the doubt. Yet I thought how different this night was from the one with Roberto when we danced, were carefree on the same beach. Everything had become fraught with significance and even danger; each day was full of surprises, most of them unpleasant.

That Roberto was dead, I found hard to believe.

We came to the edge of the hotel beach and stopped near the terrace wall.

"Thanks for taking me." Desmond said in a soft voice. He touched my shoulder and rested his hand there just that bit longer than was needed. The place where he touched was bare; his hand warmed my skin. Once again, trust of him flowed into me from some mysterious larger place them my own knowledge.

Sonja wasn't in the room. I went to bed but couldn't sleep. What was she doing? Who was she with? Could she have attacked Marian?

I couldn't believe it and neither could Captain Hernandez. She was free to go and I was not. Was Roberto dead?

I thought of his face and body. He'd spoken with such passion about his country. The night we'd spent together was still meaningful for me, had become part of the Hotel Madre Maria world would now leave. I didn't want Sonja to know what had happened to him, or to me: I wanted Roberto, Mexico, the sea, Desmond to be mine alone. A solitary selfish thought which made me wake in the night.

How close evil comes gliding beside us
We may not notice
Like a snake, evil sliding along the brittle edges
Of our normal world

I sat up, looked over, saw that Sonja still wasn't in her bed. I looked at my watch. Two a.m. Where was she? Would I have to look for her tomorrow? Why didn't she call, tell me where she was, what she was doing? Maybe she couldn't. That was a terrible new thought: that something could have happened to her; that she was in trouble. I rose, turned on the light, wandered the room. There was nothing I could do until morning. Yet fear wouldn't leave me. Back in bed it took me a long time to fall asleep and then only when I prayed,

Thursday, Day 12

S onja was in bed when I woke. The bathroom light was on and the shabby Mexican hotel room suggested not dawn, but a twilight that made my skin prickle. I got up quietly but as I dressed, she turned over, and lying on her back, began to talk. She was still half asleep. "I thought, perhaps instead of a Nazi this is Hans."

"Hans?" Then I remembered the photographs I'd found in the cosmetic case.

Half naked, shocked, I sat on my bed and waited for her to say more. She didn't. She lay on her back staring at the ceiling, than closed her eyes. I rose, dressed, went into the bathroom, came back, waited for more words to come from her, but nothing did.

"Why are you telling me this?"

"I began to think of Hans – that he is not dead. There are others they have found. Maybe he escaped. Maybe I will find him."

"Mama, I don't know what you're talking about." But I dreaded her answer. I wanted to flee, to dash out of the room, to run into the fresh, free air of the real world.

Sonja didn't look at me, instead still lay looking up, her body limp.

"In Germany I had a letter from people here. Friends sent it to me. These people here sent photographs. I thought then, maybe Hans is alive. Maybe he escaped. But there was no address, only a little information with the letter. They asked for money. To help Hans, they said, because he is old; he is ill and needs help. When I sent some, they wrote on a postcard: Mazatlan, Mexico. I remembered the city from my visits with Josef. The photographs they sent are in my cosmetic case. And it is lost, where I do not know."

The light of morning was widening outside. I turned to look. Yes, the sun was up.

"That's why you went into town?"

"Yesterday, I took some money from a bank there to give these people, but no one in the bank knows the name on the envelope."

"Mama, he must have died years ago."

"There are others they have found, who have survived. There are miracles." "I don't know what to say, Mama. Do you want me to talk to these people?"

Sonja didn't look at me, instead closed her eyes. "I think it was a trick – the people who write me, Karin." Then she opened them. "Or a joke; it is not a joke for me."

"Do you want some help, Mama? That's all I need to know." But I moved toward the door. She turned to look at me, face filled with emotion – whether it was anger or sorrow I couldn't tell.

"Never mind; he is dead. I know this now. My hope was small but I came to Mazatlan because I think maybe he is still alive. I was a fool. I think too much about the past. You say this to me, and now I know that is the truth."

She sat up – her hair wild, her voice filled with... what? *Malice?*

"Karin, before I die you must know this. I told no one until now about Hans. Not even Josef. But you must know."

I sat down again on the bed opposite her. Suddenly there was this other person between us. Hans. I knew what he looked like. I had his photographs.

"I don't need to know anything, Mama."

"Hans was your father."

My stomach roared with pain. I squeezed my wrist, digging my nails into it until the pain went there – a trick I learned in hospital. "I don't believe you."

The room was filling with morning sunlight. Sonja swung her legs down on the floor. The narrow beds, the way we sat looking at each other reminded me suddenly of the camp, of middle of the night moments when someone was frightened, or dying, and we had to move, sit up, briefly assert our own lives against the death around us. Yet how could I remember that, a child of three or four?

Maybe that wasn't true, was instead something she'd told me.

I stood up. Such memories came like brief flares of light, camera flashes lasting only seconds. I didn't trust they were my own.

My mother sighed, placed her hands on her thighs; she was wearing an old peach pale nightgown; it had risen up so that her thighs were white, naked and fleshy. Her voice was settled, but the words were rapid.

"Marian Eissel looked like Anton's comrade." She said the word 'comrade' with scorn. "When I saw her, I remembered, Karin; I do not want such memories.

"Mama, I don't know what you're talking about. I don't know who Hans is or was. Why bother to look for him? Forget him, forget everyone from that past. Forget for God's sakes, or at least let me."

"Do you think I am a fool?" she snapped, than gave a great sigh and lay back down. For a moment I was tempted to copy her, but instead moved to the window to look outside. A beat up truck was driving slowly down the road, the sound a rough splattering that was a jarring break in our customary silence. I could barely hear my mother's words.

"He was with her all during the war – Anton. You must remember her."

"I know nothing of what you're talking about."

"You must. He took you to their rooms, to his beautiful woman - Helga. She made you treats. She thought you were sweet. She cried for your hard life. If there had been no war, they would have taken you away from me. I despised her. She cried about many things and, like all men, Anton worshipped weakness in women. The great communist comrade cried and I did not. I hated them. Then Hans came."

Walking beside the sea

A black wave descends upon me

Sea spray gleams white on its edge

When I turn to watch, the wave breaks round me

A rush of cool water engulfs me

"Did you sleep well," someone calls

"Yes" I whisper

"Do you want to go on waking?"

"No. Please, no, please God, no

The morning was clear and sunny. I walked into the hotel and used the dining room bathroom; I washed my face, combed my hair there. My eyes were wide and frightened in the mirror.

You're afraid of your mother
No kidding

At the outside bar I ordered coffee and sat drinking it. I needed time to think. Running no longer seemed to matter. I'd fallen into another place and found myself yet another person. Finally I forced myself onto the beach.

As I ran slowly along the edge of the water, I saw Desmond. He was in the direction of the cave talking to three Mexicans. I debated running up and interrupting their conversation, but instead slowed to a walk, and turned to pick my way through the sunbathers emerging from hotel rooms, like rabbits from burrows. The longer I was at the hotel, the more I understood its rhythm: Every morning a human wave flowed out to meet the waves from the sea.

At a solitary breakfast on the terrace, I wrote in my notebook. Like the run, it had become a daily habit. But that morning, only the most mundane life experiences came to me, perhaps in response to the confessions of my mother that I wanted to erase.

I didn't believe her, didn't want to believe anything she said. Instead, I played with simple memories.

My first dresses in Iowa and Idaho were old fashioned cottons

I loved the words for them - gingham, calico

They felt light on my skin

Not like the raw wool of the war years

The war years seem distant here

Mexico be my land of amnesia

After breakfast, I took myself to the garden. Under the mid-morning sun, the pool looked benign, yet even in bright sunlight I saw blurred boxy shadows deep in its cloudy water. I went over to where the shadows lay, and leaned down to touch whatever was at the bottom, but found I couldn't reach far enough. Did I want to put my whole body into that murky water? I was reckless that morning. I walked down the metal steps, walked into the pool wearing my shorts and t-shirt.

I could touch ground, could touch the shapes – boxes placed side by side on the bottom, large square fiberglass boxes, sealed and secure against water. How many were there? I waded deeper, my shorts were soaked. The water was dirty, had a smell, covered my breasts, then my throat. Four large almost square cases. Then I was treading water. How many boxes might there be at the deepest end? A man entered the garden. Edwardo. I walked to the pool stairs, climbed up them rapidly. "I fell in." I said. He didn't reply nor look at me, just walked out. I dragged a lounge chair into the sun, stretched out to dry my clothes. It wasn't such a bad morning after all. I'd found out what lay in the pool or at least had begun to – and I hadn't let Sonja upset me - not for long anyway. I could defend myself just like the counselor had said.

I picked up <u>Sense and Sensibility</u>. I was being drawn into the lives of Jane Austen's. Elinor and Marianne, though I now suspected mine was as exciting as theirs. Above me, birds fluttered excited responses to one another; sunrays found my body through the tree branches, then wandered on. After an hour of reading, I closed the book, lay back, thought about what Sonja had told me that morning. Was it true? Anton was not my father? It was an awful thought. But why would she lie now, so long afterwards? Was it necessary for me to tell anyone about such a soap opera? I seemed fated to learn things I didn't want to learn, and about which I could do nothing. I had to concentrate on getting Sonja and I out of Mexico, out of the mess we both seemed to be in. But how? What part were Jason and Nathan playing? Sonja was not going to be much help, but perhaps her cosmetic case would be.

I rose and dug out it out of the lilies. When I again examined the photographs of Hans and the woman called Sophia – my mother had given herself another name -- I saw that she looked happy, but Hans was glum. Perhaps he was on his way to the eastern front. I took out the address book and looked more carefully through it. It was full of names and addresses in Germany, Britain, other European countries and North America. The notebook might be what everyone was looking for. Who could I talk to about that?

I returned the notebook to the case, hid the case in the lilies, and was back on my lounge chair, asleep in the warm air when a touch on my cheek woke me. Skin tickling, I resisted opening my eyes. The hand sought out the contours of my cheek, touched the skin gently, stroked along my neck just beneath the curve of jaw. It was a calming touch. I felt myself relaxing, but kept my eyes closed. Fingers touched briefly the tender skin of my neck once more and I opened my eyes, to look up into Sonja's face.

"So here you are," she said, "It is quiet." She looked around. The birds were silent; the sea a distant murmur. We were in an outdoor room of green leaves and ruby hearted rubrun lilies. "Did you swim today?"

"Not yet."

"I will sit on the beach for an hour. Come with me."

"Not yet, Mama. I want to doze here a little more."

"Why not in the room?"

"The sun is perfect here."

"You burn very easily, Karin. You must be careful."

"Probably Mama, yet I never am."

"She will not speak to me."

"Greta Herchmer?"

"I told you she is not Mrs. Herchmer."

"What's that supposed to mean?"

"She is not his wife."

"It is all too complicated, Mama." She began to move around restlessly.

"Good news, Karin, my cosmetic case is found."

I sat up. "Oh. Where?"

"Nathan found it, on the beach." She touched my cheek again. Her hand was gentle but I felt myself draw back. "He will give it to me. Karin, what I told you this morning – that is true. Or at least it is my truth."

"And what is that, mother dear?" My voice was grim, but so was her face. "We were lovers. Hans saved us. I believe this. It was not because of me, but because of Hans that you survived, Karin. He was German; he put us in a camp where he had friends. They kept us from death."

Should I tell Sonja I had her photographs? Right beside my chair, but hidden? *No. It's not the time, nor the place. Nor do I want to.*

"You are telling me all this now? Why?"

"We were lovers - years. Hans saved us. I believe this."

It was a lie. She lied sometimes, did Sonja.

"You cannot understand how it was, Karin. He was German, yes, but he was Czech too. Hans loved us all. He loved his mother and father; he loved me, you, Prague. But he believed in Germany too - Greater Germany, Hitler. I never heard from him after the war. I thought he died. His love warmed me, Karin. His love kept me alive after all those years of Anton not caring. Even Josef did not know. I kept the secret until now." She fumbled with her belongings, moved away from my chair.

"As soon as I'm through napping, I'll come find you," I said. I hated her. She went away. After a moment or two, I got up and went back to our room to dress for my interview with Captain Hernandez. We were meeting at twelve that day.

In the annex, two battered suitcases stood outside the door of the room across from ours. I hadn't seen any sign of newcomers on the beach or in the dining room that morning. Somehow those suitcases reminded me of a journey out of my own past. To my grandparents? Or to the camps? My memories seemed small bright beads, gathered one by one, but never made into a necklace. When I came out a few moments later, Desmond was unlocking the door in the room across from us. I stopped.

"What's wrong?" He asked.

"Nothing."

I unlocked my door again.

"You look like something's wrong."

He stood beside his open one. "What's wrong, I said."

I turned around. "Desmond, you want me to cough up what I know, think, saw, whatever, as though we were lovers or something, when I barely know you, and you tell me nothing about what you are doing. Now you are moving in across from us. How can I trust you? And then there's my mother!"

"What about your mother?"

"Stop asking me questions." I was shouting to my own surprise as well as his. "Stop shooting significant looks at me, and demanding to know what's wrong. My mother is acting weird; you're acting weird; she's telling me things I don't want to know, and I'm a suspect in a murder case."

"What did she tell you? And what is weird about me moving in to be near you?" My stomach fell when he said that.

"You were talking to some men down by the cave."

He followed me into our room. I walked around enjoying myself as delicious self-righteous anger rode through me. "You see you're not going to tell me what you're doing are you? And that's not supposed to worry me. This is the holiday from hell." He came over and grabbed my arms and gave me a kiss, a long kiss so close and sure, I felt his response rise between us, and my own reaction to it. He backed away.

"I don't believe in married people having affairs."

"Well neither do I. Too complicated"

"Too many people hurt."

He kissed me again. I pushed him away. Then we walked on the beach. He held my hand. Or was I holding his? We stopped. Desmond looked steadily at me.

"Karin, I'm trying to find out what Marian was doing. She had a reason to come here, but I don't know what it was. I'm talking to some of the locals. They skirt around it, but some admit there are smuggling rings here. I think Marian got involved, and then, crazy bitch that she was, got in over her head." He tightened his grip on my hand and began walking again. "The whole thing doesn't make sense. Her death is driving me crazy. I've moved in because I'm worried about you and your mother. And what in hell is your mother up to anyway? That dentist friend of hers is a bit dicey."

"O.K. Sorry. Don't tell me anything more. As for Nathan Herchmer, my mother and he appear to have been chasing Nazis. Does that have something to do with the murders? I haven't a clue. But the police are questioning me every day. Desmond, I do need to know one thing. Why haven't the police caught up with you?" He said nothing, just kept walking, still holding on to my hand. "Why Desmond? Why aren't you, as Marian's husband, under suspicion?"

He paused. "Everyone thinks I'm dead."

"Don't be silly."

"It's true. The crazy bitch told everyone: Her parents, the authorities, the kids. Her parents were amazed when I called them to say I was sorry about her death."

Above us, the sky was high and blue and everything it was created to be; below it the sea brilliant, with sharp hissing roar of waves coming in; above us, jeering seagulls arrived and circled in the air.

He turned, walked backwards in order to look at me. "Karin, it suited me to disappear. I was in trouble. Still am. Money trouble - I owe a lot of money. I've been chasing my kids, all over the world."

"What's your business? And what about your family?"

"I'm the world's greatest salesman. I can sell anything, and have. Cars, Insurance, appliances, houses, variety acts. Family? There's only my mother. She doesn't know about my troubles. I call her. Tell her I'm fine. She's a librarian. She can't imagine me doing anything wrong. She's like you." Desmond said. Those last simple words were like a sword thrust penetrating every organ in my body. I wanted so to believe him.

I touched him, said, "Everything I learned was from reading books the school librarians found for me. I learned English that way. They were so kind, I'm sure she's wonderful." We walked on. He still told me very little about what he was doing. And would my mother like him? No, maybe not - Sonja had inevitably disliked my male friends, and most of my female ones. Only Greg she approved of - a man both competitive and conceited, but, as she insisted on repeating to me, 'an intellectual'. She would not find Desmond intellectual. It was just after eleven. We sat at the outdoor bar and drank coffee. But I wasn't comfortable with him that day. Too much had happened and the sword of longing that had penetrated me was only complicating things. Sitting opposite Desmond, I felt myself willing him to enter me, a vision so visual it seemed to hang between us like a mirage in the desert. Yes the old dry self was blossoming, wildly, blindly, but perhaps into disaster.

He didn't notice. He was watching the waves roll in – white foam gleaming in the bright air. We sat together for awhile, communicating somehow without speaking. That astounding day when we spoke openly of what we felt, he turned to me and said, "It was better to disappear. I lived too high, too wide – giving in to her drug habit, my own drinking. Two kids – the best schools, nannies - but not enough parenting - I dropped out of sight. I had enough investments squirreled away to live for a year." The mood trembling between us was like the warm sea breeze closing in on us - unassailable for the moment but subject to reversal. "Marian was a victim of incest or so she said – it was her excuse for whatever she did. Her parents were Nazis, or rather her father was a Junker landowner – wealthy before the war. He told me he joined so he would 'survive' - whatever that means." The bar was filling with guests who ordered lunch with their drinks; the air already warm, now swelled with the odor of grilled hamburgers

"Doing contract work for the U.S. Army - buying food, produce, grain. I traveled all over the German countryside. I met Marian at her father's estate. She threw herself at me. She wanted out of there. And I was too dumb to think things through. She was the most beautiful woman I'd ever seen, ever embraced."

A waiter offered us more coffee. I touched Desmond's arm. "I'll have to go to my interview soon." Almost at once he got up, threw down change, took my hand in his strong one, a hand not large for so tall a man. Walking back into the hotel, we hesitated in front of the garden and spoke a little more about our lives. Perhaps it was the scent of the lilies – mysterious and elusive - that allowed us to do that. I told him a little about my childhood and he said more about his life with Marian. "She drew me into things. Some of it was exciting but my values slipped; it was too easy to cheat, to lie. I began covering for Marian too. I thought I was helping her but finally I realized for the sake of the kids I had to climb out of the swamp."

"Swamp?"

"Mud up to here," He pointed to his throat. "I went to a counselor. He told me some people can't be helped. They're not constructed to face their own lies and survive."

"My husband is like that."

"So were the Nazis," Desmond said. That stopped me from saying anything more.

I looked at my watch; it was ten to twelve. "I've got to go."

He touched my shoulder. "Karin, I promise. Today or tomorrow I'll go to the police and tell them who I am. And remember I'm right across the hall from you."

"Desmond, what are they smuggling?"

"I don't know. Drugs or it may be more complicated than that"

He waved and was gone.

*   *   *   *   *

Captain Hernandez waited beside his table. He looked more at home there every day. That morning, the vase beside him was filled with purple and yellow iris.

"Mrs. Carter," he gave a little bow.

"Captain Hernandez." I returned a nod of recognition. We both sat down. "Please let me know when I can leave. My mother refuses to go without me."

"Yes." I blinked. I didn't know what he meant.

"Yes, you can go. We have a suspect." I was astounded, "Who?"

"I'm not at liberty to say. But you may leave with your mother if that is necessary." He stood up. I responded by rising also. "It would be useful to us if you stayed a day or two more in order to answer questions about the circumstances in which you discovered the body. However that is up to you. That is all for today, Mrs. Carter. Thank you for your patience."

Never had I been more completely dismissed. I stumbled out. I knew instinctively that I didn't want to go. Not yet anyway. There was something fishy about this abrupt reversal. But I would have to tell Sonja before the police did. I walked up and down the beach looking for her. The sun and sky – hot and once again cloudless - had attracted its regular crowd of worshippers. Then some distance away in the direction of the casino, I spied the familiar figure of Nathan Herchmer. He was with Greta. Thinking they were attempting a walk to the casino, I followed them. They stopped and looked out to sea. Hoping to catch up with them, I walked faster. They pointed out to sea; I half ran. They began walking again; she was taking much slower more careful steps than he. I caught up with them, walked directly behind them.

"Hello there," I said. They both turned. The woman with Nathan was not Greta but Sonja. Why was my mother wearing that odd cotton dress instead of her usual white slacks or bathing suit? Why a hat the carbon copy of the large one Greta sported? Sonja did not look particularly surprised to see me though I detected a slight flutter of her eyelashes, a tightening around her lips. She greeted me with a smile.

"Do you like my new dress, Karin? Just this morning Nathan bought it for me."

Sonja in a white dress was a shock. He'd bought what the locals called a Mexican wedding dress, a long white cotton dress with lace like decorations, a dress for a young woman. Sonja did not look good in it; her hair was too gray, her skin too white.

"It's pretty, Mama. Maybe you need some bright jewelry."

"That's what Nathan said." Her voice was happy like a young girl.

"How is Greta today, Nathan?" I kept my voice neutral and polite though the question moved between us like a knife stab.

"Not bad." He was unperturbed. "Not good either. It is a question of nerves right now. I give her morphine shots to kill the pain." He said this calmly as though discussing one of his patients.

"What exactly is the matter with her?"

Sonja motioned with her lips – no. She had that earnest do-listen-to-me-you- stupid-child look that usually threw me into a temper and goaded me into doing exactly what she wanted to warn me against – a response she failed to notice. Dr. Herchmer looked straight at me, big bone firm head with college professor horn rims hanging in the air between my face and the universe. I was a patient in his dentist's chair. "Greta is near death. She knows it and there is nothing anyone can do and she knows that too, but she is angry, very angry."

"She looked all right last week."

"Last week…" His eyes widened, his words trailed away.

"Nathan is being very strong. He is thinking of the future." Sonja said with a happy lilt to her voice. That brought home to me with an ominous clarity that she was involved with him. Sonja always had a social life, but men with dying wives?

She's old enough to take care of herself. "Do you want to eat lunch, Sonja?"

"Nathan and I must eat lunch in town today."

"Is Greta going with you?"

I take all her food to her now." Nathan said. "She's too ill to eat much."

"But tomorrow," Sonja said proudly. "Tomorrow he makes a special point of getting us all together. Because I am worried about her. Yes, Nathan?"

"We all are," Nathan looked solemn. "Such a dear, dear lady."

"I'll see you later, Mama." I turned to walk away.

"Are you going to swim, Karin?" Sonja called after me. "Wait please." She trotted up. "We are going for a drive today, Karin. Will you come with us?"

"No thanks."

"I shall find you later." she promised. "Nathan said he may take me into the countryside. Perhaps we will stay somewhere for dinner."

I wanted to shout, NO. As though reading my thought, Sonja came closer and spoke in a low voice. "There is nothing to worry about, Karin. Nathan is a good driver." "Did you say he found your cosmetic case?" But she'd already trotted away.

I spent the afternoon alone - Swimming, reading, and sunbathing. Against all odds I was acquiring a tan. I fell asleep near the sea, like a child resting beside her mother. Close your eyes, the mother urges, the faster you sleep the sooner you will wake. Then the mother breathes deeply and steadily until the child is without fear and falls asleep.

The black and white dog

I'm holding the dog he brought

Is that my father?

The man dressed in white trousers and fine white shirt ?

Mama is not angry today

* * * * *

The sea went on rolling in. What a miracle! Lying on the beach beside it, I knew contentment so deep nothing could shake it. But late in the afternoon just as I was gathering up my things, a man walked up the beach toward me. I hadn't seen Desmond all day. There weren't many out sunbathing that late, it was too close to dinner.

It wasn't Desmond. This man was short and thick-bodied with cropped hair. He was wearing khaki shorts and a white t-shirt. He had a mean scrunched up face. It was Freddy from the night before. He came up and squatted down beside me.

"You're in that murder," he said. I stood up, began to walk away. "Yes."

"Some people could help you out." "I don't need any help."

"You will." He had a mean scrunched up voice too. He walked beside me.

I tried to hide the trembling. "Please go away." Everyone around me had left. I seemed then to be alone.

"I'm not bothering you." He squinted up at me. I took comfort in the fact that I was taller than he was. His skin was pasty white.

"Yes you are." I was closer to the hotel. "I'm telling you there are people who can do you some good."

"Thank you." There was still no one near us.

"Do you want to meet them?"

"No."

"You should."

"No."

"You will whether you want to or not."

"Stop threatening me."

I walked up to the closest security guard who was talking to another guest. Freddy squatted on the ground close by. "You've got that case." It wasn't a question, his voice so neutral, so chilling I wished quite sharply for Desmond. I could see one or two others coming in from the sea. I was safe enough. I pretended unconcern, spoke to the security, complained about being badgered by someone, but when we turned to look, Freddy was gone. The sun was lower by then, the birds calling more mournfully. What were they seeking – so many spiraling up and down in great crescent whirls?

I went up the stairs and into the dining room, which as always in the evening, smelled of lime and fried fish. Freddy didn't follow me. I was safe for the moment. Just so Freddy didn't know where my room was. He seemed to know a lot about me. The dining room was half full; most guests were still ordering before dinner drinks or first courses. I wasn't hungry, not at all. I went through the lobby, out the front door along the front walk, and back to my room. I sat down on my bed and began to tremble.

Who was Freddy? How did he come to know about the case? Finally I rose and changed clothes for dinner. It seemed odd not to have Sonja there preparing for an evening together with me. The maids had been in and the room smelled of cleanser and insecticide. I saw under my mother's bed, her carved handbag. I dragged it out and found a wallet in it full of money -. I counted it - two thousand dollars. Why on earth was she carrying so much? And why leave it in such an unsafe place?

At first I felt a little thrill – it might be for me. Had she relented about helping me leave Greg? Then the more predictable thoughts came. Had she intended to give to Hans? Or an even worse idea: Was she being blackmailed? Did someone know something about her? It was a horrible thought, but with my mother there were always a number of possibilities why she did the things she did.

I shoved the money back into the wallet, pushed the purse back under her bed, and went outside to look briefly around, but there was no sign of her. In the foyer I slid into the telephone booth and called Greg, but my younger daughter Ona answered. "Dad's gone," she said. "Aunt Bets is here. Mom we don't need her - really."

"Your father must have thought it a good idea. Where did he go? How long is he away? When's he due back?"

"I don't know," Ona said slowly. "Is it nice, the sea there?"

"Next time you girls are coming," I promised. We said goodbye and I went into dinner, half expecting Sonja to show up. She didn't. As I ate a shrimp salad on the terrace, I thought about Freddy. He knew about my mother's cosmetic case. But why was it important to others? And Greg. It was the middle of spring term at the university. How could he just take off? It didn't make sense. From the main dining room came dramatic guitar music. The full band had taken the night off. I went to the lobby and dialed home. This time Nadine answered. "Do you know where your dad is? I need to talk to him."

"I'm not supposed to tell you."

"Things are difficult here. Forget what you promised him."

"He said he was going down there," she said. "He said he was going to Mexico. It was a surprise for you. He said he was going to walk into the dining room and sit down across from you and cheer you up." All this was reported rapidly, not at all her with her usual fourteen-year-old calm.

"He was coming down to Mazatlan?"

"Yes."

"When did he say all that?"

"Two days ago."

"Right after I called?"

"Yes. But Mom, it's supposed to be a surprise."

"It is. But Nadine, I want you to listen to me. Tell your dad not to come."

"But he'll be mad we told you."

"That can't be helped. You tell him that we have been released to leave, that Sonja and I will be booking to leave as soon as possible. We won't be here when he arrives. Call him at his office right now."

"He'll be mad, Mom.""He'll be even madder if I'm not here. If he wants to talk to me, tell him to call the hotel." I gave her the hotel telephone number, sent both girls a kiss, and hung up. But I stood by the phones. What prompted my inattentive husband to suddenly pay attention? Was he planning to come down with his latest graduate student? Could he already be in Mazatlan? That was a horrible thought. I went back into the dining room and headed straight for my table. Roberto's friend Edward was standing by it.

"Pardon, Senora Carter. The management does not like us to sit down with the guests. But I must talk to you."

"Of course. How is Roberto? Have you heard anything?"

"Please, Senora, come away from the terrace. It is better if we are not seen talking together. Come outside with me."

I hesitated. Edwardo was a pleasant enough young man, taller and thinner than Roberto, but I no longer felt like meeting strangers

326

in the dark. "By the equipment -.I will meet you. Don't worry. It is safe down at the water. It's important, Senora Carter."

"As soon as I finish my dessert." I hadn't planned to order any but it seemed a good idea to make him wait. "I'll meet you in fifteen minutes."

He gave a slight bow, and disappeared. I ordered vanilla ice cream and made it last a long time. Did he have a message from Roberto? I remembered only gentle conversations, the muscular body of a young man. I ordered coffee and relished it, then signed the bill, left the terrace and walked slowly across the sand. A crescent moon was low on the horizon. In the shadow of the equipment, someone was kneeling; a white shirt gleamed like sea foam on waves. Uneasy, I slowed then stopped. Behind me I could hear guitar exaggerations, a mixed burst of noise from people talking and eating. "Edwardo?"

"Over here."

I sat down on the sand. Edwardo was leaning against the first aid board. He stared at me with narrow serious eyes. "Roberto, he was in pain those last days." he whispered. "I was afraid of that." "Yes, the dart entered his chest. Near his heart. But that is not how he died.""He's dead?" I was shocked.

"Yes, they killed him." He looked out to sea. "How?"

"Water. They poured water down his throat while he slept."

"That's horrible." I strained to see Edwardo's face. He was looking down.

"In the hospital?"

He nodded, "They attacked him in his bed; pulled plugs from his body."

"Who are they, Edwardo?"

He met my eyes but shifted uneasily, "There is a gang here – bad men."

"Have you gone to the police?"

"No."

"You must." I stood up. "Or I'll go."

"No. That is not safe." Beside us the sea waves gleamed white as they rolled in. "Something will happen to you?" He lifted his shoulders with expression, "Of course." Now he rose and stalked up and down in front of me. I could feel raw energy tumbling out of him. Behind us the hotel muttered and played its way through the evening. It was close to nine. He turned back, stood over me hands on hips. I stared at his muscular legs, alert tight body. His body was an aggressive one even if his voice and manner were not. "There is much trouble with the German woman, and with you and your mother." "What do you know about my mother, about me?" I snapped, foolishly because suddenly he was kneeling, pulling me roughly down and toward him. I squeaked a little with surprise. His face was against mine. "Listen to me, you foolish woman, you get out of here, because I do not want to do what I have to do."

I played dumb – not a difficult act for me. "I don't understand."

"Listen to me" He had hold of my shoulders and he had strong hands that young man. "I came to warn you. For Roberto - because he cared for you. It is not safe here for you." His breath was strong; he smelled of liquor and spicy food. I wanted to draw away but couldn't. "I tell you there is danger here for you and for your mother. Why do you walk into the swimming pool? What are you looking for?"

"Hello there, isn't it time you came for your walk with me?" Desmond swung suddenly out of the darkness. He reached down, grabbed hold of my hand, and pulled me up. My heart lifted. I was glad to see him, but he didn't stop to talk, just walked me away, leaving Edwardo still kneeling on the sand. "Come now, I wanted to tell you about my trip to town."

"But Desmond, you didn't tell me you were going to…"

"Don't look now, but there are three men just up the beach by that small grove of trees; our friend the night watchman is one of them."

"I know. He tried to get me to…"

"Keep walking up the path; and faster."

Then we were in the hotel, and in the light. He was tall and thin and harassed looking and I was glad to see him. He pushed me toward the door to the annex, but I resisted, stopped in front of the entrance.

"Wait a minute Desmond. I simply must tell you how glad I am. I must show you." And reaching up I kissed his fine lips. And surprise, he swept me back into a long kiss; held me tightly and strongly, his body so fine and firm and masculine, his smell light and untouchable and clean. What a lovely man I thought. And what a lovely kiss. It was thrilling, the bells ringing, and all the knockout sensations of surprise that is a lover's kiss.

He stepped back. "No time, come on, back to your room, you're safer there." Then he kissed me again, pressed against me harder, slipped a sly tongue down into my mouth, and pushed me away; grabbing my arm, he hustled me along into the quiet bar. It was empty. I was trembling. Fear? Desire? Both: so much was happening, so fast.

"Sit down and have a drink," he said, "I want to talk to you." The barman was watching us as I sat down, but turned back to his television -a baseball game. Desmond sat down opposite me. I grabbed his hand and held it. "Order something," Desmond growled, "And pull yourself together before you have to deal with your mother." He turned slightly to catch the game.

"Is she back?" I stood up. "We've both been told we can leave."

He looked at me. "Then why don't you?"

"I'm having trouble keeping up with her."

"I saw her a few minutes ago."

"Thank goodness." I sat down again.

"You're worried about her?"

"Yes. She's wandering around, not telling me what she's doing."
The barman strolled over I ordered tonic water, Desmond, a beer.

"Neither of you seem to be able to take care of yourselves," he
said.

"I'm doing okay."

"If doing okay is finding a dead body, and attracting lowlifes:
Congratulations."

"That's not funny."

"No it isn't. You should stay close to your room. Don't wander
around alone." He was watching baseball. I looked around. One
couple in the corner: a wide faced man with a brush mustache,
she, the heavy set blonde who'd overheard Sonja and I arguing.
The barman arrived with our drinks. I watched Desmond watching
television, thought Yes, I love this man. He turned, looked at me, and
smiled, but looked tired.

"You o.k., Karin?"

"Yes."

"I'm beat. I have to turn in. But I'm right across from you. If
anything goes wrong, holler."

"Desmond, I'm glad you're here."

"Anything suspicious - beat on the door if you have to. Damn it. The rooms should have phones."

"How'd you get the room across from us?"

"I implied a romance. O.k. Now go to bed." He threw down money and we walked back to the annex. A sea wind was blowing: waves were roaring their siren call. I wanted to run one last time before we left Mazatlan - I promised myself.

We went inside. The air in the hallway was dead still and clammy. "By the way, that act went out twenty years ago," Desmond said.

"What act?"

"The little lady is a dimwit. You're one smart woman, maybe too smart for your own good. Be careful." He was gone. I went into the room. Sonja's sweater and new white handbag were on her bed. She's gone for a drink, or a short walk I thought. I climbed into a bath and lay soaking for awhile. It was after eleven. I was weary and avoided thoughts of Roberto, and Edwardo, boxes in pools; thought briefly of Greg. Was he actually coming here or was that a lie? I tried not to think of Greta, dying and unhappy, when I thought her such a saint. I tried to think of nothing - except perhaps of Desmond, and even he was moving too fast for me. I didn't know how much I should trust him, but every time I thought about him I got warm and fuzzy, almost lightheaded with desire. That felt good, I was sure of that, but did those feelings endanger me? I liked how Desmond hadn't asked me why I was hunkered down in the dark with Edwardo, but it meant I couldn't ask him what he was doing either.

Drowsy in the warm water, I thought then of Marian's beautiful white naked dead body as it looked when I'd found her. I couldn't remember much about her face, and concentrated on recalling it. The cave was small, dark, and earth-lined, a superb coffin for so fair a woman, as though the earth had formed itself around her, and she lay a bright chrysalis, performing an inner magic. Her face had been tranquil: her chin, nose, the tilt of her head all had proclaimed a dignity that perhaps she had not had, or even reached for, in life. There had been no wounds, no sign of blood, only an odd twist of the neck and the calm of the dead, like a clock that had a voice, than stopped into a silence. Lying in the bath, my own white body stretched out before me, I thought about how she might have died. Who had killed her? Maybe she killed herself. The police had reported she was murdered, but perhaps it had been a suicide or an overdose? But why would she kill herself there – in a small cave? Did someone carry her body there? If so that someone knew the truth. I wished then that I had asked Roberto about the cave. How many people knew about it? Who took their friends there? Did tourists know about it? She could have killed herself. There'd been times when I'd wanted to die, to end everything neatly and without pain. Maybe many people have been tempted. But why in a cave alone? It seemed more likely than someone else was guilty of her death.

The door of our room opened. "Sonja?" No answer. I heard a slight scuffling sound. "Mama? Mama is that you?" The bath water had cooled. I noticed too my own nakedness. More slight sounds in the outer room. Someone was out there. I sat up in the bath. Our purses, our things were in the room.

"Mama is that you?" I spoke in a loud firm voice. Then I saw the bathroom doorknob turn. I panicked. "Who's there? Who is it? Get out of our room." I'd locked the door. I remembered Desmond saying he'd be close by. "Desmond? Is that you?" A loud bump against the door. "What are you doing out there?" Someone hit the bathroom door, hard. One, two, three - a steady thumping.

They're breaking down the door.. I flapped like a large fish in the bathwater, thinking I mustn't be trapped in the water when they break in. The steady ferocious hammering went on. I scrambled out of the tub, stood naked, was screaming. "HELP, HELP, HELP, Desmond, Desmond, HELP. SOMEONE."

The slamming stopped. Silence. I stood trembling, dripping wet on the other side of the bathroom door, listening, as though my life depended on it, which perhaps it did. Still, no sound - long moments without sound; I didn't dare open the door. How many minutes went by? I sat on the toilet seat, determined to stay there until morning.

"Karin?" Sonja's voice. I sighed, breathed carefully, and calmed my voice. I knew my mother; I must stay calm, say nothing. "Karin, did you have a nice day?"

"Yes, Mama, did you?" I hesitated a moment more and then emerged. Sonja was undressing, folding her skirt neatly over a hanger. I sat down on my bed and looked around. Nothing seemed touched. Sonja wandered around half dressed. I'd shocked Sonja

the first night by refusing to wear a nightgown. Now we were intimates together. I was sitting naked wrapped in a towel. "So you had a nice day?" Was my voice really as calm as it sounded? Sometimes I amazed myself. I was still trembling with fear. But my mother didn't notice. "Wonderful." She turned around and faced me and I saw by her flush and the tension of her body that she'd enjoyed the day.

"We went all the way to Guadalajara."

"By bus?"

"Nathan rented a car."

"Dr. Herchmer drove? Did Greta go too?"

The change in Sonja's eyes was barely discernible, a slight narrowing. "No. She has cancer." She unbuttoned her blouse. "You should call him Nathan. He is my friend. Your friend is in the garden."

"What friend?" I wrapped my towel tighter. I was incapable of standing up, of moving, but I looked around. Was there anything different, anything gone in the room?

"That tall man. He is in the garden smoking. Is he a smoker? Did you speak to Greta?" Sonja's voice was sharp.

"I saw her this afternoon. She was walking on the beach. She was there only a moment." I was still looking around. By then I'd found something different in the room. "Is Desmond still out there?" One of the suitcases on the closet floor was open.

"I don't know. Second hand smoke. You must be careful." She sat down on the bed opposite me. What we were talking was nonsense. "Karin, you must remember they are not married - the Herchmers. He is looking at apartments here. He wants to retire in Mexico."

"But not with Greta?"

"She was his office nurse for many years. They worked together, and then, as so often happens, an affair." Sonja shrugged her shoulders with an elegant gesture that I recalled from her years with Josef – a sophistication she put on or took off with such ease, it used to intimidate him. I took out a nightgown.

"How long have they been together?"

"Years. But he wanted to end it long ago."

"And she didn't want to end it at all." I said dryly. The room was warm. I felt perfectly comfortable sitting in a towel, but Sonja, half undressed, rose and turned on the air conditioner so that its decrepit racket swept through the room. "God, Mama, do we have to have that on?"

"Do you use this word God still? You know I don't like it."

"Why? You don't believe in God."

"You sound like a rough head."

"Roughneck." I walked over to look at the empty suitcase,-Sonja's large one. "Did you leave anything in that suitcase? Why is it open?"

She looked at me but said nothing. She too was preparing for bed. She walked into the bathroom: the air conditioner was racketing away and somehow I couldn't put the bones of argument down. "Mama, what I want to know is: If it's all over, why are they traveling together?"

"He thought it would be a nice way to end it, because she is going to die." Her voice was cheerful. She was putting on a new pale blue nightgown that she hadn't worn before, a scent of white shoulders rose in the air. "But she, she thought there was a possibility of reconciliation." She started the shower.

I took my towel back to the bathroom, rapidly brushed my teeth, and desperate to forget what had just happened, climbed into bed. Oh that delicious slip into fresh sheets. "Hope springs eternal is that it?" My voice was harsh.

"He told her again here. He wants to be through with it."

"Because he's interested in you, isn't he, Mama?" And your money I thought. She wandered back into the bathroom. The air condition snarled on.

"I just met him, Karin. Why do you ask about the suitcase? I must pack. I have a new dress, and today Nathan bought me some shoes and a jacket. He is fun to shop with." She came over to my bed "Nathan is a wonderful man - wonderful, wonderful." Her voice swung out like a skirt in dancing, whirling through the air, making balance out of imbalance.

"Please turn off the air conditioner, Mama."

"Was she angry?"

"Who?"

"Greta?"

"I didn't see much of her.

"He was embarrassed. She was saying some not kind things about me."

"The air conditioner, Mama."

She walked to the wall and switched it off; shrugged her shoulders again with that beautiful, unconscious gesture. "She is not a happy woman." Though I lay with my back to the room, once again I couldn't resist being lured into conversation.

"Maybe the fact that she's dying has something to do with that. And how long did the affair go on anyway?" I turned over to look at her.

"Twenty years." Sonja said briskly. She was taking off her jewelry

"Twenty years?"

"There was no marriage"

I turned my back. "Twenty years is not just an affair."

How long were you with Hans? What about you? I wanted to ask this woman, my mother, who was so calm, so tolerant, so unusually forgiving. But I was too tired.

"Let's talk at breakfast, Mama."

Sonja hung up her blouse and sweater. The Hotel Madre Maria provided only two hangers each so Sonja stole one of mine and I pretended not to notice. I was pretending to be asleep. "He is a nice man, Karin. Nathan. She is not a normal woman."

I opened my eyes and asked a question that had been haunting me for days. "What kind of cancer does she have?"

"Breast. She refused chemotherapy. She will die soon. Maybe here."

I woke in the middle of the night - a panic attack. Who slammed on the bathroom door? Why hadn't I told Sonja? How serious was Edwardo's warning? Why was Desmond outside our door? I said prayers; I prayed for Greta, and for myself - that I'd be brave. Still, the unknown was hanging over me. Not only the events that were unfolding but why I pretended nothing happened, I needed courage. Why wasn't I talking to Sonja? Why wasn't I telling her everything? Didn't I trust her anymore? Once she was the bravest person I knew. And Desmond – everything he said and did seemed honest and helpful. Why couldn't I quite trust him?

I sat up in the dark, confessed my fears. Did I expect betrayal? Perhaps my marriage has eaten away at my ability to trust others. I'll pray for that. I must include myself – trust your feelings the counselor had said. I didn't tell him that my Desa has most of my authentic feelings. She's kind of a child – She hasn't always behaved well. Karin is brave. In fact, tomorrow I will walk the road outside my window.

Friday, Day 13

The next morning I found myself wishing for a room that looked out to sea, a room on the beach where we could see and hear other people. Our window addressed only dusty land and a monotone road that followed the sea, but didn't seek it; instead wandered above it along its own lonely way. Our hotel was the largest and the last. There were no trees or bushes, only a dribbling out of motels and private cabins – shacks some of them. That morning I planned to walk that road. First I had to face breakfast with my mother. I was still shocked by the intruder in our room, but almost as much by Sonja's announcement of her growing relationship with Nathan Herchmer. It astounded me in some private place in a way that her relationship with Josef never had. I didn't like Nathan nor trust him. And I felt sorry for Greta. It seemed Sonja no longer did. But most of all I still brooded over the so-called facts about her wartime years, facts that would force me to change my entire view of my father, Anton, and my grandparents.

My mother had always been the one person I trusted. I didn't want to believe her, didn't want to think about this Hans, a German soldier. What had he to do with me? Yes, o.k., he was my mother's lover during the war. I could accept that; yes, o.k., he helped us survive through his German contacts - probably that was true – everyone had special arrangements during the war - but my father? No. Never. I resented this idea, remembering how Sonja wanted to ignore my grandparents after the war was over. They were my only link with Anton. He is my father. I know it, I believe it. His parents were the only grandparents I knew.

I lay in bed thinking about them. They are dead now – Nana and Papa, but they are good memories, a good normal past that I have, and Sonja doesn't. After the war Sonja had no one – almost an orphan – that's what she said about herself. Her parents, uncles, aunts, cousins were dead. I never met them – some died in Lidice. I remember train rides with her, the raging sound of the wheels and all the thick smells of engine and people. There's dirt everywhere, Mama said. Dirt, dirt, dirt – she didn't cry, or call out like some people, just whispered that to me.

I remember my grandparents' house in the country – the horses in the fields and my father walking with my mother. Once all of them were sitting at a big table talking as I was led away to bed and I didn't like that. Their house was bare. They had hardly any lamps and no books or pictures. Only an old couch and rocking chairs and a big mangle that Nana let me help her iron with. She didn't like too many things in her house. Papa had a workshop in a shed at the back of the house. I wasn't allowed in it because it was full of sharp tools and I could hurt myself. Sharp tools. Could Marian have died from something sharp – like the dart in Roberto's chest? Or from water poured down her throat? That would leave no mark. It's horrible to think about such things. Memories help change thoughts. They are my facts.

Nana and Papa slept in a big old room; two walls were dark wood, and full of shelves. Their most precious possessions were on those shelves. Most were sold during the war – silver spoons and china dogs and cats, little painted birds, small dishes and bowls, photographs – one wall behind the shelves held a mirror. When I saw myself in that mirror, a small serious child wearing a pinafore and white shoes, I was delighted. I belonged to my grandparents too, standing beside all those pretty little dogs and cats, birds and shepherdesses. I had the same name as my Nana, DESA. I wrote it down on little pieces of paper.

We visited them after the war, but only once. Anton was dead. He is my father. My brother Stefan was dead too. They both died in the camps, but Nana and Papa survived – rather nicely - Sonja would say sarcastically. We spent three days with them before we went under the wire. They cried when we left, said I was their family, but Mama wouldn't think of it.

Now I know why. Memories are crowding in, mixed up in time and place, not logical, not chronological. These memories of my grandparents are happy, but why does thinking of them make me cry? Anton was my father. I loved him. This hotel room is as quiet, as sightless as a closet. I must go out and take my walk up that lonely road. But first I have to face breakfast with my mother. She is still asleep.

I tiptoed out and was sitting by the pool when Desmond found me. It was early - around six. I had fallen into the habit of checking the boxes every morning, and that day there they were, deep in the water, square reminders of all the mysteries that shape our lives. I was dressed in a green sundress and white jewelry, in anticipation of my morning walk up the road.

"Have you had breakfast?" Desmond came to stand beside me. He lit a cigarette.

"The restaurant opens at 7. I haven't even had coffee. Desmond, someone was in our room last night."

He looked startled, sat down beside me. "Why didn't you call me?"

"I did. I yelled."

"When was this?"

"Not long after our drink. I was taking a bath. I'd locked the door so they didn't get in. They spent a while trying though, making a lot of noise pounding on it. You didn't hear any of that?"

"I slipped outside for a last smoke. I won't do that again. Promise."

"Desmond, what do you see down at the far end of the pool? In the water?"

He walked to the edge of the pool. "Some stuff in there. What is it?"

"You tell me."

"The water's so damn dirty I can't tell. I'll ask the manager." He vanished but soon returned. "He'll look into it - the manager, Senor Moreno." He touched my arm, pulled me up, put his arm around me. I liked that. I needed kindness that morning. "S

"Sorry you had a bad scare" I put my head on his chest. "Now look. You're going to have to be good," he said. "I mean - stay in touch. Don't wander off alone. No late night running."

I pulled away. Stepped back "I plan to walk today."

"Where?"

"Along the road. I want to see if anyone comes out to talk to me."

"Not a good idea."

"I've looked at that road for days. It seems to go nowhere. No one uses it." "Please don't." His face was serious. But he didn't offer to go with me. Desmond, it's my life." We stared at each other and he withdrew his arm.

I walked the road. The dry landscape was empty. It was still early - about ten; in the distance, a rising heat haze made the horizon shimmer. The smell was still of the sea, but also a dry mutter of sage and dust, an occasional harsh, brilliant odor of asphalt and rubber. It seemed a surprisingly modern road to glare so emptily at the sky above. Scattered across the semi-desert were small huts, each with a television aerial. None advertised any life. I passed small, mean looking motels and modest haciendas, saw ahead a man standing beside the road. His figure did not waver and, at first, I thought it was a scarecrow. Then the man walked further out, stopped by a mailbox, stood gazing up the road at me. I walked closer. He was in blue jeans, a white shirt and was hatless.

I looked away, saw a train on the horizon but didn't hear its passage. Still I walked the road. The sun was gathering me up, growing hotter and more demanding. Finally, I felt dizzy and stopped to take a rest. I wished I'd brought water. Wondered if I wanted to walk toward nowhere; thought about turning back. Then a car behind me scattered the dust and ruffled the hot air with furious energy as it passed me. It was soon gone, but gave me courage. There were other people moving through this landscape.

I continued to walk, strong steady paces. I felt a partnership with fate. Soon I approached the man, close to the pretentious brick hacienda he was standing in front of. He was looking up at the sky as I approached, but turned to look at me. My heart beat a little harder. What was I getting myself into? Yet I was not surprised; I'd half expected this encounter. The man took a step toward me. There was no traffic, no other pedestrians. I pretended to stop and adjust my sandal, than shaded my eyes with one hand to stare out at a narrow strip of the sea I caught sight of between two haciendas. I wished for a hat; the sun was too hot. Looked at my watch; it was nearly noon. But I could not delay the encounter with Marian's friend, Carl.

"Buenos Dias, Senora Carter." Carl stopped directly in my path and flashed broad white teeth with no smile to match in his eyes.

"Good morning, Carl."

"I shall call you Karin."

"Do."

"Have you come to speak with my friends and me?"

"No."

"My friends and I wish to speak with you."

"I'm just out walking."

"You have something we want."

"Marian? Roberto? Do they wish to talk about them?"

"It is better to say nothing about them," he growled.

"What do your friends want?"

"A small purple case."

"Like my mother's. You want me to give you my mother's cosmetic case. Unfortunately she lost it. She doesn't have it now. Carl, the police think I had something to do with Marian's death."

"What has that to do with me?"

"They question me every day. It's boring." I broke off our stare, turned slowly to look again at the sliver of sea between slabs of stone wall.

"Have you looked inside the case?"

"Yes. It has photographs in it that belong to her." I turned to look at him, determined to appear calm, but inwardly thinking - are you nuts Karin? Do you think you're a detective now? Get out of here. But a new stronger self was whispering too.

Stick with it. Nothing's going to happen to you. Not out in the open.

Carl shrugged his shoulders with elaborate nonchalance, flashed his broad toothed predatory smile. "I am sorry. That is all they want from you - the case."

"If I find it, you will leave me alone."

Again the teeth flashed, "Of course."

"And my mother – you will leave her alone."

"Of course, if she does nothing further that is stupid."

I didn't want to reply to that. "Then I don't have to meet with your friends, having found this out from you."

He blinked, "No."

"Just give you, personally, the cosmetic case."

"You have it with you?" He stepped as close as he dared.

We were the same height, his flesh was bronzed, his hair cut so close I could see his naked scalp. His eyelashes were burnt white and he gave off the smell of fat flesh, an aura of sudden swelling, like a mushroom that can bulge above ground overnight. I took a step back; heard a car behind me and turned around. A small battered red truck was coming up the road; it hesitated; then stopped in front of a small motel. Nobody got out.

I turned back to Carl. "I don't have it with me. It's hidden. Where do you want me give it to you?"

"Not me."

"Who and where?"

"You must bring it to the cave."

He stared at me, face turned hard. My stomach reacted to his suggestion with a punch of fear. The feeling of playing a childhood game vanished. "That sounds very dangerous and highly unlikely."

"Then we will find another place to meet."

"So I can give you the cosmetic case?"

"No, to my friends."

"And what do they give me?"

He smiled tight, teeth clenched, eyes closed, "Your life."

I looked down at the black road, stared at it, believing the sea view would no longer be out beyond us. The hot sun struck my bare neck and forced me to look up again. "I have friends too. And I can tell the police everything you've just said, the threat you've made."

"Do so." He was distressingly calm, voice flat.

"Can I think about it?"

"What is there to think?"

"Whether I want to meet your friends anytime, anywhere; it's a cosmetic case with makeup and some photographs in it – nothing else."

"Where is it hidden? We can meet there."

"I couldn't possibly tell you."

"Of course." His voice continued flat, but he didn't take his eyes off my face. Once again he gave an elaborate shrug of his beefy shoulders. His shirt, so white and normal looking from a distance, was covered with stains. "Who knows?" He smiled. "People act crazy around here. People die around here."

The house behind him was a sleek brick modern hacienda that sprouted television antennas in several places. The sun beat down and the day rose up to embrace it with sharp heat. I could see no point in standing around.

"Goodbye, Carl." I turned, began walking back to the Hotel Madre Maria.

"Where are you going?" Anger deepened his voice.

"Back to the hotel." I called back over my shoulder. "Let me think about what you said. We're leaving soon."

"Yes. One way or another, lady, you are leaving. And tell Jason to keep his fucking face out of it."

That stopped me. I had to turn around. "What do you mean by that?"

"What I said. Your mother's got some bad egg friends. Jason's a fuck head."

"He's not her friend."

"You give him that address book and your mother's dead, Mrs. Carter."

Carl put exaggerated emphasis on the Mrs. From a safe distance, I turned to watch him go back into the house. I walked toward the hotel, cursing myself for not wearing a hat: The rusted red ford drove slowly up behind me. I stopped. It stopped. Desmond was sitting in it. I walked up to the open driver window, "Hi, friend."

"Get in."

"What are you doing, Desmond?"

"Watching you play around. What did Carl have to say?"

"You know him?"

"I ought to. He's Marian's husband." Then his face changed, "Or was. He's a bastard. You should be wearing a hat."

"This is your truck."

"It is."

"How long have you been living in Mexico?"

"Off and on – two years."

"Hiding out?"

"You could call it that."

The sense of open sky and endless landscape, the threat of the day and the continuing mystery of Desmond stayed with me a long while after he dropped me at Hotel Madre Maria.

I dressed for lunch, went looking for Sonja, but didn't find her until an hour later. She was sitting by herself at a table in the outdoor bar drinking a margarita. That surprised me. It was only half past one. "How are you feeling?"

"All right," But her voice was subdued.

"Where's Nathan?"

"Greta is ill this morning."

"Is she still eating?"

"Yes." She sighed, looked tragic. "I too have not been well. All this noise and these people - I have no appetite. And the food in this bar, so mediocre."

"What does Jason do, Mama?"

She looked blank for a moment. "He works at the casino."

"Is that why Dr. Herchmer hangs around with him? Mama, does he owe money, Dr. Herchmer? To the casino?"

She hesitated then shifted uneasily. She was wearing heavy red jewelry, an embroidered white blouse and blue and green peasant skirt. She looked highly ethnic.

"Yes. But it is not our business, Karin."

"How much?"

"I do not know. It is not polite this prying into other people's money. You are too American, Karin. In Europe we do not ask about such things."

She took a solid slug of margarita.

"Sorry. Once when I talked to Greta, she said you have the gift of lamentation."

She pretended not to hear. Why was she so dressed up? But I told her how good she looked, mentioned how these weeks were the longest holiday we had ever taken together. For some reason I began to talk about the long train trip we took to Iowa where she'd first found work. "Do you remember, Mama? The train across the U.S. – all the noise, and the berths with curtains and the heads poking out from behind them; the black porters marching through the narrow passageways – the first time we saw black people."

She tried to smile. "Yes I remember. That trip made me think too much. It was not comfortable that train ride." She looked down into her drink. "Why are you talking about it? Why are you thinking about that?"

"Those are my memories, Mama. That's when mine begin - in America."

"We had no money, I remember that," she said, looking at me crossly. But I felt like pushing those memories at her. Why did she always forget the good, remember the bad? Though, in fact, the complexity of the dining car and its waiters had terrified her.

Now, to avoid more conversation, she wandered away to the restroom. I stayed in the bar and wrote in my diary. I wasn't using it for dreams by then - I wasn't having many. Instead I was attempting to catch the rush of memories that were coming to me, in this enforced wait in the Hotel Madre Maria.

After one tea and cakes excursion, we fled, and purchased only soft drinks and snacks for three days. Most of the journey, she stared expressionless out the window while I wandered around the train, hungry but thrilled by the true summer we saw out the windows. It was August and hot, the sky very blue. When we reached Cedar Rapids, people noticed our shabby, old-fashioned clothes. We were two foreign women with funny accents. But they were not unkind.

We found their food cheap and abundant. When we opened the door of the apartment someone had found us, we saw three rooms full of sturdy furniture and were thrilled with our new luxury. We were in America, land of the brave and the free. I discovered a window that looked out on a tree; I thought the lawn and flower beds beautiful, but Sonja sat down in an old armchair and began to weep - I remember that - Sonja crying, hands over her eyes, tears squeezing through them. She made happy-sad sounds. I sat beside her confused and oppressed because I didn't know whether she was happy or sad, and so longed to be outside playing with other children.

I hadn't told Sonja what I was writing. I didn't know why I was doing it. But I knew that I was growing stronger by remembering the past, that I was putting it to rest. We met for a late lunch at the outside bar. Sat and admired the beauty of the sea and sky in Mexico. It was a calm day, the sun hot. Sonja ordered tacos, I fish. We ate and drank and were careful of each other. We spoke of New York, of her going back to work, and I, to my family. We didn't mention Greg. I refused to think about him. Sonja said we should leave Sunday. I agreed. We parted with a hug. Or rather I hugged her. She planned to sit on the beach with her friends, I, to go on walking around looking at everything.

First I walked down to the sea. By then, our beach was covered with bodies; the afternoon sun was hot and pleasing and nearly everyone was comatose - not talking, simply yielding themselves up to it. I threaded my way through the dreamers and approached my other mother, the sea. I wanted to say goodbye, to tell her I loved her, marveling once again at her strength, her glamour. How certain she was, how unyielding. The sun does not command her, I thought. Nothing does. Except, perhaps, the deepness of her selfhood, her own bottomless, inexplicable depths, which man still has not completely explored, still neglects to appreciate and understand.

The moon commands her tides
Even the sea must accept guidance.

I stood for awhile, breathing in the sea smell, that of life itself, drawing it in and feeling my body and mind fill with it. Her command: Live, go on no matter what. I try to drink in her message, this mother, to remember this moment. This command is the same as the one Sonja insisted on: Strive to live!

Around me almost everyone was sleeping, a few turning, but, as in sleep, unknowingly; a few sat half propped up, drowsy, pretending to read or attempting conversation; the air was heavy and the sun unrelenting. Were they awake? I stood though and there were others who walked or played, carefully, paying respect and attention to those who insisted on sleeping. They cannot be ignored, they are the majority. I saw three men way up the beach, and the tall figure of Desmond.

Excited, I started to walk to the edge of the hotel beach, to leave the sunbathers behind. Yes, it is Desmond standing with two other men, one very short, Edwardo. Desmond is talking with Edwardo, and the other, the other...I slow, stop, uncertain, begin to tremble. He is the man I spoke to today - Carl. They stand just outside the cave. What were they talking about so earnestly? Then Edwardo looked up and saw me. He said something to Desmond, who looked too. I expected him to wave, for we were some distance apart. The noise of the sea will drown out any sound. But Desmond did not wave. Instead he turned away and the three men walked rapidly up to the land above.

Something is going on. I think that. Something is happening. Desmond is about some business unknown to me. He has dug up the cosmetic case and is now engaged in some kind of maneuver. And a great explosion of rage blows up in me. It is ferocity. It is violent rage. I hate him. I hate them all. And part of me is already marveling at how all my frustration, fear and anxiety is now melted into this one pure emotion: Rage. I want to beat them all into the ground, especially the man who has threatened me, but also Desmond. I start to run. Part of me is coolly analyzing just what madness this behavior is, but the other self, the newborn, angry Desa self is already running, running once again as Roberto taught me, down the beach toward these men who insist on playing with my life, and that of my mother's, who carry on mysteries and refuse to solve them. I am running, and then I start to shout. Come back here, you bastards, I am shouting, come back here. But the beach ahead is empty. There is not one soul on it now except me. I take a quick look back – the sleepers still lie motionless, one or two dreamers walk wearily beside the sea. Only I have changed. Only I am able to run and that is because I am angry. For the first time in my life, I am truly, deeply, horrendously angry - that is what it feels like, that is the fuel for my running.

When I reach that section of beach, it is still empty. I stand desolate. No Desmond, no Edwardo, no Carl. No one. They have escaped me.

This is an odd, unlovely beach; the great street light, an absurdity. The sand is not the white, sifted sand of our Hotel Madre Maria beach, but is mealier with tufts of grass growing out of it. Above it rises the hill, back from it, I know now, lies a large house, but I cannot see it. I see nothing.

A great well of anger still lies me, like a great wave of the sea; it is about to overwhelm me. I want out of this mess, this confusion, this threat. And where is Desmond? The noble Desmond - where is the supposed defender, the man who has promised me through his eyes and lips and voice that he will stay with me. Where is he?

I think about going up the hillside, but I know that is not wise. And the cave - I know where it is. Shall I go inside again? A little shiver of apprehension guides me. No, NO, I do NOT want to do that. But how well I remember it, a rocky edge, a little wall tucked up inside the rocky wall of the hillside. Not that far from the street light. Part of the absurdity. And looking down at the sea, I catch sight of old Juan who has ridden up on his drooping horse, almost in the same position as the morning when I emerged from the cave after finding Marian Heisel's body.

He sits on his horse, gawking at me, and I remember when I rode with him and he thrust his dirty fingers up me and then laughed. The anger boils up again and I run over to the horse, slap it hard, look up with fury at old Juan. I shout at him, "You asshole if you dare lay hands on me again, I'll tell the police, the Federales." I strike the horse again; it backs away. Old Juan looks at me, nothing changes on his face, and then he leans down and spits full in my face.

In a fury I pull at the cinch, yanking and rocking it, and then push him hard, his feet hold him but I grab his rotten coat and shove him over; he falls on the sand with a hoarse grunt and then shouts, and I am running, running so fast I am like a leprechaun because I don't want him to catch me. I don't even look back; I just run and then I am chortling with pleasure. I did it. I really did it. I pushed the old bastard down and I feel a sweep of triumph and then some surprise. What am I doing today?

I slow down, think -.as Karin likes to think - I am growing quite violent, is that wise? Then think- as Desa - go ahead, thrust yourself into life with vehemence, do that.

At the edge of the Madre Maria Beach, I stop, and winded, turn around to look up the length I have run. Old Juan stands, looking back at me; arms akimbo; his horse has staggered up and is beside him. I wonder if they can do me any harm, and then I turn around and stroll through the dreamers, the sleepy ones, some of whom are waking in order to gather drinks and change in the room for the cocktail hour. I'm still breathing hard as I head for my room.

When I walk by the terrace, I see Sonja. She is sitting alone at one of the tables. I walk up toward her, then stop. She does not see me and on her face is the terrible dark look I have not seen for years. It's not a sad look, nor an angry look, not melancholy; it is difficult to describe. Her face is so sad that it proclaims something deeper than just Sonja, as though something more powerful and majestic has entered her, expressing its dark knowledge through her. This expression I used to run from as a child. I remember it most in Florida. When we first came to the United States we stayed there. Sonja sat for hours on the beach, or in the makeshift living room under the awning in the trailer park.

Those months were unlike any other in my life. We stayed with Dede and Frank. They were an elderly couple, distant relatives of my father, Anton. When they heard of us from other members of my father's family, they invited Sonja and me to stay with them for a month or six weeks. Until you know what you want to do, they said to Sonja, and so the child can learn to play again.

I did play. The trailer court belonged to the elderly, but there were a few families with children, and I soon discovered them. Many of the old people were friendly, and knowing our story, would call me in for milk and cookies or fresh made doughnuts. They were wonderful cooks those ladies.

Dede and Frank didn't have much; they lived in Minnesota and drove down to St. Petersburg every winter. Their trailer was a modest one and they created a second room under an awning, Here they put two beds for Sonja and I, and for the first time we slept apart. Sonja had a great bed in one corner of the porch and I, a small roll away cot that had been rented just for me. It reminded me of the hospital but not of the hospital because Dede gave me a wealth of stuffed animals until I had a whole bed full of them, to pick and choose which ones I would sleep with every night. It was a dream for me as a child: The warm Florida air, the sunshine, the constancy of the days, the lack of pressure, animal friends to sleep with, children who wanted to play.

I didn't have to go to school but soon I began to catch the bus with the other children, to disappear into the elementary school, where I learned English. The month stretched out to two and it was time for Dede and Frank to pack up and go back to Minnesota. I wept saying goodbye.

We rode back up as far as Iowa with them, the state where Sonja had found work through other relatives. I loved Dede and Frank, but somehow Sonja didn't warm up to them, though she was always correct. I was made to write, each Christmas and Easter, a long letter telling them my news, but we never saw them again. First Dede, then Frank died in far away Minnesota, but their kindness helped heal me, and perhaps the long hours when Sonja brooded were important in her healing too, though I don't know, only remember Florida whenever I see Sonja's face filled with despair.

One night lying together with Sonja, for sometimes I snuggled with her in that sweet room outdoors, the air cool and smelling of orange blossoms, I dared to ask Sonja about that look.

"Mama."

"What dear?"

"Why do you look so sad?"

"I am remembering."

"Remembering what?" I was afraid I knew the answer, but didn't want to act surprised. But I was.

"I am remembering the woman I am."

"What do you mean?"

"I am remembering that I am a woman who loves life. I had forgotten."

I fell asleep puzzling over that. What did she mean?

Now perhaps, I know. I too may have fallen into forgetting who I am – a woman who loves life. Falling into forgetful sleep is easy. I can do it without even shutting my eyes. I walk past the terrace, allowing Sonja moments of remembering, return to the room to change clothes. The door is open. I'm afraid to enter so peek in.

The room is empty. I walk into it and feel the slight stirred currents of invasion, a brief, subtle invasion. Nothing has been touched. I check my jewelry, my purse, our clothes. Everything is in order.

Except for a piece of paper beside Sonja's bed – in strange handwriting, it says: "If it can be arranged, we'll do it." That's all - strange words in strange handwriting. I stand bemused, not for the first time in this Hotel Madre Maria room. I go out, try Desmond's door. I want somebody to talk to. But there is no answer and the door remains locked. I wander out of the building. I cannot think. I cannot plan. My heart is beating rapidly. I go into the front office and speak to the woman desk clerk. She's usually there in the afternoon – a slight, pretty woman with a face as worried as Senor Moreno.

She gives me a letter. How odd, I thought as I stood in the foyer of the hotel, staring at the letter. There is no postage. Only my name carefully printed across it. I sat down in one of the two stuffed armchairs in that crowded, busy little place (curious how safe one feels in small, busy hotel lobbies) and opened the letter.

It was from Desmond. 'I tried to catch up with you this morning, but no luck. I think I've found some answers for you. Can you meet me on the beach tonight at 11 p.m.? For various reasons, I don't want Sonja or others at the hotel to know I'm here. I'm checked out and I've told everyone, but except you, you darling woman, that I had to leave. If you meet me tonight at the edge of the hotel beach, we can walk up to the cave.'

Up to the cave? I stood up, astonished, and frightened. I was trembling again. It was almost a habit now at the Hotel Madre Maria. He wanted me to meet him at 11 p.m. and walk up to the cave together. After all that's happened. Is he crazy?

He'd added a short postscript: 'Don't tell Sonja because she'll worry.'

She'll worry! I felt like shrieking right there in the hotel lobby. I'm worried and it's only four o'clock. I went outside into the white hot vixen sun. I walked around the corner of the hotel noticing all the cracks and rubbed places in the stucco. An old hotel -. a beaten up old hotel, but a solid structure and still standing. Had there ever been hurricanes? Tidal waves? Fires? Murder? Had anyone ever been stood against this wall and shot a dozen times by a firing squad?

Get ready hotel; your tranquility may be over.

Sonja still sat at the table on the terrace, still looked like she'd swallowed a great dollop of sour milk. She probably had if she's been with Nathan. I sat down opposite her.

"He's a bastard."

"Nathan?"

She looks at me and her eyes are dark black olives; her skin is sallow with rage.

"You know that don't you? That he's a bastard?"

"There's a note from him for you in the room." She doesn't stir for at least three minutes, then rises and sweeps majestically away. Toward the room I notice. Sonja has no answers. I know that now. For so any years I thought she did. Her guidance, her advice sustained me. But now her answers seem small and shriveled up from lack of exercise, from lack of new ideas. She is intent on doing the same things she has done for years.

About four, I was back at the beach intending to go swimming. But first I walked over to the outside bar to get a coffee. It was empty. The one waiter hovering by the cooler was the sad-faced older man of our first week, the one who had mistakenly followed Sonja back to our room. He advanced cautiously.

"Where is everyone this afternoon?"

"You don't know?" he asked looking at me with sad eyes.

"No."

"There is a regatta today. There will be a picnic on the beach this evening. At this hour – surfing, swimming. Everyone is invited." He looked hopeful, "Lots of fun." The word "fun" was pronounced with ominous clarity. I took this to mean a sense of personal deprivation.

"Does the staff take part?"

"If they wish, me I am careful," he raised sad thin shoulders and let them drop. "Me, I am not a surf boy."

I took my coffee outside. Sure enough a great crowd was gathered along the beach to watch swimmers flail through the waves. As I walked down to join them, I saw Greta sitting on the Herchmer patio, embroidering. I strolled up.

"Greta, I want to thank you."

"I am almost finished with this." She held up the cloth. "I like to finish what I start. Sit down, my dear. Would you like a glass of juice?"

"No thanks."

"Do you like the earrings? I see you wear them sometimes."

I was astounded and almost sputtered out awkward words but thought better of it.

"I love them. Thank you so much."

"They're a pretty color."

"Sonja is jealous. She looked in all the stores, but couldn't find anything like them. Where did you get them?"

"That old man on the horse makes them. Or says he does."

"Old Juan?"

"I bought them from him. I'm glad you like them. They were a farewell gift and here we are still. I remembered you speaking about blue marbles." She smiled and patted my hand. "Come, come sit down with me."

I didn't remember telling her about Stefan or the marbles.

"Greta, I want you to know how much it meant to me - talking with you. You've made me think about things in a different way. I've been trying to find ways to forgive the unforgivable. Isn't that what Christians are supposed to do? But can those who survive concentration camps do that?"

Greta laid aside her embroidery, and put on sunglasses.

"In the camps I was an animal, a survivor. We all were. When I left I was unable to love or to forgive; I believed in nothing but my own life. But that life only began after I married. My first husband loved me and I loved him. And through that love I found I could believe in God again. Now I am a Christian. Christians must forgive. As they say – 'it is no longer an option'. Would you like a glass of wine?"

I didn't want to leave her. I loved Greta, needed her comfort. "Yes, if it's white."

"Nathan drinks a lot of wine."

She rose and slipped into the bedroom behind her. On the beach, a crowd was clustering at the far end of the beach. They stood densely packed in a circle.

I was watching the crowd. Some men broke away, ran up to the hotel. The two at the parachute ran over to the crowd. I didn't see Desmond down among them. Greta came out carrying two glasses of white wine, and began speaking as she handed me one. "I was interested in science. In the U.S., I studied science. My first husband was a science professor. We had children, a good life. After he died, I met Nathan. We've had fun together. So many good things have been part of my life. I am grateful for that."

Below us two men rushed down from the hotel; the crowd parted to let them through. Greta didn't seem to notice. We sat on the patio; she spoke of how she and Nathan had met, how they'd decided not to marry, since she had three children from her first marriage, a son who was a doctor, and five grandchildren. She talked and talked until her voice, never very strong, grew constricted and faltering. But her life had opened up before me, a warm ordinary life. She said nothing about the camps. Unlike Sonja, she seemed to have no bitterness.

She asked about Sonja and me, about our life in the U.S. I said, "My mother was sometimes difficult for me to understand, and sometimes seemed a little out of control. I was glad when she found Josef. Her anger seemed to dissipate; and later, when I left home to travel, I thought she was relieved."

"Anger is a place we go in order to survive, Karin. I think you are angry too."

I drew in my breath. Greta was sitting very still, her eyes closed.

Below us on the beach, men and women were running up and down shouting; several were waving. The crowd moved back and we saw that a man was lying on the ground. I stood up to see what was happening. He was blond, handsome, wore a white shirt and long pants. He wore wearing shiny dress shoes.

Greta rose and went inside the room. A moment later, I heard a moan and followed her. She'd fainted across a chair. I helped her to bed. She sighed and lay back against the pillows, kissed her fingers and touched my forehead. I was dismissed. She wanted me to call no one.

I didn't run down to join the crowd on the beach. I didn't want to find out who the man was. I'd already recognized Peter Baden and thought he was probably dead. So I went in the opposite direction, out on my friend the empty road, this time walking in a different direction – past the hotel up to the casino which looked far shabbier in the bright of day than at night. I was half expecting to see Sonja leave or arrive in a taxi, but she didn't appear.

I ate dinner alone. I wanted to think of, and pray for, Greta. I didn't go to the front desk, and ask about the latest dead body; I didn't sit with strangers and make polite conversation; I didn't call Irene. Nor did I search for Sonja or Desmond. Instead I sat, ate shrimp, drank a glass of wine, then went back to the room and read the last of 'Sense and Sensibility'. The silence of our room seemed profound, so I wrote memories in my diary.

Sonja clearing the table, brushing her hand across and everything flying off -papers, pencils, my book. Shouting: "Leave the room." I argued with her about World War II. Stupid ridiculous arguments, but I was just fourteen, full of book information about events my mother had experienced first-hand. Yet her experiences were one person's; she didn't particularly have a sense of the political machinations, the personalities of those who engaged in the politics and directed the war, beyond what she'd learned in Prague before the camp. I'd decided she was in a time machine and was determined to bring her up to date. We argued that fourteenth year, until she silenced me through increasingly violent responses. Later, older and at university, I deliberately asked her questions I knew she couldn't answer, told her flatly she was only educated in her own pain. Finally she gave up attempts at intelligent arguments. Instead she turned on me with tears across her face, or with angry words, while I went on stupidly poking, prying, delivering opinions. Yet I knew through it all, that she loved me.

I closed the diary, lay down on my bed. This memory was hard to accept - how stupidly cruel I'd been. Young yes, but somehow determined to change her. Why? When I owed her so much? Finally, after asking God for forgiveness, I fell asleep.

I'd told my mother several times how rude I thought I'd been, but she'd always waved me away.

Friday Night, Day 13

Once again I'm by the pool. The moon is out, low over the horizon. Dusk here is almost non–existent. The evening quite suddenly descends.

No sign of Mama. I thought we were eating dinner together. Usually we have a drink somewhere and then go to dinner. But she didn't come back to the room to dress, and I looked for her everywhere and no luck. I don't remember her saying anything about going away from the hotel. I'm worried. It's not like her.

The smell of the pool is really raw tonight. Is there something rotting in the water? But it isn't exactly a rotting smell - more one of healthy decay, of old dead plants. I never did dig up the case again – too much time spent looking for Mama. Walking around I heard people talking about 'another drowning victim'. But I don't believe it - that close to shore; he'd have to be a rotten swimmer. The water's so shallow there!

I didn't talk to anyone. But I did start thinking maybe Mama not showing up has something to do with Peter Baden's death. Isn't that horrible? Why do I think that way? That she might have done it? Maybe he isn't even dead. Maybe some doctor saved him. They covered him with a blanket when they carried him away. Oh he's dead all right. It's getting too dark to write. I can barely hear the band. Is there a dance tonight? I'd like to be dancing with Desmond. I like his body, the way it feels against mine.

That evening I wrote in my diary in the half-light for over an hour, growing more and more moody. The slightly rotting odor of the pool seemed to cling to me. I despised myself. Why did suspicion of Sonja so often erupt in me? She was my mother.

Why not first think that she too might have been attacked? Or about my own safety? Instead, I thought maybe she'd killed Marian, and then had to kill Peter Baden too. Was it because I knew the kind of anger that sometimes rose up in her, that I condemned her? But hadn't I just felt the same kind of murderous rage? Then I thought. Could these be memories from the camp that I'd suppressed? A horrible thought but I couldn't let it go. Did I remember the striking of others? Did I remember a killing of someone? Violence happened in the camps because most people were beaten down by fear, and hunger and cold. But then again, I'd read too much about all the camps. What were my memories of ours, and what had I read, or learned from others, especially Sonja?

There were others who might want to kill Peter Baden. He'd had an accident, one in which he'd narrowly escaped serious injury. He was engaged in a controversial activity – buying native art. What about Roberto? He'd been the object of one attempted murder, and victim of another. He'd been indignant about the loss of native art. What linked all the dead together? How could four deaths – for I hadn't forgotten the pool technician – be simply coincidence? I knew so little about the Hotel Madre Maria, I had nothing to go on, no answers. I was sure Desmond knew more than I, but he too had disappeared that day. Yet I wasn't the least bit worried about him.

I heard a faint sound. Someone had come into the garden and sat down in a chair on the other side of the pool. I strained to see who it was. The air was mouse grey and thick, the same atmosphere as forests at dusk. I thought it was a man and thought probably he'd say something, but there was only silence. From the dining room, the dance music came up in volume and then abruptly stopped. The band was taking a break. I waited but still no acknowledgement from across the pool. "Hello." I said loudly, keeping my voice non-committal.

"Nice night." A man's voice - light-toned and flat.

"Yes."

"I live up the beach." Not a warm voice but one I thought I'd heard before. It was odd talking to someone who mingled so completely with darkness. We said nothing more for long minutes. Around us the evening continued to deepen and our silence seemed to rise directly from the pool's waters. "Have you something to give me?" His words were a noose around my neck.

"I beg your pardon."

"Have you something to give me?"

My heart beat faster. "I don't know what you mean."

"I think you do. You have a cosmetic kit."

"I don't know what you're talking about." I stood up "I should go. Good night."

"That's too bad." The neutral voice didn't challenge, but wasn't the least bit soothing either. "I believe you have it."

"Why would I have your kit?"

"Just an idea."

"If you mean my mother's case, why would I give it to you?"

"So you do have it."

"My mother might sell it to you; I'll ask her."

"Sure go ahead. Ask her." I saw a dark shape across the way move. The man walked around the pool toward me, just as I moved quickly toward the exit, very certain by then that I wanted to be far away. Instead, I was suddenly reckless. "How much is it worth to you?"

He'd paused, was standing by the entrance of the garden that led into the hotel.

"Let us think about it." I was speaking faster and faster, "I'll tell you tomorrow. I'll ask her. Tell me your name and how to contact you and I'll let you know what my mother wants to do." I took step after baby step backwards toward the other entrance.

"Of course, I'm at your convenience - as always." The tone was polite, the voice wooden, but thick with contempt, and suddenly he was at my back, grabbing my hand and arm, pulling me around to face him. "Good night," he said and pushed me violently backwards into the pool. Caught off guard, I could do nothing but yell and pull my head up out of the water. I landed in the middle of the pool where the water was deep enough to allow me to dog paddle, but I had to spit out the brackish water; the taste wouldn't leave my mouth, nor the smell. Fortunately, I'd missed hitting the hidden boxes at the deeper end of the pool.

Jason stood back. I thought it was Jason though I couldn't see his face in the darkness. I tried to paddle down to the end closest to the annex exit, but Jason was walking along the edge of the pool following me. Yes, it was Jason – the same build of body, the same haircut. "Nothing will happen if you give it to me."

"A lot of people want that case. Why?" I'd reached the stairs at the far end, and was struggling up them. He rushed down to meet me, arriving just in time to put his foot on my neck, but I pulled back and he stamped on my hand instead. I was flooded with pain and shrieked. He pushed me back into the foul water again, this time against the fiber glass boxes. They provided enough support so I was able to grab his ankle and try to pull him into the water. We struggled. He was cursing. I yanked his ankle hard and pulled him forward enough so that he slipped and sprawled into the water, and across the boxes. There was a hard, flat slap of sound and a cry of pain from him. He lay still just long enough for me to half swim, half walk in the water to the stairs. I was up them before he could follow, and was out of the garden, walking, than running toward the annex, dripping wet and aware, for the first time, of bruises on my shoulders and side. Behind me I heard Jason still cursing. He was probably climbing out of the pool. What he didn't know was how close he was to the cosmetic case, which lay in the lilies a few feet away.

The air beyond the garden was warm and friendly; the sound of the waves a lure and a challenge; the sea smell a constancy and consolation, but I still had the taste of the pool in my mouth. As I walked out of the threat and into our room, everything seemed changed. I saw that waiting out the countdown to a murder investigation was more than worrying about my mother. I had to protect myself. I was under attack now. But I was angry too. For the first time not just afraid, but angry, and discovering that anger overwhelmed and suppressed fear. Surprisingly I was angry not only at Jason, but at Desmond and my mother. Where were they? As I approached the annex, I saw a light was on in his room. And our door was open. Sonja and Desmond were sitting in uneasy companionship on my bed. Sonja rose when she saw me. So did Desmond.

"You are wet, Karin. A late swim?"

"I wouldn't call it that, Mama."

"Are you ready?"

"For what?" I growled. I was dripping on the floor in front of the closet. I grabbed my dressing gown.

"To go to the casino; we were going there tonight. Your friend is going with us."

Desmond said, "I invited myself along."

"He didn't think you'd mind," Sonja was offended, but I didn't care. I gave a brief explanation that I'd had an accident. I didn't say anything about Jason. I didn't want Sonja to know. And I wasn't sure what I would tell Desmond.

"Are you all right, Karin?" Desmond was watching my face.

"Yes. Just let me put on dry clothes." I picked out white slacks and a white t-shirt both of which, after two weeks, weren't particularly white any more.

"Do you want to eat?" Sonja played with her bracelets.

"No. I ate already." I sounded as sulky and cross as I felt.

"I am starved. I will eat at the casino. The food there is not so bad."

I went into the bathroom, put on the dry clothes, blotted on lipstick, combed my wet hair. Dark hair, dark eyes, a flushed frightened look – I didn't look that bad. Was it once again excitement? I still felt startled, even shocked by the attack, but in the middle of the biggest mess of my life, I was busy observing myself. Sonja wandered in. "You do not look good, Karin. And those pants are too tight."

"I'm not changing again, Mama. How's your friend Jason?"

"Why do you say that - your friend Jason? Jason is not my friend, Karin."

"Let's go ladies." Peeking out, I saw Desmond standing by the door.

As we joined him, Sonja announced with a carefulness that deceived no one, "Greg called."

"Thanks." I smiled at Desmond, then at her, but not with the same smile. "How's Dr. Herchmer these days, Mama?" By then we were out in the hall. "And Greta?"

"I have a key, Karin. You do not need yours." She locked our door, "Your husband was not in Boulder."

"I know that, Mama." My voice was smooth and polite, and very thin.

"Greta does not open her door. I have not seen Nathan today. He is with her I think, because she is so ill. Where is Greg?"

"Ask him." I said. We were outdoors, in the dark; Desmond moved up beside me and held on to my elbow, which gave me a little jolt of happiness. "What happened?" Desmond was concerned, even if Sonja wasn't.

"I was shoved into the pool. By Jason."

"Do you want to report him?"

"No, because I shoved him back in too." By unspoken consent, we were walking the long way into the hotel - out on the beach, then into the door near the outside bar. Sonja was leading the way.

"Greg wants to talk to you." Sonja sounded pleased. "Very important he said. He said not to call him tonight, he's not at home."

We were out in the delicious night air, the sea smell and band music drifting in. What a difference to be walking with others! Desmond's truck was parked in front of the hotel. We drove the short distance to the Casino Royale, which sat on a spit of land north of the hotel, and walked into noise, bright lights, and the clanging jangle of casino coin and machine clatter. It was only the second time I'd been there, and I hoped the last; the huge room and its noise were like a blow. While Sonja ate a plate of fish and chips, Desmond and

I held hands under the table; then for an hour sat on stools watching my mother feed nickels and quarters into machines. She won $100, lost $200, won $75 back. By then, we were all too tired to talk, but I was the happiest I'd been all day.

I'd always thought casino gambling was one of the most mindless human activities ever devised and, for that reason, highly seductive. I'd read Dostoevsky! I tried out this theory on Desmond and Sonja; but he looked blank and ordered a beer, while Sonja impatiently waved me away from the machine she was feeding. After an hour, however, she declared herself bored. We drove back to the hotel. There was a light on in a room next to Desmond's. Someone new had checked in. Sonja opened our door. "What about a nightcap?" Desmond asked.

"No. I will see how Greta is." announced Sonja.

"Are you crazy, Mama?" I said at once. "It's too late for you to be out alone." She put on a shawl and went out. Minutes later, Desmond and I faced two large margaritas and each other. It was close to midnight and the terrace bar was almost empty. I noticed one man sitting alone at a table. It was Carl. He looked up and caught my eye, but refused to acknowledge me. Desmond rose to go to the restroom and, as soon as he was gone, I got up and approached Carl's table. The breeze was blowing in from the sea like a siren call. Carl held a Spanish coffee mug in one meaty hand and looked at me with hostility. I sat down opposite him. He scowled. "What do you want?"

"To say hello. And ask you a question."

"No. Go away. You are trouble."

"It would give me a direction. That's always useful. Who killed Marian?" "Go away, Mrs. Carter."

"Call me Karin. What if I said I'll give you an address book."

"Do I want an address book?" He looked at me with dangerous eyes. I shrugged and tried my best to look nonchalant, saying to myself: *Almost an actress now?* The other half was alarmed: *Are you crazy?*

"Carl, I answered your question. Remember? The one you threw at me when we met walking in the sea. You asked me and I answered you. You owe me. First I want to know if you made your decision. You said you would make a decision."

"It was made for me." He smiled a thin smile and offered me a cigarette, a thin French cigarette from a silver case lying on the table in front of him. I shook my head. He took one and lit it, replaced the cigarette case in his pocket. "Have a nice evening with your friend, Karin. I neglected to express my gratitude for your answer. Now excuse me, I make my own plans."

"Carl, do you know anything about four fiber glass boxes in the swimming pool?" He blinked. I assumed in Carl that demonstrated surprise.

"I do not want to see you hurt. So bold you are. But now that you know about the boxes, it is far more likely I will do exactly that."

"I'm not afraid of you, Carl."

He drew in smoke, yielded it back to the air. "You are a fool then, like Marian." He breathed smoke again. "Your friend is coming back, your great friend and Marian's ex-husband. Did you know that, Karin? That he and I shared the same bed?"

"Yes. I knew." He blinked. I turned to see Desmond headed our way and spoke more rapidly. "I will give you the address book if you tell me what the boxes are doing in the pool and who killed Marian."

"They are full of antiques - antiques and Indian relics of great worth that have been exported illegally from several countries. Illegal to export, but labeled as souvenirs. Worth a great deal so a good investment."

It was I that blinked. "Do you know who murdered Marian?"

"Was she murdered? Frieda filled Marian's pockets - Barbiturates, Valium, enough street junk to kill anybody. Marian drank too much too. She could never do both. Did my sweet red head know what she was doing?" He shrugged, "That I can't answer."

Desmond was standing beside us, "Cozy conversation, Carl?"

"This woman is crazy." Carl stubbed out his cigarette.

"I'm beginning to think so. But let me warn you."

Carl stood up. "Yes, yes, Desmond, I know what you say. Let this woman do what she pleases. We have done this scene before. You like to rescue beautiful women." He threw down money and walked away, down the terrace steps. I was afraid to look at Desmond. He said nothing just motioned me to our table where the two margaritas sat. We sipped in silence. The band had quit and the room was silent. "Sorry I was so long - a couple of phone calls. I like to check on my kids now that they are here in Mexico. It's not safe to leave you alone."

"He called me over."

"No he didn't."

"I'm glad you can check on your kids."

"I won't be around to rescue you every time, Karin."

"What time does the terrace restaurant close?" I motioned to the empty room.

"Twenty minutes. What were you two talking about?"

"My mother's cosmetic case."

"You should give it to me."

"I don't know what you are up to yet or how long you'll be around, Desmond."

"And what about you, what are you up to, Miss Mouse?" He looked at me, and then that smile. I felt little waves of guilt and silliness bubble away at the edges of my brain. I liked his voice, his eyes, and even the look in them at that moment, which I saw as a new wariness. "Justin attacked you tonight?" He made it sound like I'd made it up.

"Yes."

"Why?"

"He pushed me into the swimming pool. He was trying to force me to give him Sonja's cosmetic case. He called it 'a kit' But he really wants the diary in it, as do several other people.

"Diary? Your mother's?"

"No, a list of names and addresses everyone seems to want. It may have been dropped there by Marian. She apparently found the case which my mother had lost, or left behind at the bar. That's all I know. I haven't said anything to the police yet, though maybe I should. We're leaving, I think, this weekend."

Caution was still in those blue gray eyes, but also now a fine edge of tension.

"When did this attack happen? What were you doing?"

"Sitting by the pool."

"Alone?"

"I'm not used to being important enough to attack. Anyway, Jason asked for the case. I don't know his last name. He works at the casino."

"You don't seem very frightened."

I hesitated. "My mother knows him. He's a friend of Dr. Herchmer."

"A friend."

"I'm worried it has something to do with Sonja."

"More likely it's to do with you. You're pretty cozy with the Federales."

We finished our drinks. The dining room was closed, the waiters moving around with tired grace. We got up to go.

"Peter Baden's body was taken into town by the police." I said.

"I heard that."

"Carl wants the case too. What do you think I should do?"

He looked away, at the bar man who was cashing out. "Why do they want the damn thing? And how did they find out you had it?"

"How could Marian get the list? I assumed she put it there. But maybe someone else did that to frame her."

He stood up. "Let's look at it. Where is it?"

I hesitated. Should I tell him? "I wondered about Frieda. Maybe she found out I had it. Maybe she's left already.

"Frieda's with Carl at his place. Are you going to tell me where the case is?"

"Not tonight. I'm too tired. It's a little complicated. Tomorrow."

"O.K. We'll get it in the morning. Now go to bed." I bristled a little. Who was he to tell me what to do? But it had been a long day. Yawning, two waiters were doing a last clearing and setting of tables. Glancing over at us, they clearly wanted us to go, but somehow I couldn't quite leave, and so stood briefly at the edge of the terrace reminding myself of the smell and sound of the sea. I would soon have to leave it. Desmond came to stand beside me. Gently, he touched the small of my back. "You like it here."

"Yes." I felt tears come. "Mostly it's the sea. I like Mexico too."

"I've lived here for two years, off and on. My children like it too."

"This is all I've seen – this hotel."

"I'd like to show you Mexico City." He turned away; walked toward the hotel. "I take time off now to see my kids. If I'm not here, be careful, Karin, please."

I walked after him. "Sometimes being careful feels like death."

We walked beside the terrace, then back into the hotel, through the lobby.

"What makes you come back, Desmond?"

"You," he said still not looking at me. "I need to keep an eye on you."

"Isn't that a bit dangerous?" He didn't reply. I stopped at the front desk, found a note. Irene had telephoned again. Would I call her as soon as possible? I tucked the note away. I didn't want to break the mood with Desmond and didn't want to think about Irene. We walked along the path between the hotel and the annex. Part of me never wanted to go in, to be tamed – the self that ran at night, who sang and loved in secret. That part seemed especially precious that night. We parted at the door. Desmond looked serious, even sad. It had become too complicated: too many people, ideas, principles, secrets separated us. I whispered goodnight and unlocked my door.

Inside the room Sonja lay motionless. Usually she left the bathroom light on but that night the room was dark. I stood slightly uneasy in the middle of the room, testing the space. It felt different somehow. "Mama," I whispered. She didn't answer, didn't stir. "Mama" - my voice was louder then. Still, she didn't stir. SONJA, Sonja, WAKE UP. Still, she didn't stir. And then I thought – suddenly and with great certainty – She is dead. Immediately I felt hysterical. I could not imagine my mother would ever die. In my small world, in my childhood, she was the foundation; nothing went back further back than she. To suddenly believe she was dead that night in Mexico was devastating. *A straight railway track. I was looking down the track. It unwinds like yarn. It leads somewhere. Mama said so. But Mama wasn't holding my hand. She was with someone else. It's dark on the train. I'm afraid. Afraid she's dead. She can't be dead. I can't lose her, I can't live without Mama.* A rush of old thoughts, old memories, old fears seemed to engulf me. I stood in the center of the room, trembling. A car drove down our quiet road, lights flashing briefly through into our window. SONJA. I let her name drop into the well of silence that was our room. Then I whispered, Mama, Mama wake up. Did she lie floating in a secret pool, escaped, tranquil. Oh God I was thinking. Oh God, God. I was afraid to walk over to her bed, afraid I would find her dead there. I walked across the dark room to open our door; was banging on Desmond's. No answer. Then he was there, wearing only pajama shorts.

"What's wrong?"

"Sonja."

"What's happened?" He came out into the hall.

"I can't wake her."

"She's in bed?"

"I don't know. I'm afraid to look." I was unwinding into the cocoon of calm he seemed to create in me, but still full of irrational fear. Has she disappeared. How could she disappear? How did I know she wasn't there?

"Anyone else in the room?" Startled, I looked at him again. I had not thought to look around, had not turned on a light. "I don't know.

I know that's crazy. I was too afraid to look at her bed. No, I don't think so."

"Stay here. I'll check." He left me standing outside his room. I stepped inside it. My thoughts were intense and despairing. I held out my hand -.an old trick, from the hospital. Yes, I am still here. I can see my hand. Now alone in this stranger's room, I have two certainties: the sound of my own frightened breathing, and my hands. Memories come like flashes of lightning, brief and stark and illuminating. They seem to rush through and past me. But are they real?

Desmond came back into the room. "No sign of anyone. Come, I'll show you." He took my hand and led me across the hall, turned on the light beside my mother's bed. It was empty, untouched.

"This is ridiculous Desmond."

"She's not here. I'll go up to the front desk and alert them."

"Desmond, I am ridiculous."

"No, you aren't. Something big is going on, Karin. You and Sonja, and my dead ex wife have been caught up in it. But are you all right?"

"No. No, Desmond, I'm not. My mama, Desmond, my mama…"

And I was crying, holding on to Desmond who helped me sit down. I turned off his light. I felt so ordinary croaking away like a child, but it felt delicious to sob my heart out with a sense of loss. I was not alone; a man's warm sure body was touching mine, his arms were around me. How long had it been since Greg had held me? I hugged Desmond and went on crying for my mother, and what she had experienced and done all those years ago; for an end, too, of confusion and anger and doubt; crying for the first days at the Madre Maria, their simplicity, and my discovery of running at night by a glorious sea, and the fact that I must leave it all, and those I cared for.

We drew apart. I looked at him. In the dark he looked strong, confident. Was he really as sure as all that? But his masculine act was a good one. I loved his voice, warm and enthusiastic. "You'll see, Karin. It'll come together. It'll make sense." Someone beside Sonja was in my life. We were already somehow connected. I had a delicious feeling of belonging to someone again. I wanted him. I shivered with the thought. "I have an idea." Desmond said in a soothing voice. "Let's go back to your room and look around." I shrank a little, a tiny gesture of refusal that was based more on the pleasure of leaning against him than upon good sense.

We walked into the other room; he opened the window, let the curtains blow in the breeze. Sonja's bed was still empty. He paused a moment, gave my hand a squeeze, then let go, walked across to shut the door and turned on the overhead light. The room, stark, uneven, empty, sprang out at us - not an exotic room – the furniture ordinary, only the one obligatory picture of a Mexican boy with blank eyes. But on the bedside table under the window lay a white envelope. I walked over and picked it up. My name was on it in Sonja's handwriting.

"It's from my mother." Desmond came to stand beside me. Once again, I indulged myself and leaned against him, then tore open the letter and pulled out a single sheet of Sonja's writing paper. But I didn't want to read it.

"It's all right, Karin." Desmond said. "Do you want me to read it first?"

I realized with some surprise that he thought it was a suicide note. The thought that Sonja had killed herself never occurred to me. I could not imagine such an act by her. Not after she'd survived the camps.

"It could be bad news."

"No, Desmond." I touched his cheek. "My mother is a survivor. She believes she must prove her victory over death. She's told me that."

I read the letter. There were only a few lines hastily written.

Dear Karin, I am sorry to alarm you this way. Do not worry. I agreed to help Nathan with Greta. She wants to die at home and Nathan believes her children will want to be with her. He needs help with the journey to New York. She's close to death and very weak. There is a midnight flight direct to New York City tonight so I've left with them, without returning to find you. I will be away only a day or so; I hope you'll stay on until Monday and my return. I'll pay the costs. Everything is all right. It is that I promised to help him. You remember once or twice before I left you this way, and no harm has ever come of it. I love you my darling daughter. Mama.

I handed the letter to Desmond and he read it.

"Dr. Herchmer!"

"I don't trust the man." I told him.

"He seemed harmless enough."

"Once or twice – the way he looked at me – something there is not quite what it seems. But I don't trust any doctors now." I sat down on my bed, suddenly weary. "What time is it, Desmond?"

He looked at his watch, sat down beside me. "One-fifteen"

"I am tired. I am sorry about Greta. She's a lovely woman."

"Go to bed." He rose, turned off the bedside lampand paused by the door. "Your mom's o.k. Sonja's a smart woman."

"Is she?" My voice was bitter. She'd left like that without warning before – Michael, Josef, one or two others. 'I'm making up my mind.' she'd say. It was usually an affair of the heart that forced Sonja outside her usual caution. But what did she mean by 'help Nathan'?

"Would you like me to sleep in here?"

My confusion must have shown in my face.

"I can sleep on your mother's bed."

"I'd like that," I said. Confusion blurred into relief; I didn't want to be alone.

"I'll get my things." He disappeared across the hall. A thought struck me. Curious, I rose and walked down the corridor to the other newly occupied room. There was a light on under the door but I heard nothing when I pressed my ear to it. I tip toed back, and a minute later Desmond came in wearing a pajama top over his shorts. Without a word, he turned off the light and lay down on Sonja's bed. I did the same on mine. For a moment we were silent.

"Desmond. I wonder if you'd come and hold me for a few minutes. I don't want anything more than that, honestly I don't, but...I 'm afraid."

He was already beside me as I said these words; his strong arms went around me and I lay encircled by his warmth and his concern. Soon, I felt a rise of desire but I fought my own, turned on my side; my back was to him. "Goodnight, Desmond."

"Night," His voice was already wandering.

The blue marble, the feel of it in my hands at night. Blue was the smoothness of water, blue was the perfection of round; blue was the sky that I remembered, that contained the whole world. In the hospital I could fall sleep when I thought of blueness.

*   *   *   *   *

Darkness was fading outside the window. Not long before sunrise, I got up, walked over to the hotel where the night clerk sat reading in the office behind the front desk. I saw the clock – four a.m. in Mexico, seven a.m. in New York.

She would be up.

After we murmured sleepy pleasantries I was blunt.

"What's going on, Irene? Why did you call?"

There was a pause, an empty crackling line.

"Are you still there? Irene?"

"Yes."

"Why did you call?"

"I have to tell you something, Karin."

"What? It's the middle of the night here. I started to worry that I hadn't returned your call, Irene. You said as soon as possible. What's wrong? Is there something wrong?"

Another pause – then her voice – weak, subdued, not at all the confident Irene.

"You need to know something, Karin."

"O.K."

"I sent the letter."

"What letter?"

"Your mother got a letter from Mexico."

"I know that."

"I sent it."

It was my turn to leave the line open and empty.

"It was an old letter I found among Josef's papers. Sonja gave them all to me without looking at them. It was a twenty years old letter. I erased the date. He must have kept it from her – my dad. He'd resealed it with scotch tape. But he didn't throw it out. Maybe guilt, I don't know. When I saw it, I thought – that'll get her in the chops. She took Josef's love, took his money - I got next to nothing - a pile of old letters and photographs of my mom and me. So I changed the date and sent the letter. Have you seen it? Do you know what's in it?"

I had a sore pit in my stomach – anger or grief, I didn't know which.

"Yes, if you mean one from somebody claiming to know a Nazi refugee. Irene, let me get this straight. I'm sorry if I'm stupid but it's the middle of the night here. You sent Sonja a letter that was twenty years old, so Sonja would come to Mexico believing the man was seeking help."

"I didn't know she'd go to Mexico. I was pretty sure the man must be dead and I wanted to needle her. I was angry. I am so sorry you both got into such a mess. You are in a mess aren't you?"

"Yes."

"What's going on?"

"Sonja's on a wild goose chase. She's having fun I can tell you that. There's no desperate German refugee as far as I know." I didn't feel like telling Irene about the long lost lover. "But there has been a German tourist murdered and I found the body."

"I never expected you'd get into trouble with it. I am so sorry."

"What do you want me to do, Irene? Do you want me to tell her?"

Long, long pause. Then a timid voice from my stepsister, "I don't know. It's whatever you think is best. Should she know?" The anger I felt was because I'd always tried to stay out of the warfare between Sonja and Irene.

"Listen, right now I'm going back to bed. I've been up most of the night."

"I'll talk to her if you think it's necessary."

"Let me think it over, Irene, O.K? Goodnight." I staggered back to the room. Desmond was sprawled across Sonja's bed. Retreating to my own bed, I fell asleep.

Saturday, Day 14

I woke just after seven. The light was truthful and calm, the room, warm. Waking early by then was a habit I could not break. I looked across at Sonja's bed, and for a moment struggled to remember. Desmond still lay sprawled on his back asleep. Concern for my mother came flooding in. The cure for that anxiety, I knew, was to get up and do something physical. At home, I would rise and do housework, or in the summer go outside and garden. In Mazatlan, I'd been walking or running on the beach. Perhaps that was what I should do. But I found, lying there, that I liked looking at Desmond who certainly wasn't looking back. He was deeply asleep, like Sonja, mouth open. He was so big, so good looking. I felt lucky he was there.

I rose and tiptoed into the bathroom, brushed my teeth and washed. When I came out in a few moments, I saw that he'd had shifted slightly but hadn't wakened. I put on a sweatshirt and shorts but stopped half dressed, and once again considered him. How comfortable I felt with him, as though we'd known each other for years. Another complication, I thought yanking on shorts. Will he worry if he finds me gone? I took a pencil from the rickety table drawer and scribbled a note suggesting breakfast in an hour. I promised not to walk beyond the boundaries of the hotel. Just like I used to do for my mother - I couldn't help smiling. Would he really worry in the same irrational way she always had? Or did I simply hope he would.

Then I was outside, free. The sun was sharp and bright; the sea smells strong. An overwhelming sense of freedom flooded in. Houses and rooms were prisons. I ran on the beach, and then walked back, exulting in the seagulls that wavered and soared and complained above me. There were others out early that morning. It was Friday, a day when guests knew they'd soon be going home. I tiptoed into the water, a cool caress, and thought with pleasure that the sea will never be taken from us. Just as the child cannot supplant the mother, because the mother comes before the child, the sea came before us. But soon worry thoughts returned.

If only Sonja had not gone off in such a crazy way. How could she be helping Nathan Herchmer? Doing what? Turning around I saw up the beach, Desmond wearing shorts and a t-shirt striding down the beach toward me. I waved.

"Coffee," he growled, "And breakfast."

"Desmond, why did she go off – my mother? How can she help Dr. Herchmer? Help him do what? He's a dentist. Maybe he'll give her a job."

Desmond pointed to his open mouth, "Breakfast." He led me firmly away from the water, up onto the terrace, pushed me into a chair and sat down opposite.

"I'm starving," I said happily. Much too happily for someone who had just lost a mother. Somehow at that moment, I felt overwhelmingly confident that Sonja was all right, that everything was all right. Greedily I sucked down my coffee. Desmond refused to speak, but lit a cigarette, then forced two coffees down. He was a big man, virile; everything he did seemed open, even overwrought. And yet I still didn't know much about him. He didn't talk about himself. But then, did I talk about myself? That seemed to be what we had in common.

With our eggs, the waiter brought a newspaper to Desmond. That must be his ritual – Desmond's - coffee and eggs on the terrace reading the paper. I ate mine and looked out to sea. Why did I feel more companionship with a man I'd known a week than with my husband of fifteen years? And where was that husband? Why had he told the girls he was coming to Mexico? Why had I ordered eggs when I rarely ate them? Nothing made sense anymore. Desmond looked up from his paper.

"You should inform Captain Hernandez that Sonja is gone."

"Yes, I suppose so." I didn't look forward to talking to Captain Hernandez.

"First talk to Senor Moreno, the manager. He can notify the police." He went back to his paper.

"That's a good idea."

"And you can tell the police about me. You can even quote me."

"What do you want me to say?"

"Let's talk after we eat."

A half hour later, we sat back and looked at each other. He lit another cigarette.

"I know something about Marian. It may or may not be relevant but you can be the judge. You saw her body. Tell me if the police should know."

I was relieved because it had nothing to do with Sonja, and curious. Also flattered that he thought I could make a judgment call.

"She was pregnant – Marian."

Shocked I sat back, stared at him.

"Pregnant? How do you know?"

"She told me." He said simply. He waved the waiter over and signed the check.

"She wanted me to help her keep the baby. She didn't want an abortion. I said no. I said she was already a lousy mother, and didn't

need another kid to abandon. We had a fight. She called me names."
He sat back, looked at me. "It wasn't my kid."

"When was this?"

"A couple of nights before her death; our first conversations were about that."

"What are you going to do?" I drank the last of my coffee. Tried not to judge a woman I didn't know.

"Maybe I was wrong. That's what I think. You saw her body."

"Untouched," I said gently, responding to his distraught look. "Beautiful and calm. Go with me to the police interview today."

He shook his head. "No. I have to collect my truck. It's in Mazatlan. And I did have business in Mexico City so I'll make some phone calls to postpone that if I can. If I get back in time I'll go with you. But tell the manager right away that I need to talk to the police."

In an hour it was done - promises were made by Senor Moreno, but as I stood in the lobby with him, I saw Greta Herchmer head for the desk, followed by a porter carrying two suitcases. Immediately I was alarmed. Where was Nathan? My mother?

"That's Mrs. Herchmer." I said to Senor Moreno. He looked up with practiced non-committal calm.

"Yes."

"I thought she left."

"Her husband did. Excuse me, Senora, I have work to do." He went into his office and closed the door.

I walked over, spoke to her. "Greta."

She gave me a quick, startled hunted look. Her face was drawn, haggard.

"I thought you'd left."

"I was too ill to go last night." She said in a throaty reluctant voice. She moved to the front desk. I followed her. The slender clerk was busy with a Canadian man checking out with maddening deliberation. Greta and I had to wait him out. I reached over to hold her hand.

"Is something wrong Greta?"

She looked at me, pain in her eyes. "Nathan and Sonja left for New York last night. Your mother took my seat. I do not know why she wants to go. I don't need her help. My children will meet my plane."

She dropped her handbag and crumpled against the desk. I grabbed her arm to keep her from falling. Even the clerk was traumatized into coming over.

"Is Madam ill?"

She nodded her head. I helped her back to a small couch against the far wall.

"I'll get the doctor," The clerk vanished into the manager's office.

Face drawn, Greta sat slumped against me. I put my arm around her, felt her thinness. She was much frailer than I'd thought.

"Did you know about my mother?"

She nodded her head; her eyes were full of tears. "But not until last night. They made these plans without me."

"My mother left a note saying she'd agreed to help Nathan take you back." "Oh my god," the words were wrenched out of her. "I didn't want her to go." She looked at her hands. "He's mad - foolish, extravagant, a liar. Your mother…"

"Is she in any danger?"

"I don't know. He's changed. Something… forgive me…I will wait in my room." She rose. The desk clerk waved to the sturdy bellhop and he helped her into the elevator.

* * * * *

Captain Hernandez was the same. Silent and unsmiling, he sat behind his makeshift desk, the chairs he'd chosen for both of us as severely straight backed as before, in the middle of a small dining room in Hotel Madre Maria, He still made me nervous, but that morning I had Desmond with me. He'd changed his mind, changed his plans, had come with me.

"I've brought a friend, Captain Hernandez."

"A lawyer?" His tone was one of disapproval, his glance icy.

"No. A friend."

Uninvited, Desmond sat down in another straight-backed chair close to Captain Hernandez. "I have an interest in the case," Desmond said, and stood up again to walk over and hold out his hand, which the Captain took with reluctance. "Desmond Nicholson."

"Good afternoon," Captain Hernandez said coolly. "What interest do you have, Mr. Nicholson?"

Desmond sat down. "I knew Marian Eissel intimately."

"Oh?" The word was neutral, but Captain Hernandez straightened in his chair.

"Here? Did you know her here?"

"Here, there, everywhere."

"You are a clever man, Mr. Nicholson."

"Not really. If I were clever I wouldn't be standing in front of you."

"You are not standing, you are sitting. Do you wish to speak to me alone?"

"Mrs. Carter and her mother had nothing to do with Marian's death. They had no reason to harm her. They didn't even know her."

"Ah." Captain Hernandez raised two immaculate shoulders, "You are an expert on the case I see. We will talk, Mr. Nicholson. Mrs. Carter, I must ask you to leave."

I took out Sonja's letter, rose to go. Desmond stood up too. I paused in front of the desk. "My mother, Captain Hernandez, I'm concerned about her."

"Yes," Captain Hernandez's looked blank.

"She's left hastily, in the middle of the night. She's with Dr. Herchmer. I don't know where they went or why. Mrs. Herchmer doesn't know either. Mrs. Herchmer is ill and is now on her way home. My mother left me a note."

"Have you the note?"

"Here." I gave him Sonja's letter. After reading it, he looked up at me.

"Do you suspect she is in danger? She was advised she could leave."

"I don't know what to think. I'm worried. They left in the middle of the night, with four murders here."

"Four murders? He stood up, walked to the window. I glanced at Desmond. He was rocking on his heels with speculative dignity.

"A swimming pool repairman, Marian, Peter Baden, Roberto."

"The life guard? Who told you he was dead?"

"One of his helpers."

"His name?" Captain Hernandez had a pen ready but I decided to be vague.

"I don't remember. Should I be worried about Dr. Herchmer? He said he was a Nazi hunter. Are there Nazis here?"

Desmond shot a warning glance at me which the Captain intercepted.

"A Nazi hunter. Yes. Dr. Herchmer frequents various resorts in South America; occasionally he comes to Mexico. He has a list of so-called suspects. He does not belong to any reputable organization, nor is he Jewish. As far as we know he hunts Nazis on his own time, and from his own inclinations."

"Why?" I asked in a near whisper. All I could think was what on earth had Sonja gotten herself into?

"We are not sure. In the past he has denounced them. He does not always find Nazis you understand. Sometimes they are cases of mistaken identity."

Captain Hernandez straightened his papers, tapped them against the table so they were sharply aligned, then shaped them into a neat pile. "Why is your mother with such a man? Foolish perhaps. Or worse. Now then, shall we discuss your acquaintanceship with Marian Eissel, Mr. Nicholson?" Captain Hernandez patted the papers tenderly. Desmond sat down again at the Captain's table. The Captain looked over at me. There was no doubt he wanted me gone, but I was reluctant, took out a note I'd written that morning.

"Wait," I said and walked over to this irritating policeman from Mexico City. "What do you mean foolish or worse?"

The good Captain looked up from his paperwork.

"The last few Nazis that Dr. Herchmer traced died shortly after his visit. Or so it is thought. Some were old men. Germans, Austrians. There is no proof. Only rumor. And rumor..." he shrugged those narrow immaculate shoulders, "Now please, Mrs. Carter, I must excuse you."

I said nothing, simply slipped the folded note on the top of his pile of papers. I knew Desmond was behind me and couldn't see what I'd done. I looked at the Captain and shook my head slightly. He blinked, paused, and then slipped the note under his top paper. As soon as he did that, I left the room.

The rest of the morning, I lay on the beach. I didn't want to do anything but soak up sun and try not to worry about Sonja. I missed her - her chatter, the look of her plump body on the beach, the identification I could make with her as my family. I prayed she was all right. After a lunch alone, I went back to the room to sleep and read but could do neither. My resources were poor - one crummy paperback and a mother who'd vanished. So I called my daughters. Nadine answered the phone. "We're fine Mom, Everything's okay. Aunt Judy is cooking up a storm."

That worried me. Why was Judy, a kind neighbor, cooking at our house? How long did Greg plan to be away? I hung up and wandered around but everything worried me that day: the sea, the sky, the pool - none of them gave pleasure. When I got a message from the front desk that I was wanted on the phone, I rushed over, heart pounding, expecting the worst –and got it.

"I'm up the road," Greg said.

"What?"

"I'm in Mexico."

"Why?"

"To see you. I've rented a car. I'll be there in half an hour. Where do we meet?" Typical. I didn't know if I wanted to meet him but he was planning the time and place.

"On the hotel beach."

He meant it when he said he'd be there in half an hour. I had just enough time to get furious and throw on some beach clothes.

As soon as I saw his crew cut and trim body, I hated him again, hated everything about him – that eternal look of certainty, the fact that he had all the money, and sneered at academic prestige which I could never have. As usual he managed the first verbal blast.

"I broke up an important seminar to come down here because Sonja said you needed help." His face was flushed, his never very attractive eyes narrowed down to hawk sized slits. "Look, Karin, it's over. I want a divorce. I want someone in my life that cares about me – ME - and I've found her."

He was shouting by then; semi-comatose sunbathers all around us were roused up. Like somnolent seals, they lifted their heads in wonder at the two of us standing eyeball to eyeball, toe to toe, shoulder to shoulder. But it was hot work being that angry. I sat down on a beach chair. "I didn't ask you to come down here. I didn't ask for your help."

"You're an attractive woman, Karin, and you're bright, but you're all over the map, chasing things that aren't important. I need someone who spends a little more time on me. ME!" He certainly loved that two letter word. "A little more time" I translated into constant grooming.

"GREG, LISTEN TO ME FOR A CHANGE!"

"Your mother called me. She sounded desperate, said you were trapped here." I sat down on the beach. He remained standing, continued shouting: "YOU ARE THE MOTHER OF MY CHILDREN AND I DON'T WANT YOU TO GO TO PRISON FOR MURDER." He usually didn't like shouting. This must be an emotional state I'd never seen him in before.

The seals definitely had their heads up, now were thrusting up shoulders, balancing themselves awkwardly to get a better look. Abruptly I stood up again, which didn't allow Greg to lord over me.

He was sensitive about being an inch shorter. "Greg, I didn't ask for your help. And I didn't murder anybody."

"I do not care. I'll cross a few palms with silver; you can be out of here tonight And we're divorcing, is that agreed? We can even fill out the paperwork while I'm here."

I picked up a handful of sand; it was dry and hot, I let it pour through my fingers. He was so capable, Greg. I felt odd twinges of gratitude that he was so damn capable, so intelligent. I would never be like that. I would be "all over the map" the rest of my life. He went on talking loudly to the back of my head. "I'll make some money available to you right away. You need some job training, or to finish your degree. O.K. KARIN?"

"O. k."

"I understood from Sonja that you've been threatened. So get yourself out of here. I've booked tickets for you and your mother for Monday afternoon, but you can switch them to tonight if you want to."

"Monday's fine, Greg. Sonja's not here today." I said in a meek, small sized voice. Problems were being dissolved completely - so easily, so permanently - while I played in the sand. A few more days in Mexico, some money to survive on – my heart suddenly leapt with joy and I stood up, walked over and kissed his sweaty cheek. He jumped back. Of course, he didn't know that Sonja was temporarily vanished, that neither she nor I were in danger, nor held against our will anymore, that I was in love with someone else – I didn't think he'd want to know any of that at this point in time. "There have been murders here, Greg; something is going on, something bad."

"So what? Murders are going on everywhere. Get the fuck out of here, Karin. Go home and look after our daughters."

"There's something I have to do first – to make a difference."

"What kind of difference can YOU make?" There it was – the familiar sneer in his voice. At least he wasn't shouting. "You're not about to do anything much but get yourself into further trouble. This is a seedy place and a pretty corrupt bunch of people as far as I can see. I was going to stay at this hotel, but took one look at it and drove us down to the Mazatlan Princess."

"Us?"

"Jane's with me."

"Jane? Your latest?

"My future wife. I've left an envelope with five hundred dollars in it at the front desk. Put it to some use. We'll do the paper work for support for the girls when we get home." He was walking away. I hated him, feared him, and admired him. Some part of me regretted losing forever such a rational, successful, self-obsessed person.

"I have to participate, Greg, don't you understand?" I called after him." I can't walk away from evil when God's put me into the middle of it." He didn't turn around, just snarled, "God! You've put yourself into it. You can walk right on by, Karin." Then he turned around and let fly, and all my regrets vanished. "YOU ARE FUCKED IN THE HEAD!" The beach bodies lifted their heads again. We all watched him walk back toward me looking so furious I became frightened. He'd struck me once or twice. "You are a meddler, Karin. Meddlers are always in trouble. I'm bored getting you out of jams. You're on your own now. God can help you next time."

"He already has." I said in a stiff, stupid, little voice.

"Oh shut up." He turned away again, but I didn't want to let it go. Besides I wanted to make sure that money was waiting for me at the front desk. He'd played that trick before.

"Did you come all the way to Mexico to tell me that and leave?"

He walked back again, teeth clenched with rage. "I came here because I owed it to your mother. She's been decent to me and she's called me twice because she didn't like what was happening to you here. She's doesn't like the men you're playing around with either. But this is it: This is all I'm doing. I'm out of here. See you in court." He marched up the beach toward the hotel.

It was one of those days when the sea seemed to be singing as the waves rolled in. I noticed tears in my eyes and wondered why. Nothing new was happening between Greg and I – just that it was out in the open air. I felt, for the first time, the depth of his hatred for me as well as my own anger at him. I followed him, softened my voice.

"Did you say you had a car, Greg?"

"Yes."

"Would you give me a ride into town?"

"Why go this late in the day?"

"I have to buy some things. No one will know I left the hotel if I go with you."

"Is that a good idea?"

"It's safer. And you said you'd advance me some money."

"You don't need to go shopping."

"I do."

Walking up the beach together, we were still the old married couple, carrying on harassment as an everyday chore. We stepped through the somnolent, once again indifferent to us, and then walked through the hotel.

"I don't think it's a good idea, Karin, taking you into town."

"If I get this shopping done, I might be able to leave tomorrow."

"I can't come to your rescue; I've got other things to do."

I pushed all the buttons. "I need to buy some women's stuff. The hotel shop doesn't have much."

"What kind of stuff?" Wheels were grinding behind the hawk slits. "You don't need Kotex." *Low blow Greg, good thing I don't care.*

"I promised some women here I'd help them look for what they need." Secretly, in my mind, I was pretending what they might 'need'. Greg was embarrassed and annoyed. We were in front of the hotel. I smiled sweetly. "Old women do need special things. These are two sweet old women." I was lying beautifully and was quite proud of myself. Mrs. Jones and Mrs. Allen had already left.

"Oh Christ, get in the car." Greg said. "Here's the money I promised you."

On the way into town we talked about our daughters. Jane, having been left at their hotel, Greg and I were at our best in the closed confinement of the automobile. Early in our years together, we took trips, and our silences and conversation mingled comfortably. Those are my happiest memories of our marriage - the two of us alone in the Valiant, spinning along an empty highway somewhere in the western U.S, Greg holding forth on subjects of interest to him, and I occasionally spilling over with indignation about something political or irrational. Outside on either side of the car, the landscape of hills and valleys and light and high clouds would unfold with breathtaking majesty somehow ennobling us. The landscape in Mexico worked the same magic until we entered Mazatlan that day; then he asked. "Where do you want to go?"

"Anywhere in the center of town - I'll take the hotel shuttle bus back. Thanks Greg." Almost immediately, he pulled over beside a large enclosed market. "See you."

He drove off as soon as I slammed the door shut, bur five minutes later pulled up again beside me on the sidewalk. He turned off the ignition, leaned out the passenger window. "Karin, where the hell is that paper work you were going to do for me, before you left. There was some stats work and typing."

"Greg, our last conversation -you wanted to leave me."

"Forget that conversation. Nothing - it means nothing. I need that paperwork as soon as I get home. I have an important meeting next week. You said it was done."

"Did you ask the girls?"

"They don't know anything."

"Have you looked in the study?"

"I looked everywhere."

"Greg, you want to leave our marriage. I can't be in charge of your projects or your possessions anymore."

"I'd like get myself out from under this mess we call our home. It's so damn disorganized I can't find anything.

"Did you look in your car?"

"Of course I looked."

"In that brief case you decided to keep in the trunk so that important papers wouldn't get mixed up with the girls' homework?" Silence.

"Did you?"

"No."

"Maybe that's where the papers are. Greg, I hope you meant it about our marriage. That it's over."

"Yeah, I'll look in the car. I seem to remember the briefcase was out there."

"Greg. It's over."

"I'll talk to you when you get home." He started the engine, put the car in gear.

"I want to talk now. Here in Mexico. You came all this way."

"I said we'd talk about it when you got home. I'll try to meet your plane."

"No, I want to say it now. I want a different life, Greg. I want to separate, to divorce. I want you to warn the girls."

He closed the side window and drove away.

I found the largest market and wandered for an hour until I found exactly what I wanted - Address books, the same size and black color of my mother's. I bought two. They weren't the same quality as her leather one; were cheap cardboard copies, but who would notice?

Then, just for the fun of it, I bought a third bright red one. I went to a sidewalk restaurant, ordered an icy cold bottle of Mexican beer, and watched the world go by for awhile. How glorious to be in town, to have money again! Feeling reckless, I paid for an early supper, then walked up and down streets until I found a hardware store, where I bought a small camping shovel, a flashlight and batteries, some plastic bags, and a canvas one to carry everything in. Finally I caught the shuttle bus back to the Hotel Madre Maria, and was nearly there when I thought suddenly, why didn't I buy some books to read? I stopped scolding myself - my own life was now as exciting as any book.

Back at the hotel, I tried calling my daughters, but they were both out. Saturday – what did I expect? They had so many activities and enterprises, many friends; but fortunately no serious romances yet. When I hung up the receiver, I walked out into the sunshine. I'd taken the next step. I was going to leave Greg, or he was leaving me. He said so anyway. The kids will be hurt, but maybe not surprised, and the first step, the hardest step had been taken.

At seven I called Irene from the hotel, and asked her to tell me more about the letter she'd found. We shared facts and opinions; soon anger and love came tumbling out as well, because we were sisters.. All she could say was that she'd found the letter unopened among Josef's effects. The envelope had been addressed to Sonja's New York address, with a postmark dated twenty years before, but the letter itself was undated, nor was the signature legible. We speculated about the men and women in the photographs. When I told Irene that Sonja had said Hans was my real father, she sighed.

"Oh, Karin, how horrid - do you believe her? She's such a liar sometimes."

"Why lie about that?"

"You tell me. You know her better than I. But if you ask me liars can't help themselves once they get started." Unable to confess my own new ability to lie for good causes, I shrank inside, but didn't want to let her go when she said goodbye. I hurried to ask about her son, husband and friends all of which she worried about. She was a worrier, Irene. I said good-bye but she wanted to keep talking.

"Karin, take care of yourself. That writer George Eliot said. 'Don't be afraid to be the person you were supposed to be'. Think of yourself as lucky – two families and three fathers."

After hanging up, I wandered back out to the beach, and slept on the sand.

I dreamt Sonja walked up to me blithely smiling, bent down to kiss me as she had so many times returning from an evening out with Michael, or one of her other friends "What were you worried about you silly girl. I had a wonderful time." But Sonja had not returned. Instead Desmond was sitting beside me, hands on knees. He was staring at the paragliding concession. I yawned, sat up. Two men were packing up. I looked at my watch: Six o'clock. "Desmond I'm glad to see you. How was your interview?"

"You're right," Desmond interrupted, "Edwardo is the key. Let's talk to him." "Together? I don't particularly like the man. The key to what?"

"Let's talk to him right now." Abruptly he stood up, then turned to help me, and looked surprised when I wasn't instantly ready. I reached out a hand and he pulled me up.

"Edwardo will know some of those bastards, maybe whether they had anything to do with his buddy's death."

"What bastards? What buddy?"

"My friend Carl, your friend Jason, Roberto"

Edwardo was not happy to see us. He and Desmond spoke together in Spanish then switched to English. "Captain Hernandez -" Edwardo spat on the ground in front of him. I wanted to be away from there, to be the unencumbered tourist of a week ago, away from this growing hotel nightmare of lies and counter lies. But I still cared about who killed Marian Heisel, and whether Edwardo was telling the truth or not. When I asked him, he said only, "Senora, I have no answers for you. Go away, I am busy." He turned back to the paraglider equipment.

"What about your friends?" Desmond asked.

"I have no friends."

"The cosmetic case."

"I don't talk to you."

"We can get it to you – the case." Desmond said then. I pinched his arm but he refused to look at me, instead stared out at the horizon. "I know nothing about that." Edwardo went on rolling up canvas. The beach was nearly empty by then, everyone inside as evening drifted in with the waves.

"We can meet you this evening after dinner and give you the case, if that is what you want it. Or know someone who does." Desmond spoke to no one in particular.

"You want to buy me a drink?" Edward spoke rapidly and glanced at us. He was still squatting on his haunches, face half hidden.

"We would like to buy you a drink." Desmond was still looking out to sea.

Edwardo stood up, "O.K." The words were casual but a change had come into the dialogue, a movement that promised event. "We need some news"

"News?" Desmond said, still speaking to the horizon.

Edwardo's face was blank, insultingly so, "Of the lady."

"What lady?"

"My mother," I said. It was only the second time I'd spoken. "She's gone somewhere with Dr. Herchmer, a guest here."

Edwardo glanced at me, dark eyes in an unsmiling face. "I know nothing of the lady, your mother, or the doctor." He walked closer. "You are careless with them I think."

Desmond moved so that he stood between Edwardo and me and said, "Maybe you have friends who know who are the killers here."

"I have no friends."

"Unhappy man," I said, hoping to sound sarcastic but failing.

"No. I am happy." Edwardo shouldered the canvas and walked away.

So did Desmond – in the opposite direction. It was all so sudden I was left standing in the middle and having to run to catch up with him.

"Do you think he knows anything Desmond?"

"Haven't a clue, but we may see in a day or two, or even tonight."

"Why would they tell us anything?"

"As trade for your famous cosmetic case - which is where?"

The light was already sifting away, into sand, into sea, into trees and buildings. I pretended not to hear. "I'm a little nervous about all this, Desmond."

"Good." He stopped and placed himself in my path. "Now, oh beautiful one, the blasted cosmetic case, where is it?"

I stumbled to a halt. "It's hard to explain. No one knows exactly where it is except me, and I like it that way."

"Are you going to tell me?"

I hesitated. "I buried it."

"Where?"

"Maybe it's safer if only I know."

He came back, took my arm and walked me forward. "No. It is not safer. Little lady, you are in trouble with some mean men."

One last hesitation, then I stammered out "In the garden beside the pool."

"We don't dig up the whole garden do we?"

"Underneath the rubrun lilies."

"Show me."

"Let's have a drink, first." I whined, but he was already striding away.

I'd almost forgotten the lilies. Their scent was familiar by then, as was the smell of the stagnant pool – both reminders of its lure and its threat. In the late afternoon sunshine, the water looked withdrawn, neither sinister nor comforting; but above all dirty and forlorn – an unwashed bag lady of a pool going about some private unappealing life. The lilies were the only flowers blooming; neglect had silenced all the others. I stopped. Desmond halted too.

"Right over there." I said.

"Don't point, tell me quietly."

Really the way he ordered me around was like a parent to a child -
that and the heat, and the melodrama of everything to do with what
was turning out to be weeks in Mexico, had turned me irritable.
"Don't speak to me like I'm a child."

"Don't raise your voice."

"There's nobody here."

"How do you know?"

I walked over to Desmond and took hold of his hand. "I planted
them right at the foot of that big bunch of flowers."

"You did a good job. I never would have guessed."

"Desmond, are we going to dig the case up right now?"

"Tonight, after dinner; first I'll take you to dinner."

I shoved enthusiasm into my voice. "Great idea. But later - I need
to rest."

As soon as we parted, I went back to the room and got the canvas
bag with the shovel, the plastic bags and the extra address books. By
then it was that nicely dim time of day when people scurry inside, or
go to the bar to hide from the spookiness inside them. I know because
I do. I went back to the garden and quickly dug up the nest lilies, took
out the cosmetic case, which wasn't wrapped in anything because I
was not that organized, and removed the black leather address book
full of names and telephone numbers and addresses of people that I
didn't know, but that everyone else seemed to want to get to know.

I put it in my pocket, and then pulled out one of the cheap ones I'd bought, stuck it in the cosmetic case, zipped it up, and then thought of the photographs. Sonja would want to have them back; I'd have to figure out what to tell her.

I unzipped the bag again, took out the photos, then wrapped everything in a plastic bag, and reburied it under the lilies. Poor lilies, I thought, your tender roots are being disturbed. However, they seemed to be thriving. As I walked away I thought: I have a better idea. So I dug up the case again, removed the black address book and put the cheap red one in. Then I planted everything as before.

As I patted the lilies down, I was giggling. They looked so innocent. Thank you darlings, I thought as I left them. Stress was turning me silly. Once back in my room, I wrote Greg's name and university telephone number in the other two black address books and put them back in the canvas bag. I lay on my bed and tried to nap. I was meeting Captain Hernandez in half an hour. He'd left a note at the front desk requesting a meeting as soon as possible. Restless, I decided to go outside and indulge in a communion with the sky, air, the earth – all of which I didn't want to forget. I won't I promised them as I walked around; it was still hot, a rich berry lushness that seemed more inviting than it ever had, now that this day was close to my last. I had felt every kind of emotion toward the Hotel Madre Maria, and all the people and events experienced in it, and now it seemed, I'd become fond of it. Once home, I thought, I will try to recall this, like an old cinemascope movie - the colors of the changing sea, the sharp gleam of sand, the endless ever mounting sky, and all the people and events my mother and I had experienced. I walked slowly, requiring myself to take in memories like snapshots.

Saturday, Day 14, Night

Captain Hernandez was waiting by the hotel's front door. He gave a neat polite perfunctory bow. "Good evening Senora."

"Good evening"

"You wish to speak together for a few moments?"

"Yes." I was determined not to go into his makeshift office, or to sit before his tidy pretend desk. "Can we go somewhere quiet? Outside?"

"Of course."

We went outside. I was leading. It felt odd – the police captain letting me take charge. I walked us into the garden and we sat down in two straight chairs. He shifted his so it was facing mine. The pool was a thick square of black resting beside us. A young couple entangled on a lounger across from us sat up; they waited but when we didn't move on, rose and walked out. Her blouse was unbuttoned and they were holding hands.

I looked up, only a few stars were visible. It was only just dark.

"Senora, I am happy to speak with you for I am troubled."

"So am I." I kept my voice neutral.

"For two weeks you are here and you have done nothing but stir up trouble."

I was surprised. "Me? Stir up trouble?"

"Trouble," he leaned forward, took off his hat, put it on his knee.

"In what way?"

"You have found a body."

"Several." I couldn't resist the cheap shot. "Yes, that was inconvenient wasn't it?"

"In an inconvenient place."

"Inconvenient to whom?"

"To some people."

"The neighbors."

"Yes. But also..." He shifted, slightly but still sat ramrod straight.

I made sure I lolled back in my chair. Desmond had definitely improved my ability to be annoying.

"You have witnessed several acts of violence."

So he did know what happened to Roberto.

"I'm not trying to do all those things. I'd like to remind you that I was attacked, that my mother and I may be in danger too."

"Yes. I remember you spoke of that. But why you, a simple tourist? It makes no sense to me."

I thought about rising, getting out of that ever darkening square of privacy, of silence, the pool motionless beside me. But instead, I leaned back and looked up at the sky and gave a little half laugh. "No sense at all. But that's not why I asked to speak to you. What a beautiful evening! You said I was free to go, that I was no longer a suspect. Am I still thought to be guilty of something?"

"There are certain customs here that must be respected."

"Of course."

"There are businesses, and friendships that are based on those businesses."

"I see."

"And you have disturbed some of these friendships."

"I'm sorry."

I could barely see his face, the darkness had deepened. I tried to relax. I looked up at the stars again. Yes they were still sane and wonderful. I breathed slowly in and out, gathering it as Roberto had taught me.

"What do you want me to do, Captain Hernandez?"

"Go home and sleep in peace." The words were gentle, but his voice was not. "We have made it possible for you and your mother to go home immediately. I have arranged it so you do not have to come back for the inquiry. You will be asked nothing."

"And if I should volunteer it?"

"That would be unwise." His dark eyes gleamed in the dim light. "Not because I am eager to let these men go, or their businesses to continue."

"I'm glad you said that."

"I am concerned for your safety, and what you are doing is not always wise."

"The wise thing is to be quiet?"

"To go home, as I said, and be safe. Do not worry about this matter. You have been on holiday. That is all."

"But bad things have happened here. And my mother hasn't yet returned."

"That is true. But she will return; I am confident."

"Still I'm worried. We're leaving Monday."

"We will make inquiries if you wish."

Three people walked along the tile path beside the garden. They were talking noisily and halted to peer in at us. The Captain and I waited them out in silence.

"You found a body - you, a simple tourist, so this is a disturbing experience. Why then did you go back? It was to look for something. Something you found. Did the life guard learn you went back, or what you found? Is that why he died? If he is dead."

His voice had quickened, become raspy with irritation. Did he know what had happened to Roberto? I wanted to ask about Peter

Baden, but didn't dare. I noticed the pool, suddenly, a strong fetid odor.

"Captain Hernandez, a few days ago I sat in this garden listening to a man say the same things you're saying - go home and forget about this place. A man named Jason who works, I've been told, at the casino. He threatened me. Am I in danger?"

"Of course." We leaned forward like cozy friends with choice gossip to share. "You say you are a nice person on holiday. But you find, not only a dead woman, but something two competing gangs both want. Therefore they want you."

"I don't like that. And wondered what part did Peter Baden play? Is he dead too?"

"You knew Senor Baden?" At last I had surprised him.

"Not really. But we talked."

"Then you have made yourself even more seductive. I doubt we can protect you."

I liked the way he said 'seductive'- such an ominous exotic tone.

"I agree these 'two competing gangs', as you call them, want what I found. Though its my mother's possession some of what it contains doesn't belong to her."

"Do you wish to tell me what that is?"

Why did I feel he already knew the answer to his question? I couldn't see his face, only that of a shadow opposite me.

"You're not really a police captain are you? Or if you are, you're not in charge of this investigation. Where are the other policemen, the reports, the formalities?"

He didn't move. Captain Hernandez was very good at not moving.

"I have a friend waiting for me in the bar, Captain Hernandez. I'll do as you suggest and leave Monday. All this is much too complicated for me. But I'm waiting for my mother to return. As soon as she does we'll go. She knows nothing about all this."

I stood up. "Thank you for your warning. I have a present for you. Here is what everyone wants - an address book. No matter who you are, it is safer with you than with me. Also the pool is full of large boxes. I think if you were real police you would have discovered them, would have taken them out and opened them. Maybe you are an actor one of the gangs hired to impersonate a police captain. Anyway the address book is all I have to bargain with. Please, tell everyone I don't have a clue what the names in it mean. I want to make sure my mother and I leave in safety. Goodnight."

I dropped the real address book on the ground in front of him. When he bent over to pick it up, I slipped away. I was suddenly voraciously hungry.

*   *   *   *   *

Without Sonja, without anyone who knew us, the dining room seemed much larger; the dance floor contained only Desmond and I as we moved together with a delicious familiarity. There was none of the awkwardness of the first time we'd danced. He held me warm and tight; his heart beat through to me in those thin cotton clothes we both wore. His aroma reminded me of desire.

There were few diners left, yet the band played with enthusiasm – the same band that had played one week before – they looked no different, sounded no different yet everything was changed because I loved that man. With Roberto I'd felt an awakening but Desmond was solid, was inescapable fact, though I still didn't know him well.

"Too bad you're married; I'd follow you home."

"My husband has been consistently horribly unfaithful."

"You didn't tell me that."

"He was here today."

He stopped dancing. 'You didn't tell me that either."

"He wants a divorce. It's going to be easier than I thought."

"He came to the hotel?"

"Yes. But he's not staying here. He's in Mazatlan with his lady love. I hope we don't run into them at the airport Monday."

"You're leaving Monday?"

"I hope so. It depends on Sonja. She isn't back yet."

"Let's go." He tried to walk me off the floor but I resisted.

"Let's just finish this dance."

The music, a flamboyant tango nobody wanted to dance to, ended, and he succeeded in leading me back to the table. He didn't sit down. "I ran into Edwardo again. He said he couldn't come to the bar for a drink. Can you meet Jason there? I'll go alone and talk to Edwardo.

"Why bother? He's not going to help. Forget it. But yes I'll meet Jason."

Looking distracted, he finally sat down and picked up the menu. I moved closer to study it with him. He regarded me with a swift stark look. "You stay safe."

He looked around, responding to the noise and energy in the room. Minutes went by; I sat back, relaxed. Our drinks arrived. At first we didn't talk, just sipped. I thought: This may be my last margarita in Mexico. Minutes later, Desmond leaned forward, stared straight past me. "Look kid, I have to tell you something. I think I love you." He was talking rapidly, but not meeting my eyes. "That's pretty heavy for me. I don't want to fall in love with a married woman. I believe in staying single or staying married and not mixing them, and adorable as you are," he looked into my eyes, "don't sit too close. And for God's sake stay out of trouble. I may not always be there."

That was a lot of words to come out of that man. I couldn't think of a reply so I ordered pineapple ice and smiled a lot. After awhile we found an excuse to dance in each other's arms again.

Later as we walked across from the hotel, we avoided the dark pool, the garden like a blank slate. Without a word, we entered the annex and sailed like members of royalty to our individual doors. We both knew we had things to do, errands to run, people to meet. After twenty minutes, I heard his door open and then the outside door. After twenty more minutes, I too went out, across to the indoor bar, by then no longer quiet, but crowded and smelling of smoke and exaggeration.

Serious drinkers crouched in corners, while parties of newly arrived tourists laughed loudly as they looked around with half startled eyes. The television in the corner was tuned to a football game with no sound. One table crowded was crowded with overweight Europeans, another with overweight Americans. They all dressed alike and looked happy to be at the Hotel Madre Maria.

Jason was as brutal looking as I remembered. We sat down at a small Formica topped table in a corner by the door. Immediately a waiter appeared to take our order; a man I'd not seen before, sturdy and middle aged with a gray mustache. He looked more stockbroker than hotel waiter. He eyed me carefully and asked for our order in English.

"Scotch."

"Tonic."

"The waiter looked doubtful, "Gin and tonic?"

"No, just tonic"

"You're not drinking," Jason scowled.

"I only drink with friends."

When our drinks arrived, at first we didn't talk. We were on the edge of negotiations. That's what I had suggested in my telephone call to him at the casino.

I sat forward. "Sonja and I are due to leave Monday, if she gets back in time."

He had 'I could care less written all over his face which only inspired me.

"I'm worried. We should get out of here. I had an interview this evening with Captain Hernandez. He said there's a criminal war going on here and that Sonja and I are in danger. Is he from Mexico City?"

Jason held his glass in a strangler's grip. "How should I know? He can't make you leave."

"Well I told him if so many people wanted the cosmetic case, I might as well keep it. That's safest isn't it?"

"Fuck you." He growled.

"Nice. You're nice. I thought you wanted the case."

"I want what's in it."

"What's that?" I tried for innocent and succeeded in sounding coy. "There were a number of things in the case – my mother's makeup for one thing. Is that what you want?"

"Fucking bitch," he said quietly into his glass. "I told you what I want. I met you here to get it. The police know nothing about me. Unless you open your fucking mouth."

Senor Moreno came into the bar and looked around; he saw us and came over to our table. Moving as quietly as a cat, he seemed to part the waves of noise.

"Pardon me, Senora. The Captain..."

"Captain Hernandez." My heart, for some unaccountable reason, lightened.

"He would like to speak to you again but in his office."

"Now?" Jason sat silent opposite me. "It's very late. I was about to go to bed."

"He said it was important, Senora."

"Both of us?" Across from me Jason winced. He motioned the drink waiter over. "My mother is not back from a little excursion"

"Just you, Senora. For a moment only. Before you retire. It is late I know." Looking sorrier for himself than for me, he took himself away again.

"Jason we need to talk. Do you want to wait for me here?"

He scowled. "What does he want?"

"I'm going to find out."

"I'll be in the outside bar in an hour. I want the address book."

"Really? Oh my," I said sweetly, and got up to go.

He took a slug of scotch. "I like your mother. Let's keep her safe."

"That's a deal!" I managed a perky voice.

Captain Hernandez was a shadow in the dark room. He stood behind his desk.

"Senora."

"Please call me Karin."

"You are a brave woman."

"Or a stupid one."

"I am from Mexico City. I came to investigate the death of one of my men."

"Roberto?"

"No. The repairman. He was here to find out more about smugglers. He was murdered and he was my friend."

"I'm sorry."

"So am I."

"There's more than one gang?"

"Two. They fight over the address book because it is full of the names of customers and couriers for one of the gangs. How did you acquire it?"

"It was in a cosmetic bag I found outside the cave."

"The morning you saw the body?"

"Yes. It was my mother's case, with her photographs and make up in it so I took it. Then later I found the address book in it. Marian must have put the book there."

"Or someone else." He bowed. "Thank you Karin. Please forgive me for imposing upon you so late." I was once again dismissed but this time I didn't mind.

I went outside to the beach. Jason strolled down from the bar toward the water. I walked in the same direction. There were others out - couples leaving the bar, a waiter carrying a tray. The lights were still on in the bar.

"Jason." I said loudly; others on the beach looked over at me. "Jason. Look what I've got." I held up one of the cheap address books I'd bought in town. I waved it in the air. He swerved toward me, but I rushed down to the edge of the water and waved the book again. "See. Here it is. Come and get it."

Then I waded into the water and began clumsily running against the waves. Looking back to shore I saw Jason was approaching. Hip deep in the water, I heaved the book as far as I could – about three yards. Bracing myself against the waves, I watched it until it sank from sight. Then I was wading out and running up the beach. Jason swerved and had nearly caught up with me when a noisy pack of hotel guests surged between us and stopped to look at the sea. Jason turned back, hesitated for a moment at the water's edge, and then waded in. I walked into the hotel, out again through the front door, across to the annex.

Desmond's light was on but when I knocked on his door he didn't answer. Trembling a little, I unlocked my own door and turned on the light. No Sonja. The room was empty. I double-checked the doors and windows, undressed, lay on my bed. My pulse was racing. I was waiting for a knock on the door. None came. Was Desmond out meeting Edwardo? I got up went across to his room and knocked several more times but no luck. Somehow, after all that had happened that night, I didn't worry about him because I was strangely happy. I'd done something, something energetic, that seemed good and right. Or maybe not good, but energetic. Somehow I was discovering an old but essential part of myself

I went to the window and looked out at the road. It seemed friendlier. Above it, millions of stars hung out. The sky was not nearly as dark as before: Re-finding the Desa child in me has meant that I've also found the obnoxious teenager, Desa became. I blame her on America. She'd thought America let me be brave, let me fight back; only the fights I picked had to do with my mother, with Sonja's odd, unpredictable, emotional responses to life in the New World.

My mother went away with Michael. How many times? I lost track. With very little warning and no apology and she always came back smiling. It made me angry. Something about Michael made her do things like that. Things that made me feel I didn't matter. That year she bought chiffon dresses, wore makeup and jewelry, took dancing lessons. She went around smiling, hummed popular songs, read poetry. Michael didn't buy her anything but he did send flowers –often – and that thrilled her. I hated him. When he tried to be friendly, I was rude. I shunned him and berated my mother. Sonja wouldn't listen, or pay attention to all the obvious signs – obvious to me - that their relationship was doomed.

He was an English professor at the university, married to another professor. He had two children; his son was in my class at school. Michael was big and burly with long blond hair that he wore in a ponytail. He had square white teeth displayed on every possible occasion and wore scented cologne lotion when he visited my mother. Sometimes he came to the house in the evening. As the year went by they became bolder – twice he stayed the night, though he lived in a huge house on the edge of the campus. When they went away together - four times, always suddenly - my mother left notes explaining she would be 'at a conference for two days'. She'd never left me alone before, and I found it hard to endure. We lived in community apartments and she put me in the care of one or another of the other mothers there, but I resisted going into their apartments, or eating at tables where a whole family gathered around a home cooked meal. Sonja and I had never had that and never would.

I was only thirteen, and didn't dare challenge her directly, not after the first occasions when I pointed out that (1) he was married; (2) she, not he, could lose her job; (3) if my friends found out they would despise me; (4) Michael was revolting.

She told me to be quiet, to leave them alone.

I slashed his tires several times. At first he blamed an irate student but finally accused me. I lied, said I was innocent. I went into his office when he'd stepped out and stole papers and books from his bookshelves, or left letters pretending to be in love with him. Once I sent a complaining letter to the Dean of his Department. When he took to locking his door, a bottle of pills labeled poison appeared in his mailbox. Another time it was a voodoo doll I'd made, though I don't think he knew what it was. Twice pizzas were delivered to him at the English Department. For a long time he put these antics down to students; he was a tough marker and not particularly well liked, but eventually he again accused me. I denied everything. But then I went too far. I wrote a letter to his wife and told her about the affair. She attempted suicide. His son started setting fires; Sonja cried for days; Michael came around to talk to me.

I admitted everything, was sent to a counselor. But I'd succeeded because their affair ended. The following year Sonja left to take a job in New York. When she met Josef there I kept my distance and my mouth shut.

I don't like this memory. I am filled with the irritation of guilt and fear. Did someone from the Idaho send the letter and photographs? Around me the annex floated in silence. It took me a long time to fall asleep.

Sunday, Day 15

I woke because of a sound. It was early morning - I could tell by the meek light through the window – the sound was familiar - a door opening. I thought sleepily that's funny I locked the door and then, rolling over, saw Sonja. She slid like a phantom into the bathroom and I wondered if I'd seen her at all, or if she were a dream like the one I had before, but then I heard the toilet flush and running water.

She came out and sat down on the bed opposite me and, like my dream, she was smiling, her face flushed and happy. No, this was not a dream. This was really Sonja, my dear beloved mama. She held out her left hand. There was a large diamond on it.

"Mama, you didn't..."

"We are to be married, Karin, I tell you how happy I am. Nathan Herchmer is a wonderful man, so thoughtful, such a gentleman."

"Mama you couldn't."

"I am in love, Karin," she raised her body up stiffly, assuming a mantle of dignity and I couldn't help the tug of admiration I often felt toward her. She was so certain, so authentically herself. It seemed she never doubted, or worked at being like others. Still I was aghast at the abruptness of this latest transformation.

"Sonja, you decided in one week to get married?"

"At our age, why not?"

"Whose idea was it? Can he contribute financially?"

"He will almost be a wealthy man."

"Almost?"

"Enough. He will not take my money if that is your question."

"But what about his wife?"

Irritated, she stood up, walked to the closet. "Greta is not his wife."

"She assumed the role of wife."

"He was sorry for her. She has been in his life for a long time. But they have not had a relationship for many years." She came back over to sit down on her bed again. "Why is he to be with her all his life? She is a drinker. She is a terrible alcoholic. Three times she went to a sanatorium. Three times he paid for everything. He has told me these things. She does not stop. This was the last time. She promised him this holiday she will not drink and she was all right the first days, but then, after the murder...."

I sat up, slipped on a shirt. "I find all that hard to believe, Mama. The only one I've seen drinking is Dr. Herchmer. I thought she was dying of breast cancer."

"She is. But also she is alcoholic. Did you think you could not be both? Cancer does not make someone noble."

"Are you talking about Josef?"

Startled, she looked at me, then rose, and disappeared into the bathroom again. "That is better forgotten – his torment. Do not speak to me about him, Karin."

"What about the Nazi hunting? Don't you remember, Jason bragged about it but you were upset." I raised my voice so she could hear me in the bathroom. But I lay back down, shaken by these new facts.

"That no good – to brag. He is a bum. Nathan does not brag."

"I'll bet. Listen, last night I talked to Jason. What do you know about him? He said he knew where you were. I was worried. Why did you leave me only a note?"

She came back into the room wearing a nightgown, and sat on the edge of her bed. "We went to Puerto Vallarta. It is a pretty town."

"I thought you went to New York. To help with Greta."

"She didn't want us. She didn't want me to go. Then she didn't want Nathan at all. So our plans changed in the middle of the night. Such an argument they had and Greta so sick. She called her sons and they said, 'if Nathan comes with you we will punch him out.' So violent these Americans, but – Nathan. He wanted my help. He does not speak German." Her eyes were dark with fatigue, but sparkled with excitement too. Jason? I know nothing about Jason. But Nathan does not like him. He works at the casino, I saw him there."

"Is Dr. Herchmer still gambling?"

Her face tightened. She crawled into bed, under the coverlet, put her head on the pillow, sighed with pleasure. "I wish to sleep. Maybe we found a Nazi this time, Karin."

My heart sank. I remembered Captain Hernandez's words, "Nazi? How?"

"We rented a van. We slept in it. I like such adventures, Karin. Nathan is fun. My life is nearly over, so dull, so much sadness in my life. I need some fun, Nathan says."

"Nathan is fun?"

"We went to a man's house in Puerto Vallarta. Another old man lying on a bed, he was emaciated, thin and old. Eighty-eight he said. He barely talked. I think his mind was not good. He was ill with a wasting disease. If that was Nazi, never mind. I was not interested. But Nathan said that we should talk to him, and he spoke to the wife and asked her to leave us alone with her husband, but she would not. She was a Mexican, a very ordinary woman but smart too. She stayed with this Karl." Sonja clucked her tongue in disgust. She had turned on her back, was staring at the ceiling. "He was a Hungarian. Afterwards we had a fight in the van."

"You took the Hungarian away with you?" Horrified, I sat up.

"No. No." She said impatiently and sat up too, "With Nathan. He did not believe me. I said he spoke German with Hungarian accent. I said still he could be a Nazi and be a Hungarian, but Nathan said I was avoiding the truth. So I said some nasty things to him. I told him that like all North Americans he made complicated history too simple. You know that Karin. All history is one person's history, one person, another person, each person knows something different, especially in Europe where we were all given such terrible choices. Nathan said there is good and there is evil - that is all. Stupid simple man I said. Oh I was angry. I called him Stupid Man, also North American Ignoramus and Big Jerk. You would be proud of me, Karin, I was angry."

She lay back down, sighed, "Such a terrible fight."

"Forget about it, Mama. Forget him. Don't look for problems."

"Nathan is not a problem."

She sat back up like a shot. "I will marry him."

I looked over at her. Her chin had gone stubborn, she meant what she said.

"When?"

"Soon."

"In Mexico?"

"Maybe."

"New York?"

"That could be."

I got up, threw on shorts and a shirt, staggered into the bathroom. "Why Mama? Why do such a stupid thing?"

"It is not stupid. It is my life. Not yours, Miss Know–Everything. I do not think marrying Nathan is stupid. I am in love."

I chose silence.

"He apologized. He took back all the silly remarks and said that something had gone to his head and that we would be married. But I think he wanted also to come back to the hotel and make sure Greta was all right. She is very sick. Perhaps we cannot marry while things do not look good for her."

"It is awkward." I called from the bathroom. "But she's left already."

"Will you come to our wedding?"

"No." I came out, sat down on my bed to put on running shoes. "He is a very odd man." I said. "But I won't make trouble, I promise you. I've got problems of my own."

She looked over at me with the trusting eyes of a child. "Am I such a fool? Why have I said I will marry him?" I knew she didn't want me to go out just then, but I raised one eyebrow and she had the grace to laugh. "You make faces at me."

"I'm amazed Mama, that's all. I was worried about you. I'm glad you're back."

"So am I," she closed her eyes. "What problems do you have? I mean some new one you have? Something has happened while I am gone? Tell me. I missed you. I will meet you for breakfast in an hour or two, but first some sleep, a little, please."

When I returned from my run and first coffee, she was up and dressed and engaged in her makeup ritual. I changed clothes, sat watching her. It seemed strange to be together again. So much had happened.

"Is Dr. Herchmer staying in the same room?"

"He is in Acapulco today."

"I saw her – Greta - when she was preparing to leave. She looked pretty sick."

"Oh." Sonja seemed not the least bit interested. She was staring into the mirror, examining the ravages of the night close up.

I went to the door. "I'll wait outside, Mama."

"I am coming. Karin, Did you talk to Captain Hernandez again?"

"Yes."

"He is a strange policeman."

"You're right Mama. But I've come to trust him."

She said, "Let me meet you in the dining room."

When I left, I slipped a note under Desmond's door that said, 'Sonja's back'.

The maids were cleaning the room next to his. Someone had been there, had come and gone without ever being seen.

I wandered outside. Walking into the garden, I saw lilies scattered in a jumbled mass; they'd been uprooted and thrown around; the ground beneath them was dug up and exposed. I poked the earth. The cosmetic case was gone.

Only Desmond had known. Unless someone had seen me digging it up. I stood beside the flowerbed, appalled by the treachery of it. Why did Desmond take the cosmetic case without telling me? I thought of others who might have - Edwardo or Carl. Even Frieda or Nathan Herchmer. Sonja? It was after all her case. But how had anyone but Desmond have known where to look? Well, I thought whoever it was, they'll be disappointed when they open up the case. Captain Hernandez has the real address book, I have the photographs. The purple case contained only cosmetics and a cheap red address book with my name scrawled in it.

When I reached the beach, it was empty. I stood desolate. No Desmond, no Roberto, no Sonja. I thought then: This is an odd, unlovely beach, the great lights on it absurdities, those crummy umbrellas over the aging beach chairs and the sand – not the white sifted sand you'd expect but some mealy gray with tufts of grass growing out of it Ugly. Everything here is ugly. That morning I saw nothing as it was. Like a great wave, regret, guilt, and anger all rioted inside me, like a great wave they were about to overwhelm me. I wanted out of this mess, the confusion, and the threats. And over and over again I thought - where was Desmond? Why had he dug up the case without telling me – the supposed defender, the man who promised me through his eyes and his voice that he loved me? And where was Sonja – the Mama that wanted never to let go of me? She was letting go with a vengeance. Both were leaving me. Even Greg was leaving me.

I began walking. Fast, up the beach. I didn't know where I was going, but there was more anger in me than regret. I thought about going up the hillside, thought about the cave. Should I go inside again? A little shiver of apprehension guided me. No, no, I did not want to do that, and besides there was no time, my mother was waiting for me, but how well I remembered it, a rocky cavern tucked inside a rock wall. Not far from an absurd street light. I turned to go back.

I refused to run, why bother? I walked slowly, and at the edge of the hotel beach, winded, stopped and glanced back. Old Juan was standing up, arms akimbo by the street light. I wondered if he could do me any harm, but at that moment I didn't care. I thought, never mind I'm leaving tomorrow, leaving all this mess and that particular jerk behind. I strolled through the dreamers, the sleepy ones waking up beside the sea, toward the hotel to meet my mother.

Then I stopped. I needed to run, to run beside my other mother, the sea. And I did, up and down the beach, in and out of the water. I remembered the first Sunday at the Hotel Madre Maria -how joyful I felt. I stopped, my feet in the waves, and prayed, prayed my thanks for my stay here, for all the people, good and bad that I'd encountered, and for the self knowledge that was directing me now. Thank you God, for all of this -forgive me for not thanking you enough. And when I opened my eyes, all the ugliness was gone. It was the Hotel Madre Maria as I had seen it the first Sunday morning two weeks before.

Time for breakfast with my amazing mother I thought, marching up the sand.

At breakfast I asked Sonja about the murders.

"About what?" she said devouring her bacon and pancakes. She poured blueberry syrup on the pancakes, definitely not a Mexican breakfast. The key to Sonya's mood was her appetite and she had a remarkably robust one that morning.

"The murders."

"Yes, this hotel. Three murders. Like a movie. But the most terrible was that young woman." She was still stuffing in pancakes.

I eyed my colorful fruit plate with doubt, even fruit looked heavy that morning.

"Who do you think did it – killed Marian and the others?"

She stopped chewing and looked at me with surprise. "Why will I know?"

"Surely you have opinions."

"None," she said emphatically and went back to eating pancakes. Then put down her fork, and looked into my eyes, "Haven't I seen enough murders in my lifetime? They were all murderers there – every single person that ran the camps had blood on their hands. Please don't talk to me about what is happening here."

We ate in silence for some minutes. I offered her some of my fruit which she took.

"Did you know I found your cosmetic case?"

"Nathan thought you did. He thought you will give it to me. But I do not care because I bought a new one. Did you see it? The new black one I bought?"

"No. How did he know I had it?"

"Someone took it from the table in the bar when we were all together there. He thought it was you. But he couldn't talk to you. You weren't friendly, he said. But maybe one of those German girls took it. They were not nice, those girls."

My mother was methodically eating her way through the pancake stack in an aggravating way. I wished then that I was opposite Desmond who ignored me, but in an intelligent offhand way. My mother's aggressive passion for food was normal, but not the way she kept throwing challenging glances at me while she ate. And why mention the German girls again? Why decide to marry so suddenly? Did she really love this Nathan Herchmer? I sat back, reminded myself to speak carefully.

"You're sure you want to marry him?

"Nathan?"

She shrugged her shoulders in a dramatic offhand way. "Why not? Sex is good for old people."

"Mama!" I was shocked. She'd married Josef nearly as suddenly and that had turned out all right. But it had never struck me that she and Josef were passionate lovers.

"Remember to call me Sonja, my darling."

"Your old case is lost. But I rescued the photographs."

She looked up. "Good. You keep them. He is your father I think."

"You think?"

"I do not want to talk about such things now, Karin. Anton or Hans, what do you care now? They are both dead. I loved them both. You can do the same."

I could feel my temper rising again. "Anton was my father. This Hans - I don't even remember him."

She pushed her plate aside, wiped her lips, and lipstick on the white cloth napkin, a habit I hated in her when I was a teenager. "Please, Karin. Enough of this talk."

I sat back, "O.K. But, Mama, what is going on between Jason and Nathan?"

"Why do you say 'going on'?"

She was dressed in one of her splashiest outfit, a chartreuse, white and pink long blouse over white trousers. It made her look slimmer, taller, and younger "Why do you care about Jason? There is nothing important between them. Except gambling. I do not like him. The young man is a flirt."

"Jason a flirt - Jason?"

"A playboy."

"And you weren't interested?"

"All the time he asks about you."

"Jason? Me?" I acted surprised.

"He wants to make you his special friend. He says to me - your daughter will make a good special friend. I would like to spend some time alone with her. Can you help me? He should not say this to me. Your mother, he tells your mother such things. I did not like it. No."

We were eating in the dining room but near the windows. The beach below was filling up with people. It was another day of sun worship. My mother took note.

"This hotel beach - packed like sardines. Still I like it. Did you know Nathan found it for me? I met him in New York. Yes, I admit it. A little, a little I knew him. Here we got to know each other much better. But, Karin, it is our last day here in Mexico. You and I, we must spend some time together. Nathan I can see in New York. Shall we go for a swim?"

She looked so appealing in her brilliant blouse I couldn't refuse her, though wheels of thought and apprehension and anger still churned away inside me – a not unfamiliar feeling around my mother. But usually I forgave her everything. Today, facing years of Nathan I wasn't sure. Sonja was hopelessly childish about what she did and those she involved herself with. But I remembered that love took away her harshness, evaporated her cynicism. Mexico had already lightened her mood, invigorated and strengthened her - as it had me. "You look glamorous this morning, Sonja."

"I try, I try."

"We should do this holiday again," I said to her," Only without murders."

"I have money for you," my mother said, "For your university courses."

'You've given me enough, Mama. I'll have to pay you back."

"Don't pay me back. Take it. I want to help you, Karin. You make mistakes, but I want that you and the girls do not suffer. I want that you finish your degree. Then you can start something new. I too start something new. I have a new job."

I flushed, thrilled for her. "That's wonderful. What kind of work?

"Nathan's receptionist."

Oh no, Mama, no, I thought but didn't say.

"Mama"

"Yes, my darling."

"Are you leaving tomorrow?"

She looked at me with surprise. "Of course, you are leaving tomorrow too."

"I don't know. When is Dr. Herchmer leaving? Nathan, I should call him."

"I don't know. He thinks still he can help Greta."

"She's a nice lady."

"Is she?" Sonja's voice was neutral.

"Did you speak to her?"

"No. There was already trouble between them." The sharpness had returned to my mother's voice.

The dining room was full that morning; guests were eating, drinking, smiling, scowling, above all talking - discourse amongst the civilized – or so I liked to think. But I was rememberng her voice from the camp, a voice that was often fierce. She didn't speak much, didn't talk to others, not even to me. There was no sentiment, no soft words from her, only a tight hold on my hand, the demand of where was I going and what was I doing. Some of my memories have nothing but the flat slap sound of her voice above the voices of others, across the deep silences that sometimes engulfed all of us. That sharp crack was the whip that drove both of us through each day, sometimes through the nights.

The second year as privileged prisoners Sonja gained work in an office as a relief clerk. Everything improved for us then and we had more food. Sometimes I've wondered if she found other ways to earn money too. But I no longer want to ask.

That Sunday morning I'd watched my mother eat and thought of the miracle of our lives. Thought then how I loved her, sometimes feared her, and occasionally hated her. What did she feel about me? Probably the same mixture. I no longer resented the fact that she had had so many escapades, so many men, while I was supposed to live a quiet respectable life in an unchanging, seamless world. It had been a burden living that sensible life for my mother. I wanted to discover what life could also offer me, to escape the tyranny of practicality, if only briefly, before old age caught me in its net of obligations. But did she feel the resentment of the old for the young? The anger of the person with a painful life toward someone with a safe one? I never felt that. That morning in Mexico we sat a long time talking. A waiter arrived again and again, pouring fresh coffee, the aroma and taste comforting us. I was still poking my way through the mango and orange slices. And for the first time, telling my mother about my marriage.

"It's been a lie for years. I'm sick of talking to women on the phone who are trying to track him down, of hiding the facts from the girls. They're growing up. I can't keep it from them forever." At last we were talking about what mattered to me. "There must be something wrong with me, something undesirable that he needs to constantly run away from. We haven't had a relationship, a normal husband and wife relationship, for years. Am I married? Or am I just a servant, a thing?""

"I'm sorry Karin." She stared at me for a moment, and took a sip of her coffee. "Greg is like Anton," she said calmly, "He was no good too."

"Don't say that! He was my father."

Carefully, Sonja put down her knife and fork.

"Sometimes a woman doesn't know. Two men in her life – how can she know? I was lonely and afraid. It was wartime. What are you, a child still? You are more like Hans than Anton that is what I think now. And please, you are not a thing. You are a beautiful woman, more beautiful than that young German woman. And now you look happy. Not like when you arrived. You looked terrible."

"You noticed."

"Of course," she said calmly, eating last shreds of pancake and sighing with satisfaction. Her plate was clean. We cannot escape the camp in that respect. We must always finish all food. It was a wonder we were not fat. "Are you in love with that man?"

"Desmond?"

"He is a rough man. He was married to Marian Heissel."

"I know that."

"Perhaps he killed her."

My eyes filled with tears, "Oh Mama, why say something so complicated?"

"It is really quite simple," she said calmly pushing her plate away and drawing the coffee cup closer. The dining room was emptying, people rising, jamming on sun hats and sunglasses, gathering tote bags, discussing what to do that day.

"Simple, there is nothing simple about all this."

"Simple." she said authoritatively, and opened the carved handbag she'd claimed she'd lost. Was she still carrying all that money around? She took out a lipstick and began painting a thick layer on her mouth, an act so archaic I wanted to wince.

'You found your purse?'

"Nathan had it. Karin, it is simple. Life goes on." She said this with great authority. "That is all. Life goes on, with us or without us. It does not matter what happens to us. It rides on, and over us, through our bones, on it goes, dragging us with it, or tearing us apart, or carrying us on its back; it always goes on. Leaving us behind or taking us apart, we cannot stop it, or choose the way we ride or whether we ride. Life goes on, my darling daughter." She was staring at me, and I felt the steel that was Sonja enter me. When we rose to leave, I asked what she was going to do that morning.

"I will go to the beach," she said. "I must enjoy this last day of sunshine. New York in March?" She gave a dramatic shudder. "You must remember how that is."

"I do. It's cold in Colorado too."

"Come back and live in New York. Bring the girls."

"And Dr. Herchmer? What if you are living with him?"

"I accepted his engagement ring. And we spent those nights together. In my mind I am as married, but the rest is up to him. We will marry but first he must release Greta." She touched my arm. My word it was complicated. It was hard to remember my mother was over seventy. She flushed a little. Her eyes looked frightened. She leaned against me and spoke softly. "We look for Nazis."

"You aren't marrying him because of that, Sonja, please don't tell me that."

"Of course not, what do you think I am?" But her voice was still a whisper. We were walking out; she was still clutching my arm.

"But it does attract you – the idea?" I asked.

"A little. To seek them out, to track them, to force them finally – all of them – to see what they have done, so smoothly, so easily, without guilt or conscience, to believe finally when you are old, that God does work his judgments, that woven into crime is also, a little, such a little, punishment, I like that idea, yes. Nathan says that he feels called to do it, that it was as though God guided him to take the first steps."

"Mama, you worry me. I was worried last night."

"Did you find my note?"

"Yes."

"I told you not to worry."

"There have been several unsolved murders, Mama, don't you understand? I couldn't trust the note. I can't trust anything because everything can be something that it didn't promise to be. Everything can turn suddenly and look different so that you understand nothing, and what was familiar is strange and what was strange is curiously familiar. That was what was happening here with me, and then with you, and I hope you haven't turned yourself inside out for Nathan."

We were at the annex door. The sun was hot. A warm wind was blowing fine brown dust in from the road. I was still anxious, but

Sonja was calm. "No, no, my dear child, I am all right. I will put on my bathing suit now. Will you swim with me? I sit alone. We are two women alone in the world today."

I hadn't heard her say that in many years. And it was no longer true. I thought that she was afraid of the waves, was physically weak though not admitting it. She needed someone with her to test herself against them. But I begged off. My real concern was with Desmond. I hadn't seen him that day. So first I went back to his room and knocked but there was no answer. Then I went to the pool. How desolate it looked with its torn and scattered flowers. Almost all the lilies were dead.

I wandered into the hotel foyer and found at the front desk a message from Greg.

I telephoned immediately, wondering about the children.

"Everything's O.K." Greg voice was calm. "Thanks for calling."

"Greg. I'll be home in a couple of days."

"Karin, I wanted to tell you something."

"The children?"

"No, no, I told you, everything's fine."

I waited; he was stumbling, unusual for such a know it all, fix it now man.

"I don't want a divorce."

I was stunned. I was back in the glass booth. I sat down.

"You haven't found someone?"

"No,"

"I thought there was a young professor."

"I don't want to get a divorce, Karin."

"Greg. You are in love with someone else."

"She's too young. She doesn't understand me. You do."

"No, I don't. Why tell me this over the phone?"

"I want you to think about it."

"Like hell you do. You're a coward. You always have been; you always will be."

The anger was rising up but part of me couldn't connect with it because this was a routine we'd already endured - name calling, accusations. Our marriage was at an end even if he wouldn't acknowledge it.

"I'll wait until you're calmer."

"I want a divorce, Greg."

"We'll decide when you get back."

"We already have." I hung up, willing at last to let it out - all my anger and humiliation. Maybe he would tell the kids before I returned but I doubted it. It looked like he wanted to torture me a bit more and make me tell them.

I begged some matches from the front desk clerk, then wandered out to the terrace and looked forlornly at the spot where Desmond and

I had breakfasted several times. No sign of him. On the waterfront, the parachute concession hadn't opened up

I walked down and saw Ramon, one of the new young men who ran the concession, sitting on the ground fiddling with some equipment.

"Hi, Ramon. You haven't opened up this morning."

"Only me today."

"What news of Roberto?"

"He is better."

I sat down on the sand beside him. "Edwardo told me he was dead."

There was a long perceptible pause and then Ramon said, "He was like dead. But he is alive. I saw him yesterday."

"I'm glad."

"It was good," Ramon said, "That he was so sick."

"Where is he?"

He looked at me, smiled, but shook his head.

"Edwardo? Where is he? And Manuel?"

"They went to town."

"Do they have another business?"

Ramon looked out to sea, his voice grew sad. "It is better not to ask questions. Otherwise we end up like Roberto." Ramon looked sideways at me. I was reminded of Old Juan with his mournful face.

I wandered around the hotel, restless, unable to settle myself. I'd run out of reading material, hadn't read for days! I decided to walk the length of the beach. The day was warm but the wind made midday bearable. I ran some of the way up toward the cave, passed it, and then walked to the very end of the sandy beach. I hadn't been there before; the sand disappeared into a jumble of large rocks, a bleak little place, with old fallen timber. The perfect place to think deep dark thoughts. I sat down, knees up, and looked out to sea.

The familiar islands were telescoped into each other in the distance. Waves rolled in with a firmness that discouraged swimming. The ground was dirty. A few gulls swooped over the water searching for food. Yet that place and that day were like every other day beside the sea and the certainty in its pattern was comforting. I wanted to think about my life, not Roberto's nor Sonja's nor Desmond's. How had I become such a voiceless personality, living lives for my mother, my husband?

Greg had told me the truth. He'd said he wanted a divorce. That was the healthiest response he could make and was the truth. My being away had helped. But the children mattered to him, as they did to me. I didn't want to face the hurt of the children either. If he wanted to change us back to old selves, to squeeze ourselves into an old relationship based on pretence for their sakes, that was impossible for me. I needed to know myself as I had come to know this sea, this beach, day by day - a slow aggregation of knowledge, small pieces that delight in the moment but are drawn into consciousness slowly. I wanted that everywhere, before old age, before death. The pretenses had to be broken; especially the one Greg and I had once thought our truth.

My pretense had been that I didn't need Greg for comfort or companionship. But in fact, like all people, I needed those qualities. Thinking this, I noticed I could hear nothing but waves rolling in. If someone spoke to me from that distance I wouldn't hear him. If I called for help, no one would hear me. Struck by that thought, I looked back at the beaches some distance away. They were all nearly empty, On Sunday there was a buffet lunch on the terrace at the Madre Maria; everyone got there early since the hotel sometimes ran out of food. On one private beach a young girl sat on a stone wall swinging her legs, on another, an elderly couple dozed under an umbrella. But why did I so often chose to be alone? Must I? Could I become more like my mother, seeking out friends wherever she went.

Sitting on the sand, feeling the heat of the sun penetrate my thin blouse and bite into my newly tanned tanned legs, I felt a little skip of joy. Something was moving my life forward again. Whatever relationships I achieved in the future – and I prayed it would include Desmond – any relationship must be as honest as I could make it. I had to learn to see pretense for what it was before I linked my fate to another human being. Then oddly I thought of Myrna.

In the distance I saw a man walking in the sea. Behind him the hotels and motels stretched out into the distance. The sun was intense, so bright it made the air shimmer, the heat was rising as the afternoon hours spread themselves across the sea and sand.

Myrna was blonde, medium height and slender - a very attractive girl. I roomed with her in the college dorm but after two years she quit to become an airline stewardess. That was in the years when a stewardess conveyed glamour, and attracted instant interest from men - this Myrna knew how to enjoy. I'd been so attached to Sonja that the world of young women, one of fluctuating alliances and energetic competitions, was strange and uncomfortable for me. To take a break from university, I worked six months in New York at an accountant's office to raise the money to go to Europe. Sonja didn't approve. She didn't think it safe. As Czech refugees we might be caught and returned to our unhappy country. I should finish my education first. She worked away at me, urging me not to go. Telling me she needed me. But Myrna had the energy and drive and stubbornness to get us both there, to organize my first experience of travel, which I came to love as an expression of personal freedom.

The man in the distance was moving toward me, sometimes walking in the water, wincing as he stepped fully onto the hot sand.

He must be barefoot, I thought. I watched as he stepped back into the shallow water and resumed his walk. He was in shorts, was of medium height, and had a compact muscular body. Did I know him? I couldn't make out his face; he wore a sun hat that hid it.

By the end of my first year of university I understood that young women liked to learn as many intimate details about each other as they could. Confessions were constantly in the air. Yet that was exactly what Sonja had warned me against. I'd been taught never to speak of family, my father and brother, about her, or our health, and especially not to reveal what I thought or believed. All these were tools given to an enemy. What people knew about you could be used against you.

Myrna never asked such questions. On our first trip to Europe together, Myrna and I developed the ability to attract men, or rather, Myrna had it and I tagged along. Men were drawn to her, caught up with both of us, and vented their anger on me when Myrna danced away, skillfully slamming glass doors between herself and their companionship. I remember assorted dinners with strangers, rides in cars when we had to leap out; but the real problem rested with me, with my refusal to be discourteous, my insistence on commitment to friendship with every acquaintance. Some men stung by refusals, usually initiated by Myrna, grew angry.

One drunken American stood in the streets of Paris, grimly holding on to the edge of a taxi so that it could not drive away, as Myrna had instructed the driver to do. The disappointed man began thumping on the glass, shouting words like "cock teasers" while Myrna, a little drunk, jumped out of the taxi, ran up the road in front of us, threw up her hands in the air, and giggled madly. I wanted to be her at such times, wanted to be running like an elf out of responsibility and hurt, instead of an earth mother attempting to stanch the wounds of the bleeding male egos left behind. In the end Myrna and I had to part somewhere along the rail journey to Barcelona. When a long amorous beginning between Myrna and a French businessman unfolded before my eyes, my nerves gave way and I pleaded a necessary trip to Geneva. We wrote for awhile; she managed a visit me one summer, but events had changed us. She married the French businessman, lived in Paris for seven years; and when her marriage ended, worked in N.Y. as a stockbroker and became hugely wealthy.

The man was closer, once again wincing with the heat of the sand on his bare feet, but now moving slowly up the beach. Behind him the hotels and motels stretched out into the distance. He was moving regularly arms swinging a little in the rhythm of his walk. As he came closer I saw he was clean shaven, his chest covered with dark aggressively masculine hair. He was about fifty.

He was looking straight at me. He didn't smile. It was unnerving. There was not a flicker of emotion across his face. I didn't like the feeling of sitting when he was closing in on me, so I stood up, and was half poised for flight as he walked closer. His mouth moved. He appeared to be saying something but I couldn't hear the words. Then he was close. It was Freddy.

Where was Myrna when I needed her? Freddy was breathing hard and smelled of sweat. Once again I was back in the camp and the solder pulling me away from Sonja; my mother shouting we had papers; shrieking as she held them out, the guard instead snapping me back against the wall; I felt his anger.

Freddy walked past without looking at me. Where was he going? I stood and caught my breath, caught too the self within that was calm and rational. Freddy must be just another gringo wandering around. The next minute my arms were grabbed from behind. Why did he do that? My rational self asked. I waited, but no answer came.

"You talk to Carl." Freddy said.

"I'd love to."

"I'll take you to the house." He let go of my arms.

"O.K. What's your name?"

He didn't reply. We walked back along the beach side by side. The elderly Mexicans looked up at us from under umbrellas with some curiosity, but no true interest. The young girl on the wall went on swinging her feet. She was in a bikini.

Sonja will be looking for me to go swimming, I thought. Too bad.

Near the cave we walked up the side of the hill. A narrow trail above led to a staircase. Freddy said nothing and neither did I.

I slipped once and he didn't offer to help, just waited for me to right myself. I felt like apologizing for my lousy climbing shoes. We were at the back of Carl's house. Please let me see the blue sky again I prayed as Freddy led me inside. We went up some side stairs and then he opened the door to a room, pushed me inside the house and shut and locked the door.

It was a bedroom with a narrow bed covered with a blanket against one wall, a small table and lamp next to it. On another larger table was a jumble of articles. I went over and looked at them -.a makeup kit and some pills, a daily diary, black with gold letters, a wallet and a cigarette case with no cigarettes in it. I picked up the black wallet and opened it: Marian's credit cards, driver's license, a book seller's card. They were all in German but the name was clear. Marian had been in this room.

That her things were in a room where I was a captive somehow frightened me. I was in deeper than I'd expected. I tried the door – locked. I walked around – we were on the second floor; the front view was of the road and the mountains. After awhile I lay on the bed and rested. I heard dishes clattering below. Delicious smells wafted up. Someone was preparing dinner, or a late lunch. I thought, for once I'm hungry. What time is it anyway? I hadn't worn my watch for almost a week. How long would I wait here? Finally I dozed off.

I woke up when Frieda slammed into the room. She was carrying a tray with a small coffee set on it. She smashed the tray down on the big table. She was capable of making a lot of noise. She was wearing a low cut, blue and white sundress and a teeny tiny apron. She looked pretty but her mouth was still a wide slash in a mean face.

"Carl will see you in an hour. They are meeting now. Carl's bodyguard is stupid. Carl is angry with him. But you are stupid too."

I nodded my head. I agreed with her. She said a lot more but her German accent wasn't easy for me to follow. I noticed for the first time that the wall cupboards were painted blue. In fact there was blue trim everywhere in contrast to the white walls. The wooden bed had a sun design at the back. The toilet was in the shower stall.

"Marian - she was disgusting. She tried to cheat Peter. She came to Carl and she said Peter wanted her to take his share. She tried to take two shares, hers and Peter's. When Carl caught her she said Peter made her do that. I don't believe her. I know Peter. I have known him for years. He played it safe. Marian was a bitch. She told Carl she was pregnant. She said the baby was his. She said Peter couldn't have children. Maybe she was lying. She was a liar. She knew about Carl and me. They were divorced but he decided he wanted that baby. It was his baby, he said. Marian told him – No, she will have an abortion and go with Peter. Who knows what she was doing?"

Frieda was standing over me as I lay on the bed. I didn't dare sit up. She waved at the dishes on the tray. "For you I made coffee. Marian was repulsive. She was crazy. She made Carl angry. Carl is a bad man when he is angry." She went out. The rational self said. - That is one unhappy lady.

Do I care? The other self snarled. *Just shut up*

To pass the time, I thought about Myrna again, Myrna waving her hands behind glass while an insulted male vented his anger. Myrna had no chinks in her well made armor. She simply started to laugh at the absurdity of men and commitment dissolved like a sandcastle when the tide comes in. What would Myrna do in this situation?

She would keep track. She wouldn't fall asleep. She'd be ready to run. She would do what had to be done. I felt in the pocket of my jeans. The fake address book was there. How stupid they were for not finding it! I drank the coffee which was not bad considering the delivery system.

Frieda came back into the room. She talked at me again. This time she said some sensible things, some surprising things. She unlocked the door and told me to get out and get out fast because that was safest for me. Thank you, I mumbled out of a dry mouth. She went out again. I closed the door. I didn't trust any of them. Instead I went out on the balcony. It was crummy. There was one bushy plant in a corner; otherwise it was covered with bird shit. But it did provide a good view of the road and a side path, both led back to the Hotel Madre Maria. In the other direction lay rows of hills and mountains and endless sky. I went back into the room.

I took out the matches I'd gotten at the hotel, and the fake address book that had been in my cloth bag the whole time, and put them down on the floor of the shower stall.

I tore the cover off the address book, then piled matches on the pages and set fire to them. It took a little doing but adding toilet paper helped. Soon all that was left was a sad little pile of ashes and part of the cover. I drew an arrow on the floor pointing to the pile with Marian's lipstick -why ruin my own? – and the words -Address Book- next to it.

Just in case somebody noticed.

I looked at my watch. I'd been captive for just over two hours. I crept down the stairs. The downstairs smelled of fried fish. I heard voices in the kitchen but a side door had been left open, so I slipped out. The narrow path beside the road was dusty but I stuck to it because I couldn't believe I'd gotten away. The house behind me was silent. After I'd walked out of sight of the house, I moved over to the road. I walked quickly but it was still hot and I had to slow down. As

476

I approached the hotel I saw a man walking briskly toward me. He was tall and thin. It was Desmond. I started running toward him; he walked toward me faster and faster.

I took his hand. He looked distracted, almost ill.

"Are you all right?" he said

"I'm o.k."

"I'll walk you back and then I have to take off. I've sold my truck."

His truck was parked in front of the hotel. He climbed in and tried to smile.

"I've turned myself in to the police. I'll find you later."

"You killed the rubrun lilies when you dug them up."

He started the truck. "I'll explain everything tonight."

He drove off. His car rattled ominously.

It struck me once again how white the light was late in the day - a dissolved color, evaporated into the air, and whatever color was left looked bleached. Was it leached of vital elements? I felt shaken, exhausted; and angry, but I was hungry too, and so went into the hotel to look for Sonja. I found her sitting with Nathan Herchmer on the terrace. They both had plates laden with food and were chatting amicably. They looked like two large cats splitting a canary between them. I walked over and said, in my calmest most rational voice, with the politest, most subdued language I could muster.

"Hello, Mama, Nathan. Mama, I'm sorry I missed our swim this afternoon. Would you excuse me if I take a few snacks back to the room and rest?"

My mother's mouth opened a bit. She knew something was askew but she couldn't quite fathom what, besides she didn't really care. She wanted that time with Nathan, The rational self muttered, but the newer one just spat out: *Jealous are you?*

I swallowed hard. Letting hard thoughts trickle out meanwhile staring at Sonja

"Of course we don't mind, dear." Sonja smiled majestically. "Nathan and I will keep each other company."

Of course, I thought, gritting my teeth and striding away, of course you will. I gathered a plate of tacos and salsa - there was very little else left - and wandered across the terrace - which was full of people enjoying afternoon cocktails – down the stairs, toward the garden, but then saw, in front of it, a barrier, and a large sign in English and Spanish: : <u>Garden Pool Open Tomorrow.</u> I peered in.

The pool had been drained. The boxes were gone. Two workers were scrubbing the tiles. That was fast, I thought, impressed with Captain Hernandez's efficiency. But I mourned my private place, my secret pool. I went back to the beach and sat under one of the umbrellas and tried to eat slowly while I churned through the day's events.

What exactly had Frieda said to me? I tried to remember.

Marian was pregnant with Carl's child, but told everyone it was Peter's baby. Except Carl. She told Carl he was the father. She was going to have the baby no matter what and then all of a sudden she was going to have an abortion. Was that why she was murdered? I remembered Carl said that Frieda had given Marian too many drugs. Had that been deliberate? Marian's death had something to do with that baby. Then I remembered Frieda had said something later about that.

Had Frieda said something about any of the other deaths? Roberto's wounding and Peter Baden's drowning? She had certainly warned me enough times about Carl. Was he responsible for them?

The rational part of me jumped right in -Who else? I didn't find that rational at all. Perhaps the rational self was by then the most unbalanced part of me because it consistently tried to find simple answers to a world grown more complicated by the hour.

Something was going on yes, but it wasn't my job to answer all those questions.

I thought about Desmond. What did he have to do with all the confusion? I was sure he'd dug up the cosmetic case. But why had he turned himself into the police?

"I am so tired of thinking," I said out loud.

"You don't like me much, do you?"

It was Nathan Herchmer, standing much as he had so many days before, staring at me with uncanny tenseness.

"Not really"

"Because of your mother?"

"Partly."

"She wants to help."

"Help with what? We've had this conversation before, Nathan. My mother doesn't need any more trouble."

"More?"

"Than her life has been. She deserves only good things."

"She wants to be part of the punishment."

"I'm not so sure of that."

"It is very natural. It brings conclusion, a closure." He sat down beside me.

"Catching a Nazi brings conclusion to what? It doesn't alter memory, or change events, take away the wasted lives or the suffering. It doesn't change any of that."

I'd finished my food. I stacked the dishes under my chair to make it look like I was about to leave.

He leaned over the table toward me. "It gives hope."

"For what?"

"Punishment exists. The guilty are punished. Sooner or later."

"Much, much later I'd say."

"Action tilts the perspective." He was full of eagerness, of energy, leaning forward and stabbing a finger into the air. "You understand, my dear, perspective is still very much in the world. That tilt has saved my life several times."

I refused to ask him to explain what that meant. I only wanted to get away. "Captain Hernandez said you're not legitimate. Not in what you're doing."

"Captain Hernandez..." Nathan Herchmer's voice was contemptuous. "Don't you find it strange that there is only one policeman sitting in a rented room on a makeshift chair? Why, let me ask you? Why is there only Captain Hernandez?"

I gathered my dishes and stood up.

"Please. Let me carry those dishes in for you." He took them from me. "Like all of us, Captain Hernandez has his own game to play." He balanced the dishes and slowly we walked together into the hotel. Then suddenly, I had to stop, a severe sensation of terror was engulfing me.

I sat down breathing hard, hyperventilating -an anxiety attack -the first in a long time. Nathan Herchmer turned and looked at me, shook his head and went on with the dishes into the hotel. I rested my head against the webbed backing of the chair and looking up at the blue sky, rode into the fear. I was overwhelmed by feelings from childhood, from the hospital, the camp, the separations from Sonja, the terrors that aloneness held. Memories came of cowering in bed, failing to breathe, the roughness of the sheet against my cheek, strangers around me. I remembered it all as I fought the panic, using the weapons I remembered had helped me survive as a child: The blue marbles in my hands, the stick doll against my throat, the voices and hands of kind strangers, Sonja's determination. And I owned so much now as an adult - friends like Myrna, my daughters and mother, Desmond, and yes Greg, love and faith. – in God, in human beings, the sea and the sky.

The panic vanished. Confidence flowed back into me. I could go home. I was ready to begin something new there. There were things I could do, questions I should answer.

* * * * *

Senor Moreno still had the sleek, alert look of a coyote. He didn't smile, but moved rapidly among various tasks. I spoke to him as he stood at the switchboard answering calls in a low rapid monotone voice.

"We are leaving tomorrow, Senor Moreno."

"Of course, Senora. Buenas Tardes, Senor, un momento."

"You've closed the garden."

He cast a quick stark look at me, "Si."

"And drained the pool. Will there be water in it tomorrow?"

"Buenas Tardes, Yes, of course. Excuse me Senora, the telephone."

"Where were the boxes taken?"

"I do not know. Buenas Tardes, Senor, un momento."

"Were any of the guests under suspicion?"

He turned to fix on me an icy stare. "Senora we are told nothing."

"You know nothing."

The phone rang again. He turned his back. I wandered away.

"Mrs. Carter," Senor Moreno's voice. I turned back. "This call it is for you."

My heart lifted, it must be Desmond. "I'll take it here."

I went to the phone at the end of the front desk.

"Hello, Karin."

Greg's voice. "Is everything going okay?"

"Yes. Are the girls there with you?"

"They're fine. Will you be home Monday night?"

"Yes. But very late. I'll stay in Denver overnight."

"Listen, Karin. Forget about that last conversation. It meant nothing. It's best we both move on. Don't you agree?"

"Yes. Yes I do. Greg."

"Still we need to talk, to make arrangements. When can we get together?"

"I'll call when I'm back. In the morning. Bye."

I walked out into the late afternoon sunshine. What had changed his mind this time? Where was he anyway? I would have to go home and find out. I walked out on the beach. I just might finally become an adult. The beach was covered with bodies. The sun was still hot and pleasing and nearly everyone was comatose. I walked down to the water, threading my way through the dreamers. When I approached the sea, saw how certain she was, how unyielding. The sun, though it turned her dazzling, did not command her. Nothing did – except perhaps her own bottomless, inexplicable depths, and perhaps the moon and night. I stood before her, breathed in her life, her will to go on forever.

Sunday, Day 15, Night

Walking up the beach, I passed a pregnant woman reclining in a beach chair and suddenly stopped. I'd thought of something else Frieda had said that afternoon in Carl's house: "I didn't want to kill her. Only the baby."

I remembered Carl's words too - that Frieda gave Marian too many drugs. It had been a deliberate act then - Frieda was not a generous friend, but a jealous rival. Should I tell anyone? Captain Hernandez? One woman's word against another about a third – men rarely seemed to validate that sort of information.

In the distance I saw Desmond walking up the hillside with two men. They looked like Edwardo and Manuel but I couldn't be sure. They disappeared from sight, and I turned back to the hotel. Was he giving them the red address book? I regretted putting my name in it. I saw Sonja sitting alone on the terrace and started to go up to her, then stopped for on her face was a dark look. Not my mother's usual sad or angry expression, nor but instead a more powerful mood, as though some hidden self was expressing itself through her. I went back to the room.

*   *   *   *   *

The door was open.I stood outside afraid to enter. Finally I went in. The room was empty and looked untouched, but still I felt slight stirred currents, an invasion, a brief, subtle visit. Checking our jewelry, purses, clothes, I found nothing missing. But on my bed was an envelope with my name on it from Desmond.

'I've told the police everything and now I need to tell you. Meet me tonight about 10 on beach in front of the hotel, and we'll go for a last walk.'

I went outside into the late day sun. I went around the corner of the hotel, noticing once again all the cracks and rubbed places in the stucco. A solid structure though and still standing. What a marvelous old lady, this hotel, I thought. Why had Desmond written a letter? Should I do what he asked? Go out on the beach late at night? He was always asking me to meet him late at night; last time I'd turned him down. I went outside again, after locking the door.

It was already early evening, the sky sinking into sunset through gray clouds that would soon color the sea. Sonja still sat at the table on the terrace. I sat down opposite her. "The door to our room was open."

"The maids do that -very careless."

"Very young though."

"He is a bastard." She said, not looking at me.

"Nathan?"

"You knew that? That he is a bastard?"

"No. But maybe a flake and maybe a con man." I felt myself shrinking into a child self, mourning a Sonja angry at the world, at whoever had breached her defenses. Her hands were clenched into fists. She wore none of her rings. I risked triggering her anger. "What's happened Mama?"

"A bastard." Once again she refused to meet my eyes, instead moved her head from side to side. As a child I would feel the energy boiling around her, unseen yet there but never knew, could not know why. Perhaps for me the end of childhood came when I no longer wanted to find out, only to get away.

The evening wind was rising.

"He will marry her."

"Greta? I thought they were married when I met them."

The fury swung out, striking me. "Are you a fool? I told you the truth. They are not married."

"Legally living together that long is considered a marriage."

She stared out to sea. "Go away."

"Mama, they've lived together for years. You knew that."

Her teeth were tight together; she spoke through them. "He is a liar. That I know."

We sat in silence. I rubbed my palm against the table, smooth squares of parquet or imitation parquet. In Mexico one never knew which. The slick smoothness was pleasing. I didn't order a drink, nor did Sonja; we just sat together on the terrace, waiting for an evening wind to calm us. I wanted to talk about Desmond's letter, but she would not have listened, her own pain was too extreme. So often in our life together it had seemed that way.

A couple sat down at a table near us. He was fleshy and dull looking; she, plump with too much costume jewelry on a thick neck. They looked over at us with curiosity.

I stood up. "Let's go to dinner, Mama."

Sonja stayed in her chair, "I am not hungry. Who is he?"

She gestured at a thin Mexican youth approaching our table. He looked worried.

"Can you two ladies come down to the parachute with me?"

Sonja face was white, sharp faced. "Who are you?"

"This is Ramon, Sonja," I said, I turned to him "Both of us?"

Ramon carried his baseball cap in his hands. He had full strong white teeth, wide gentle eyes. "Yes. There is someone who wishes to speak to you."

"No." Sonja shook her head emphatically. Ramon looked at me. I nodded.

Hat still in hand, he walked toward the stairs. I followed him. Behind me I heard Sonja get up; hurry to catch up with me. Ramon went out and down the beach. The parachute concession was closed. The wind was up, slapping the waves and I wondered suddenly if there were other places in the world I wanted to be at that moment. I decided there were.

Ramon went around the corner of a small closed concession shack on an empty stretch of beach, and there joined Roberto who lay on the sand, back against the wall, a bandage clearly visible in the v of his short sleeve shirt. He smiled at me.

"Hey, Karin, you are still here."

I sat down beside him, forgetting for a moment Sonja, who came up behind me.

"Mama, do you remember Roberto?"

"Of course."

"Roberto, did they release you?"

"No, but my friends did."

"I'm glad you're okay."

"If you two want to talk," Sonja snapped. "I shall go back to the room, Karin."

"Yes, Mama," but I didn't move and neither did she.

Roberto looked past me, at her. "Listen ladies, I must talk to you both."

As he spoke he pressed his hand against his side as though talking was painful. Ramon went to stand at the edge of the shack and keep watch. When I saw that, I felt an inner gasp of alarm. Were we in that much danger near the hotel? The sea slapped into the shore beside us, a steady forceful sound.

"Ladies, you must go home."

"We are. Tomorrow."

"Maybe tonight go to another hotel."

I rose and pulled back to stand beside my mother; I put my arm around her. Another warning. Somehow I was not surprised, but I was angry. I didn't know yet what part Roberto was now playing.

"A lot of drugs are here, a big." he paused, "circulation - this beach. Not the hotel guests, they are tourists right? But there is also a big market right here, a lot of drugs coming here, nice and quiet; nobody pays attention."

"Some of the hotel employees are in on it?"

"Yes. But it is not so simple as you think. These men are smuggling native art from other countries too. That is the way they bring the drugs here. Some of these things are real. They are valuable, but many are imitation. It is against the law to take out the valuable from their countries so they hide these things here. Now there is a fight," he demonstrated with two fists, "Two gangs fight here. More happens every day. It is dangerous to know this. When I came to know all this, they struck at me." His voice sank to a whisper; his brown eyes were drained of life.

I knelt down beside him. "Don't say any more. It hurts to talk doesn't it?"

"Yes, but Karin you are in trouble here. Leave tonight with your mother."

"We understand." I said.

"I don't." Sonja snapped. She stepped forward. "What does he mean?"

"Drugs, Mama."

She turned abruptly. "Come Karin," she walked away, jerkily, without grace.

I hesitated, still crouched beside him.

"It's better to stay away, and say nothing." Roberto looked at me. There was no tenderness in his voice or his face, that hour was over. But there was in the man, a painful sincerity. I could not doubt his words.

Rising, I saw Sonja already half way across the beach, on her way to our room.

"What about Marian, Roberto? Do you know anything about her?"

He looked away. "I tried to help her. A pretty lady. She wanted to have a baby. Then she wanted to get rid of the baby. Then I said I would not help her."

"And Peter Baden? Is he dead?"

"The blond man from Europe? A trickster. I don't know. He goes back and forthbetween the gangs. He makes trouble but they both cooperate with him." He looked into my eyes again. "You see Karin. This is a bad place to be right now. Please go quickly."

"Thank you, Roberto." He bowed his head somberly. I leaned forward to give him a soft quick chaste kiss, and then touched his hand. "Take care."

At the edge of the shack I turned back. "Will you be all right?"

He smiled. "My father told me - about my mother -.when I was in the hospital.

After I was born, she was sick." Roberto pointed to his head. "In her mind."

"Postpartum depression. It happens."

"They did not know how sick she was. She walked into the sea when I was six weeks old. She never held me, fed me. They didn't want to tell me."

"Are you sorry you know now?"

"The truth does not hurt. Only lies or silence."

"You must go, lady." Ramon came back. He was nervous. "We must move him. Before the hotel security comes."

"Who's helping you, Ramon? Edwardo?"

"No."

"Edwardo and Manuel are in one gang." Roberto whispered. "Be careful."

I walked away. Sonja was gone, and the beach was empty.

Ramon came up behind me. "Lady, we need money. We took him from the hospital but we need a boat to take us down the coast tonight. We have no money."

"I'll see what I can do. I'll try to walk beside the shack this evening."

"Not the shack. We must move him. I will find you. Thank you, Roberto, is a good man." Ramon backed away.

The wind was strong by then as it rose up from the sea. My heart lifted. Slowly pieces were coming together. Perhaps Desmond too would reveal what he knew.

In our room, Sonja was lying on her bed, eyes closed.

"Did you believe all that?" she said in a dry voice.

"About the drugs, yes."

"A lie. That is what they all do. Lie."

I turned to look at her. I felt for her such love and need, but also sometimes great weariness. My mother's fires were too deep, and unpredictable. I could not match them, nor support her against all those she was angry at.

"Would you like to have a drink, Mama?"

"We were just there."

"Shall we join some other guests?"

"On a last night I do not wish to see new people." Her voice was vehement; she turned her back.

I lay on my bed and surprisingly fell into a short delicious sleep. When I woke the evening had begun its game - the deepening disappearing light, the mellowing sound, all the familiar gentleness of mood, broken by bursts of machine gun laughter from tourists gathered in the bars. Sonja's bed was empty. I heard her in the bath. She was running water - my mother was crying -the sound was of sobbing mingled with running water. I would come home from school in Iowa, Idaho, New York and would hear my mother crying in the bath, as though the waters of her life were running out..

I listen to her and envy her the certainty of tears. I have not cried in seven years. Perhaps I will learn how, I thought. Often my mother, when speaking of the camps, would say: "I had to teach her not to cry." And I don't remember her crying there. So I'm glad she has that reclaiming of her inner self - which is what tears are for – a drawing up of the inner waters of the soul. Perhaps one day I will learn how to do that.

I was saddened by those thoughts and so walked out of the room into the evening. I'd thought about asking Sonja to loan me some money to give to Ramon, but that was impossible. I was, by then, certain she would refuse. I went for a quick walk along the waves. The evening was advancing, the sun setting with a gold rimmed elegance. I had dressed for dinner in a long skirt. I found I was singing a dumb little song I'd made up as a child in Florida: "Oh never, ever would there be a boy like you and a girl like me." There had been no boy in Florida, but there was one in Mexico.

When I returned to the room, I heard Sonja splashing in the bath. She wasn't crying anymore. I reached under her bed, and pulled out her carved handbag. I opened it. The money she'd waved at me a few days before was in a white envelope with my name on it. I took out two hundred dollars, closed the envelope, and shoved it back into the purse. The sound of bath water running out made me rush. I pushed the purse back under the bed and shoved the dollars awkwardly into my wrist wallet and left the room. Ramon had said he'd find me, but I was tempted to look for him.

He sometimes worked as a bellhop so for awhile I sat on a bench outside the front door of the hotel and watched people arriving from the airport in the dilapidated Hotel Madre Maria van. How well I remembered arriving! A trio of married couples climbed out. One man carried his own luggage with irritated contempt. Two tightlipped tourists held on to half a dozen small bags. A jaunty young couple gave all theirs to a bellhop. I became interested in the many different ways people treated their luggage. After a half-hour I saw Ramon. He was walking slowly up the road so I strolled after him. I passed him, and looking swiftly over, saw that he recognized me. I tore off the wrist wallet so that it fell in his path, walked a short way into the dusty distance, and then ran back, jogging, though I wasn't dressed for running. He stopped, picked up the wallet, stepped off the road until I passed.

Sonja was dressed, red-eyed, but pretty in a white crepe dress I'd admired before.

"You look lovely, Mama."

"Thank you," she said primly, "our last night." She sounded hurt and sad, and in me rose the same question that had haunted me as a child whenever she cried. Had I done something wrong? A question never answered by Sonja.

"Is this a serious drinking night?" I asked and tried to smile. "Shall we order a bottle of wine?"

"Wear that lovely new black dress you bought in town."

"It's too dressy."

"It is pretty on you. And wear my pearls with it."

Obediently I changed into the black dress and put on her pearls. I'd worn that dress for Roberto and didn't want to remember the cave, but I decided to please her.

"Are you glad we are going home, Mama?" I called out from the bathroom where I was putting on makeup. I was tan, freckled really, which pleased me. Whatever else the week had been; it had not been bad for my looks.

"Yes, I need my work."

Looking into the mirror I looked into myself. You stole from your mother. I whispered. Never mind I will pay her back. She wanted to give me some money anyway. Excuses. But my eyes reminded me I was stronger, that someone, or something, was inside watching over me, whether I slept or tried to hide, or ran away or sought amnesia - something good was minding the store in Karin.

* * * * *

The nightlight gleamed against the sheets. My mother crawled into bed. She was determined to go to bed though it was still early. I leaned down to kiss her goodnight, knowing it was the last time for a long time. She sighed with pleasure. The quiet evening together had calmed her. I noticed again how she smelled of flowers – gentle ones.

Often she used perfume or scented soap, but I remembered that even in the camp her smell was of a light agreeable sweetness.

"Sleep well, Mama."

"Be careful."

"I will."

"That man you go with – he is a loose nut. Do you love him?"

"Yes, Mama."

"Love is good, yes," she turned her face to the wall. "But you can't trust men. You must remember that, Karin."

"I will, Mama."

"You be back early."

"Yes, my commandant. Shall I turn out the light?"

"No." She turned to gaze up at me. "It was good the dinner - and to be with you. Why not again next year – we will go on a cruise."

"A good idea. I'd love to do that."

I picked up my jacket and scarf, paused. "What happened to the Herchmers Mama? Did you hear from them tonight?"

"No." her lips tightened. "Never mind. It is better we do not talk of them."

"Goodnight, Mama."

I was down the hall and outside. The moon was out that night, the stars, pale. There were others out walking; the murmur of voices was everywhere. On the terrace the band was playing the same South American urgencies. I was learning their repertoire.

I walked down to the edge of the sea. It was calm; waves were rolling in one by one with a sedateness that was deceptive. It seemed my mother the sea had relented, had succumbed to civilization and would now behave well, forever and forever. But of course she would not. I drew in deep breaths of the odors of this larger parent. Hers was not a gentle sweet smell, but the lustiness of passion and being. The being I knew I wanted to draw myself into. So that when I died I could say I'd lived.

"I missed you."

I jumped with surprise and turned to find Desmond standing next to me.

"Sorry I didn't mean to startle you." He took hold of my hand. "How are you?"

"Fine."

"And your mother?"

"She's fine too." I dropped his hand.

"When time are you leaving tomorrow?"

"Listen, Desmond. Why do you just vanish that way? Where have you been? What's going on?"

I waited but he said nothing. Instead he took my hand again and this time I let him hold it. Without another word he brought that hand up to his lips and kissed the inner palm, a gesture so delicious my body prickled with desire. Oh that fatal softening!

"I'm sorry," he said softly, kissing the palm again. "I should have known better than to lie to you."

We stood side by side gazing at the sea.

"Have you been lying, Desmond?"

"I'm up to my neck in this affair."

"Marian?"

"Probably I murdered her."

"You don't probably murder someone, Desmond. That's like being almost pregnant. Haven't you taken any university English classes?" I spoke in a lighthearted tone, and then struck by the ghastly of the analogy, exchanged looks with him.

"I told you I was with her one night."

"Yes."

"It was the night Marian died."

Without thinking, I walked away, leaving Desmond standing on the beach watching me. He didn't say a word but instead seemed to blur into the odd slanting light of the beach spotlights. I began to run, to smooth the edge of the sea with small steps through the shallows, exactly as I did that first day two weeks ago. I ran clumsily, not having run much for days, remembered Roberto as I did so, and whispered a little thank you to him for teaching me how to run without shoes, and with humility. I promised too I would help Sonja whenever she needed me, to show more love for her. Desmond stood waiting, hands in pockets, head back - he was watching the waves, perhaps he too was making promises. When I came across the sand toward him, he walked forward to meet me in the half dark, his face a white blur, the outlines oddly sharp, while the fullness was indistinguishable.

"Did you really kill her, Desmond?" I asked. My voice was steady.

"I don't think so," he said simply. "I hope not."

It was not the answer I'd expected.

"Marian was the mother of my children. That's why I came down here – to see her, to beg her to reconsider custody. We'd been divorced for three years. When she fell in love with Carl she followed him down here. Later she took the children out of their schools in Germany, away from their grandparents, out of my life. I've been pursuing them ever since. When I followed her down to Mexico City and saw the way she was living, I knew I had to get the kids back. She was into drugs again, traveling all over the map. At first she pretended to me that she was with them in Mexico City, but I found out she was away most of the time. She'd left them with some Mexican couple. She even let me take the kids when I arrived. I guess she figured I wouldn't dare abducted them. But I have. They're hidden away now, still in Mexico City but with American friends of mine. I should have tried to take them out of the country right after

I got here. I don't know why I didn't. I guess some kind of mistaken sense of fair play. They were upset enough as it was and they love – loved - her." His voice broke a little, "They don't know. They ask about her."

Desmond's voice weakened; he took my hand again. "When I had them safe, I came back here to talk to her. I left her a note. She insisted we meet after Carl had left - so he wouldn't get jealous. Apparently he was a jealous man though he didn't look it. But she was by then sashaying around with Peter Baden. They'd cooked up some fraud together."

"Frieda told me that."

"Frieda ought to know. She was an old girlfriend of Baden's. She was no friend to Marian. She'd moved in with Carl. It was Frieda who told me where to meet Marian. Baden was by then in the hospital. Marian insisted Carl wasn't in the picture anymore. I don't think Frieda believed that. That night I walked up to the end of the beach to the cave. Actually, I saw you - you and your friend. You looked beautiful and I wished I weren't trailing along to plead with a woman who didn't love me for a chance to take care of our kids.

She came down from the house on the cliff above. She was laughing, really quite wild. She said we had to talk so nobody could hear us because there were some touchy people around; then she literally drove me into the cave. She started taking off her clothes.

She was really quite out of her normal behavior and I realized she was on cocaine - maybe some additional trash. She was still so beautiful – you have to admit she was a beautiful woman – you saw her. She was like strong music or a glass of champagne; she was always like that."

He was speaking rapidly while we both stood staring in the sea, into waves that chased each other up the shore.

"Very beautiful," I murmured. It was odd to be standing in the darkness listening to him talk about another woman. Not at all the way I'd let myself begin to dream. Not at all what my heart wished.

"I wanted her all over again, as though there was no bitterness, no years apart. It was – I can't explain it - her again, the familiar but also there was something wild, driven about her responses, and then she died in my arms. I felt it, felt her rising up against my chest, only it was her spirit incorporating itself into me. It was an eerie feeling. And she said nothing, she just ... wasn't breathing. I was attacked with such a sense of horror I bolted out of there, ran up the beach, got back to my motel room, tried to sleep, but couldn't. When I calmed down I realized she'd probably died of an overdose or a bad drug combination and I hadn't recognized her condition. Had I known there might have been something I could have done."

We stood in silence. He said nothing more.

"Why did you want to meet me tonight?"

"To tell you – I wanted you to know the truth. Marian had your mother's cosmetic case. She'd taken it, or Frieda had, and Marian was going to return it. I think. Anyway I recognized it. I knew it was your mother's and grabbed it when I ran out of there. But I dropped it. That's how it ended up on the sand."

"Marian put the address book in it."

"That was her dodge – the address book. She was trying to sell it to the highest bidder. I've turned myself in to the police. They've been great – given me a few days to sort my affairs out. It's partly the drug dealing I was once part of, but they seemed to believe me when I told them about the circumstances of her death. Someone had already reported seeing me with her."

"Desmond, how can I believe you? You dug up the case without telling me."

"I wanted to see if it my name was in it, the name of my friends in Mexico City, friend's in Europe. Marian's. But you pulled a trick on me."

"Yes. But weren't you trying to sell the address book to Manuel and Edwardo?"

He looked startled. "You saw us?"

"What were you doing there?"

"Pretending to buy drugs - The men I talked to insisted they didn't know anything about them. I may have complicated things. They were pretty surly. Suspicious."

"The police knew?"

"It was part of the deal I made with them."

"Oh Desmond, we are up to our necks in it, aren't we?"

I lay down on the sand and stretched out as though to press myself against the strength of the earth. "Lie down, Desmond."

He looked down at me stretched out at his feet. I guess he thought I was suggesting something more complicated. "Stretch out, touch the earth." I said in my new command voice. He lay down beside me. For long moments we lay side by side staring up at the stars, still persistent in the face of all our threat, the immensity of the universe pressing into our own smallness. Desmond rolled over on his side facing me; I turned to look at him. He stretched out one hand and touched my arm.

"Did I kill her?" His voice was husky.

"How can I know, Desmond?"

"That was what our whole marriage was about. I was a weight pressing against her, demanding from her, demanding her. That was what she said anyway. So it was eerie, her death – like I pulled the very life out of her yet reason tells me I couldn't do a damn thing." Than he briefly cried, big rough sounds, an animal noise. I couldn't think of anything to say, as always when faced with emotion I'd fled, was somewhere high above observing. He turned and lay on his back, and once again we stared up at the palette of distant worlds stretched above us. I felt like a rag doll, arms flung out. Desmond was stretched out on the sand nearby; both of us staring up at that singing sky, signpost for our own mortality, the smell of the sea everywhere; its sound drilling us into humility.

I turned on my side. "Desmond."

"What." He stared up, his body silent.

"Desmond, I want to sleep with you."

"I know."

"I'm married."

"Yes."

"But still I want you."

He scrunched across the sand like a kid; his hair thin and awry, he looked almost ill with fatigue, and sad, sad and yes, frightened. He also looked curiously hopeful.

"Desmond, I'm going to kiss you."

"Good."

We kissed and it was a slow gentle rise of feeling between us and for me it seemed a long time since I'd cared that much, or felt such swooning into the heat of being. He pulled away roughly. "I can't. Can't you see I may have killed her? I don't know. I've got to know."

Raising my head I saw behind Desmond in the distance, a dark figure separating from the darkness of the distance. "Maybe we should go in, Desmond."

He came close again; his face was next to mine. "I need you, Karin, your help. I've done everything I can. I've still got the kids to worry about; I've been driving back and forth to Mexico City to check on them. And I still don't know."

"Know what?" A man on a horse. They were walking slowly, majestically toward us. I only knew one person that could be. Desmond didn't notice. "I spoke to my friends there, even talked to my son and daughter. Asked them what they knew about their mother. They couldn't tell me anything. They rarely saw her. And Baden – everybody here thinks he faked his death to get away. I saw his car in town. There's no body, no reports on him."

I sat up. "Desmond," I whispered, "That old man – Old Juan. He's coming up behind you."

Desmond turned and sat up. "What a character." His voice was indulgent.

"Desmond." I cut across his words with my fear, my knowledge. "He's not friendly. He might be angry. I attacked him; pulled him off his horse."

I looked around. There was no one on the beach but us, no security guards, no tourists. It was after midnight. The lights shone down on an empty stage.

"I can't imagine he'll do us any harm." Desmond voice was still easy, but he stood up. "I'll take you back to your room."

Old Juan was closer by then, his steady approach menacing.

"Desmond," I whispered, 'I'm afraid of him."

"Come on," he said, "start walking."

He held out his hand to pull me up and then suddenly I felt an overwhelming sting of pain in my hand. I cried out. We both looked at a blossom of red gushing from the back of my hand. I saw a long pointed needle there, blood was pouring out. Weak from pain, I sat down again. Desmond shoved me flat.

"Lie still," he said hoarsely, "Play dead."

I did as he commanded, lying with my face down on the sand, which was dry and smelled of seaweed; all of me was concentrated in my hand. My head was spinning.

Desmond bent over me.

"Are you all right," he asked in a loud voice. I looked up at him.

"Play dead," he whispered, "He's coming closer. Karin, say something. What's wrong?" Once again his voice was raised for the old man to hear.

Blood from my hand was seeping into the sand, a dark urgent coloring. I looked over at it. That was my blood, my neutrality destroyed. I closed my eyes, and then opened them when I felt Desmond move away. Don't leave me, I thought and made a small motion of protest, but by then Desmond was shouting as he ran down the beach.

"Help, this lady needs help; you over there, we need your help." Old Juan was motionless astride his horse.

Desmond ran toward him. "Do you hear me, man, get down." and then Desmond reached old Juan and, without another word, grabbed hold of him and pulled him off the horse, which shied and skittered away. I turned and struggled to my knees to watch, holding my hand which was scattering blood around me.

It was a dangerous fight, Desmond was younger and stronger, but Old Juan was wily and had a knife. They were exchanging blows, circling, all the world out of some archaic western film; Desmond not able to get close to old Juan who wielded the knife with a savage circling thrust. Desmond began to shout. "Help, help, murder, help; Karin yell for help, we've got to get rid of this bastard."

I stood up, and was screaming. Shakily, I looked around for a security guard. Where were they all? Old Juan pulled away from Desmond and lurched down the beach toward the corner of the bay where the cave was, the horse scampering after him.

"Help, stop that man." Desmond was running after him, but only a short way, then he turned and ran back to me.

"Are you all right, Karin?"

"This hand is awful."

"Is the dart still in it?"

"No. It must have dropped on the ground. Oh God, it hurts." I felt his arm around me. He helped me back toward the hotel and safety.

"Should we tell the police, Desmond?" I asked as we entered the annex.

"Not tonight," he said grimly, "come into my room. Don't wake your mother."

"But she might be in danger."

"I'll check on her," he said, and opening the door of his room, pushed me in.

He thrust on the light. The room was bare, but full of a tobacco smell.

"I'll get something for a bandage." I'd forgotten for that moment my hand and I looked down. There was a real hole in my hand near the wrist, blood was still running down. Desmond came back with a white washcloth and wrapped it carefully around the hand and wrist, knotting it with an absurd little knot.

"Sit down," he commanded, "You look pale."

"I feel pale." I stumbled over to his narrow double bed, looked out a window which faced the dark beach, heard the sea waves roaring in. I put my head down on the pillow. I felt faint.

"Just rest there," Desmond opened his door, "I'll check on your mother."

"The door's locked."

"Where are your keys?'

"In my pocket," I mumbled. A great delicious weariness was rolling over me. What seemed an instant later, Desmond was back.

"Your mother's sleeping. And that's what you're going to do."

I struggled to sit up. "I'd better get up then."

"Lie down," A moment later, Desmond was standing beside me brushing his teeth. "You're sleeping in here."

"I can't." I was still struggling to sit up and not doing a good job of it.

"First, you're too weak," he inserted the toothbrush back into his mouth and talked through it, "and second, it's too dangerous. I'm not letting you out of my sight tonight."

"Desmond. I'm getting tired of mean people."

"So am I."

That was the last thing I remembered until morning.

Monday, Day 16

I woke up to sun and silence and Desmond's empty room. For a moment I was bewildered, our room – Sonja's and mine – didn't receive the morning sun and in my confusion I somehow thought I was home in Boulder. Then I remembered the events of the night before. I sat up. A sparse room – Desmond had only a scattering of essentials – his toiletries, a towel, a jacket. I didn't even see a suitcase.

The morning sun was peaceful. In the camps during the winter, the sun was a blessing. Here by the sea it moved from friend to opponent as the sun rose higher.

Where was Desmond? I was sitting, half drawing in the sun, but with that thought gave a little squeak of alarm. Was I crazy? Last night, he'd told me his ex-wife had died in his arms while they were making love. And I'd slept in his bed without a care in the world. Why did I continually forgive him, excuse him? When I was with Desmond I trusted him totally but once away, what he said and did worried me more than I cared to admit. It was a long time since I'd trusted anyone so much. Yet I felt no need to reach for my diary. I didn't even know where it was.

I got up and dressed. My shirt and pants were filthy and there was blood on the shirt. My hand seemed fine though still painful if I put any pressure on it. When I opened the makeshift bandage Desmond had wrapped around it; it looked o.k. - a small but deep wound. How will I explain this to Sonja? I thought.

I didn't have to worry. Sonja was making up her face when I turned the key in our door. She was wearing an interesting black turban, and black stretch pants with a turquoise and blue top. She was adorned in all her rhinestone jewelry.

"Good morning, my darling," she said cheerfully. "Your friend Desmond told me you hurt your hand. He said you spent most of the night looking for a nurse."

"With no luck," I said. How easily that lie came out. "Where is he?"

She shrugged. "How in the world could you put your hand down on a spike?"

"It was stupid wasn't it?"

She turned around to look at me but I was already headed for the bathroom.

"Oh, there was some dreadful news," she said in a loud voice.

"Come tell me about it." She followed me to the bathroom and stood in the doorway. I began to run a bath. I'd already peeled off my dirty clothes.

"The pool in that garden where you often sat. To think you probably were sitting there when that…thing was down there."

"Down where?" I climbed happily into the bath.

"The pool."

"What thing?" I sank up to my neck. The hot water was glorious.

"They found a body in that pool."

I sat up in the bath "Who?"

"That nice young man – the one you talked to."

My heart nearly stopped. She can't mean…"Who, Mama?"

"That young man. Peter Baden. They found his body in the pool. They said he'd been dead for days."

I stared at Sonja. She stared back at me. We shared a sense of both horror and astonishment. We'd been so often near that pool, especially I, who'd sat beside it many times, when it held a secret, a large slug of flesh hidden beneath its closed eye. I couldn't help a little shudder.

Sonja vanished. "I'll get some coffee. I'll meet you on the terrace," she called back and shut the front door. I heard the lock catch. I listened for that catch because once again I was afraid. Naked in my tame bath, I was afraid of all waters, of all men, of everything. Sometimes I was afraid of myself.

I got out of the bath and toweled myself dry; my body was reddened and soft from the heat of the water. Her body had been cool, a white of perfection, then the thought came – suddenly, starkly - what if I had killed Marian? The spurts of violence that I'd fallen into were not typical of me; what if there were a part of me wandering about, scattering violence, a secret even to myself? That was such a curious idea I wondered why it had occurred to me at all. Were such thoughts temptations? Reminders of our own possibilities of guilt? How could we be sure real evil wasn't present in our lives?

All questions I could not answer. My sixteen days in Mazatlan had taught me that I had no answers to the real questions that came from the world around me.

I dressed and went outside. The sun was very hot. It was about 10 in the morning, but already I could feel its lash. On the terrace Sonja sat wearing a sun hat and sipping coffee. Desmond was with her.

"He's telling me about his trip to Spain," Sonja was smiling. Her makeup was perfect. She did not look 71. "How he was robbed in Madrid. They accused him – the police – didn't they, Desmond? - treated him as though he were guilty of a crime."

She was smiling chattily at Desmond who was also smiling. They were happy together, those two and I was left out of that good humor, having walked by the empty pool, once my sanctuary, my closed eye. Workmen were filling it again with blue clear water. I thought guests will be swimming in it by next week, will open their eyes underwater and see everything clearly. Nothing will be there. I will not be there.

"Coffee please," I murmured to the waiter, "Coffee and hot milk, plus toast.

"Eat a good breakfast," my mother said, "You know you must, Karin. We go to the airport by one o'clock."

"Maybe later, Mama, first coffee. Desmond, how are you?"

He smiled a gentle reminder of our closeness. Yet there was something different about him that morning, something sharp and a little distant. He was up to something. Why bother asking, I thought, when the sea dances just beyond us. Thank you, Sea for being there, and the sun and sky for resisting the earth's gravitational pull.

Or was it the other way around?

They had not replaced the rubrun lilies. Could they be replanted? No, I must accept the removal of my flowers too. With my coffee, the waiter brought, instead of toast, a slice of coffee cake, served with orange slices spread into decoration on a wide peasant plate - a happy accident, because toast was North American and the cake was Mexican. I was entering the world of opened eyes that morning, slowly carefully eating my way into knowledge.

"You are guilty of the crime of being a stranger, Desmond." Sonja said and patted his arm lightly. "That is a crime. People don't like strangers. And we don't like playing that part. That is why we take care of ourselves on holiday. We eat and sleep carefully, with concentration; we pay attention to our feet and luggage, for then we can slip into every reality like a foot trying on a new shoe. The shoehorn is the truth of what we need to survive whole. I learned that a long time ago."

"And you still follow this advice," Desmond smiled.

"Of course, I make friends wherever I go. That is one need I have. Otherwise it is the practicalities."

I thought suddenly, oddly, absurdly of the blue marbles, the gleam of them in the white and brown of the hospital room. I clutched one in my hand, held it tight. The thought made me dizzy that morning, as did Sonja, the odd slanting light and the loss of the rubrun lilies. Too much had happened and it had accumulated and yes, I thought, I am a stranger here but sitting with people that I care about, who care about me.

"You are quiet, Karin," Sonja said. "Are you still asleep?"

"I wish I were."

"Nathan called." Sonja gave me an odd insinuating look.

"Where is he?"

"He and Greta are in a hotel in N.Y. City. Much nicer, he said, quieter than the hospital. She didn't want to go to the hospital. But Greta is too ill to stay at home. He wanted to call me in New York."

"Sonja."

"To talk," She shot a quick half-shy glance at Desmond. "a job."

"I didn't ask why, Sonja," I said. "Just wondered if Nathan had told her kids where they were."

"I didn't ask."

"If they contact you, what are you going to say?"

"They don't know me. He will introduce me as a new employee. I already said okay. I need a job."

"Mama."

"It's something I have to do," Sonja said, and first looked down at the table, then out the window, stroking with soft tentative fingers the spoon lying beside her plate. "You can't understand."

"Maybe I can." Desmond and I exchanged a lsmile.

"No, you can't," and my mother's voice was fierce; she looked at me then with a bright hard look, the brittle face that I feared as child, the face of remembering in Florida. "I know that now, Karin, you do not share my memories. Always I thought I must make you remember but I was wrong. But these people, Greta and Nathan, they understand. They help me remember."

"Why remember?" Desmond asked in a soft voice.

"Each of us has something to do, each of us. I have finally found something I really have to do - after all these years. Besides survive."

"Chase Nazis?" I cut in with anger.

"Yes, maybe. But at least not forget what they did."

"Nathan is not a nice man, Mama."

"No, maybe not - many of his family in Europe died in camps."

"You saw enough of him and still want to get involved with his stupid plans?"

"It is confusing. I was confused. Yes, I admit this."

"And you're not now?"

"No."

"Then let's not talk about it today, Mama. Do you mind?"

She looked both relieved and a little hurt. We sat in silence. Desmond looked out to sea. What was he thinking? My stomach was churning, not with coffee and cake, but with thoughts that oppressed me. Ever since Sonja had told me about Peter Baden, I'd once again taken responsibility for not knowing something. Who had killed him? And then I thought, I'll never know. Half a dozen people probably wanted him dead, any of whom could have killed him. I, a stranger here, have been warned again and again to go home. Let me go home in peace I prayed; if ignorant too, well so be it.

"Children," Sonja said, and stood up. "It is time for a swim - last day, best time." She smiled a little wanly but with that charm that, once again, made me love her. For a long moment, we stood, paused by the table, the three of us. "Will you swim, Karin?"

"Of course, Mama, I'll change my clothes."

Desmond rose with us. "I have things to do, and people to see. Later."

Sonja reached over and gave him a hug. "Until we meet again," she said.

*   *   *   *   *

How at ease Sonja and I were that morning. Our last day seemed precious as we played in the sea – or rather, Sonja tiptoed and I danced. She insisted on carrying her beach bag with a towel in it into the water, and then struggled to hold it high enough to keep it from getting wet. The sun was a bright friend above us: we met the waves together and apart, laughed again and again at our failures to stay upright. Surprisingly only a few guests were out. We were resting on our towels on the sand when I saw someone running up the beach, the faraway beach where the cave lay. It was a Mexican running very fast, waving his hands. I heard faint shouts. Sonja sat up. She was in a two piece suit, a bright green one that I liked. She didn't notice the runner; her full mouth was turned down in a slight frown. He arrived, the messenger. He was shouting in Spanish to the lifeguard of the day. Then they were both running up to the hotel.

All around us the sea stretched its tentacles - the sea soup, the true smell of being, the waves breaking into white garlands, with a roar so constant, we had become accustomed to talking above and around it. We turned away from the latest Hotel Madre Maria drama now unfolding; instead lay as close to the water as we dared. Sonja slid down to lie next to me and we talked in our friendliest, most confidential tones.

"Nathan was worried about Greta. He thinks she will die there. Cancer is such a terrible death. Karin, what do you think? Should I try to help them? Nathan does love her. He is trying to help her find her peace, to go her own way in her last days."

"No. No, please Mama, go home, rest. Look for work, or wait for Nathan to call. Call Irene; she'd like to talk to you. Later – in New York –there will decisions to make."

"You will visit me in New York?"

"Yes."

"And the girls – they will come, perhaps to university. You remember – I said I would help them?"

"Thank you, Mama."

"Not Sonja anymore?" She was smiling.

We ate seafood for lunch – shrimp and crab. Sonja couldn't finish her plate and I refused to finish it for her. We lingered over coffee, ignoring the irate glances of tourists waiting for tables. The dining room was full, was large, bright, and sane as always. It was our last meal together.

"You didn't really push him into the pool did you, Karin?"

"Yes, I did. It was so tempting. He was sitting there spouting nonsense."

I had invented for my mother's benefit a dramatic encounter with Captain Hernandez that had nothing to do with the facts.

"He could have drowned, Karin."

"Maybe it would be a policeman test."

"You think he's a policeman? Nathan says…"

"It's like witches. Throw a man into water; and if he's a policeman he sinks."

"Karin, how can you act so? This policeman could make trouble for you."

I knew her awe of them, the awe of all that generation Europeans who had been through the war. I had given Captain Hernandez status in her eyes.

"How is your hand? Such an odd wound."

"I put my hand down on a table in the garden."

"Let me see it," she was pawing in her handbag looking for her reading glasses.

"No, Mama, it will be o.k."

"Don't go near that garden. The body - how did a body get there?"

"Let's not think about it, Mama."

"Did you find out what happened on the beach this morning?"

"Let's not think about that either."

I didn't want to know anything more about the Hotel Madre Maria, or Carl or Frieda, or Freddy. The runners had come from the beach below Carl's house. More revenge? More combat? Mexican vendettas were a habit here - time for us to leave.

Sonja and I parted outside the dining room. At the front desk, I made arrangements for her departure, and mine. There was a message from Greg to call him. "When are you coming in?"

"Tonight I hope, but very late."

"Karen I do love you. Forget those other things I said."

"I can't forget what you've done, that's the trouble. We should divorce. That's what I want. You said there was another woman."

"No, I didn't."

"Greg, you're not making sense. You want a divorce. You said that."

There was a silence. "No, I didn't."

"You did."

"NO."

"You said there was someone named…." I couldn't remember her name.

"Jane."

"Yes. Where are you, Greg? Are you with the kids?"

"No." he said, "I'm busy." He hung up.

I stood in that funny little second-rate telephone booth and was surprised. I'd said what I wanted so easily, with such certainty, though the step itself was momentous.

I called Irene. She wasn't home. I left a message telling her we were leaving and that I'd come to New York sometime soon and that Greg and I were through. Then I said, "I love you Irene, and I need you in my life."

I walked out into the sunshine, walked toward the beach.

"Stick with your friends, with your Mama, stay close. Then you'll get away." It was Carl – muscular, powerful, mean. His hands were on his hips. He wore only khaki shorts. He was standing on the terrace above me. I could smell the bite of his aftershave; on his bare chest, a gold necklace gleamed.

"Why don't you just leave me alone?"

"Because you won't stay out of other people's business and you get in the way of people and you make other people do things they don't want to do - cute trick burning the address book."

I looked at his face. A look of ? …well it was not admiration that was for sure. In the bright hot light of mid day it occurred to me maybe it hadn't been such a cute idea after all. Then I found myself asking the sort of question that got me in trouble before.

"What happened today, Carl? Up the beach?"

"If I tell you, I'd have to kill you. Maybe I will anyway."

"It was a very small address book, Carl."

'Lady, it had a lot of names and addresses in it."

"I'm going home today, Carl. Trust me. I know nothing, nothing at all."

*   *   *   *   *

Standing outside the hotel with her luggage, Sonja was once again wearing the interesting black turban, black stretch pants, and turquoise and blue top, wearing again her rhinestone jewelry. There were only five guests going on the afternoon flight. Sonja got on the bus with the other three and attempted conversation with a tepid narrow eyed blonde woman named Trudi, who, I'd already been informed by my mother, had been married four times. Desmond put his arms around me as we stood by the van. "Desmond, we have to say goodbye."

"Do we?"

"I'm going home to sort myself out. I'm getting a divorce."

"There's another flight late tonight."

"You're staying here tonight?" My heart beat faster.

"Yes."

"You'll have to protect me from Carl."

"I won't let you out of my sight, believe me."

"I'm quite sure I love you, Desmond."

"Prove it." And he smiled a wicked smile.

Then we were in the van, Sonja and I driving away from the Hotel Madre Maria. Desmond stood watching us go. I knew I was leaving someone very important to me. My mother and I waited in the airport together. She was leaving first for New York.

The airport was noisy and we were both tired. We drank coffee at a white plastic table. "Well Mama, we're saying goodbye again."

"My darling daughter. Why so far apart? Come to New York."

"I will. Soon. I love you Mama."

"I love you too. You are everything to me: Past, present, future."

It was time for her to go. We kissed goodbye. I watched her get on her plane then went to my counter, changed my ticket to a later flight, walked out of the airport, got into a taxi, and was back at the Hotel Madre Maria.

Desmond was sitting under a beach umbrella drinking a beer. He stood up, smiled, walked over and held me.

I'd been in his room before. I'd even slept in it. But that afternoon as we entered it, we walked into a sun that filled its plainness with a white gold heat. I was a stranger entering a man's privacy for the first time. Desmond shut the door and with a simple gesture locked it. Across the hall, my room - mine and Sonja's – was far away, my mother vanished. Desmond went to the window, pulled the venetian blind so that the dazzling blue sea was hidden, the sun shadowed.

"It's going to be hot," he said in a wry voice. The room had a seaweed smell.

"Yes," I said and noticed my voice was husky. I still stood beside the door. Desmond walked to the bureau and unfastened his watch.

"Take off your clothes and lie on the bed," he said in an everyday voice, laying his watch on the bureau. The words were not a command and not an entreaty. They were an organization of this event, a taking charge of a scattering of two people, a reorganization of two psyches into one, and the meeting of two bodies in a simple dance.

It had become almost geometrical in that sense and, without a murmur, I did as he instructed. But as I took off my clothes I felt shy; I didn't know this man. Desmond stripped off his clothes with a quick pair of gestures - the shirt, the pants.

He had no underwear, his shoes must have vanished. I was still parting myself reluctantly from each article of clothing. I was wearing a summer suit, a blouse, sandals. Why did it take me so much longer?

I removed my bra and Desmond, lying on the bed, gave a satisfied sound in response, a pleasure sound that instructed me. I removed the bikini pants, drawing them down slowly, still reluctant to be naked.

"Come here," Desmond said and he was watching me, his eyes warm and glowing, a strange blue green, the color of the sea, and as I moved toward him, heat began in me, warming my nakedness from within.

"It is hot," I murmured, and slowly, with humility stretched myself beside him.

His body was warm, but contained. He was muscle, sinew; he was male, all that the male body asserts - control, protection, strength.

I lay beside him, falling in love with him, flowing out toward him, the most pleasurable yielding in life. Like the sand departing with the waves, and returning to land again, that act we enter into becomes the giving out of self, the taking back of self; stability is not knowing safety and yet knowing it.

"I've come home," I murmured to myself. I didn't know if he heard. He was instructing me with his hands, guiding me to rise up on him, to straddle him, to invite and taunt him. I was his child, his need, his wife.

It was a long slow afternoon, the sun hot behind the muted barrier we had placed against it. We took our time and our pleasure, discovered we were both direct people, and simple hearted. We discovered that something greater than ourselves moved between us, as though we were lifted up into inner selves with greater knowledge and surer purpose, discovered also that we admired each other and found in each other a statement of that opposite sex we have always liked.

We discovered too that we wanted to continue another time; something had begun that was not finished. We did not know how or when or where that knowledge between us would finish, but we did not want it to. From that one long slow hot afternoon I came to love Desmond and believe he loved me. Everything else was briefly washed away into pastels – my children, my mother, Greg, my ambitions, my dreams – they all lay beyond that old hotel room, which looked out on a sea where islands stretched along the horizon. I rested with my arm around Desmond's neck, my knee on his bare legs while he slept - that delicious drugged sleep of the sated, the completed. I barely heard the door to my old room open. Barely but I did hear it. It must be Sonja, she must be back - I fell asleep thinking that. And when I woke Desmond was gone and the room was dark. I'd slept into evening and with evening came darkness.

I dressed and went across the hall to my old room. When I opened the door I saw that everything in the room was smashed. The mirrors were broken, the window, Sonja's hand mirror, which she'd left behind. The mattresses had been slashed and the stuffing pulled out. Our clothes were scattered all over the floor and beds. Everything was torn, slashed, everything dismembered and violated. Shocked, I stood and looked at it. And I saw Sonja lying on the floor in a pool of blood.

"Desmond!" I shrieked, the fear in me trembling up into a spiral that threatened to dismember me too, "Desmond!" Just as he came into the room, Sonja turned her head and looked up from the door. "Don't worry," the Sonja face said, "I 'm pretending to be dead. I am all right."

"Sonja," I whispered, but had an odd hushed feeling that I didn't want to go too close in case she was a mirage, a murdered being, a ghost.

"Don't worry," she said, her face and voice faint like smoke. "I'm pretending."

"I know that, Mama, I know that," I thought in the dream. But I was crying.

"What's going on?" Desmond said, and his was the voice of reason. He came over and took hold of my arm and held me close and his being was reason too.

"I don't know, "I whispered." Is that Sonja there on the floor?"

He looked down. "No," he said, "that's some clothes. Sonja's not there."

I looked again. I saw that he was right. I hadn't seen her at all.

The second time, I woke into light. Desmond was still there lying beside me.

We were hot, sticky, naked.

"Oh Desmond, "I whispered, "I had an awful dream."

He opened his eyes and kissed my nose. "So did I." he said.

"That's nice." I murmured turning over so my bare bottom was against him.

"Is it?"

"What time is it?"

"What was your bad dream?"

"Sonja. I thought she was dead."

"She's a nice lady," he protested.

"Sometimes," I said. I'd risen and begun to dress. Desmond put his hands under his head and watched me. The room smelled of sweat and roses. It was nice. Perhaps the roses part was only my imagination; the sweat surely was not. I set aside the venetian blind and looked out. The sun was invisible heat, low and departing.

"It's gorgeous out." I turned around. Desmond was dressed. Sure it's easy when you wear no underwear.

"I want a cigarette," he said.

"You smoke a lot."

"I've given it up. Just try a few once and awhile.

"I don't care if you smoke."

531

"It doesn't matter if you care or not." He looked at me, challenging.

"Tough aren't you?" I leaned over and kissed him. But I felt the tension in his arm, like an alert animal, ready to spring away.

"Was I in your dream?"

"Yes, you were my hero."

"Good," he said. "Unfortunately you weren't in mine. However, you are in my life now. You are, aren't you?" He looked like a boy when he said that.

"We'll make it work. Will you call me?"

"When it's right, when I'm right."

We were dressed. I didn't want to go outside, to the real world, to all the mysteries I could not solve. But it was time to catch my plane. I looked at Desmond as I opened the door. He didn't smile and neither did I.

I like remembering him as he stood outside the hotel. He was waving, looking disheveled, a little dejected, but extremely loveable. The Hotel Madre Maria, on the other hand, looked bland and insignificant as night pressed down upon it.

Afterwards

'Failure to Thrive' – that's what the doctors call it. My mother is dying, but without cancer, heart problems, or organ failure. Even her brain, despite minor dementia, works very well. When she wakes, she is hungry; when she sees me, she wants to talk. She remembers the good past we share, never mentions the tortures we endured. But she has lost interest in the future.

This visit, we've been remembering our visit to Mexico. I like going back to that time in Mazatlan, filling my thoughts with the sea and its sounds, the smell of all that thrives there, even some of the things and people we enjoyed. I brought along my diary and I read bits of it to her (not all though!). She loves to listen to me read aloud from the Walt Whitman poetry paperback I carried at the Hotel Madre Maria. I bought Rubrun lilies for her too; they are in her bedroom – Stargazer Lilies they call them in New York.

I am saying goodbye. Sonja wants to die. She misses Nathan. Yes, she and Nathan were married. For years, they lived a dance of life. He was a borderline crook and she loved it. He didn't get any of Greta's money, but they spent all of Sonja's and his; - he didn't have much after four wives and five children. They hunted Nazis on various trips. I don't think they found any. But the search allowed them to go all over the world, on a great many cruises, and discuss strategies over glasses of wine.

Desmond was given six years in a Mexican prison for involuntary manslaughter. He appealed and the sentence was cut to two. His mother took on the responsibility for his two children until he was free. Now they live with us and I've come to love them.

I left Greg, and he left me. We brought up the girls with dual households in Colorado. They are grown now. Nadine is in graduate school at Columbia, and has been living with, and looking after, her grandmother. Ona is finishing university at the Univ. in Boulder and will marry this fall.

Desmond and I are doing all right. We run a travel agency in Colorado, specializing in bringing Germans over for summers in the Wild West, and escorting Canadians and Americans down for winters in sunny old Mexico. Desmond and I and our families spend a lot of time in Mexico. While he was in prison, I received a letter from Captain Hernandez. We began a correspondence and eventually he invited me to visit him in Mexico City. He promised to pay for my hotel room. A solid Catholic, he would never leave his wife, but admitted he'd fallen in love with me. He wrote to tell me so and he has very neat handwriting. I was terribly tempted; he was such an intriguing man and, at first; it appeared Desmond would be in prison a long time. But I knew there could only be Desmond. Now, we are together night and day after twenty years of marriage. I work at remembering every moment of every day we spend together.

When I reread Whitman's poem in "The Sleepers' about the sinking of a passenger boat, and the desperate but failed attempted of a male swimmer to make it to shore, I think: I rescued Desmond. That's what my husband has told me, over and over. But I tell him - you rescued me too. Maybe that's what our purpose in life is: to rescue each other. Maybe that's what God designed us to do.

Printed in the United States
By Bookmasters